I **INI**

Julie Forester Books

J.F.
Books

Marmalade Martini

Julie Forester Books
First Edition

ISBN: 978-1-9999121-1-6

Acknowledgements

Liz, for putting up with fiction and real-life
getting a little blurred at times!

Angela Green and Carl Westmoreland
for their first-draft reading
and honest, constructive criticism.

Carrie O'Grady, my fantastic, creative editor.

R.E Bradshaw, who got me thinking:
"What if…?"

Cover photograph Marmalade Vodka.
Adapted by the author by permission of
© Chase Distillery Ltd.

Dedication

To my E.M.B.

ABOUT THE AUTHOR

Julie has enjoyed action-packed, thrill-seeking experiences in life, including jet-skiing, motorcycle trail-riding, powerboat racing, fencing, karate, scuba-diving, flying airplanes – and even considered a career as a stunt woman! These days, when she's not writing, her interests incline towards the arts, from painting and drawing to live music and theatre.

Her background is in education, for which she holds a first-class university degree with honours. Writing fiction has always featured somewhere in her life, whether professionally, or as much-loved creative hobby. So, when offered the chance to become a published author, she seized the opportunity without hesitation.

She lives with her wife outside north London, surrounded by beautiful countryside. Living just a stone's throw from their quirky little local pub, it is not unusual after a weekend walk to find her enjoying a pint of real ale at the bar.

A frequent visitor to the UK's vibrant capital, London is the inspiration and setting for this novel, Marmalade Martini.

Social media / Website:
https://julieforesterbooks.simdif.com

LIFE
ISN'T ABOUT
WAITING FOR THE STORM
TO PASS
IT'S ABOUT
LEARNING TO
DANCE IN THE RAIN

Vivian Greene

CHAPTER 1

Jamie was standing halfway across Shaftesbury Avenue on a pedestrian island, gasping for breath, her heart thumping. Still drunk, she doubled over, willing the nausea to pass. Her wrist, now painful, had started to swell. The past few hours had certainly been bizarre. How could an innocent meeting have become so complicated?

A low rumble of thunder grumbled overhead. Seconds later, the heavens opened in a torrential downpour. Jamie had only her new denim jacket to shield her from the deluge. A useless gesture, but she flipped forward the collar.

Stupid bloody jacket. She hadn't particularly liked it in the shop the day before, and she liked it even less now. But she knew perfectly well why she'd bought it – and it had been nothing to do with augmenting her wardrobe.

Jamie shivered to her core. Her jeans clung to her legs, wet to the skin, and water was starting to seep through the canvas of her Converse pumps.

She stumbled across the road. The rain was getting heavier. She needed to get home. Wincing as her bruised wrist flexed, she searched through everything she had that had a pocket or a zip. Where the hell were her keys?

Jamie scanned the length of the street, searching for a shop doorway in which to shelter. She crossed a narrow, one-way side road. A flashing neon sign caught her eye, so she made a dash for it. Getting nearer, she was relieved to see a luminous ‘open’ sign above the door of a bar called Alchemy. Why had she never noticed this place before?

Chest still tight, Jamie stopped briefly in the dark entryway. She didn’t generally wander into bars alone – much less ones she had never been in before. The splash of running footsteps and high-pitched squeals came up from behind her. Jamie wasn’t the only one caught out by the rain.

“’Scuse us, love,” said the taller of the two women. They manoeuvred past her down a few steps and pulled open the door, wobbling on silly-inch heels.

Jamie stepped to one side. The sticky heat of the bar wafted out from inside. She leaned across the small stairwell and spontaneously grabbed for the door handle before it closed. Decision made! Following in the wake of the two women, she was immediately hit by the heady smell of candles and burnt orange peel.

She entered a dim, vault-like archway. A converted Victorian cellar, walls bare brick and floor of paving slabs and cobblestones. Antique, dark-wood tables were occupied by chattering groups of people, huddled around free-flowing candles in bottles that had left rivulets of white lava on the tables. Wall-mounted church candles continued the theme. They had dripped down the black cast - iron brackets, creating fragile stalactites of wax.

Various bottles were lined up along glass shelves, spanning the length of the wall behind the bar. They were cleverly backlit to illuminate the range of coloured liquids like an apothecary's hoard. Behind the shelves were mirrors, creating the illusion of opulence and spaciousness. The bar curved towards the back of the maze-like building and disappeared into the depths of three other dimly lit arches.

It was at least fifteen minutes since Jamie had escaped. Surely, by now, Alex must have noticed that she had left the pub, and be wondering where she had got to? Jamie took out her phone. Useless. The battery was flat.

Three more people crashed their way through the door – wet through but laughing and immensely pleased to have found shelter. This wasn't just a short summer shower, it seemed.

Resigned to the possibility that she was going to be stuck here longer than she'd expected, Jamie decided to make the most of it. Besides, after the night she'd just had, she needed another drink.

Seizing the opportunity, she headed for a newly vacant barstool and reached into her jeans pocket, flinching at a stab of pain from her wrist. She pulled out a scrunched-up ten-pound note and some loose coins. If this was all the cash she had, she wouldn't be able to afford the cab fare home, as well as a nightcap. What the hell. Home would have to wait. It would be easier to solve the problem of the lost keys later in the day when she was thinking more clearly.

Jamie leant across the bar to pick up a cocktail menu. Pushing her sodden fringe from her eyes, she skimmed down the page in search of the cheapest drinks. Drops of rain from her hair smudged the ink. Wiping the menu with her sleeve only made it worse. Now the print was only partially legible – hopeless without her reading glasses.

The bartender came to the rescue. “Here, use this to dry yourself off.” She offered Jamie the linen cloth over her shoulder. “It’s only been used to polish the glasses. It’s clean.”

“Thanks.” Jamie could feel her usually sculpted, spiked hair was now a flattened, dripping mullet. She quickly rubbed her head and handed back the cloth, catching her reflection in the glass behind the bottles. It wasn’t a pretty sight, but she didn’t want to draw attention to herself by fussing further over her hairstyle malfunction.

To preserve the illusion of composure, Jamie casually peeled off her wet jacket. For the first time, she took a proper look at her recent purchase. Bleach-splashed, augmented with chains, zips and safety pins, patched with badges and odd squares of tartan, it really was dreadful. Jamie gave it a shake and draped it over the seat of her barstool. She sat down on the makeshift cushion. Her comfort, however, was short-lived – damp started seeping into the seat of her jeans.

She shifted her weight uneasily, trying to look as though she was concentrating on a replacement cocktail menu.

"Typical English weather," the bartender smirked. She slid a bowl of peanuts in front of Jamie. "What can I get you?" She made eye contact.

Jamie held her gaze. "Surprise me," she said, realising she hadn't yet selected a cocktail. "It'll have to be under a tenner, though." She apologetically smoothed out the ten-pound note onto the counter.

"I'm guessing this is hair-of-the-dog time?"

"You wouldn't be wrong there."

"Well, now, let me see..." The waitress turned to scan the bottles on the shelves, giving her concoction careful consideration. She took what appeared to be a jar of marmalade from the chiller cabinet. Then the theatre of her art began.

Jamie watched her pour the contents of a bright orange bottle into a shaker full of crushed ice. She lost track after that. A skilfully trained mixologist, this woman provided the full works, and Jamie appreciated the spectacle of her juggling act.

Eventually, tasting from the end of a dipped-in straw, and approving of her creation with a nod, the bartender finally offered a lighter flame to a slither of orange peel, twisted it and dropped it in the drink. Routine complete, she stood back, waiting for Jamie's reaction.

"I feel like I should be holding up score cards after that performance." Jamie took a long sip. Still drinking, she gave a thumbs up. "Oh, wow, now *that's* good."

"Excellent!"

"What is it?"

The woman tapped the cocktail menu in front of Jamie. "Call it breakfast."

Jamie read: Marmalade Martini. She liked this woman's sense of humour. "Any toast and a mug of breakfast tea to go with that?"

The bartender turned to serve the next customer.

"What do I owe you?" Jamie picked up the ten-pound note and waved it in her direction.

The bartender glanced back. "On the house," she replied with a smile.

A free drink? Why? Jamie watched the bartender fill the customer's order, then take a wineglass from the rack before returning to Jamie's section of the counter.

"It's okay," the woman added. "I'm the owner of this place." She slowly polished the wineglass. "Anyhow, you look like you could do with a nightcap," she said with a wink. "Heavy night, was it?"

"A free drink? I must really look rough if you thought I needed alcohol *that* badly." Jamie noticed the smile lines around the woman's eyes and mouth – deep and expressive. Jamie was an 'eyes' woman, and this woman used hers to communicate. Trying not to stare, Jamie took note of her simple, almost symmetrical, pear-shaped face. She had a strong, strikingly chiselled chin, and a slight Romanesque bump on the bridge of her nose. Her highlighted auburn hair was centre-parted and pulled back over her ears into a short ponytail, barely reaching the base of her neck. Was she wearing make-up? If so, it was expertly applied. For a fleeting moment, Jamie toyed with the possibility of there being a shared chemistry worth pursuing here.

But the woman's attention had already turned, as a new person's custom proved more appealing. Jamie watched, mesmerised, as the bartender held the gaze of the next guy at the bar, striking up a similarly attentive conversation with him. There was something about her; he, too, appeared taken in by her charm.

Damn. Jamie knew it was irrational, but she had already entertained the notion that the bartender had singled her out for special attention. It seemed not. She was, after all, in the hospitality industry, and without a doubt was good at her job. Jamie made a mental note that not every woman that she found attractive was necessarily gay.

Her thoughts were interrupted by the nudge of an elbow, which caused her to spill her drink over her lap. The man on the stool next to her was flailing his arm while trying to remove his suit jacket. He turned, realising what he had done. "Oh – what an idiot." He took a paper napkin from the counter.

"Thanks." Jamie said accepting his offering. "This pretty much sums up my day," she said, half-seriously, thinking out loud.

"That was so clumsy. Can I buy you another drink?"

"Nah, you're all right. Anyway, I'm already soaked through from the rain."

He looked embarrassed.

"No, really, I'm fine," she reassured.

"I wouldn't hear of it." He waved at Jamie's bartender. "Could you get the lady the same again, please?"

"Of course." Half-smiling, she looked at the empty glass then back to Jamie. "Well, that certainly went down well."

Jamie reluctantly conceded, too tired to argue the point. "Ok, just a coke, though please."

There followed a conciliatory conversation between the strangers. They chatted about the weather and other banalities. The conversation then moved to their respective professions.

"An architect? That's a stroke of luck," the guy said. "Do you cover domestic work, like people's houses?"

The fresh drink was delivered.

"I never turn anything down until I've assessed what's involved," Jamie answered.

"It's just that someone I know is currently pulling apart an amazing period townhouse – I think it's Victorian. They're looking for someone to take on all the architecture and the modernising. Is it something that might interest you?"

Jamie was very attracted to the idea. A bespoke blank canvas? It sounded right up her street. "Tell you what, pass on my details and I'll take it from there."

He took the card she handed him and tapped at his phone. "JB Architects? Canary Wharf?"

"Yes, that's me."

"A-ha, small world." He held out his hand. "Mike Norbury. You designed one of our branch offices, about two years ago… Keeble and Norbury Insurance Company? Royal Tunbridge Wells in Kent?"

"Yes, I remember," Jamie said, taking his hand. "Small world, indeed."

"There was a very complimentary article about it in Metropolis. Did you read it?"

"No, I don't believe I did." Jamie had long since lost touch with buying and reading every article that featured her designs. She didn't need to any more.

"I'll pass on your web-link right now, if you like?"

"Sure, why not," Jamie said, still dabbing her sticky thigh.

He tapped once more. "There you go – all done."

"Thanks."

"Not a problem at all – and it helps to clear my conscience, having caused this." He pointed to her legs. "I'll put in a good word and keep my fingers crossed for you."

Jamie lifted her glass of coke as thanks.

*****

Three crisp clangs filled the cavernous space. The bartender tugged on the rope of a large brass bell hanging on the back wall. The room fell obediently silent. "Last orders, please, folks," she called out. "Closing up in fifteen."

People began to emerge from the depths of the inner vault, grudgingly putting on jackets or peering despondently through the small, high windows at the rain beyond. Most people had not anticipated the unforeseen change in weather, having dressed for a humid summer evening. One or two moseyed to the bar to take advantage of the last drink of the night, prolonging the unavoidable wet journey home.

The bar quickly emptied. The hustle and bustle had dwindled to the murmur of a few last punters, eking out the dregs of their drinks.

Then the door behind Jamie opened again, sending in a blast of the chilly night air. This time, the chill lingered; the door had not been closed.

Someone nearby muttered their irritation. The flames around the room guttered. The candle on the table nearest to Jamie blew out, pitching the surrounding customers into gloom.

A couple nearby turned their heads as a formidable-looking man – six-foot plus – bulldozed his way through. Head down, wet trilby jammed low on his forehead, he was completely obscured behind the upturned collar of his black leather trench coat. *I've stepped into a John le Carré,* thought Jamie.

Without stopping to look around, the man strode purposefully to the back of the room – through the archway, reappearing round the other side of the bar. He was aiming headlong for the bartender, who was standing alone in a narrow doorway to the side of the back bar, unaware of his presence. She looked tiny, shadowed by his austere demeanour as he towered behind her.

Jamie sensed the intimidation.

Then the woman spun round. Her body tensed, and her face changed. It seemed that this was an uninvited visitor. She mechanically stepped backwards, further into the recess of the doorway, manoeuvred by unseen forces.

Then she clutched the man's hands. His whole body visibly relaxed. They were, for a few brief minutes, engrossed in their own intimate conversation.

The bartender was almost completely blocked from Jamie's view behind the man's large frame. His back was turned. Jamie watched him gently kiss her forehead. They were locked in an emotional embrace, oblivious to anyone else in the room. They spoke quietly, surreptitiously.

Jamie glanced at Mike next to her, wondering if he had noticed her snooping on private business. It appeared that he shared her embarrassed curiosity. Both he and Jamie were transfixed.

The trilby man's back stayed turned to Jamie throughout, but she could see just enough of the bartender's face, every now and again, to register the intensity of their exchange. The room was no longer buzzing with noise and music, and although Jamie hadn't meant to eavesdrop, the man's words leapt out at her.

"I love you." He held his palms up to the bartender's cheeks. "But I just can't be here any more."

"Love you too," she replied, fighting back tears. "Call me when you arrive, yeah?"

He nodded, then pulled back to move away. His hand slipped down her arm to her fingers. He kissed the back of her hand and let go. "I've got to go now."

"Do you have to leave now? This morning?"

He looked at his phone. "I have a plane to catch, Kate." The words caught in his throat. "I've made up my mind. I need to make a fresh start. There are opportunities in America that I couldn't dream of here. I'm not planning on coming back."

The couple finally disengaged.

Jamie still couldn't see his face; his hands reached up in such a way that she was sure he was now wiping away tears. He stood rigid, then turned brusquely.

Jamie watched him go back through the arch, the way he had come. He didn't look back. She was conscious of his close proximity as he passed behind her. She watched his back as he took large strides past the few remaining customers, then walked out into the rain.

But Jamie was now less interested in him; she was concentrating on Kate.

Mike Norbury had already made up his mind. "Bastard," he said, under his breath.

"Yeah. Very harsh," Jamie agreed.

Meanwhile, Kate stood motionless, facing the wall – absorbed in thought. Presently, as though snapping out of a trance-like state, she scrambled for her rucksack under the counter, and took out her phone. After tapping the screen, and waiting impatiently for the connection, she spoke rapidly. "Chris? It's Kate... please don't hang up... listen, I'm going to fight for this – for us…"

Mystery man has a name, Jamie thought.

"I can't let this be goodbye," Kate continued. "I need to talk to you one more time. I'm just leaving work, and I'm going to get to the airport, before the plane leaves... yes, yes, I'm sure... Chris...? Please wait – I'm going to get to you as soon as I can, but I need to tell you I'm not..." Kate disappeared through the little door at the back of the bar.

"Well, that's me done," Mike interrupted, putting on his jacket. "I've got quite enough drama with my own marriage; I don't need to be sucked into watching someone else's break up in front of me. Nice meeting you, Jamie."

Left alone, Jamie realised that she had completely misinterpreted what she'd hoped were flirtatious signals from Kate earlier. She turned the base of her empty glass round and round slowly on the bar, watching the pattern of the wet circles that it left behind.

*****

Another blast of cold air hit the back of her neck.

"Oh, my God, Jay," came a breathless voice.

Jamie recognised the voice without turning.

"What in God's name was all that about? What made you take off like that? We've been going nuts trying to find you."

Jamie rolled her eyes, stood up slowly, and reluctantly turned around.

"I've been ringing and texting you and got worried when you didn't answer. I sent Gavin out on his bike. He just messaged me to say he thought he saw you come down here but couldn't follow you down the one-way street. What the hell was all that going on with those two women earlier on? I know you have got yourself into some situations, Jamie, but jeez – that woman looked like she was out for revenge or something." Alex barely took a breath.

Jamie held up her phone. "The battery died."

Wearing only a thin cotton blouse, open sandals and linen trousers, Alex was thoroughly soaked. Black lines of mascara streamed down her wet face, mingling with smudged eyeshadow. Her long, mousey-brown hair, usually salon-perfect, fell lank, clinging to her scalp.

Jamie's stock reply in such circumstances was to make light of this spectacle. It was very amusing, but Alex would be appalled if she could she see herself. However, even Jamie recognised that, on this occasion, being the joker was not a good move. She could see that her friend was far too upset.

"My God," Alex grabbed Jamie's wrist, distracted from her barrage of questions.

Jamie gave a little whimper.

"What the…?" She lifted Jamie's left hand up to the light to get a better look.

Jamie looked at her swollen and bruised wrist. Her usually loose watch felt tight. There were nasty scratches up her arm, scabby with dried blood.

"What in God's name happened tonight, Jamie?"

Jamie just couldn't help herself. "The handcuffs tied to the bed weren't such a good idea, then?"

"Not funny!" Alex yapped. "And don't you dare fob me off with your usual crack-a-joke bullshit, Jamie Barker."

It was true. Jamie's tendency, especially with Alex, was to make light of prickly situations with humour.

"I don't have my door keys." Jamie attempted to deflect the conversation. "I can't get into my apartment."

"What?" Alex wasn't amused.

"Should've seen me half an hour ago, I was in full-body pat-down fury in the middle of Shaftesbury Avenue trying to find them."

"What are you going on about? What's that got to do with the state of your arm? I despair of you, sometimes." Alex pouted. Something clicked. "Oh, no. That woman hasn't nicked them, has she?"

"Whoa, easy, tiger," Jamie protested, waving her phone above her head, miming a peace flag. "I surrender. Have a little compassion, Alex. I'm the victim here."

"Don't you throw that card at me." Alex's voice was strained. "You wandered into the pub and totally ignored the people you were *supposed* to be meeting up with. Oh yes, and you ended up bolting for the exit, fending off some screaming banshee. Who was she?" Alex didn't wait for the answer. "If you insist on being the victim for sympathy, Jay, you need to fill me with the details. I've been watching out for you all night. Give me some credit and show more respect to your *real* friends."

"It's not that straightforward, Al," Jamie tried to explain. "It got complicated."

"Why doesn't that surprise me?" Alex turned and clicked her fingers across the bar. "Are you still serving?"

Jamie's bartender didn't even look up. "Last orders have been called already." She turned away. "I'm closing." Her voice was flat, her behaviour a total contrast from minutes earlier. She now looked fragile.

"Ooh, great customer service," Alex sneered. "That attitude is really going to get the public flying through the doors."

"No, don't be nasty," Jamie said. "Her fella just walked in and dumped her. He was stood right there," Jamie pointed opposite them, across the counter. "He just ended the relationship right in front of everyone and walked out."

"Like that's my problem?" Alex tugged at Jamie's sleeve. "Come on." She took out her phone. "It's nearly twenty past two, for God's sake. I'm calling a taxi. You're crashing at ours tonight. God knows, it wouldn't be the first time. A pot of coffee and an explanation is in order. Neither of us is in any fit state to be going anywhere right now. And thank god you took my advice to give me a spare set of your keys. We'll get them and go to yours later in daylight."

Within minutes, the bar was virtually empty. Jamie slipped down off the stool and picked up her denim jacket. She and Alex were the last to leave. Jamie glanced back to Kate, who was now close behind them. Her arm was thrashing unsuccessfully at the sleeve of a thin raincoat; her other arm was rearranging a rucksack, mobile phone and set of keys.

The rain was now just a light drizzle. Kate hurriedly pulled the door shut and stabbed the key a couple of times into the keyhole, fumbling with full arms.

"Oh, damn!" Her phone dropped to the floor.

Jamie was just near enough to spring into action. "There you go," she said. She wiped the wet phone on her jeans as she waited for Kate to sort out a free hand. "You don't want to be losing that."

"Come on, Jamie. Get a move on, will you?" Alex griped.

"Thank you," Kate said, taking her phone with no discernible interest at all in Jamie's chat. She rearranged everything in her arms and scurried towards the first of the two waiting cabs nearby.

Jamie watched. She liked Kate's style, her dress sense – a flattering, feminine blouse and a shapely bum fitting snugly into her faded jeans.

But now, as Kate walked away, Jamie started thinking how differently the poor woman carried herself since the incident with Chris. She suddenly seemed lost; burdened with a heavy kind of sadness.

Alex was on Kate's heels. "Come on, Mother Theresa, the other cab must be ours."

Jamie followed, watching Kate as she bundled herself into the back of her cab.

CHAPTER 2

"Drink this." Alex thrust a mug of sweet black coffee into Jamie's hand. "You know where the pillows and duvet are," she added, flopping back and sinking into the large leather chair next to the sofa. She kicked off her sandals, planted her feet heavily on top of the coffee table and exhaled with a loud, exaggerated sigh. The thump of her heels shook her mug of tea. It slopped over the table. Jamie sprang forward to clean it up.

"Just leave it!" Alex groused. "I've been running across London after you tonight." She started messaging on her phone. "God knows where Gavin's got to – he's still out looking for you too." She thumped her phone down on the arm of her chair. "Are you going to tell me what went on this evening? How did you end up at that medieval dungeon?"

"Dungeon? I disagree. I'd go back there again," Jamie said. "Interesting decor and great atmosphere. It had a great cocktail menu, too," she added.

Alex pulled a face. "And you're supposed to be the architect?"

Jamie smiled at Alex's predictability. "I would expect no finer appraisal from you, Alex. Anyway, I might have landed a job offer out of this evening, chatting to a guy at the bar. It was one of those 'right time, right place' moments."

"Never mind all that squit," Alex huffed. "And don't change the subject. What happened tonight?"

Jamie adjusted the ice pack around her wrist, wishing she could occasionally just close her eyes and switch off from Alex's noise.

Alex, on the other hand, was in the mood for interrogation. "Well?"

It looked like Jamie wouldn't be going to sleep any time soon.

"I'm not going anywhere, so talk!" Alex was resolute, arms folded.

Jamie knew the stance well. There was no way Alex would be convinced to wait for a more convenient time for an explanation.

"Well," Jamie began, uncertainly. "You know the denim jacket I was wearing tonight?" She took a gulp of coffee. "I bought it yesterday from Contemporary Retro – that shop we browsed in last weekend."

Alex grimaced. "That crappy charity shop, off Brick Lane?"

"It wasn't a charity shop."

"Sure it was. It was rammed full of 70s and 80s crap," Alex said. "Why anyone would choose to trawl through racks of someone else's cast-offs and pay a premium for the privilege is beyond me."

Jamie added a heaped spoonful of sugar to her coffee.

"Bonfire fodder," Alex declared. "All of it… and how did the place describe itself? 'Upcycled Fashion

Fusion'? Per-lease! I know your wardrobe, Jamie Barker, and that jacket certainly has no place in it."

Alex was right. Jamie's fashion sense was quite particular, although her work and social attire were totally different. Outside business hours, she usually slobbed in a pair of jeans and a t-shirt. For work, she presented a totally different persona, with tailor-made Gresham Blake or Savile Row suits, fitted shirts and designer shoes.

"Hang on," Alex held up her hand. She thought for a moment. Then her mouth opened. "Oh, my actual God – I remember. You were drooling over that tall, skinny American woman at the till? The one with the skinhead haircut."

"Alex, you are a master of exaggeration," Jamie said, pushing her head back against the sofa. She considered her next words, adding, "She was more like Demi Moore's G.I. Jane, I thought," Jamie said attempting to justify the drama of the evening by making the subject of her attraction sound more appealing.

"You know what? As soon as she opened her gob, I knew you would be incapable of resisting that American accent. God, Jay, I can read you like a book." She started her finger-wagging. "And don't pretend you were drawn in by the wonderful selection of clothes."

Jamie laughed, knowing her purchase had had nothing at all do with fashion.

"One sniff of an accent and boyish good-looks, and you're off like a whippet at the races." Alex was trying not to smile.

Jamie gave a slow nod. "You know me too far too well," she agreed.

Alex grabbed a cushion from behind her and hurled it at Jamie's head. "You are so damn predictable, Jamie Barker."

Jamie grabbed it mid-flight and laughed, relieved that Alex had lightened up a little since her earlier reaction.

"Go on then, what happened *this* time?" Alex said.

Jamie took herself into the kitchen area to top up her coffee. "If you *must* know, I went back to the shop yesterday morning."

"And...? What happened?"

Jamie sat back down. "Originally, my plan was to go in on my own and suss out where the land lay – try a bit of harmless flirting."

"Without me cramping your style, you mean?"

Jamie leant back in her chair, not sure if she really wanted to share the details of the day before with Alex.

*****

"Once upon a time I was falling in love
But now I'm only falling apart
And there's nothing I can do

A total eclipse of the heart…"

Jamie listened to the song that was playing. Feeling oddly furtive, she browsed through the racks, acclimatizing to the unique, second-hand aroma of stiff leather, old sweat and incense. Enough hanging about! She randomly grabbed for the first thing she saw that looked to be size twelve-ish. It was a denim jacket, hanging in what seemed to be the 1970s punk rock section. Bleach-splashed, augmented with chains, zips and safety pins, patched with badges and odd squares of tartan, it was evidently intended for someone half Jamie's age.

A voice spoke over her shoulder, above the volume of Bonnie Tyler's classic. "Fine choice, if you don't mind me sayin'."

"Ha!" Surprised, Jamie jumped, letting out a nervous laugh. She was caught off guard – addressed by the very person she had come to see. She turned, still clutching the jacket to her chest. The shop assistant was just as appealing as she'd remembered. And her boots were very cool.

"You know, I'm old enough to remember this stuff from the first time round," joked Jamie, waving at the rack of shredded, paint-splattered denim behind her. "Somehow, they don't seem quite as shocking as they used to."

With a polite smile, the woman eased the jacket out of her hands. "Let's just see how it sits on you," she said. Within minutes, she was buttoning up the full length of the jacket – a little too slowly for coincidence, Jamie hoped. She had to bend down to reach the last buttons, and Jamie resisted the urge to stand on tippy-toe to get a better look at her delicious brown eyes. "There," said the assistant. "Now that's what I call a perfect fit. And you know, I'd say that particular jacket is just the right shape for your figure, ma'am… accentuates all the curves."

After that, there was only one thing Jamie could do.

*****

"I hadn't intended to part with sixty-five pounds – it just happened. She was very persuasive."

Alex made a performance of pretending to splutter out her tea. "How much? Sixty-five quid? Persuasive? Is *that* what you told yourself? She was probably more interested in securing an easy sale. She probably saw you coming a mile off, you muppet!"

"Well, she seemed keen, and my radar was picking up the signals, but I couldn't be one hundred percent sure."

"So?" Alex leant forward, her eyes peering.

"So I decided I would go back later in the afternoon before the shop closed up, when it would be less busy, to ask her out for a coffee… or something."

"And…?" Alex's persistence intensified.

"And…" Jamie said, peering over her mug, "when I went back…"

Alex craned her neck further forward.

"She wasn't there any more," Jamie concluded.

"What?" Alex's face lit up. "The American bird wasn't working that afternoon?" She burst into loud, crowing laughter. "Bloody priceless!" She lay back and theatrically spread herself across the sofa. "And Ah'll think of *some* way to get her back..." She pressed the back of her hand against her forehead. "After all, tomorrow *is* another day."

"You are such a comedienne." Jamie laughed along at the annoying inevitability of Alex's taunting. She threw the cushion back at Alex. "And your Scarlett O'Hara accent is dreadful."

"So? What's that anticlimax got to do with the woman you were with tonight, then?"

"I'm not finished yet."

Alex waved her hand with regal impatience, encouraging a speedier delivery.

"Well, I needed cheering up, so I popped into Costa to grab some chocolate cake and a coffee."

Alex puffed out her cheeks and made a 'pile on the pounds' barrel shape with her arms.

Jamie tutted. "Anyway, I got chatting to a woman on the next table in Costa, who happened to be sitting on her own. She was having a coffee too, as you do... and one thing led to another... as it does..."

Alex buried her face in her hands. "Oh God, this is painful. It just gets worse. So this was the woman you waltzed into the pub with earlier?"

"Yup."

"You invited a complete stranger out for a drink – at the same place you were supposed to be meeting up with us?"

"Pretty much, yup," Jamie said.

Alex shook her head again. "You are such a tart." She huffed. "So, to sum up…"

Jamie braced herself.

"Number one, you got fleeced for a crappy 1970s Bay City Rollers cast-off. Number two, you got blown out by the Yankee-Doodle, recycle-retro-queen – and all you ended up with was a crap date with some floozy you picked up at a coffee shop, half an hour later?"

"Pretty much."

"Knowing you," Alex continued, "she probably seduced you with some irresistible chat-up line. And *please* don't tell me you two shared more than a skinny latte in between Costas and arriving at the pub?"

Jamie didn't answer.

Alex spun around. "Oh, my God, Jay – no! You didn't…?"

"Alex! I only just met the woman. What do you take me for?"

"I'm just asking," Alex said. "Anyway, I still don't get why this all turned out to be so complicated." She picked up a tea towel.

"Yeah, believe me, that very same thought had already crossed my mind."

"I give up," Alex moaned. "Did you at least find out her name, before you discovered she was psychotic?"

"Jamie tipped her head and forced an emotionless smirk. "Very juvenile. Her name is Sophie."

"You know, when you walked in with her, the rest of us were all wondering who she was. To be honest, I took one look at the pair of you and decided you didn't want anyone else sharing the company. Anyway, so what's the story with the commotion at the bar? The bruise and scratches on your arm?" Alex's hands were now firmly on her hips. "I'm not dropping this, Jamie."

"I can see that," Jamie surrendered. "That was when things got strange and messed up."

"You're telling me," Alex agreed, sitting down. "I don't understand why she didn't at least come and say hello to the rest of us."

"It wasn't personal. We were just having a drink together – nothing heavy, so no need for grand introductions."

"Nothing heavy?" Alex flapped the tea towel. "Surely a simple, civil hello wouldn't have been too much of a hardship?"

Jamie got up and went to top up her coffee. "I was actually enjoying her company until it became apparent that Sophie wasn't holding her booze."

"Go on?"

"Everything was going great at the start. She was just like she'd been in the café. She'd had a couple of vodkas and was relaxed and chatty. After an hour or so, she kept checking her phone."

"Rude!" Alex said.

"Well, she had already mentioned that a couple of her friends might be coming to the same pub later. It was only when she nodded rather sheepishly at someone behind me that I realised her friends had actually, turned up."

Alex took out her phone and started checking messages.

"Pot? Kettle? Black? Rude?" Jamie complained.

"Oh, shush! Just carry on."

"I asked Sophie to call her friends over – to come and join us for a drink. She seemed to think the idea was hilarious, but I didn't get the joke. Anyhow, she made it clear that she definitely wasn't planning on inviting them over."

"I saw her go up and buy a bottle of wine at the bar."

"I already told her I wasn't drinking wine," Jamie said. "She said she was planning to drink it solo."

"Oh God!"

"Yeah. The problem was, the copious vodkas she had been downing had already started to kick in. That was when she began to get all touchy-feely."

"Touchy-feely? She was all over you like a rash."

"Alex!"

"Tetchy." Alex held up her hands. "Let's call a spade a spade here. Your love life of late hasn't gone much further than one-night stands or a weekend jolly, at most."

Jamie frowned. "I've not found the right one yet. I'm still searching." She knew better than to admit that she still believed in the magic of love, and trusted she would one day find her forever soul mate. If Alex heard that, she would no doubt howl with laughter.

Alex raised a lackadaisical, open palm, directing Jamie to carry on, then moseyed back to the kitchen area.

"Sophie's friends were sitting on another table somewhere behind me. She kept looking over my shoulder at them," Jamie said. "Then suddenly, out of the blue, Sophie morphed into a horrible, out-of-control creature. She started raising her glass, and mouthing obscenities across the room at them. I sure as hell wasn't going to stick around to watch her get messy. I suggested we call it a night – go our separate ways and join our own friends."

"I noticed she took the bottle of wine with her," Alex said.

"Yeah, she did." Jamie put her mug down. "Blimey, Alex, you really were watching everything, weren't you?"

“Absolutely. Someone needs to, since you seem incapable of looking after yourself most of the time.” Alex looked at Jamie for a reaction that didn’t happen.

“She started talking to two women at another table. She didn’t sit down with them, though.” She mashed the teabag against the side of her mug, then hesitated. “Actually, Sophie started gesturing like she was pointing you out to her friends. It was hard to see because other people kept walking in front of the table and blocking my view. When I looked again, Sophie had gone and one of the women that she was talking to had got up and was walking towards you. What the hell did she say to you? Your face was a picture.”

“I was just about to settle my bar tab and come join you guys when I noticed a woman looking straight at me and powering across in my direction. She looked like she’d had quite a lot to drink and was hurling abuse. I had no idea Sophie had just been speaking to her.” Jamie held her mug with both hands. “Oh yeah, and get this – the woman accused me of screwing her girlfriend, although her description was more colourful than that.”

“She what?”

“Yeah – seems that I tripped over a relationship that hadn’t quite ended yet.”

“Oh, my God!” Alex announced dramatically, adding, “Mind you, the whole bed-hopping thing is a known phenomenon amongst gays, isn't it? I think I read that in a magazine once.”

Jamie let Alex's ignorance wash over her. "It's a damn shame that Sophie conveniently forgot to share that little gem of information with me."

"No kidding."

Jamie nodded towards Alex's mug. "I think it's dead."

"Huh?"

"The tea bag. It must be stewed to death by now."

"Oh, knickers!" Alex poured the lot down the sink again.

"And your lesbian cheating comment just now was a shitty thing to say, Alex."

"Oh, never mind that," Alex said. "Stop being so sensitive and get on with the gossip."

Jamie's head ached. She needed the bathroom.

She came back into the room, inspecting her sore arm. "The woman wouldn't leave me alone. She'd got it in her head that I had no business being with Sophie and began to get aggressive. The guy serving at the bar was getting twitchy, and I decided it was best to leave her to it and make a quick exit."

"Seems logical." Alex got a comb from her bookshelf and pulled it through the damp tangle of her hair.

"Well, I wasn't going to stick around and risk getting ejected by the owner, but I hadn't anticipated that this woman would follow me outside, either. It could have been worse. She was drunk and wasn't that steady on her feet."

"So, Sophie basically did a bit of shit-stirring then legged it to a safe distance to watch the fall-out, and did sweet F.A. to check you were all right?"

"Pretty much," Jamie said. "Sophie stayed in the pub, while her not-so-ex-girlfriend was busy escorting me outside. She was more upset than angry. I don't think she meant to hurt me. It all got out of hand. She sort of wrestled me to the floor."

"Hell hath no fury like a lover scorned, eh?" Alex quipped.

"No kidding. That's when she started grabbing my clothes; alcohol had made her beyond being reasoned with. I sure as hell wasn't going to wait for her inner Rottweiler to be unleashed. I could just about cope with the nails, but no way was I going to wait for the teeth." Jamie inspected her wrist.

Alex laughed out loud.

"Sophie eventually came outside and tried to calm her friend down. That's when I ran," Jamie continued. "I heard the woman screaming after me, but I just wanted to get away from it all."

"Brilliant. This could only happen to you, Barker."

Jamie closed her eyes.

"Do you need another ice pack on that arm?" Alex opened the freezer door.

"No." Jamie didn't feel like accepting any empathy from her friend just yet. She was still defensive about Alex's brainless comments.

"And your keys – did they fall out of your pocket?"

"I've no idea. It was only after I'd stopped running that I even noticed they were missing. If they had fallen out, it's possible she picked them up, I guess. I need to retrace my steps."

"I know your key fob is pretty unmistakable. Anyone who knows you will recognise they're your keys. It baffles me that you have your swipe-card attached to the key-ring as well. Anyone could get past your security front entrance. Honestly, for someone so intelligent…" Alex said. "Well, all I can say is, thank God she doesn't know where you live."

Jamie scrunched one eye closed and peeped from the other. "I gave Sophie one of my business cards."

Alex raised a derisive eyebrow. "You reckon she's going to pop over and drop your keys through your letter box, like a Good Samaritan? Yeah, right. I think not. You're a loose cannon, Jamie. You were just the same at secondary school."

"That's unfair, and untrue."

"And here we are again," Alex said sternly. "Jamie's in pursuit of yet more fluffy little romantic dalliances."

Alex was right, thought Jamie. It was just like secondary school – in more ways than one.

When they were teenagers, Alex had always been privy to the highs and lows of Jamie's romantic escapades, but she had never made any secret of being baffled by same-sex relationships, even when Jamie came out to her at the late age of 25. Alex had been the most popular girl in the year group and was always surrounded by adoring admirers of both sexes. One morning, she actually chose to sit next to and speak to Jamie – the insignificant tomboy, who was poles apart from all the other girls in her clique. Jamie, who could hardly believe she'd been singled out, waited to become the butt of some cruel teenage joke. Thankfully, the punchline never came.

From then on, they stayed friends, falling into a lazy pattern of hanging out together. Alex could be a pain in the arse, but she was a known quantity and usually fun to spend time with. It was what it was.

CHAPTER 3

The sound of a key in the front door made both women look up.

Even though she had no religious belief, Jamie looked skyward and mentally thanked the lord – the arrival of Alex's husband provided an excuse to stall any further cross-examination. She got to her feet and faked a stifled yawn. "My head is pounding. I'll just go get a duvet and let you two get off to bed."

Gavin stormed through the lounge door. Even through the visor of his full-face motorbike helmet, the glare directed at Jamie stopped her in her tracks. She sat down again. Gavin wasn't about to offer Jamie an easy ride. He tugged angrily at the tight strap under his chin. It refused to budge. The crash helmet and his thick, full-face beard muffled his swearing, but there was no mistaking his Scottish accent. Wearing only khaki shorts and a t-shirt, he was completely soaked through. Gavin finally heaved off his Arai helmet, still cursing profusely. His tirade of anger was aimed full-force at Jamie.

"Still raining, then?" Jamie joshed, speaking before thinking.

Alex looked daggers, forewarning Jamie.

"Glad someone finds this amusing." Gavin threw his gloves across the coffee table, spilling Alex's cup of tea for the second time. He swore again although made no attempt to clean it up.

Jamie opened her mouth, primed for confrontation, but was well and truly cut down by Gavin's steel-cold eyes.

"I'm fucking sick of your high-maintenance melodramas, Jamie." Gavin's top lip curled. "I don't even want to hear the explanation behind this one. I'm going to bed."

He left the room, slamming the door, not stopping to give his wife their usual goodnight kiss.

Any other day, Jamie would have given back as good as Gavin was dishing out. Usually, they were equally matched sparring partners, but tonight Jamie held back, knowing that Gavin had put himself out – she didn't have a leg to stand on with this one. His angry response was a reminder to Jamie of his true feelings about her friendship with Alex.

Now that Gavin had left the room, Jamie turned to Alex. "Look, Al, I'm shattered. I need to get a couple of hours' sleep before heading back to my place. I won't disturb you guys. I'll just slip out when I wake up, if that's okay? I don't think that Gavin would be too happy to find me here when he wakes up."

"Don't be a plonker. I'm not leaving you to go to your apartment alone. If that woman did get your keys, you have no idea what you might find when you get there."

"That's a very unlikely scenario and rather extreme scare-mongering, don't you think?"

"Anyway, Gavin is on shift work, and will be

asleep most of the day tomorrow," Alex said. "I'm sleeping in the guest room so as not to wake him. I'll leave him a note to tell him I've gone with you. Come and wake me before you leave."

"Really, there's no need to come –"

"No arguments! Get some sleep and I'll see you in a short while."

Alex wasn't waiting to negotiate, and Jamie was too tired to argue. She peeled off her jeans, lay sideways on the two-seater sofa, hugging her knees to her chest, and pulled the duvet over her head. Minutes later, she fell into a cramped and all-too-brief sleep.

Jamie woke abruptly to the harsh slam of a china mug on the counter.

"You still here?" Gavin growled. He was already through the door, heading back to bed, and didn't care about the answer.

"Of course I'm still here, you dick!" Jamie mumbled at the closed door.

Jamie had always believed that Gavin didn't particularly like or trust her. Not long after his wedding to Alex, he'd been foolhardy enough to accuse her of harbouring ulterior motives towards his wife. Granted, he'd been very drunk, but Jamie never forgot the accusation. The following day, when Jamie reminded him, he conveniently denied all recollection. They never spoke of the incident again, but their communication from that point was always loaded with tension.

It was nearly ten to five. Jamie realised she should leave. Minutes later, she was creeping down the stairs from the second-floor maisonette in Bethnal Green, and she closed the front door as quietly as she could.

Jamie heard the bathroom window squeak open above.

"Wait up!" Alex's voice rasped gruffly through the gap. "I thought you were going to wake me?"

Jamie shushed back. "It's still early. Go back to bed."

Right on time, the faint chime from the Bow bells of St Mary's church could be heard in the distance as it signalled the hour. The morning air was still but warm. It was promising to be another hot day.

The window above squeaked again, then thunked shut. Jamie kept walking.

*****

The sky was a cloudless blue. The morning sun cast slivers of light between the buildings of the London skyline. Condensation shimmered above where the sun warmed the still-damp roads and streets. From this perspective, walking past Old Spitalfields Market, Jamie thought she caught a glimpse of the tip of the Shard across the Thames, towering majestically above the surrounding metropolis. On days like this, Jamie thought London was truly the most beautiful city in the world.

Alex’s footsteps and breathless gasps followed close behind Jamie. “Slow down, will you? It’s not the London bloody marathon.” She tugged at Jamie’s arm, bringing her to a halt. Jamie winced a little, supporting her wrist.

“Coffee, I need a coffee,” Alex begged, pulling Jamie in the opposite direction towards the nearest double espresso and croissant. “It’s Sunday. Where’s going to be open now? Why can’t London be more like New York?”

“Come on, Carrie Bradshaw,” Jamie laughed. “We’ll go to Café 1001 on Brick Lane. It opens at six.”

“‘Carrie Bradshaw’? Which decade are you living in?”

“Alex, you’re more interested in your coffee than seeing me home safely, aren’t you?”

“You know I can’t operate without my morning coffee, Jamie – particularly on a Sunday morning. Anyway, if we are going to do our detective work, we need time to think through our plan. We’re on a mission to solve a mystery.”

Jamie wasn't surprised that Alex’s gusto was less about concern for her and more about the excitement of being involved in the thick of it all.

Forty minutes later, they were climbing the stairs, coffee cup in hand, to the top deck of a quiet W15 bus, heading towards Mayfair. The bus retained the lingering stench of Saturday-night vomit and stale beer

– a stark contrast to the Monday-morning smell of aftershave and freshly showered commuters during rush hour.

"So, tell me." Alex pushed a discarded kebab box off the seat and onto the floor before sitting down. "I bet you didn't think about a couple of fundamentals before you headed home this morning?"

Jamie sighed. Alex always put on this air of superiority when she wanted to point out what she thought was blindingly obvious. The next forty-five minutes were likely to drag.

Alex took a wet-wipe from her handbag and wiped the grease off her fingers. "Some people are so disrespectful. Didn't their parents teach them to use a bin?"

Jamie looked at the fast-food box on the floor. "Good to see you're setting an example, then."

Alex ignored her.

"Please enlighten me." Jamie closed her eyes in anticipation. "What *are* the fundamentals I've apparently forgotten?"

"Well, number one," Alex said, keen for the chance to educate her friend. "What were you planning to do exactly, once you got to your place – with no keys? Bearing in mind only *I* have your spares?"

"Call you, I guess, or call out a locksmith, and contact the company responsible for the security swipe cards to our flats?"

"Which brings me conveniently to question two –

how would you have made that call?"

Ready with her answer, Jamie plunged into her pocket for her phone. Her self-assurance was short-lived.

"Ah!"

"Yeah, exactly. A knackered mobile is a great help." Alex waved her own phone triumphantly. "Alex Forbes bails out Jamie Barker, yet again. Good thing I came with you, huh?"

Jamie rolled her eyes at Alex's insistence on playing the indispensable martyr.

*****

When they finally arrived outside Jamie's flat, they both stopped and looked up towards her balcony on the top floor. The sun glared off the windows so that it was impossible to see inside, and for a moment Jamie felt oddly detached from the property, as if she'd never set foot in it before.

The man she'd brought it from had been a successful New York divorce lawyer whose high-profile clients had included A-list actors and rich celebrities. This apartment was just one of his two continental pied-à-terres.

She'd only just been able to take on the mortgage thanks to her inheritance from her late father. In the four years since, she had kept up the payments through sheer hard work, building up her own architectural

practice and expanding her roster of private clients, whose tastes
in homes ran to luxury and bespoke detail.

"Come on." Alex took the lead, striding on ahead.

Alex already had Jamie's spare key in her hand. She swiped the ID card through the security scanner and walked into the main entrance.

As usual, Alex went straight for the lift – where Jamie and Alex usually parted company. Jamie routinely opted for the stairs, taking two or three steps at a time, aiming to beat the lift. This daily micro-workout was her excuse for avoiding the local gym; she'd convinced herself that she just didn't have the time for regular exercise.

This morning, though, Jamie followed Alex. She sensed safety in numbers, and was disinclined to be the first through the door into her home. No doubt Alex would make some smart comment, she thought. She wasn't let down.

Alex pinched at Jamie's waist. "Not like you to take the lift. I thought you'd want to work off that croissant-filled muffin top."

Jamie's heart beat a little faster as they walked the short distance from the elevator exit then along the corridor. She quickened her step, taking her spare key from Alex as they walked.

At the door, she hesitantly slotted her key into the lock, holding her breath. She turned the key more slowly than normal, prolonging having to face what she might find beyond. She gradually pushed the door half open.

The sound was enough to disturb the silent occupant. Amelie leapt up from the sofa, raced down the hall and threw herself into Jamie's arms.

"Hey, gorgeous. Did you miss me?"

Typical of her rag-doll breed, the fluffy grey and white cat instantly relaxed into a firefighter's lift across Jamie's shoulder. Totally trusting her owner, Amelie's front paws and head dangled down Jamie's back. Deep, rasping purrs emanated contentedly from the creature. Relieved, Jamie nuzzled into Amelie's soft fur.

"I can't believe you didn't train her to do that." Alex swung her bag off her shoulder and shut the door. "What's that?" She peered at what appeared to be a bubble-wrap envelope on the floor. It had been pushed out of view as the door had opened.

Jamie's name was written across it in thick, black capitals. She picked it up but refrained from opening it, staring at the letters.

"Oh, for God's sake, Jamie!" Alex snatched it away. "It's only a frigging envelope – not an Oscar nomination." She tore it open.

A card fell to the floor.

This time, Jamie grabbed it before Alex. It was a cardboard beer mat for Meantime London Pale Ales. There was writing on the back.

Alex squinted, childlike, over Jamie's shoulder.

"There's a note, too. It's from Darren." Jamie had noticed his name before reading the note. She went back to the writing above. "It says: *These were handed in*
behind the bar last night."

Alex delved into the bottom of the envelope. She took out a set of keys on a red key fob, dangling them in Jamie's face.

"Darren. What a superstar."

Darren was a friend of Gavin's. He had worked part-time for the last eight months behind the bar at The Coal Hole pub.

Jamie showed Alex the card. There was a phone number on it, with *please call* written across the bottom. She could generally recognise a number from the last three digits, but not this one. "I have no idea whose this mobile number is."

"You'd best get your phone charged up then, so you can check."

"Lend us your phone. I'll call now," Jamie suggested.

"No way." Alex was quick to respond. "I'm not getting involved. I don't want some freak being able to access my mobile number. Use your landline if you're so keen to ring now."

Jamie was curious, but not curious enough to call right away.

Alex looked at her watch – more a reflex action than from a need to know the time. "Right. It's too early to call the pub now, so I could go in and ask Darren tomorrow if he can tell us more?" She clapped her hands excitedly. "Ooh, it's like playing at detectives."

"Please don't do that, Alex." Jamie was firm. "I don't need your interference. I'll deal with it in my own way."

"Fine!" Alex harrumphed.

Jamie tossed her keys into a wooden bowl on top of a drop-down shoe cabinet in the hall. She tugged at the laces on her shoes before kicking them off and placing them neatly into their designated drawer, then walked towards the kitchen. Amelie trotted alongside, circling in expectant figures-of-eight around Jamie's ankles.

"Come on, you soppy bag of fur, you need feeding."

Alex followed.

"Shoes!" Jamie ordered, pointing at Alex's feet.

The cat meowed plaintively, frightened by Jamie's raised voice.

Alex tutted and deferentially slipped off her shoes, placing them neatly next to the drawer cabinet. In all the excitement, she had forgotten about Jamie's domestic regime.

Jamie's apartment was meticulously clean and tidy, kitted out with quality furnishings and appliances. The artist in her craved light, which now streamed in through large, east-facing sliding doors at the far end of the main room. To make the most of the daylight,

Jamie's architect's drawing board stood in front of the balcony doors. Tucked in the corner was a small desk, complete with a laptop. Like the rest of the place, this office was methodically and precisely organised, with rows of alphabetically arranged architectural journals and interior design publications and magazines. On the wall, opposite, was a built-in shelving unit full of novels, DVDs and CDs. Each had their designated place, also arranged alphabetically. Alex had once lambasted Jamie in front of friends at a party for taking up so much wall space with shelves of CDs. She'd accused Jamie of having a secret stash of TDK cassette tapes stored in a cupboard somewhere, ready to take to the Antiques Roadshow, along with her collection of Betamax videos.

The only indication that this was someone's home, rather than an immaculate show-house, was the evidence of Jamie's creativity: a dozen or so unwanted design plans for a client in Kensington, screwed up and tossed arbitrarily around her drawing board. Even the kitchen area looked unused. Jamie had never quite got to grips with the Aga and lived off easy options that involved minimal preparation, or a quick ping in the microwave. She couldn't see the point of spending precious work-time preparing meals for one. She preferred to work late and order in a take-out, or grab a sandwich on the go between the office and home. That way, she only needed to worry about a quick shower and usually a whisky before falling into bed.

Her career always came first – and that, she believed, had nothing to do with the fact that her romantic life was in such perpetual chaos. Alex, of course, had not failed to point out the error in her thinking.

The large bi-folding doors opened out onto a nine-foot-long, glass-fronted balcony, providing a fabulous panoramic view across Hyde Park and beyond. It was a cleverly enclosed construction and not overlooked by anyone. Outside, four chairs nestled snugly around a small, round table. A shallow puddle of rain sat in the indentation on the seat of each chair.

Jamie unlocked the bi-folding door, flinging it across its frame. She connected her phone to the charger on her desk. Within seconds, it started madly pinging, indicating the missed calls and messages. She flicked through and deleted them, pausing to listen to a rambling voicemail: *Hello, darling. It's only Mum. I've just left you a message on your home phone, too – you never seem to be around when I call and I've not seen you for months – poor love, you must be working far too hard. It's just not healthy – Anyway, I've spoken with your sister this morning – she's fine, but she tells me you're still being elusive and impossible to pin down – it's upsetting her, darling... I've been meaning to ask you both to come for lunch one Sunday. You both need some sea air and good home-cooked food in you... She loves you, and misses you terribly, you know, Jamie... Anyway, I've not called to lecture you – Please call very soon, darling. Love you.*

Jamie frowned. It had been a long time since she had been in touch with either of them. But she couldn't dwell on it now. There were more pressing things to occupy her mind. She deleted the message before walking back to her balcony.

Looking across at the park, she inhaled a long, deep breath and breathed out slowly. "Know what, Al?" she declared presently, pointing towards the wall. "Life is not about waiting for the storm to pass, it's about learning to dance in the rain."

Alex followed Jamie's gaze to a framed canvas hanging above the white leather sofa. It had the sentence that Jamie had just recited, printed across a black canvas background in large, multi-coloured capitals.

"Deep," Alex said, deadpan.

"These last few days have got me thinking. I need to sort my life out."

Alex air-played an imaginary violin.

"Seriously – I need to start reclaiming my life. I'm the wrong side of forty and look at me. Rattling around in this amazing place. More money than one person can spend, and never enough time to really enjoy it. I'm tired of work dominating my time. I'm tired of dead-end Friday-night flings. I'm tired of dreading Sunday mornings alone. I'm just tired of being single, Al."

"Eureka. The phoenix is finally rising. It's time to move along the aisle inside in that little old bus called life." Alex delighted in her wit; Jamie did not.

Alex pushed for a more satisfying response. "She whose name shall not be mentioned has been out of your life for over four years now."

The pit of Jamie's stomach turned involuntarily. A sense of emptiness reminded her that the wounds from the knife in her back were still raw.

"Do you miss her?"

"Stupid question," Jamie replied.

"You've been hiding behind your work for way too long now. Stop allowing the past to influence your future." Alex looked at the words written on the canvas. "It's time to start dancing, honey." She chortled to herself. "But you didn't do much dancing during last night's downpour, did you? More like running away from getting your nose punched."

Jamie knelt on the sofa to reach the picture on the wall. She pushed the corner down a few degrees, to correct the slight offset tilt.

"So, time for that online dating now?" Alex teased.

"Haven't we already had this conversation? I'll do things my way and in my own time."

"I did offer to write your profile for you."

"Yeah, and the answer is still no."

"But getting a friend to write your profile is the best way to get across your true and honest personality… so they say. I read it in a magazine somewhere."

"Give it a rest, Alex. This is getting boring."

As expected, Alex couldn't let it go. "Who knows, maybe it's time to start batting for the other side, for a change?"

"What a puerile and fatuous statement," Jamie answered.

But Alex wasn't done. "Anyhow, whatever your preference, how else are you going to get yourself out there again?"

"Oh, just drop it, will you?"

The phone on the desk rang.

Alex's nose wrinkled. "It's Sunday. It's not even nine o'clock yet. Why the hell do you keep your work extension connected on a Sunday?"

Relieved by the distraction, Jamie went to pick up her business landline next to her drawing board.

"You're not actually going to answer that, are you?"

"Hello, J.B. Architects, Jamie Barker speaking. How may I help you?"

Alex huffed disapprovingly.

Jamie listened, adding the odd, single-syllable affirmative. "Uh-huh… yes… right…" She propped the phone between her chin and shoulder, took a pad and pencil from her desk, then started jotting down details. After several minutes, she looked towards the clock on the wall. Almost ten to nine. "Today? This morning? Little Venice? No – It's no problem at all. I could get to you for twelve-thirty...? No...? Okay, twelve is fine."

Alex tapped at her wristwatch. "I give up," she said, too loudly to be subtle, and made for the door. On her way out, she took a sticky note and marker-pen from Jamie's desk and scribbled over it. She ripped it off, slapped it on top of Jamie's drawing board and left the room. The front door shut.

Jamie hung up the phone and peeled off the note. *GET A LIFE BARKER* was scrawled across it. She screwed it up and tossed it into the bin, peeved that Alex knew exactly how to locate her Achilles heel. But it
annoyed her even more that she allowed it to bother her.

*****

Suited and booted, with her lucky cufflinks on, Jamie turned the key in the ignition, relishing the rich growl of the engine. Her car, a red, seven-speed, convertible Audi R8 Spyder, was her baby – an older model, but nevertheless loved like an old pal. She pumped the accelerator, enjoying the echo within the confined space of the low ceiling, and thought about her dad.

Encouraged by her father, Jamie had developed a fascination with engines and indeed anything mechanical as a child. One summer holiday, her father had taken her to visit a family friend, who happened to be in his garage, preparing and renovating a 1964

Marcos GT 1800. Not afraid to get grease on her hands, Jamie was a quick learner. What she discovered about stripping and rebuilding a 1.8-litre engine set her up for a lifelong curiosity; it was a huge, formative influence on her career. Thirty-odd years on, she still smiled every time she heard the song Greased Lightning, remembering how each time the song came on the garage's radio, the mechanics would take turns to croon the lines while re-enacting the car-renovation scene.

At that age, Jamie would often spend Sundays exploring the local fields and rivers with her father. He introduced her to fly-fishing and hunting. Anything worth keeping, Jamie carried home, where she learned to skin, scale or pluck the kill, then prepare so it was ready to eat. Similarly, the distinct aroma of the lubricating oil WD40 always reminded Jamie of the post-hunting ritual with her father – stripping and cleaning the shotgun rifles on her mother's kitchen table.

This was when Jamie's father first started to call her a tomboy – the son he didn't have – and made her feel proud.

*****

Canary Wharf loomed in the distance. It was a hassle having to trek out to her Docklands office just to get the files she would need, then all the way back to Little Venice for her noon meeting. But Jamie was enjoying the drive. The roof was down, her Ray-Bans were on, and Walking On Sunshine blasted through the speakers. Jamie tapped out the rhythm on her steering wheel, singing along to the lyrics, and took a cursory glance at her driver's mirror. She moved her gear stick and signalled, edging forward to turn right.

"Shit!"

A sickening squeal of tyres on tarmac caused Jamie to stamp hard on the brake pedal. The smell of hot rubber preceded the unnecessary, over-zealous pounding of a car horn. A black London cab pulled up beside Jamie. The driver leant out of his window, his cap pulled low over his eyebrows. "Look where yer going, sweetheart." His glance turned to the Spyder. "Give the sports car back to yer husband and drive sommink you can handle, darlin'."

Jamie bristled. She fought the impulse to reply. She failed. "Imbecile!"

She was met with a gawp. He had no idea how to respond, and retaliated feebly, mumbling some inaudible profanity at her.

This specimen wasn't worth wasting any more of her precious time and energy on. Jamie was well versed in dealing with alpha-males. Such individuals were commonplace in her line of work – usually building foremen or surveyors in hard hats with large clipboards and even larger egos. Successful women like Jamie seemed to make men like this nervous. She was used to being taken less seriously and spoken to as if unworthy of her status.

But Jamie was smart and exceptionally good at her job. Although sometimes conscious of having to prove herself, she invariably ended up earning the respect she deserved.

The taxi wasn't empty. A bewildered-looking passenger was sitting in the back, mobile phone pressed to her ear. She began exchanging words with the driver while trying to scramble out of the cab. Looking flustered, she thrust a banknote through the window. "Keep the change. I'll make my own way from here." Her tip for the driver looked more like an excuse to flee the situation as soon as possible, instead of a reward for his excellent service.

The cab driver beat a retreat, accelerating up the high street after a macho handbrake wheel spin. He left as he had entered, in a cloud of burning rubber – a final testosterone-fuelled attempt to have the last word.

Jamie watched the woman zigzag between the traffic, fingers tightly around her phone. She looked terrible – had she been crying? As she approached Jamie's car, her slow steps were leaden, her conversation intense.

Jamie listened.

"No, not really… It's all been just been horrible. I feel strung out and exhausted… Yes, I did… And thank God Chris agreed to listen and let me be honest about my feelings…"

Chris? Jamie listened harder.

"No, I'm all right, honestly… Actually, I could really do with a hug… Can you come and meet me maybe…?"

The woman then looked directly at Jamie. She offered a nod and a gritty, half-baked smile.

Jamie had been right: it was Kate from Alchemy. She tracked her in the rear-view mirror as she disappeared round the corner into a side street. It appeared that Kate's trip to the airport to stop Chris leaving had not ended well.

Her night must have been even more eventful than mine, Jamie reflected. So, what the hell had happened to the woman after she'd left Alchemy?

CHAPTER 4

After the phone call to Chris, Kate hadn't been able to clear Alchemy fast enough. If there was even the slightest opportunity to give the relationship another chance, she would fight for it. Once she had called the cab to Heathrow, she just wanted everyone to hurry up and leave the bar. The few remaining people didn't put up too much resistance as she ushered them through the exit.

Once outside and preparing to lock up, she'd clumsily dropped her phone. One of the final two customers had kindly picked it up. Kate recognised her to be the chatty, rain-soaked woman from earlier. Kate noted the immaturity of the other person – making fun of her friend's thoughtfulness by calling her Mother Theresa.

Two London black cabs were already waiting outside Alchemy. Kate walked towards the one in front. "How long will it take to get to Heathrow, Terminal Five?" Kate clambered into the back, pushing her arm through the sleeve of her jacket.

"'Ow long do ya want it to take, darlin'?" The cab driver scrutinised her through his rear-view mirror.

"As quickly as possible," she added. "Without getting pulled over or becoming a road accident statistic." She waved a fifty-pound note over his shoulder.

He took the hint and registered the urgency,

spurred on by the cash incentive. He pulled his flat cap firmly down to just beneath his eyebrows. "At this time? About forty-five minutes, love…give or take. Leave it with me." He gunned the engine. "Ever watch Starsky an' 'utch, did ya?" He laughed to himself.

Kate didn't reply.

"Seventies double-act cop show. David Soul and Paul what's-his-name, wasn't it? Loved that show, me." He tunelessly hollered the first line, "Don't give up on us baby –" Failing to finish the lyrics, he ended the phrase with an equally discordant whistle. "Great show, awful song, though. Dave should've stuck with 'is acting." He gave an uneasy shuffle in his seat. "Mind you, with a jumper like that, I thought that Paul bloke must 'ave been a poofter." He guffawed.

The last thing Kate needed was a lengthy cab journey with a chirpy cockney who clearly overrated his comedic skill.

"So, Heathrow... Going anywhere nice?" He spoke eagerly at her into his rear-view mirror.

"No." Kate avoided his eyes.

"Oh, right. No suitcase. Meeting someone coming home then, are ya?"

"No," Kate said. "Someone leaving, actually," she added, wondering why on earth she was divulging her personal details.

"Oh, right. Nice. A friend? Husband?" He looked inquisitively at her reflection.

Kate bristled; she wasn't about to be coerced into

explaining more than she wanted to. But – typical Brit – rather than be honest, Kate was politely apologetic. "It's been a long day. I'm not in the mood to talk about it if you don't mind."

Content to listen to his own voice, the driver droned on. The subtlety of Kate's earlier request for a quiet journey was lost on him. He appeared totally unfazed that his passenger offered nothing in response to his monologue. This guy was relentless. Either ill-mannered, ignorant or both. The experience wasn't helped by his erratic driving. This had all the hallmarks of being a painfully long journey.

Once at Heathrow, Kate got out of the cab and sprinted across the concourse to reach the terminal with time to spare. But this was only the first part of her mission. The clincher was still to come – to persuade Chris to hear her out and consider giving their relationship a second chance.

*****

Walking back to the taxi, Kate's head started to ache. The conversation had been emotional, heated, painful and unresolved. But she could do and say no more.

As luck would have it, she got the same cab driver for the journey home – and the return trip was just as horrible as the first. Again, he continued to talk at Kate via his rear-view mirror, with intrusive, nosy questions, intermittently peering over his shoulder to engage and sustain her attention – a style of driving that terrified Kate. She spent the trip gripping the edge of the seat, white-knuckled, head down, staring steadfastly at her knees, swallowing back motion sickness – anything to avoid engaging with his eyes. Anything to avoid being reminded of her father.

The journey ended prematurely when the cab driver nearly collided with an innocent woman in a stationary open-topped sports car. He stopped the taxi and launched into a repulsive exhibition of road-rage.

Kate couldn't take any more. She leapt out, pulled out the first banknote from her purse and posted it through the gap in the window at the driver. She would make her own way from here. As she left the area, her first thought was to phone Richard. She needed a friend.

"I got your message," Richard explained, having heard Kate's abridged version of events. "But you had left for Heathrow already. Are you sure you're okay? You don't sound too chipper, sweetie."

"No, not really."

"Oh, Kate, poor love. The whole thing sounds just ghastly."

"It's been horrible."

"But you managed to get to Heathrow in time, and talk it over?"

"Yes, I did," Kate said. "And thank God Chris agreed to listen and let me be honest about my feelings…"

"I'm just walking over London Bridge to my car, so
if you need me to come?" Richard said.

"No, I'm all right, honestly," Kate replied.

"Are you sure? You sound a tad wobbly to me, sweetie."

Kate thought again. "Actually, I could do with a hug… can you come and meet me maybe?"

"Tell me where to find you."

Through the duration of the conversation, Kate slowly passed the length of the red, open-topped sports car. Then, the coincidence became apparent; the driver was the woman who had picked up her phone earlier – the marmalade martini customer… *Jamie wasn't it*? *Wasn't that what her impatient friend had called her?* Kate mustered a smile, but wasn't sure if the woman even recognised her, so she hurried on.

Further up the road, Kate slowed her pace. She saw Richard up ahead, jogging towards her. As he drew closer, she saw he held a fistful of tissues. Seeing them somehow allowed Kate to let go. Richard grabbed her for a hug and Kate sobbed onto his shoulder.

"Typical. Last night of all nights you're dealing with a crisis at work, and it wasn't my shift." Richard handed over the Kleenex. "Have some of these. And tell Uncle Richie all about it, sweetie." He linked arms with her and led her towards his car.

By the time they got there, Kate was calmer and able to string sentences together without dissolving into tears.

Richard opened the passenger door to let Kate in before settling himself in the driver's seat. "But you managed to get to the airport in time?"

"Only just," Kate said. She started tearing up again. "And then, when we talked just before I left Alchemy, I thought it might still be possible to salvage our relationship."

"So, that's a positive, isn't it?"

"As soon as I shut up the bar, I just went on what felt right. The one person – my rock and my soul mate – was about to leave my life for good. I couldn't let that happen. Not without putting up a fight."

"And Chris's response to all this?"

"I'm not sure yet. I just need to wait – allow some time to think things over." Kate wiped her eyes. "I've said what I needed to say," she sniffed.

"Blow!" Richard instructed.

Kate blew her nose. "And thank you for these." She held up her tissues.

Richard bowed his head with closed eyes and hand on his chest. "At your service. Armed and ready for all eventualities, sweetie." He pushed his fingers through his hair, checking himself in his driver's mirror and stroking one of his freshly trimmed eyebrows. "You never know when a fistful of tissues are going to come in handy."

Kate blew her nose again.

"Oh!" Richard frowned, having caught sight of his shirt in the mirror. It was stained with an amalgamation of Kate's snot and tears.

"Sorry," Kate said, catching a little whimpering sob in her throat.

"Oh, shh, shh…" he consoled, gently touching her arm. "It's nothing that won't wash out." He started dabbing at his collar with a tissue.

Kate realised she'd forgotten something. "Oh, Richard, I'm sorry," she said. "I'm so preoccupied by my own problems, I completely forgot to ask you. How is your grandmother?"

"Listen to her, will you?" Richard pointed at Kate, and spoke to an imaginary person. "*She's* the one who's just gone through the mill, but still manages to think about other people? That's very sweet of you to ask – and such a Kate-ish thing to do." He stroked the back of her hand. "The op went fine – bless you for asking – and she's recuperating comfortably in hospital. We just need to wait for a few more days to find out exactly how much mobility she has."

"I sent her some flowers and a card, to the hospital," Kate sniffed. "She should have received them."

"Thank you. She'll appreciate that. But I'm here for *you* at the moment, not to talk about my granny. Tell me what happened at the airport."

"If I'm honest, I'd lost all hope that Chris would even give me the time of day – particularly after everything that Tig has done."

Richard's eyebrows lifted. "Tig?"

Perhaps now, Kate deliberated, was the time to tell Richard the details? She looked earnestly at him.

"I'm here for you, Kate. You can tell me as little or as much as you want to, sweetie." Richard swivelled with difficulty to face his friend – the best he could for a six foot one and three-quarter man in the cramped seat of a Mini Cooper. "But it's not very cosy or comfortable sat here, is it? Shall we go somewhere else?"

"How about back to Alchemy?" Kate suggested. "It will be quiet. We've got until six before we need to open."

"Let's do it." Richard started the engine.

*****

As they sat across from each other at a table in front of the bar, Richard's questions became rather more direct. "Sweetie," he said. "I realise, reading between the lines, that your brother has been a bit of a tit over the years..." He looked at Kate.

Kate smiled, realising that he was waiting for her permission to continue with his inquisition. "What do you want to know, Rich?"

"Well, obviously I know bits and pieces. For example, I'm aware that Tig has stuck his oar in between you and Chris more than once, and that Chris obviously still loves you, but whatever your brother has said or done this time, it's been enough to put a pretty damaging rift in your relationship. I also know that you hardly ever see Tig." Richard folded his arms. "That's as much as I do know."

"We've worked together for – just over a year and a half now, isn't it?"

Richard counted on his fingers, like a child on an abacus, mouthing each number.

"And you've been nothing short of a good, dear friend."

"Not to mention your personal shopping stylist and all round good-egg," Richard beamed, reaching out to hold the back of Kate's hand as it rested on the table.

Kate drew breath and wondered where and how to begin. "Ever since..." No, she wouldn't start at the very beginning. "Chris is not the first relationship that my brother has destroyed, you know?"

"No?"

"Oh no. He is a very angry, jealous man who has been controlling and interfering in my life for years."

"Really?" Richard sat attentively straight and appropriately serious.

"He first started interfering…" Kate checked herself again. "It started little by little, at first, when I was barely an adult myself. He made it his business to vet all of my relationships. He was fiercely overprotective of me, shooting daggers at any other man that came near me. The few relationships that I formed over the years were sabotaged by his jealousy. You see, in Tig's head…" Kate thought better of how much she should share. "Well, he was just very angry and jealous."

"Why?"

"Would you mind getting me some water, please?"

"Sure, sweetie." Richard jumped up and bounded to the bar. He returned with a half-pint of iced water.

"Basically, my brother's interference with my life is the reason why I am where I am with Chris now – the one relationship in my life that I dared to call 'the one'."

"But from what you've said, the break-up is not yet a *fait accompli?*" Richard asked encouragingly. "There's still hope?"

"The thought of Chris actually leaving my life for good…" Kate wiped the rim of her glass with her thumb. "The thought of that being a reality… is more than I can cope with." She thought. "If Chris has really gone for good, I won't forgive Tig this time." She paused again, conscious of what her next words actually meant. "I think – I think I hate him, Richard."

"Hate?"

Kate could tell that she had shocked her friend.

"Struth! I can't quite believe that those words have actually come from your lips. You are probably the most gentle, considerate person I know, Kate. I don't think I've ever even heard you swear."

"Thank you for coming to meet me, Rich."

He looked dismayed. "You might be my boss, but you're also a dear friend. I would hardly leave you stranded, would I? And from what you've just told me, I'm quite upset with myself that I didn't twig there was more going on between your brother and Chris."

"Why would you? I've never spoken to you about it before. I keep my personal life pretty private. You aren't a mind reader."

"True. I'm good, but not *that* good."

"I'll cope." Kate brushed it off. "It's just another of life's hurdles to get over, I suppose." She looked towards the bar and stood up. "We really need to start preparing for the evening shift."

Richard looked suspiciously at Kate. "You're shutting down on me, aren't you?" he said. "But I'm not going to push it. Anyway, can't Kieran do the bar-prep when he comes in later?"

"I might own the place, but I lead by example – you know that. I like to keep busy."

"I have a splendid suggestion. How about indulging me? Let me get you something a bit more interesting than water?" Richard leapt up. "I've concocted a fabulous new cocktail. If you like it, perhaps we could add it to the menu?"

Kate took one of the paper drink coasters from the table and screwed it up. "You don't need to make up an excuse to have a drink, Richard," she teased, throwing the paper ball at him.

"It's good to see you smiling." Richard took himself behind the bar. "I promise, you will love this." He started to gather the ingredients for his invention. "So, can you tell me why your brother is so jealous? I don't mean to be rude, but his behaviour…Well, to be blunt, it's not normal, is it?" He scooped ice into the shaker and looked at Kate, who had followed him behind the bar. "I know it's none of my business."

Kate was cutting up limes.

"Were you ever friends, as in happy and close?"

"Yes." Kate stopped chopping. "We were inseparable as children."

"Really?" Richard put down the cocktail shaker. "So what happened?"

Kate rummaged in her rucksack under the counter and opened a side pocket. "Here." She handed Richard a dog-eared photograph wrapped neatly inside in a clear plastic bag. "On the day after he was born. I went with Dad to see my new brother in the hospital."

"Oh yes," Richard smiled, peering at the picture.

"As you can see," Kate pointed at the photograph. "I walked into the hospital with both hands full – one hand holding my dad's finger, the other clutching the paw of a Tigger the tiger toy, as in Winnie-the-Pooh?"

Richard peered harder. "Very cute. That's outside the London Hospital, Whitechapel, isn't it? Where my Granny Olga is recovering?"

"Yes, it is. My dad's brother, Uncle Peter, took the photo."

Richard handed it back. "How old were you?"

"Seven, nearly eight." Kate stood staring at the photo. "That was the day I invented my brother's nickname."

Richard wiped his hands on a towel, temporarily abandoning his creation. He took up his listening pose, the pad of his three middle fingers over his lips. "Let me guess. Tigger the tiger? That's short for Tig, yes?"

"Yes. Mum and Dad still hadn't agreed on his name, even on the day he arrived."

"Now that sounds like the build-up for an entertaining, anecdotal wedding speech," Richard smiled.

Kate smiled back and carefully returned her photo to its safe place.

The landline phone rang. Richard leant across to answer it, while Kate finished slicing the limes.

"That was Kieran. He won't be working his shift tonight. He's got man-flu."

"In this heat?"

"Mine is not to question why. I'm just the messenger," Richard said. "But I'll cover his shift tonight, if it helps you out."

"Are you sure?"

Richard looked at his watch. "I will need to pop off home first though."

"Of course."

"Like, now?" He was on the verge of apologising.

"Of course, Rich. You go. I'll finish up here."

Richard gave Kate a hug and a kiss. "I haven't forgotten our conversation. I need to hear the rest of that story." He stood back, both hands on her shoulders. "You really have been through it, haven't you, sweetie? Let's hope Chris sees sense and can see past your brother's selfish nonsense – whatever it is he's said or done?"

"I hope so, too."

CHAPTER 5

Jamie's jacket pocket vibrated.

"Jamie Barker? It's Lucy Davies here. I'm ever so sorry for the inconvenience, but would you mind awfully shifting our twelve o'clock appointment on an hour…?"

Jamie was very glad for the delay. The incident with the taxi meant her timing was out of kilter, and she could now relax, knowing she wouldn't be late for her appointment in Little Venice. It meant she had plenty of time to go to her Docklands office and sort out her paperwork. But before she had time to rev up the Spyder, her phone vibrated again.

"Did you ring that number yet?"

"No, not yet, Alex. I'm only just leaving to get to my appointment. It's been delayed and I'm running late."

"What? You've had practically all morning to call. Aren't you even wondering?"

"It's not really a priority right now, Al. I've been held up by some imbecilic cab driver who nearly trashed the car."

"Oh God, not the Spyder?" Alex did not sound sincere.

Jamie didn't react to the provocation.

"But you're okay, right?" Alex expressed unusual concern, but scuppered any hint of sympathy with the wisecrack, "You must be all right, or you wouldn't be talking to me now."

"Yeah, I'm okay. Just hacked off." Jamie looked at her watch. "I've got to go."

"Phone me before five, yeah?" Alex hung up without giving her a chance to answer.

Jamie knew Alex's mind. She didn't feel she needed to wait for Jamie to say yes; her compliance was assumed. *She takes me for granted*, thought Jamie, realising that she'd never admitted this obvious truth to herself before.

*****

"Jamie Barker, I hope?"

Jamie was met at the door of a magnificent mid-Georgian townhouse, with a warm smile and reassuringly firm handshake. "I appreciate you coming here at such short notice."

This certainly wasn't the person Jamie had spoken with on the phone earlier. "I believe it was a Lucy Davies who called me this morning?"

"Ah, yes, my delightful Lucy – such a scrumptious little creature." The gentleman finished his sentence thoughtfully, taking a long inhalation from a cigarette. The tip of his tongue caressed his top lip. He swallowed the smoke.

Jamie balked, wondering what kind of image he could possibly be conjuring in his head. "Are we talking about chocolate cake, a chihuahua or a fully-grown adult, here?"

"Who, Lucy?" The man seemed confused by Jamie's question. "Lucy's my P.A., my life-management guru. I'm completely hopeless without her." He laughed, suggesting that there was more than a grain of truth in the statement.

"And you are?"

"Oh, my manners. I apologise." He threw the cigarette down, stubbing it out with the toe of his leather brogue. "I've still not introduced myself, have I? Carl Silverton. I'm the owner of this property." He took Jamie's hand to shake it again, bouncing around from one foot to the other like a nervous child. "You were kind enough to give your details to my friend last night –" Carl's other hand slipped over the back of Jamie's to tighten his grasp. "Please, do come in, Jamie."

The handshake lingered, allowing time for Jamie to notice the gorgeous spicy-woodiness of his Creed aftershave. Still attached, Carl invited Jamie to enter, scooping her past him, his fingertips pressed with inappropriate firmness into the small of her back. Her direction forcibly steered, Jamie scampered past like a child. Once inside, she reclaimed her space, moving stealthily out of Mr Silverton's reach. He frowned at her like a reprimanded puppy.

"So." She moved on from the introductions, reminding herself she wasn't actually five years old, irrespective of how she felt right at this moment. "You need an architect, Mr Silverton?"

She bent down and opened her briefcase to retrieve a notebook and pen, then stood upright to find Carl, midway through lighting another cigarette, studying her with half-closed eyes. He extinguished the match with his first drag of smoke and flicked it across the hallway.

"A girl in a trouser suit without heels? What an interesting statement."

"Shall we get down to business, Mr Silverton?" Jamie was already forming opinions.

"But of course," he answered. "Why wouldn't we?" His question sounded genuine; his eyes, now wide, looked confused.

Jamie endeavoured to return to the purpose of her visit. "Perhaps you should take me round – to get a feel for what I might be dealing with here? You can talk me through your vision as we walk."

"All right, then," Carl agreed. He didn't move.

"Shall we?" Jamie pointed down the hallway with her pen towards the back end of the house.

Carl's eyes were still glued to Jamie's shoes.

"Mr Silverton…?"

Kick-started into motion, Carl led the way along the corridor like an excited schoolboy.

Jamie followed, noting his crisply laundered, pristine white-starched shirt and Jacob Cohen jeans. She started to take in her surroundings, but realised that her first impressions had been hijacked; first, by Mr Silverton's strange behaviour, and now, by the cloying, sweet stench of marijuana.

She refocused.

Carl stopped a few feet ahead and stooped down to pick up a large nail off the floor tiles. "You come highly recommended, Jamie Barker," he said. Still bent double, he looked up obliquely at her, his cigarette hanging from his mouth. "And I've already done my homework on you."

Once again, Jamie pointed with her pen down the corridor. Carl chuckled to himself, deep and chesty. Distinctively masculine.

The front hallway was stunning, covered with the original, Victorian ceramic floor tiles. Although now damaged and littered with cigarette butts, they were unmistakable by their duck blue, black and terracotta colours and their tessellated geometric design. Two doors led off to the left and right. The left door was closed, while the right was ajar, and led to a partially gutted kitchen. Midway down the corridor was a staircase. At the end of the hallway, twelve or so feet ahead, was a generously proportioned, empty room. Probably the drawing room in a bygone era, it had a large, sash bay window. The floorboards were freshly stripped back, and an open fireplace was partially uncovered, crying out for loving restoration.

"So many quirky, original features," Jamie said. "It's so rare to see a property like this remain untouched these days." She was in her element.

Carl looked pleased, then suddenly became animated by another frantic sparkle of energy. "I'm *so* glad you love it, too," he said.

For a moment, Jamie saw the little boy in him again.

"Seventy-four years," Carl said, stopping to admire everything around him. "Seventy-four years the previous owner lived here. A widow, I believe. She died recently at the grand old age of ninety-two… found upstairs in the top floor bedroom." Carl lit another cigarette. "A beautiful, stunning, happy family home… once upon a time." He spoke through the plume of smoke, both hands in the front pockets of his jeans. "Loved and lived in."

Jamie could see an emotional change in Carl's expression but couldn't decide what it meant.

"When I first looked around, it was all virtually unchanged, stuck in a time warp since the house was built." His eyes were on the ceiling, trance-like.

Jamie bowed her head funereally, all set to allow Carl a little time for his moment of contemplation.

"Come on!" Carl instructed. Jamie was caught by surprise.

He raced off along the hallway, invigorated by another injection of energy. “You have a house to see,” he laughed, sweeping his arms wide, like a circus ringmaster. “Let the tour commence…”

Jamie hardly had time to take breath as she was marched round the property by Mr Animation. Carl gabbled on like an auctioneer as he whisked Jamie up four flights of stairs and through and five bedrooms, on an unusually brief whistle-stop tour. When he eventually led her back downstairs to the large kitchen, her head was spinning.

Carl pulled out a wooden chair from a beautiful but battered farmhouse-style table. A convenient dumping ground, it was hidden almost entirely beneath a mound of clutter – a mish-mash of newspapers, paperwork, receipts, take-away containers with leftover food festering within, empty food packets, beer cans, wine bottles. Carl hastily cleared a small space, sweeping most of the crap straight onto the floor. He invited Jamie to take a seat.

“Smoke?” he offered Jamie a cigarette.

“No.”

“Tea, coffee?”

“Just a glass of water would be fine,” Jamie replied, taking her seat. The dust and cigarette smoke were starting to irritate the back of her throat. Carl had already lit up and half-smoked at least five cigarettes since her arrival.

"Coming right up." Carl rinsed one of numerous mugs from the sink, filled it with tap-water then set it down in front of Jamie.

One look at the rim, and Jamie knew the mug would be going nowhere near her lips. She noticed the writing around its circumference: *To the best daddy in the universe with love from Martha.*

Carl wrongly assumed her reason for studying the mug so closely. "Martha, my daughter," he said, puffing up with pride. "There's another cup lying around somewhere. That one's from my son, Rubin."

Carl strolled to the fridge and fetched himself a can of beer, which he opened and started drinking before pulling up a mismatched chair from the table. He sat down.

It was Jamie's first chance to look at Carl up close. She guessed him to be in his early 50s, although his thick silver hair made him look older. Dark rings surrounded his deep-set eyes. He looked fatigued, like he carried the burden of the world on his shoulders, and yet he had this curious, contradictory, bubbling abundance of nervous energy and enthusiasm.

She pressed on, interested enough – for now – in the job to give Carl the benefit of the doubt, despite his unconventional introduction. "This is a novel approach, Mr Silverton," she observed. "It's generally customary for the owner to employ an intermediary to manage all this early, mundane groundwork."

"Is it?"

Jamie wasn't sure, but his tone seemed to have the sarcastic lilt of someone who had just been preached the obvious. She waited to see if he would go on, or qualify his question.

He didn't.

She continued. "Yes, I wouldn't normally be meeting up with you until later on in the process – to thrash out the fun, creative bits."

"And you can't beat a good thrashing!" Carl said, totally unreadable. He exhaled smoke from the side of his mouth and took another drag from his cigarette. "What can I say?" He leant forward. "I like to know what's going on. In my experience, you *have* to micro-manage if you want a job doing properly."

"Really?" Jamie said, leaning back in her chair. "That must be exhausting. It also suggests you don't trust the experience or expertise of other people to get a job done."

"Not at all. What can I say? I'm just particular. I have standards."

Jamie considered the veracity behind this statement, patching together the contrasting extremes of her experience so far: the unappetising reception, the disgusting kitchen. And yet here in front of her sat an obviously affluent, well-dressed, well-groomed man. It was a very curious set-up.

"Tell me more about your house, Mr Silverton. There are several things I will need from you – property and legal paperwork – and I certainly need a clearer idea of your specific requirements." Jamie sat poised with notebook and pen. She met his eyes, realising how attractive they were. But she hadn't yet got the measure of the man. "I like to get to know my clients," she added.

Carl's eyes widened a fraction. "I'm aiming to keep and restore as many of the original features as I can, but intend to bring this shit-hole back to life for modern living."

Shit-hole? Jamie was stunned. His description seemed inconsistent, given his emotional reminiscing earlier. "Neglected, yes; shit-hole? Absolutely not. I can see amazing potential in this magnificent building. It needs some T.L.C."

"Don't we all?"

"So, what *exactly* do you want from me?" Jamie was rather more abrupt than she'd intended to be.

The edge of Carl's mouth twitched into a smirk. "So many questions. All in good time. Relax, chill out a little." He lit up another cigarette, inhaled and studied the cylinder in his hand. "Filthy habit," he mused. "I really should have a go at vaping some time."

Jamie noticed Carl's left hand. His wedding finger had the indentation of a recently removed ring.

"Another drink?" He peered into Jamie's full cup.

"No thanks, I'm fine."

Carl rattled his own, now empty beer can, crushed it in his hand and threw it across the kitchen into the sink, with practiced accuracy. "Thirsty work, all this painting and decorating natter."

"*I* certainly won't be picking up any paintbrushes, Mr Silverton." Jamie asserted her significance, following up with a wry smile.

Carl got up and went to his fridge. This time, he reached for the freezer section and pulled out a bottle, then picked up a mug from the sink draining board.

Frustrated, Jamie let her pen drop to the writing pad. "Have you ever done this before? I don't mean to sound rude, Mr. Silverton, but have you *any* idea what I'm here to do?" Her last sentence came out as a hapless,
doubtful laugh.

Carl sat back down. He opened the bottle – Grey Goose vodka – and poured himself a good double-plus measure. He knocked it back. He poured himself another, lit another cigarette and sat back, hands clasped behind his head, still grinning. He was no longer the little boy; he had turned into a rascally teenager. Then he proceeded to explain his job, which had something to do with overseas banking. "But it's all too complicated to bore that pretty little head of yours with the details."

Jamie had no interest whatsoever and was grateful that he spared her the explanation.

"Tell me, Jamie Barker," Carl said at last. "What do *you* see here? What would *you* do to this place?"

Jamie proceeded to give a brief synopsis of the key points and her "must do first" suggestions.

Carl very quickly slumped into what looked like catatonic boredom, preferring to engage, instead, with his mobile phone. She continued explaining her plans, in spite of his rudeness.

Eventually he butted in. "All sounds bloody marvellous. When can you start?"

Jamie doubted that he had been listening to a word she was saying. Time for a little test. "Which part of my plans do you think will need micro-managing, Mr Silverton?"

Carl's character switched yet again. "Jamie Rose Barker," he began.

Rose? Jamie sat upright, thrown back into childhood memories of bracing herself for receiving a dressing-down from her father. She hated her middle name, and her full name was definitely not on her website. She couldn't even remember when she'd last used or seen her full name in print.

"What more can I say, Jamie." Silverton's puppy-dog eyes pleaded sympathy. "Let me tell you a little more about myself…" He made himself comfortable in his chair, his voice becoming soft and lyrical: a father preparing to read his child a bedtime story.

Jamie was lulled into listening, curiously mesmerised.

"I'm an unhappy, lonely man. I've been divorced for nearly three months and I'm struggling. My ex-wife announced one day that she was bored of the relationship and frustrated that I was never home." Carl poured himself some more vodka. "She never complained during the twelve years she enjoyed the trappings of my success, though – the bitch," he said under his breath. He drank and poured himself another.

Jamie watched his eyes become gradually less attractive as he fumbled between his cigarette in one hand and mug of booze in the other. At one point, he lost coordination and attempted to raise both items to his lips, quickly realising what he had done. She stopped herself from laughing.

"She's got a substantial divorce settlement out of me, though. She's got exactly what she wanted – a very comfortable, independent future. Cheers!" Carl raised his glass.

Jamie was certain the salute to his ex-wife was not offered in the spirit of kindness or generosity.

"What can I say? I'm a hard-working man, Jamie. So, I drink too much, smoke a bit of weed and score a couple of white lines now and again? Big deal. It's my recreation – my therapy."

Jamie looked at her watch. She was beginning to understand the true meaning of the term 'sensory overload'.

The confessions just kept coming.

"Martha and Rubin? Did I tell you about them?" Carl was losing the ability to look straight.

"No, no, you didn't, Mr Silverton," Jamie said.

"My children's mother has taught them to hate me, Jamie... well, they hate me until they bloody well want something from the Bank of Daddy – the greedy little shits," he added. "Do you have kids?"

Jamie shook her head.

"One man rattling around in this old place is bloody lonely." Carl stopped talking.

The two of them sat, staring at each other across the pile of crap between them.

Jamie was exhausted. Her initial optimism and enthusiasm were fast evaporating. At what point had this business meeting become a psychotherapy counselling session?

"Mr Silverton. If we can come to some kind of plan of action before I leave, then maybe agree to meet up again and move this project forward that would be marvellous. We haven't exactly achieved very much yet, have we?"

"Haven't we?"

Carl used exactly the same sarcastic tone of voice that he'd used earlier. Was he mocking her? Jamie couldn't tell. This time, he was somehow sharper with her.

"Jamie, I've had heard nothing but excellent things about your work through the London property grapevine. I have no doubt that I want you as the girl for the job... if that's what you were waiting to hear?" Carl said.

His words sounded like throw-away sentences, without any trace of a sincere meaning. Jamie decided it was the drink talking.

"So," he slurred a fraction. "Why don't you bugger off back to your little drawing board, apply the magic of your creative genius, and let my lawyer know about that paperwork you need…" Carl pulled a business card from his inside breast pocket. "And we'll take it all from there, hmm?" He held out the card.

Jamie took it without looking at it and put it into her own breast pocket. She got up. "I'll be in touch shortly, Mr Silverton."

Carl escorted Jamie to the front door. She put her hand out to bid adieu, and he grasped it as firmly as he had on her entrance. This time, and with a whisper of aggression, he turned the back of her hand and kissed it. Like before, the intimacy of his action felt wrong.

"You know, it's so refreshing to have a pretty girl to talk to," he said. "One man rattling around in this big old house…"

"I'll be in contact, Mr Silverton," Jamie repeated.

"I can promise you one thing, my dear," Carl said. "This little bachelor pad needs some of that T.L.C. you spoke of earlier. You get it fit for purpose, and I promise to make it very much worth your while."

Jamie exited Silverton's house feeling oddly grubby. In principle, she had sealed the deal, but her sense of achievement had been tarnished by the whole experience. For once in her career, she wondered if she should pull out of the job. After all, nothing had yet been agreed in writing.

Thinking over Silverton's parting words, she shuddered. She slipped her hand into her trouser pocket and pressed the door lock on her ignition key. Several feet away, the doors on her Spyder clunked open. She made haste, relieved to be returning to the safe haven of her car. Once in the driver's seat, Jamie locked herself inside – something she never usually did.

The last time Jamie had locked herself inside a car was during an eight-week road trip across South Africa. Jamie smiled to herself, remembering the day she had approached a red light at a lonely junction on the outskirts of a remote township – a prime location for opportunistic youths to lurk in the shadows, ready to jump any unsuspecting foreign driver. Two lone women were an easy target. Jamie refused to listen to that little voice of reason that told her fear is 98% perception and 2% reality. Too scared to stop, and fearful for their safety, Jamie secured the SUV doors with lockdown, held her breath, eyes forward, and stomped the accelerator hard to the floor, skipping the lights. Once they were through, the car filled with raucous, adrenaline-charged whoops of Amazonian bravado. They were invincible. Sarah's face flashed into Jamie's mind. She pushed the image aside as quickly as it had entered.

To distract herself from the memories, she searched in the map pocket on the inside of the door and pulled out the beer mat. She stared at the number on the back, thumbing the edge of the card. What was the point in phoning the number? She'd had her keys returned, didn't she? But then why would this person, whoever it was, ask her to call back? Jamie took out her phone, ignoring the missed call from Alex, and dialled carefully. It went to voicemail. "Hi, my name is Jamie Barker. You left your number... erm... I'm ringing to thank you for handing in my keys at The Coal Hole pub..." She tailed off, wondering how to conclude the call. "Erm... anyway, look, thanks again."

Jamie hung up, satisfied this call would be enough to keep Alex off her back, but was annoyed with herself for doing it. Yet again, she had allowed herself to be influenced by Alex. When was the last time she had rung a total stranger? Never! Perhaps she should have insisted that Alex phone the number herself, since *she* was so keen to find out who the person was?

On the journey home, Jamie thought more about the whole thing. After the previous weekend, she had no inclination to deal with any more screwballs. She would block the number – by far the most sensible way to conclude the whole thing. But then she was sidetracked by a text message from Alex: *Where are you? Will call you at* 5

*****

Once Jamie was home, she decided to give herself the rest of day off from work. Silverton's plans were on her 'to-do' list, but instead, she spent a lazy late afternoon and evening on her balcony, overlooking the transient groups of people dotted across Hyde Park, sprawled out under the shade of the London plane trees. From here, Jamie watched the world go by, equipped with a selection of papers and copious pots of fresh coffee. This was her kind of Sunday heaven. She needed to make time for herself like this more often.

"So?" Alex questioned later – the first and only opening word of her promised five o'clock return call.

Having answered the phone, Jamie purposely dodged the question that she knew Alex had specifically phoned to ask. It was a rare chance for her to have the upper hand, and she wanted to retain it for as long as possible. Instead, Jamie nattered on, telling Alex all about her lazy afternoon on her balcony in the sunshine. Eventually, she feigned a casual second thought and added, "Oh yeah, by the way... I rang that number."

There was silence.

Jamie was loving the power.

"And?" Alex's tone was one of frustrated anticipation.

"Not much," Jamie said eventually, smiling to herself.

"So? Who was it? What did they say?"

"Nothing. They didn't pick up. I left a voice message."

"Are you going to ring back?"

Jamie thought for a bit. "Nope."

"Aren't you curious?"

Jamie maintained the silence for further effect. "Nope." She almost laughed aloud.

"Well, that was all a waste of bloody time, wasn't it?" Alex sounded annoyed.

"My time wasted, not yours, Al." Jamie wasn't going to be sucked into justifying her actions.

"Whatever."

Without seeing Alex's face, Jamie couldn't fully understand her meaning. "I didn't ask you to come with me to my place this morning. It was your choice, let me
remind you."

Another wall of nothing.

"What's the problem, Alex? I've got my keys back; I've called and said thank you. Job done. Anyway, why do you even care? What do you expect me to do? Post them a medal?" Jamie hit her thigh. She was legitimising her actions – exactly what she hadn't wanted to do.

It was Alex's turn to dish out the silent treatment.

Jamie took back control. "I've got to prepare plans for a client tomorrow morning. It's a bit of a crazy schedule this coming week, so I'm going to have to work late most nights. I'll call you before the weekend." She waited, listening.

"Whatever!" Alex replied.

The call ended.

CHAPTER 6

The following days were, indeed, very busy for Jamie. On Friday night, she got home from work at twenty past eight – by far the earliest that week.

Hanging up her work suit, Jamie thought about her last call from Alex, and how her reaction had been over and above her usual weirdness. But she was determined not to indulge Alex's peevishness.

Jamie pulled on a pair of shorts. They had originally been bought for jogging; in reality, they were only ever used in stroll-mode, across the length of her apartment. Trying to get one hand through the armhole of a t-shirt, she managed to scroll to 'speed dial' with the other hand. "Hi, Pedro's Pizza…? Yes, Jamie Barker. Can I order my usual, please? Yeah, peri-peri and extra jalapeños... Great, cheers. See you in a bit."

She wasn't going into town tonight; this was destined to be a chilled, lazy night at home on the terrace. Jamie took an ice-cold beer from her preposterously enormous fridge. She pulled out a damp cardboard box, still containing a portion of congealed pizza from the previous week, and dropped it into the bin. Apart from seven bottles of beer, two pints of milk and a hunk of Cheddar cheese, the fridge shelves were bare. Jamie offered her beer to the wall-mounted bottle opener and took a long, refreshing swig straight from the bottle. Within a few gulps, it was half-empty.

The bi-folding doors were already open fully. The table on the balcony was laid with a plastic plate. A folded square of kitchen roll, doing duty as a napkin, was tucked inside a redundant beer glass. The table was ready for dinner al fresco.

Jamie leant her head back on the balcony chair, eyes closed, taking advantage of the full rays of the warm setting sun on her face. The light saturated her balcony in a golden honey glow. A relaxed peacefulness hung in the streets and park below. The leaves shivered in the gentle breeze, and dappled sunshine shimmered through the canopies onto the grass.

Jamie opened her book to the place marked with a corner of the page turned over; a crime thriller by her current favourite author. She had read it before, but it made a very worthy repeat read. She loved the feel and smell of a real book.

By 12:20 am, she had migrated back inside to the comfort of her sofa. An open box of half-eaten pizza sat on the counter behind her, along with three empty bottles of Budweiser and an empty glass of Scottish single malt whisky. Her book had dropped to the floor.

She woke with a start to the sound of her phone ringing. Still half asleep, Jamie didn't answer fast enough. By the time she'd located her mobile, lodged between the sofa cushions, she saw a voicemail had been left. It was Alex's number. As Jamie went to listen, a text came through. Again, it was Alex: *You didn't call me this week? Thought we were going out tonight? Need to speak with you ASAP.*

Jamie listened to the voicemail. It echoed Alex's obscurely urgent text. Neither message explained exactly why Alex expected an imminent response. It couldn't be that important, Jamie decided, or Alex would have been more specific. Jamie wasn't about to call her back right away, at this time.

On waking the next morning, at 9:43am, Jamie gradually stirred and reached for her phone. There was yet another voicemail, along with two more text messages from Alex. The voicemail was left at 4:38am, garbled and slurred. Alex was patently the worse for wear after a boozy night out in town. Her voice was drowned out by the sound of loud music and shouting people having a good time. The gist of the texts, yet again, implored Jamie to contact her. The last, most recent message, read: *Need to talk to you. Will be with you at 10am.*

"Oh, piss off!" Jamie flopped backwards onto her pillow. Why couldn't Alex just back off and leave her alone for a couple of hours? Jamie texted back, knowing full well she wasn't being truthful: *Don't waste time coming over – I'm out this morning. Nntr.*

Jamie threw back the duvet, got out of bed and went into her en-suite to take a long soak. Her appointment with the bathtub was a legitimate reason not to answer her front door to anyone.

After twenty minutes of relaxing in the bath, a flannel over her face, she heard the buzzer go off.

Alex?

Jamie's heart sank. She increased the volume on the bathroom sound-system, held her nose and sank down, fully submerging herself into the tub. Whatever she couldn't hear, she figured she could legitimately ignore.

Having finished her bath, safe from further interruption, Jamie now stood enrobed in a towel, staring into the large bathroom mirror. Both hands gripped the edge of the sink, and she studied her face in the glass. Her eyes were drawn down to her solitary toothbrush in the double toothbrush holder. She vividly remembered the fluorescent green toothbrush that had once occupied the vacant tumbler next to hers, and how Sarah had always insisted on having her own tube of toothpaste – even though they shared the same brand.

Jamie made the mistake of allowing her mind to wander further, remembering how she used to sit on the end of the bed and watch Sarah in the bathroom – how she would marvel at Sarah's damp body, as she stood naked, cleaning her teeth, exactly where Jamie stood right now. She loved how the condensation formed perfectly between the cleavage of Sarah's breasts. She remembered how she would follow the drips of water from Sarah's wet, jet-black hair, slowly meandering towards the indentation at the base of her spine.

Once upon a time, Sarah was a funny, passionate woman. The memory aroused an involuntary response in Jamie.

Then her daydream was extinguished as she looked down at the cracked tiles on the bathroom wall and recalled the day they had been smashed. Sadness and anger took over in equal measure, like a massive caffeine rush, and Jamie found herself speculating on that million-dollar question that had led to so many fitful, sleepless nights – for how long had Sarah been weaving her tangled web of calculated lies and deception?

*****

Jamie swapped her towel for the bathrobe hanging on the back of the door. She could smell the unmistakable sweet, woody aroma of her favourite Sumatran bean. Somewhere, in one of the other apartments, someone was brewing fresh coffee.

Enticed by the aroma, Jamie headed for the kitchen.

"Shit!" Her shout came out as a strangled squeal as she jumped back, grasping her chest.

She wasn't alone.

A second voice screamed in unison – a startled response to Jamie's unexpected appearance. Then the glass smashed to the floor.

"Oh, buggeration!" Alex pranced from one foot to the other, trying to avoid stepping on the bits of glass and coffee strewn across the kitchen floor. "You scared the shit out of me. A cloth – get a bloody cloth."

"*I* scared *you*? Why the hell are you even here?" Jamie ran into the bathroom. "Get the dustpan and brush under the sink," she ordered, returning with a handful of clean bath towels.

"Bath towels?" Alex stared with horrified disbelief. "Really?"

"Just get that sorted." Jamie threw the towels on the floor by Alex's feet.

The next twenty minutes were spent mopping up coffee and delicately sweeping up shards of glass from the smashed coffee pot.

"What the hell were you thinking, Alex?" Jamie bawled. "You've just barged into my home uninvited. Didn't you read my text? I already told you not to come. Or did you just choose to ignore it and disrespect my wishes?"

"What did you expect?" Alex hurled back. "*You* didn't reply to me last night, so technically *you* let *me* down. You said you'd come for a drink last night. Where were you? It didn't occur to *you* to call me?"

She was trying to make out she was the wounded party.

"You are priceless, Alex. Do you do these things on purpose? Do you make it your conscious goal to try and wind me up?"

"Of course not. I needed to talk to you. I thought you wouldn't mind. Wasn't that the whole point of giving me your spare keys?"

"You having my keys is for *my* convenience, not yours."

Alex reverted to spoiled-child mode, and whined, "I was waiting until you had finished in the bathroom. I was going to surprise you and bring you a coffee."

"Grow up, Alex." Jamie scrunched up the bath towels and pushed them into the bin.

"They look brand new. Why are you throwing them away?"

"Stained with coffee and covered in bits of smashed glass? Don't be so dim. Do *you* want to take them home to clean?"

Alex shrugged.

"Your reason for barging into my home uninvited had better be worth it, Alex."

"As it happens," Alex gloated, "I have an extremely good reason." Her next words oozed from her lips. "I was planning to tell you last night. But, woo-hoo…" She lifted the lid of the half-empty pizza box. "It appears you've had a memorable night in alone with a pizza?" She scowled at Jamie. "Breakfast?"

Jamie tightened the tie around the waist of her bathrobe. "I'm going to get dressed, so you'd better make it quick."

"What are your plans for tonight?" Alex pulled out a chair from under the kitchen table and sat down.

"Why? And don't make yourself too comfortable, you're not staying. I need to get ready for a meeting with a client."

"I have a surprise for you."

"If barging uninvited into my home is an indication of your idea of a surprise, I'm not sure that I want to know," Jamie said flatly, heading back into her bedroom.

"Bet you'll love this." Alex was sanctimonious.

Jamie didn't answer.

"What time are you free later?"

Jamie's attention was piqued but she didn't want Alex to know she was curious. She was relying on the fact that Alex was rubbish at keeping secrets.

Jamie emerged from her bedroom fully dressed. "What exactly have you got planned, Alex?"

Alex had started to read one of yesterday's papers at the dining table. "Can you meet me later?" Her eyes didn't shift from the page.

"I suppose so. Not before five, though."

Alex folded up the paper. "Six then. Meet me outside the Apollo Theatre at six tonight."

"Okay. A night at the theatre, is it?"

"No," Alex replied. "Better."

"Better?"

"Good, you're starting to wonder. I was banking on that." Alex got up to leave and turned around in the frame of the doorway. "Six it is, then." She took Jamie's apartment keys from her pocket. "Shall I leave these with you?" She jangled them at Jamie.

"No," Jamie said. "Hang on to them. I'd prefer that you kept my spares."

"Too right," Alex laughed as she walked out of view. "God forbid that you lose your own set," she called from the hallway.

"Ha-ha, very amusing." Unlike Alex, Jamie wasn't laughing.

The front door pulled shut.

*****

Jamie checked her watch. It was nearly 2.30pm. She had spent most of the afternoon working on the plans for the Little Venice project. The initial presentation was ready for the meeting that afternoon.

Jamie was prepared to source and coordinate a specialist, bespoke service. She felt she had successfully got the gist of Silverton's requirements, and he was thrilled that she was not simply concerned with the physical space, but that she appreciated an understanding of his day-to-day existence was integral to the success of this transformation.

She closed the portfolio with a huge sense of satisfaction. This was going to be a stunning project.

What Silverton hadn't yet grasped, though, was that Jamie's approach was by no means particular to him. This was always how Jamie operated, with any client. To her, a home should flow. It needed to fit seamlessly into the client's lifestyle. She was paid good money to sum up who her clients were through a luxury environment that reflected where they stood socially.

But Silverton saw it differently. He seemed to think that Jamie was offering him some kind of special treatment; that she was doing him a personal favour. He had started to refer to the 'synergy' of their 'special relationship', and it didn't make Jamie feel comfortable.

Jamie stood up from her drawingboard. "Phase one complete and ready for inspection, Silverton." *Silverton*? Jamie realised that, even in her head, the man wasn't *Carl*, or even '*Mr* Silverton' – he was simply *Silverton*. Impersonal and detached. It was a pity the man was such a smarmy creep, Jamie decided, smiling at her unethical aspersion as she packed the paperwork.

Jamie arrived for her appointment, having eventually located the room within a large office block. Silverton wasn't alone. His companion, John Hunter, greeted Jamie with a damp, limp handshake. John's opening gambit was direct. "So, what's your opinion of London's multi-billion-pound luxury building projects?" He gawked at Jamie. "Although you probably don't get your hands dirty with anything *that* highbrow."

Jamie chose to say nothing in reply. She didn't need to explain or exaggerate her experience and connections. Where was this man heading with this challenge? She didn't yet understand his angle.

"Fact!" John blundered on. "Seventy or eighty percent of the high-end, new-build properties are snapped up behind closed doors before the ink is even dry on the planning permission."

Who was this man? Jamie took an invisible, slow inward breath.

"It's those fucking foreign investors from Hong Kong, Singapore and Malaysia. They're buying up our new-builds with no intention of ever even living in them. They sit on their nice little investment nest-eggs, shafting our own potential home-grown buyers." He stopped and sized up his audience. His eyes searched for a reaction.

Jamie didn't oblige, quietly assessing his xenophobic hostility.

It turned out that Hunter was Silverton's lawyer. He was invited to oversee the meeting and check that Silverton's building contract was properly agreed and put in place. A dour man, Hunter looked to be well past retirement age. His fat gut and bloated, sweaty red face had all the indications of someone who had lived life to excess.

The lawyer's presence did not deter Silverton from directing lewd, inappropriate comments at Jamie. Sadly, Hunter was of a similar mould. He didn't bat an eyelid at Silverton's chauvinism; in fact, he seemed to rather enjoy and even encourage it. They bounced off each other's banter with all the offensive vulgarity of a 1970s sitcom.

The tipping point came when Jamie found herself invisible.

"My God, man," Silverton said as he poured two glasses of whisky and handed one to John. "One sure-fire way to brighten up these meetings, don't you agree, would be if Jamie treated us to a glimpse of her legs?"

Hunter nodded keenly in agreement as he knocked back his liquor and handed his glass back for a refill.

At this point, the meeting was near concluding. Jamie slowly packed up her paperwork, organised it neatly into her briefcase and stood up. Before she left the room, she turned to the two men still sitting at the desk.

"Gentlemen?" She used the term reluctantly.

Both men looked at her.

"I've given my position a great deal of thought over the last few days." Jamie had both men's attention. "I'm not prepared to continue on this project if our future meetings are going to be conducted in the same way our last couple of meetings have panned out."

Their gormless expressions indicated that neither man had the faintest idea why Jamie had made this comment.

Silverton's lawyer pulled his glasses off the top of his head, positioning them on the end of his nose to look through them at Jamie. "I should remind you that you've just undertaken an agreement with my client… *Miz* Barker."

Jamie knew all too well that his sexual ambiguity with her title was intended as an insult. Was he *really* that thick?

Hunter looked over the rims of his glasses at Jamie. "I certainly wouldn't advise you to be in breach of contract."

"I'm surprised that I need to remind *you*, Mr Hunter, that there is no binding obligation. We have merely discussed the contract, have we not? It has yet to be signed by Mr Silverton." Jamie knew the legal rights and systems of her profession inside out. She was not intimidated.

"Now, now, people," Silverton flustered. "How on earth have we got ourselves into this troublesome little conundrum? John, stop behaving like a fool." Silverton's imploring was pitiably unconvincing. "I'd be heartbroken to lose Jamie, just on account of…" He was clearly unable to give Jamie's reaction any credence.

It was pathetic, but Jamie was fascinated to hear Silverton's interpretation of her criticism.

"Jamie – I can see you are upset," Silverton faffed and prevaricated. "Is there anything I can do to put things right, hmm?" He was wrestling to make sense of everything. "Is it the money? I'm prepared to negotiate."

Jamie's lack of response didn't help him.

"What is it about our previous meetings that have caused you so much grief, my dear? I *was* a little over-enthusiastic last weekend, but what's a man to do? You're a woman, and you listened – you're easy to talk to." A nervous laugh intensified. He blustered on anyway. "John has looked after me for decades and can get a little overprotective and twitchy at times. He's all bark, aren't you, John?" He glared at John for confirmation.

John had already risen from his chair to collect his coat. He didn't respond in agreement or otherwise to Carl's imploring.

What a complete and utter arse. "You really have no idea, do you?" Jamie said at last. "Neither of you have a clue how obscene your comments are, do you?"

There was not a flicker of reaction.

"This would be entertaining if it wasn't so offensive. You both behave like a pair of teenage schoolboys. No, actually, it's worse. You don't even have the excuse of raging hormones controlling your idiocy."

Silverton looked across again at John, who had now stopped walking towards the door. He turned around, first looking at Carl, then to Jamie. He was keen.

Jamie continued. "I've held my tongue several times already when you were extraordinarily unprofessional and insulting. From what I've experienced so far, I have every reason to neither respect nor trust either of you. And Mr Hunter, believe me, I shall be steering people away from your services, should anyone require a recommendation for a lawyer."

Both men looked at each other. John let out an ugly, coarse laugh. He had changed his mind about leaving and was walking back into the room, taking off his coat again. "Fucking feminist. I know your sort, you vapid, uptight little bitch."

For a split second, Jamie wanted to laugh at his insane explosion – until, that is, she noticed Silverton's reaction. Silverton initially appeared shocked by John's outburst. He then slid to a thin-lipped smile, which Jamie could only read as proud admiration.

John looked back excitedly at Silverton, before directing his black look to Jamie. "Do you *know* who I am?"

This was one of those moments. Jamie racked her brain. "No, should I?" she asked, with calm curiosity.

A proverbial red rag had been waved at the bull. Getting closer, John crossed the line into Jamie's comfort zone. He was large, standing tall, looming over Jamie's considerably smaller frame.

"You would testify to hearing that, wouldn't you, Carl?" John ignored Carl's lack of agreement. "We have a verbal threat – to drag *your* good name into disrepute, and destroy *my* reputation? Sounds very much like defamation of character, madam. Dangerous words."

Jamie was too wrapped up in trying to comprehend the last ten minutes to even consider the point in question. It didn't matter much, as she wasn't given the option to reply.

"I could crush you within a week. Trust me. If I throw shit, I make damn sure it sticks." Still in Jamie's face, John peered over his glasses. "Are you ready to lose everything, *Miz* Barker?" He was peculiarly excited.

This contemptuous over-reaction was totally in keeping with a man who had just had his balls metaphorically squeezed by a feisty female. Jamie was not thrown by his bullishness, nor his officious, puerile attempt to reduce her to a quivering child. It was somehow pitifully amusing. She wasn't going to roll over and put up with his bully-boy tactics. Her retort was totally composed.

"Are you threatening me, Mr Hunter?" Jamie stood staring point blank at John, letting him know, in no uncertain terms, that she wasn't the slightest bit overawed by him. "Are you *sure* you want to continue down this path?"

John was stoked: it was written on his face. Jamie suspected that he wasn't used to being challenged, and certainly hadn't expected any kind of dissent from *her*. He probably considered her protestation as exciting sport.

"Oh no, trust me," John repeated. "I never make litigious threats, only promises." He nonchalantly took off his glasses, cleaned them and squinted hard at Jamie, accentuating the ugly, fleshy pouches beneath his eyes. "Just try me, little girl." He licked his top lip, now moist with perspiration.

"I see." Jamie took out her phone. "If *that's* how you want to play..." She flicked the screen and waited. "Hi. Yes, it's Jamie Barker... No, it's not a social call... I won't go into details right now. How are you fixed for time...? Yes, professional advice..." Jamie listened carefully to the answer on the other end. "Great. Thank you. I'll see you Monday."

John's brow furrowed. "Calling the cavalry?" he ridiculed.

Jamie disregarded him.

"I wouldn't bother," he crowed. "It would be a futile and extremely expensive battle."

Jamie put her phone away. She walked towards the door and reached for the handle. She looked back at the two men over her shoulder. "Just try me," she said coolly, then left the room.

The minute she knew she could no longer be seen, Jamie grabbed her phone again and hit redial. "Jesus Christ, am I so glad you were free to take my call."

"This is an unexpected pleasure. I'm surmising your call was in an official capacity?" There followed the offhand sound of a cigarette being inhaled, then loudly exhaled. "Your Jamie Barker introduction was a giveaway."

"Listen," Jamie spoke in a hurry, speed-walking to her car. "This is important. I've just had a run-in with a complete twat. John Hunter – a London-based lawyer. Name ring any bells?"

"Jonathan Hunter? Why the hell are you having run-ins with *him*, Jamie?"

Jamie thought through her explanation.

"Were you with him when you called me just now?"

"Yeah, absolutely – he was breathing down my neck, in fact."

"I thought as much from your voice. Jonathan Tarquin Hunter is a ruthless, sleazy bastard. His reputation precedes him for all the wrong reasons."

"So, can I see you before Monday then?"

An infuriated huff. "You call me out of nowhere with *this*? What's going on, Jamie?"

"Oh shit. Not the best choice of person to have a run-in with, then?" Jamie replied thinly.

"I can hear you've been shaken up. But listen, John Hunter is no match for *me*. Small fish, darling – small fish."

The reassurance was overwhelming. "That's good to know," Jamie said, following up with, "I'm sorry..."

A deep sigh came after a long wait on the other end. "Well, I'm tied up for the next few hours. Call me later – and listen – no need to sweat the small stuff, okay?" she added. "Honestly Jay, trust me."

Jamie had just heard that exact same promise made only minutes earlier, but then, it was delivered as a threat. "Thanks. Lin. You've no idea how good that is to hear."

"Sure, I do," Linda replied confidently. "Anyway, that's one advantage of having a barrister in the family." She took a breath. "I love you, sis."

Jamie closed her eyes and smiled. "Love you too, Linny."

CHAPTER 7

Linda was a chip off their father's block – also a lawyer – and she had been eager to make her dad proud and follow in his footsteps. She was older than Jamie by nearly nine years. Both women had always been ambitious. Linda's working diary was always full, and her services frequently head-hunted. As with Jamie, Linda's notorious ferocity proved to be lucrative.

It had been weeks since they last spoke, but for Jamie, this chance to make contact, even in a short phone conversation, felt irrefutably right. There was no denying it, Jamie adored her sister, but she blamed herself for their estrangement. The disintegration of contact had been a gradual spiral over the last few years. For now, though, Jamie could put all her angst to one side. She had touched base with Linda, and could now concentrate on her evening ahead with Alex, knowing that Linda, as always, had her back.

Running late, Jamie just about had time to change into jeans and a shirt before shooting out again, but was still twenty minutes away from the Apollo Theatre. She texted Alex to forewarn her. Before Jamie entered Hyde Park underground station, Alex replied: *Way too crowded here – will wait by theatre entrance – look for red dress.*

This was a first. They didn't usually have difficulty locating each other, even in central London. Jamie sent back: *Red dress? New purchase? Okay – See you soon.*

The underground train was full and airless. Jamie stood squashed between sweaty armpits and tourists, clinging to the overhead grab rails. She was glad it was only a ten-minute journey to Piccadilly Circus.

Coming out from the busy underground station, Jamie hit a wall of people surging on both sides of Shaftesbury Avenue. There were people walking across the road through the slow-moving traffic and frustrated drivers. Snatches of their conversations reached Jamie's ears, and she realised why there was such a crowd: it was the weekend of the West End Live show in Trafalgar Square – a spectacularly staged yearly event, showcasing snippets of London's best live theatre and musicals.

The short walk, which would normally have taken no more than about five minutes, was, at this rate, likely to be double that. Now a good fifteen minutes late, but closer to the theatre, Jamie started scanning the crowd. She fully expected Alex to be incapable of resisting a snarky dig at her tardiness.

At last she spotted Alex. The red dress was a great beacon. Alex was standing near the steps to the theatre doors, several feet away, surrounded by people.

"Alex!" Jamie shouted, waving madly.

It was too noisy. Alex couldn't possibly hear. Jamie lost her amongst the sea of milling revellers. A brief gap appeared. Alex could no longer be seen. Jamie

pushed through and reached the place where she had been standing. Now bent over, her back turned, Alex was
faffing with something on the ground.

"Al, it's mad out here. What's with the new dress? You hate red."

Alex stood upright.

"Oh, sorry," Jamie said. "I thought you were someone else."

This red dress didn't have Alex inside.

Jamie looked round, head-hopping, trying to see the right person.

"Jamie Barker…?" the woman in the red dress queried, offering a lovely smile.

"Erm, yes?" Jamie stepped back to take a better look.

"It's Rachel…" She moved towards Jamie, arms open for a hug, like a long-lost friend.

Jamie took another step back and studied the woman in front of her with half-closed eyes, trying to put the name and face together.

"It's me – Rachel. Rachel Westgate?"

"Do I know you?"

"Are you serious?" Rachel also stood back, crestfallen.

"I've no idea who you are," Jamie explained. "Should I?" Feeling foolish, she followed through with a dopey, knee-jerk chuckle.

"So, when in the last hour did *you* get cold feet?"

"Honestly, I really don't know you," Jamie insisted. "Were we at university together?" She was grasping at any possibilities.

Rachel's attitude changed. "Pulling out *now*? At least be honest with me, Jamie. You haven't even got the decency to let me down gently *before* I wasted my time travelling all the way down here."

Jamie could only offer an attenuated, "No, truthfully, I…"

Rachel butted in, "I wish you'd been honest sooner. It's pretty pathetic that you've got this far just to end up wasting my time."

"What?"

"The internet dating."

"*What*?" Jamie gasped. "Internet dating? What internet dating?"

"I've made a five-hour train journey to get here today… we've agreed all this… what's wrong with you?" Rachel looked close to crying. She hoisted her handbag onto her shoulder and peered like a meerkat into the crowds, presumably searching for an exit route.

Jamie regained her faculties. "Look, Rachel, I *really* don't understand what's going on." She took a step forward to position herself just in front of Rachel. "I can't leave you on your own this like this. Could we maybe just go somewhere less busy so we can talk?" She placed an apologetic hand on Rachel's shoulder.

Rachel shied away, and Jamie stepped back.

"So what's gone wrong?" Rachel implored.

"Something is going on here," Jamie said. "I at *least* owe you the time to make sense of this."

In a sudden, angry U-turn, Rachel proclaimed: "Actually – why the hell *should* I let you get off that easily? You're damn right, this *does* need an explanation, and you can start by getting me a very large glass of wine."

"A glass of wine is the least I can offer under the circumstances," Jamie agreed. "I just need to call someone first. God knows where she's got to. I'm meant to be meeting a friend here – quite literally right now." Jamie took out her phone and panned a sweeping glance at the hordes of people, hoping to see Alex.

But then she stopped short. "Shit!"

Rachel looked at her, worried.

"Red dress?" Jamie's phone was poised to call Alex.

"Pardon?"

"Never mind," Jamie said, "My *friend* Alex can wait." She pushed her phone back into her pocket and nodded forwards, gesturing towards the mass of people with her chin. "Come on, Rachel, I'm getting you a drink."

"Go on then," Rachel agreed, already trotting after Jamie, who was purposefully making inroads between the people ahead.

Jamie went on, leading in the direction of Alchemy. All the while, she was piecing together the evidence, with a good idea who was behind all this chaos.

Inside the cocktail bar, it was cool and dark. Jamie blinked away the sunshine. Her eyes took a few seconds to readjust. The candles had not yet been lit. It was early evening and the place was empty. There were only

a few other people occupying the stools at the counter.

The first thing Jamie noticed was that Kate wasn't there. Instead, there was a young, fresh-faced man. He looked barely old enough to shave, let alone be legally serving alcohol. He acknowledged the two women with a nod. "Good evening, ladies." He checked his watch. "Yes, it's just turned evening. What would you like?"

Drinks bought, the two women sat facing each other – somewhat uncomfortably – at one of the small tables just in front of the main bar.

Rachel took a couple of much-needed gulps from her chilled Chardonnay. She placed her drink on the table, moved the unlit candle holder from the centre to the edge, and leaned in, staring hard. "I've only seen your profile picture. I'm still getting used to this four-dimensional experience." She reclined in her chair and folded her arms. "So, who *are* you, Jamie Barker?"

Jamie checked her phone before calmly putting it on the table. "You really need to help me here, Rachel.

I have no idea who you are, but you seem to know me. I have my suspicions who is to blame here, though."

"Blame? Fantastic. That makes me feel *so* much better." Rachel indignantly took another swig of her wine.

"No, no. You misunderstand, I didn't mean it like that. I think I've been set up. Somehow, I don't think it was a coincidence that you were waiting outside the same theatre where I was expecting to meet my friend."

Rachel looked suspicious. "O-kay?"

Jamie searched her brain for a more lucid and plausible explanation. "Have you spoken to the person you were planning on meeting today?

"Yes, I did," Rachel said, with irate frustration. "What a ridiculous question! I spoke to you on the phone this morning. You sound completely different in person."

"Excuse me, ladies." The bartender leant across to hold a fire-lighter to the candle between them, then moved on to the next table.

"That explains it," Jamie continued. "Humour me for a second." She thought for a few seconds. "About this meeting today – did you tell the person you spoke to that you were wearing a red dress today?"

"What? You know we did." Rachel downed another huge gulp of her wine. "You said you wouldn't be able to find me if you didn't have something to look out for…" She pulled her head back in disbelief, shaking her head. "Jamie, I don't understand what you are saying. This conversation isn't helping. Who have I been speaking to these past few weeks, if it's not you?"

"*Past few weeks*?" Jamie just about managed to swallow her wine.

Rachel put her glass down.

"Please, I really need you to explain, Rachel," Jamie said. "I think this is beginning to make sense,"

"But I texted you all the arrangements this morning. I don't understand what you are going on about."

Jamie had an idea. "Would you mind showing me the number of the person you've been talking to?" She tried to look across at Rachel's phone screen for clues.

Rachel didn't need to show Jamie anything. She reeled off the mobile number from memory.

"Oh God, you've learned it by rote. That's serious." Jamie looked directly at Rachel. "That's not my number."

"It isn't?"

"No. As I suspected, it's my friend Alexandra's number."

"Oh...?"

"You, or rather *we,*" Jamie corrected, "seem to have been set up. I don't know why, and right now, I don't know what to say apart from sorry." She pushed her hands into the pockets of her jeans. "I'm as much in the dark as you are with all of this – honestly."

Rachel gathered herself then reached for her phone.

Jamie leant forward. "Are you okay?"

Rachel didn't reply. She got to her feet and waited. "Hello...? *Alexandra,* it's Rachel Westgate... you *really* are one very nasty, devious bitch." She cut the call, pouted and tapped at her mobile. "That's *her* deleted and blocked." She dropped her phone back in her bag and knocked back the remainder of her drink, half standing. "Thanks for the wine, Jamie. Pity we were meeting under false pretences. But there's really no point in hanging around, is there?" She stood up and put her bag strap over her shoulder. "And Alex? She's *really* your friend?" she concluded, shaking her head.

On that note, Rachel walked.

Jamie sat alone for several minutes, trying to take in everything. The more she thought it through, the more she began to seethe. Finally, she picked up her phone and dialled, reaching the voice message. "I'm *so* bloody angry with you right now, Alex. I don't care what you are bloody well doing – get your sorry arse down to The Coal Hole, *now*." Jamie put her phone back on the table and covered her face with her hands.

"Hello."

Jamie looked towards the voice.

"Lovely to see you here again," said Kate warmly.

Jamie had been too involved with Rachel to even notice Kate's arrival. How much had Kate had seen or heard, she wondered?

"That all looked rather uncomfortable. Are you okay?" Kate asked.

"No. Not one of the most scintillating dates I've ever experienced," Jamie replied, poorly supressing her exasperation.

Kate hesitated and took a step back. "Do you want another drink, maybe?"

"No." Jamie rose to leave. "I've got things to sort out."

"Is your friend coming back?"

"Fuck knows!"

Kate frowned.

"She's no friend of *mine*," Jamie added fiercely. She was already planning the tirade she would unleash on

Alex when she saw her.

Kate made a face. "Well, excuse me." She promptly about-turned and walked to the other end of the bar.

Jamie's conscience pricked. She realised Kate's intention had been to pull the conversation back to a civil interchange – but she wasn't prepared to hear it. She was still too wound up, and wasn't calm enough to stay and explain it all to Kate.

*****

The street was still heaving. It was a likely to be a good twenty-minute walk to The Coal Hole pub. A message from Alex came through: *OMG She was sooo rude! Bet you are glad you escaped that 1!! See you in 30.* Jamie heaved deeply and held her breath for a few seconds, her anger stewing. She made a detour through Leicester Square Gardens, allowing some head-room to consider how to tackle Alex.

Jamie reached the pub first. Twenty minutes later, Alex flounced in. “Cheeky cow. Listen to this,” she said, flapping her phone at Jamie. “She called me a nasty, devious bitch. Who does she think she is?”

“The very same question I was going to ask *you*!” Jamie was trying her best to stay calm. “Drop the crap, Alex. What have you been up to? And what’s all this about my apparent internet dating?”

“Tetchy! It was only an online profile I set up. I was trying to sort out your love life.”

“Sort out? My life isn’t a bloody filing cabinet. More to the point, we’ve already had this conversation and *still* you went and did all this behind my back? I can't understand how you thought it was okay to do such a thing. Pissed off doesn’t even begin to cover it, Alex.”

“Really? I was only trying to help,” Alex said pathetically. She started picking at a beer mat. “That’s why I wanted you to hurry up and call the number that came with your keys.”

Jamie was exhausted. “What?”

“I’ve been planning this little online meeting for weeks,” Alex revealed, triumphantly.

“You did *what*?”

"I was worried that whoever had left their number on the beer mat might have been a secret admirer." Alex was annoyingly good-humoured. "You might have ended up getting all loved-up before my cunning plan had fully evolved. I would have ended up looking like a real prat…"

"*What*?" Jamie cracked, starting to realise the plot. Somehow, she couldn't envisage this conversation ending well.

"Don't you get it?" Alex continued to explain, her enthusiasm effusive. "I've been covertly undercover. I've been match-making and planning the perfect online date with a woman who *could* be the love of your life. I didn't want some other female muscling in and spoiling things with Rachel at the last minute." Alex was positively bouncing. "Hey-ho, looks like Rachel won't be the love of your life after all. Win some, lose some, I guess."

"That's just psycho-nuts, Alex," Jamie said, her anger simmering. "Do you even give a shit?"

Alex's Cheshire cat face dropped, but only briefly. Childlike, she bounced back. "Anyway," she chundered on excitedly, "get this – your online profile got over sixty views in the first hour – *sixty*! At least twenty of them wanted to find out more about you. Talk about fish in a barrel. There's plenty more where *she* came from."

"Bloody hell, Alex. As if *that* knowledge would make all this any better? What were you thinking?"

"I didn't reply to anyone else – only Rachel," Alex explained, by way of excusing her actions. "She seemed ever so nice and was extremely persistent in getting to know you – and not in a needy, lesbian way."

Jamie glared at Alex.

"Setting up your profile was dead exciting, though. It was like watching the bids going up on eBay." She hit the counter with her palm. "Boom! Get in there, cupid."

"What fucking planet are you living on?"

Alex laughed. "Mind you," she said, "there are some *really* scary-looking women out there. I couldn't tell if some were male or female. What's all that about, anyway?"

Jamie didn't answer. The futility of any response was all too apparent.

Alex started to do her 'pretending to tidy up' routine.

Jamie's heart sank, recognising this ritual of misdirection only too well.

"*What*?"

Alex looked innocent. "What?" she echoed back, pleading ignorance.

"I know you too bloody well, Alex. And you're hiding something."

Alex stiffened in preparation. "Well, erm," she continued with her confession, "saying I only replied to Rachel wasn't *strictly* true."

Jamie squared up. "What the hell is *that* supposed to mean?"

"I thought a man had made a mistake on their profile and had accidentally set themselves up as a woman. All I did was message them to check if they had set up online with the correct gender."

"You messaged them *that*? That was *me* you set up on that profile, Alexandra. You had no right to say anything in my name!"

"No harm was done," Alex sniffed. She ruined the attempt to mollify by adding, "Actually, her reply was quite snotty and aggressive."

"And that surprises you, Alex? Jesus, she had every right to be bloody angry, as did Rachel. You don't get it, do you? You can't just play around with people's feelings for your own entertainment."

"It wasn't for *my* entertainment," Alex said, preparing to stand her ground.

"Alex, you must have known that Rachel made a five-hour journey to get down here, thinking she was meeting me. She even memorised your mobile number. No one does that."

"She did? Really?" Alex looked pleased.

"It's not a damn joke, Alex. This was obviously important to her. She had expected something real. What other crap did you feed her on *my* behalf? Have you deleted my profile? If not, I'm standing over you to watch you do it. Right now!"

"No, it's gone. It was one of those free-for-the-first-month trial offers."

"I swear it, Alex Forbes, if you ever pull a stunt like that again..." Jamie was trying to think of a suitable consequence.

"Anyhow, the free month has expired already, and *I'm* not paying for your internet dating subscription."

Jamie slowly, despondently shook her head.

"But I've kept a copy of your profile that I wrote, if ever you decide you need it," Alex said pointedly. "Seems a shame to waste it."

Jamie was reminded that there were two facets to Alex's personality that were set in stone, and they were equally unattractive. First, she would never apologise. Second, she was, in her mind, never wrong about anything, and her point of view was always right. She never took responsibility and always presented herself as the misunderstood victim.

"You are so unbelievably immature sometimes, Alex." Jamie started thinking aloud and muttered, "I sometimes wonder why we are still friends?"

Alex picked up her jacket from the back of the chair. "I'm going to collect some dry-cleaning and I'm meeting friends at nine."

She left.

Jamie doubted that Alex had even heard any of what was just said. Her incorrigible attitude made it impossible to tell. Honestly, though, Jamie didn't care very much today. She finished her drink and left for home. The walk to the underground station allowed her some more time to think.

Putting Alex out of her mind, she thought back to her talk with Linda. Jamie had been a pretty crap sister of late, but at least the incident with Silverton had allowed her the opportunity to try and mend broken bridges. Hopefully her sister could find time to meet up before Monday. She suddenly felt she had to know, and she pulled out her phone.

"Of course I can make time, Jamie," Linda said. "You're my baby sister. I love you. I've bloody well missed you, you scatty cow. I've no idea what's been rattling round in your head these last few weeks. We've got loads to catch up on." There followed one of Linda's chuckles, reassuring Jamie that all was right with the world.

Jamie craved a few hours with Linda. Time with someone grounded, rational and uncomplicated; time with someone who would kick her back into touch with normality. Linda had always had the knack of doing just that. Jamie realised how much she'd missed her sister, too.

"Alchemy, did you say? Okay, that's a new one. Yeah, I'm all up for an evening out. Luck would have it I'm in town today. I finished a case at the Old Bailey yesterday, and I'm there right now to pick some files. I'll meet you at the bar as soon as I can. Excuse the attire, I'm still in my work gear," Linda explained. "You'll be there before me. Don't wait, though. Get stuck into a bottle of something cold and fizzy. *You* can commiserate the last few shitty days, and *I'll* be celebrating another win in the bag."

"Wow, another legal case won? Well done, sis," Jamie said with enormous pride.

"And while you're at it, go for a bottle of your fave," Linda offered. "My treat, and no arguing."

"Veuve Clicquot, huh? Nice one. You'd best get moving then," Jamie jested. "Or I'll have polished it all off before you arrive."

"Well, it's as much for me as for you. Sounds like I'm in for an ear-bending session tonight." Linda chuckled, reinforcing the backbone of their sisterly camaraderie.

"Tell me about it," Jamie half-joked. "My gripe is not just about my run-in with John Hunter; I've just had another classic Alex episode. Prepare yourself."

"Always," Linda promised. "Nothing much fazes me these days where Alexandra Forbes is concerned. Don't
hold back on my account."

Jamie wriggled in her seat, torn between admiration and gratitude for her sister's unfailing support, and her own uncomfortable realisation that Linda's generosity might be less forthcoming if she knew what Jamie knew.

CHAPTER 8

It was not that much busier in Alchemy than when Jamie had left there earlier. There was a bustling anticipation amongst the bar staff in preparation for the evening ahead. The table that Jamie had previously occupied with Rachel was empty. Jamie pulled up a chair, staking her claim by slipping her jacket over the back of it. Kate was at the other end of the bar, prepping. She was making no effort to acknowledge Jamie, or even serve her.

Why on earth *would* Kate go out of her way to make superficial small talk? Jamie hadn't exactly been welcoming or friendly on their last encounter.

Kate waved to her colleague from afar, instructing him to tend the bar. Since Jamie was the only one waiting for service, Kate was making her position very obvious.

The barman was the young man who had welcomed Jamie and Rachel earlier.

"Could I get a bottle of Veuve Clicquot and two flutes for the table?" Jamie wasn't going to start until Linda arrived, but didn't want to sit without something to drink. "And could I get a soda and lime over ice too, please?"

Presently, the young man arrived back at the table carrying a full tray, which he carefully arranged on the table. Kate was not far behind, carrying the ice bucket.

She placed it next to the table then beetled off to the far
end of the bar.

The male bartender showed the bottle of Veuve to Jamie for her approval.

"Just leave it unopened, please. Someone is joining me shortly."

He plunged the bottle into the ice, then folded and placed the cotton serving napkin across the top of the bucket. "Just give one of us a nod when you're ready for that to be opened."

As the room gradually got busier and customers jostled for their place at the bar, Kate was obliged to serve people along the length of the counter. Earlier, she had pointedly avoided serving near Jamie's table, but now the sheer numbers of people made that impossible. At one point, they happened to catch each other's eye. Jamie offered Kate a smile, as a signal of apology for her churlish behaviour earlier, but wasn't sure if Kate noticed or even cared one iota.

Jamie downed the remaining soda and lime, wondering how much longer she would have to wait for her sister.

"Have you finished with this?" Kate appeared, hovering just behind Jamie and pointing at her empty glass. "Can I clear your table?" She spoke robotically, lacking any warmth.

"Sure." Jamie handed up her glass, offering a peace-making smile in return.

Professionally matter-of-fact, Kate asked, "Another drink?"

"Yes, that would be great, thank you, Kate. Same again, please." Jamie was willing Kate to look at her. "A soda and lime."

Kate was not engaging. She turned to go and fix the drink.

Jamie tried an impulsive ice-breaker. "Thank you, by the way."

Kate looked around.

"For your concern earlier today."

She gave a wary half-nod – an indication of only partial exoneration.

"I was discourteous and rude. I apologise," Jamie added. "I can see that you were just being kind. Like I said, I've not had the best of days." Having attempted to calm the storm, Jamie tried a different tack. "Anyway, how are things with you? *You* were having a pretty tough time too when I last saw you?"

"It wasn't quite how I anticipated my day ending, either," Kate offered warily. She was amicable but still frosty.

Taking Kate's answer as an indication that she'd accepted her apology, Jamie added, more through nosiness than sincere concern, "You were put in a really tough position the other night. I really felt for you."

Kate didn't answer.

"So," Jamie explored further. "Did you get to sort things out with – erm – Chris, wasn't it?"

Tight-lipped, Kate stared at Jamie.

"Anyway, I hope you got to the airport okay."

Kate remained silent, her expression and reddening cheeks warned Jamie that her prying had overstepped the mark.

Thinking rapidly, Jamie back-pedalled. "Anyway, it's worth coming back here even if it's just for one of your fantastic cocktails."

Kate adjusted the cloth over the ice bucket. "Looks like you've got some celebrating of your own to do tonight?" She glanced between the two empty champagne glasses, then looked at something behind Jamie, prompting her to step back, away from the table.

"Hey, hun." Linda swanned in. "So sorry to have kept you waiting." She squeezed Jamie's shoulder.

Jamie stood up to greet her sister, who lovingly enveloped her with a kiss and a bear hug. Stood together like this, they were chalk and cheese.

"You're over twenty minutes late," Jamie scolded jokingly.

"I know, I know. I'm a crap date." Linda took her seat.

They sat holding hands briefly across the table.

"I've missed you," Linda said.

Kate looked on, before interrupting. "What can I get you?" Her question was aimed at Linda.

“Oh, yes please.” Linda looked at the ice bucket. “You’ve not cracked open the bubbly yet, then?”

“I was waiting for you. It’s been so long, I’m surprised the ice hasn’t melted completely,” Jamie teased.

“Could we have a couple of large bottles of fizzy water? And would you open the champagne, please?”

“Sure. No problem.” Kate went off, returning with the water and a couple of tumblers. She pulled out the champagne bottle, drying off the base with the cloth. “I’ll replace the ice bucket for you, ladies.”

Drinks poured, Kate stood back. “Anything else, Jamie?”

At that, Linda’s eyes popped, and she disclosed one of her impish grins. Unseen by Kate, she glared at her sister, mouthing Jamie’s name to mimic Kate’s first-name familiarity.

Jamie glared back, kicking Linda’s foot under the table.

Kate disappeared into the back of the room, through one of the archways.

“First name? Very cosy.”

“Linda, you’re dreadful. Kate’s just a sort of friend.” Jamie said.

“Kate, the sort-of-friend, isn’t someone I’ve heard you mention before.” She picked up her glass. “Cheers!” She put the flute down, her inquisitive eyes on Jamie all the while. "It’s amazing what you can pick up just by walking from one side of a room to the other."

"Such as?"

"Well." Linda sat forward. "First, you don't know her well enough to make introductions. And second, from what I could observe, the body language was a giveaway. She went scarlet with embarrassment but looked stand-offish… And third, you had your 'I need to appease this awkward situation' expression plastered over your face." Linda stroked an imaginary beard on her chin. She half-closed her eyes. "Your big sister deduces there is a story to tell here, Ms Holmes. I feel it in my bones."

Jamie had to laugh. "And that is why you are a barrister, my dear." She enjoyed her sister's powers of deduction, which, in this instance, were totally accurate. "Perhaps you should have been a detective?"

"Sweet Jesus, no," Linda said, half-seriously. "Wouldn't pay enough to get me out of bed in the morning, sweetheart."

Now was the perfect time to give Linda the lowdown on everything that had happened in the past few days.

"Perfect. I'm all ears," Linda affirmed, glancing down the wine list. She tucked the wisps of hair from her fringe behind her ears. "How about another bottle of Veuve to go with your story?"

"Give it a chance, you lush, we've still got this bottle to get through yet," Jamie ticked her off, smiling. "And I hope you're up for making a night of it and still planning to stop over at mine tonight?"

"Wild horses wouldn't, and all that," Linda affirmed.

Eyes closed, Jamie took a sip from her glass. "Ohhh, that is dangerously good."

Linda unbuttoned her suit jacket – a little tight for her full, somewhat chunky frame. She slipped it over the back of her chair, straightened her skirt over her knees and settled herself comfortably, facing Jamie, ready to listen.

Linda's round face was crowned by a tight-curled bob of shoulder-length red hair, perfectly cut and styled. The freckles across her nose and cheeks were quite pronounced, even beneath her flawless foundation. Her eyes, framed by stunning, subtle make-up, gazed curiously at her sister, tempting her to reveal all.

It was a compelling invitation.

For Jamie, spending a few quality hours with her only sibling was always a pleasure. Linda could be trusted to give honest, down-to-earth advice. Jamie had missed it.

For tonight, though, Jamie made the most of her sister's precious time. Once she had completed her saga of events, they had almost finished the bottle of champagne.

In keeping with Linda's astonishing patience, she said very little throughout Jamie's account. She listened, refraining from interrupting. Finally, when all was said, Linda leant back.

"What do you think?" Jamie said.

"So, that explains Kate's reaction earlier," Linda observed. "Did she get to make things up with her boyfriend, do you know? Before he left for America, I mean?"

"I'm guessing not. Today is the only time I've seen her since the incident with the taxi. She was in a right state. I did ask her about it, but she didn't like me poking my nose in where it doesn't belong. That was probably when *you* saw her."

"Sod's law," Linda said, glancing across at Kate. "You chance-meet with a bloody good-looking woman who's not gay. I must say, though, she's got an engaging way about her. I was hoping there something romantic brewing with that one."

"No chance," Jamie said, a little wistfully. "I mistakenly wondered if she might be playing for my team when *I* first saw her, but she's trying to reunite with that Chris bloke."

Linda giggled, her gaze still following Kate round the room. "If I had a pair of tits like those, I'd be chuffed to bits."

"Chris is a lucky chap," Jamie chuckled.

Linda looked down at her own breasts, cupping each in either hand and hoisting them up. "Mine started dropping south years ago."

Both women laughed.

“Drinking this isn't going to help my weight loss regime, either.” Linda raised her glass of champagne to Jamie. “I’m so jealous – ever since I can remember, you’ve been able to glug and pig out all you like, and you never seem to put on a pound. You’ve obviously inherited the skinny genes.” She raised her glass again. “Oh well – Dave prefers the buxom, fuller figure. Just as well, I guess.”

Linda and her husband Dave had a solid relationship, each healthily independent of the other. He was asked to join one of the leading financial protection companies in New York, as a Real Estate Portfolio Manager. It was time limited, but three months away from London still seemed a long time. Neither of them had wanted children, and so their only responsibility was to Buster, a Staff-cross that they had rescued (or rather been chosen by) from Battersea Dog’s Home.

Linda poured the remaining champagne into Jamie’s glass. “To Dad!” she said affectionately, and put the empty bottle neck down into the ice bucket. Jamie recognised the gesture as one of their father’s. He always did this with wine bottles, indicating to the waiting staff that another bottle might be required.

“I don't know why you waste your time on Alex,” Linda said, picking up the wine list again. “She’s always been selfish. I honestly don't understand what you get out of the friendship. You know all too well my opinion of that woman. Anyway, I've said that so many times, it's boring." She continued looking at the wines. "So, what next? Same again? Bottle of white? Cocktail? I'm hoping you aren't working tomorrow, because I'm planning on a long, well-earned lie-in at yours in the morning." Linda added. "But I assume a nice pot of your fresh-ground Sumatra is off the breakfast menu?"

"Oh, stop now." Jamie wasn't serious. She could forgive her sister anything. "I should get Alex to pay for a new bloody coffee pot. And no, I'm not working new
tomorrow."

They agreed on a bottle of Pouilly-Fuissé. This time, it was Linda who went up to order. As it happened, Kate was not at the bar.

Jamie gulped down a couple of glasses of water. She didn't want to be facing a hangover in the morning, so was glad that Linda had taken precautionary measures by ordering the water – another very useful tip learned from their dad.

Linda threaded her way back to the table, open bottle of wine and glasses in hand. "The bar is really busy. Table service could be slow, so I thought it would save valuable drinking time just to bring the bottle over myself. Another ice bucket is on the way… So, what about that number that was posted with your key? Are you planning to ring again?"

"Why? I've left a message."

"And you're not curious?"

"Linny! You're sounding like Alex," Jamie moaned. "No, I'm not curious."

Linda poured herself a glass of water and drank it all. "I suppose there's no real reason to ring again. You've let them know you have got your keys back and they'll have your number from the voicemail if they really want to get in touch."

"Crap! I knew I'd forgotten something. I meant to block the number once I'd left the message. I remember now – I was sidetracked by a text from Alex."

"Why block it?" Linda poured the wine. "You might

as well have not bothered to leave a message. Whoever this person is, they've gone to a lot of effort to get your attention. As much as it pains me to say it, for once in my life, I'm inclined to agree with Alex."

This was a rare comment for Linda. She had never got to know Alex very well, because she had flown the nest aged twenty-four and moved to Canada for a couple of years' work experience, just before Alex had become one of the fixtures and fittings in Jamie's life.

Back in the UK, Linda didn't warm to Alex from the onset. Her first impressions didn't alter over the years, either. She was just relieved that she didn't have to spend too much time with her. When she socialised with Jamie, she preferred to do it without Alex in tow.

"Alex's explanation for that blind date thing was appalling. Who does she think she is?" Linda chided.

Jamie recounted the whole agonisingly embarrassing event, promising that Alex had not heard the last of it. Right now, she was not in any mood to deal with Alex again tonight.

Linda took out a pouch of tobacco from her handbag and started rolling herself a line to smoke outside. “I just don't get the point of Alex’s friendship,” Linda said, licking the edge of the cigarette paper. “In my opinion, for what it's worth, she comes across as pompous and totally selfish. You invest far more of your precious time in her than she deserves.”

“I'm kind of used to her,” Jamie explained. “Anyway, I don't ever remember a time when she wasn't somewhere in the background. She’s always factored in my social circle. Better the devil you know, so they say. When she’s on form, she’s good fun to spend time with.”

Linda snorted. “I just think she takes the piss, that's all.”

“Well, I'm old enough to make my own judgements. I’m no fool, Lin.”

“I know you aren’t, hun, but I just don’t like the woman – never have. Trying to understand the world according to Alex seems way too complicated.” She tapped the end of her roll-up on the table. “*I* certainly couldn’t be arsed with her shenanigans.”

Kate appeared at the table. “Your ice bucket, ladies.”

"Saturday seems to be a good night for this place," Linda observed, looking around the room.

"It is," Kate agreed. "Thanks to the music festival in Trafalgar Square today. It's brought more people in tonight. It's generally not this busy until after ten." She gave the table a needless wipe with a cloth. "Are you both off anywhere else tonight, or staying put here?" She looked at each woman in turn, inviting either to answer.

"Now, there's a thought," Linda mused. "Depends on what excitement you have in mind for us later, Jay."

"The night is but young," Jamie gave a conspiratorial wink.

"You have more stamina than me, honey. My plan is to be snuggled in your bed by midnight with a hot chocolate."

"Looks like you two are on track to enjoy the rest of your weekend, then?" Kate said.

Jamie watched her walk back through the archway to the rear of the building.

"Oi!" Linda spanked the back of Jamie's hand across the table. "She's straight, remember? Out of bounds, little sister."

"I know, I know," Jamie conceded. "Doesn't stop her from being too darn cute, though."

Linda took out a little mirror from her handbag and reapplied her lipstick.

"So," Jamie changed the subject. "What do you think about the charming John Hunter? Based on his threat, should I be contacting my solicitor? Getting you involved would be a conflict of interest, wouldn't it?"

Linda was nodding. "Technically, yes. I can offer you pro-bono legal advice as a barrister, but as your sister, my opinion wouldn't count for representation or litigation. If you officially had to go down this path, you would require legal services."

"Technically? What does that mean?" Jamie looked unsure.

"Well, ordinarily, my connection could be questioned on the grounds of my capacity to maintain my professional independence. Jonny-boy Hunter would pounce on that. In this case, though, there shouldn't be a problem. This all seems pretty cut and dried. Jonathan has no evidence to make his defamation of character hogwash stick. Unless, that is, you know something you haven't told me?" Linda's serious question indicated a legal obligation.

"I've never met the man before," Jamie said. "But he is the kind of person who I'm sure must have acquired a few enemies over the years."

Linda scrabbled around in her handbag. "I reckon his little outburst was meant to frighten you into paralysis. All this will only need a simple phone call to clear up, giving me authorisation to represent you if it comes to that. Leave it with me." She pulled her lighter from the depths of her bag. “Unscrupulous dinosaurs like him need teaching a lesson. He is an unconscionable ass and gives the rest of us in the legal profession a bad name. Off the record, I have plenty of dirt to dish out on him, if he insists on playing dirty.”

Jamie nodded back, satisfied that Linda could handle just about anything.

“But hold that thought.” Linda stood, straightening out her skirt. “I need a nicotine fix. I’m going to nip outside for a quick smoke.”

Once Linda had gone, Jamie sat cradling her glass, gazing at her wine and thinking about the afternoon. Remembering Alex’s tactless stupidity made her feel angry again.

Kate was behind the bar. They happened to look at each other. Kate half smiled. Jamie responded with a similar, uncomfortable smirk.

Then Kate came over to the table. “She’s gone? But this one is coming back this time, right?”

Was Kate being amusing or serious? Jamie didn't know her well enough to read her, and hardly knew what to say. “Why wouldn’t she be?” she replied brusquely.

Kate gave another of her half-grins. “Well then, enjoy the rest of your evening, Jamie.” She walked back to the bar again.

Linda came back, accompanied by the lingering smell of cigarette smoke. Jamie waved her paper serviette in front of her nose. “The smell of lingering fag smoke is just vile. Don't you get sick of everything reeking of nicotine?"

"Next year, I'll quit. My New Year's resolution," Linda promised.

Jamie knew full well she wouldn't.

"So, back to Carl Silverton," said Linda, taking her seat. "I'm really surprised that you're even considering taking up his offer of employment. Particularly given your unsavoury introduction at his house."

"He's certainly odd, but I'm sure he's quite harmless. He's a fossil of the era when smacking your secretary's butt as a reward for bringing your morning coffee was the acceptable norm."

"Well, Anastasia, this reminds me of a book I once read," Linda said mischievously. "Are you sure his name is Carl Silverton and not Christian Grey?"

Jamie spluttered on her mouthful of wine. "Oh, jeez, I didn't think of that," she laughed. "You didn't *actually* read that detritus, did you?"

"Don't get me started. Fifty Shades of World-currency-in-my-pocket-thank-you-very-much! Film rights too. She must have laughed all the way to the bank."

"You wouldn't recommend the book, then?" Jamie smiled.

"Recommend it? I couldn't finish it. How it ever got past the editing phase is astonishing. Everything about it is just plain wrong on so many levels. Dave and I started reading it together, for a bit of bedtime titillation," Linda chuckled. "We ended up in convulsions, it was so bad. I think the word 'inner-Goddess' must have appeared on every page at least twice." Her chortle turned into a full-blown laugh, until she could hardly get the words out. "It was about as sexy as an eye test at the opticians." She wiped the laughter tears from her eyes.

Her giggling was infectious.

"I mean, honestly," Jamie added, joining in with Linda's merriment. "The story is supposed to be a modern-day setting about a twenty-two-year-old virgin, who doesn't even own a mobile phone or a laptop… *really*? And we are supposed to *believe* that?"

The sisters collapsed into a cackling pile of silliness. And it felt great.

Once the hilarity had subsided, Linda reverted into the big-sister mode, intuitively protective. "Anyway, I don't need to meet Silverton in person to decide I don't like or trust the man. My opinion is based entirely on your account and the friends Silverton keeps – or more specifically, his choice of lawyer."

"He is quite creepy," Jamie agreed.

"You just watch yourself, young lady. I know we've been joking about him, but he sounds like a prize schmuck to me. The way you've described him makes my flesh creep." She shuddered. "I don't know how you can even stay in the same room as him."

"The man is a very rich fool."

"I hope the money is worth it," Linda said doubtfully, adding, "how have you managed to bump into so many obnoxious pillocks in such a short space of time – of both sexes?"

Jamie was tickled by her sister's observation. "I'm beginning to think Alex is right."

Linda looked up.

"She called me a nutcase magnet the other day."

The corners of Linda's mouth turned up. "Well, if the cap fits…" She wavered, then countered with. "Damn it! That's the second time I've agreed with that woman today."

"Steady, girl," Jamie smiled.

*****

When they finally found their way back to Jamie's flat, the darkness inside was broken only by the blink of the blue light from the answerphone. Jamie checked the message. It was her mother, again, asking for Jamie to get in touch; she'd not seen her in ages, and she worried again that her little girl was working too hard.

"That reminds me, Mum's been getting on at me too about you," Linda said. "She feels like she never sees you these days." Linda waited for an answer.

"Come on, Jamie, Mum's on her own now. She needs to see us more – both of us," Linda added. "It's not just my responsibility, and Suffolk is not exactly a million miles away."

"Yeah, I should make the effort, I suppose." Jamie was markedly lacklustre.

"It's harder for her nowadays. She and Dad used to love coming into London, staying with one of us for a few days to catch up on the London culture – a theatre trip, a meal out or a visit to an exhibition."

"True."

"I'm going up to see her in a couple of weekends' time. Come with me, she'd love that – a weekend in Southwold." Linda slipped off her jacket and threw it over the arm of the sofa. "It would stop her getting so paranoid. She thinks you are avoiding her."

"You know what it's like," Jamie said. "I'll need to check my work commitments first." She deftly picked up her sister's coat and escaped towards the spare room to hang it up. "Anyway, more important right now is time with my sister and a hot drink. Cuppa tea?"

Jamie and Linda were still nattering, after several pots of tea, at twenty past three in the morning. Their evening had been fun. It had allowed for precious time to touch base again – like a childhood sleepover.

"I can't recall when we last made time for just the two of us like this, can you?" Linda asked with a smile.

"Nope."

"It's certainly been over a decade since I stayed the night here – just you and me." Linda looked at her watch. "Look at the time. I'm far too old for late nights these days. I need my beauty sleep." She got up and went towards the spare bedroom, unbuttoning her blouse midway. Her skirt, which had been removed about an hour after she'd taken off her coat, was now draped over her arm.

"There are hangers in the wardrobe," Jamie said. She was pouring herself a whisky to take to bed. "Nightcap?"

"Not for me, thanks." Linda walked into the bedroom.

"And grab a t-shirt from the bottom drawer if you want." She could hear Linda crashing around, hanging up her clothes and then pulling out one of the drawers. Jamie walked into the spare room to find her sister sizing up one of Jamie's t-shirts. It was obvious there was no way she'd get into it.

Linda folded it neatly back into its place. "I'd forgotten how long it's been since we last did this," she said. "Either I've grown, or you've shrunk." She took a black, ample-sized dressing gown that was hanging from the back of the bedroom door, and slipped it on.

"Blissful, silk too… that's so much better. Night then."

"Night, night," Jamie said, leaving the room.

"If you get up before me," Linda called out, "don't wake me before midday. I'm *so* tired."

Jamie walked back into the bedroom presently, with a glass of water. Linda had already clambered into bed, looking relaxed and nicely mellow. Jamie put the tumbler by her sister's bedside – something she always used to do when they shared a bedroom as children.

Linda kissed the air at her sister. "Little things," she said. "It's the little things that make the difference… like phoning your mother and older sister more than once in a blue moon."

Jamie's phone buzzed. She took a quick look.

"Are you going to switch that thing off? Who'd be pestering you *now*?"

Jamie tipped her head to the side and slowly cocked an eyebrow, implying that the answer was obvious.

"Tell Alex to jog on and leave you alone for one night," Linda said, typically frustrated on Jamie's behalf. "I hope you aren't giving her the satisfaction of a reply? She doesn't deserve one, you know."

Jamie showed Linda the black screen. "I've just turned it off. There were two text messages and a missed call. I've deleted them."

"Good!" Linda answered. "Now, get yourself to bed, Half-Pint, and sleep well." She blew her sister a kiss. "And thank you for remembering my bedside water."

*****

Linda was still asleep when Jamie woke. It was nearly 11:30am. She crept out to the kitchen to make tea and coffee and get a few rounds of toast on the go.

Linda plodded into the kitchen, still wearing the black dressing gown. “Morning,” she yawned loudly. She plonked herself down onto the swivel chair at the breakfast bar. “Smells yummy,” she yawned again, rubbing her eyes.

Jamie thickly buttered a couple of slices and presented them on a plate to her sister along with a large mug of tea. Curious to know if Alex had managed to exert some self-control overnight by resisting contact, she turned on her phone. “Someone’s left a message.”

“That bloody woman! She can’t even leave you alone for one night.” Linda wiped the melted butter off her plate and licked her finger.

“It’s a landline number. I don’t recognise it.” Jamie listened to the voice message. Her initial indifference gradually cascaded into a turmoil of emotions.

Linda stopped drinking. Her brow knotted anxiously as she watched Jamie’s changing expressions.

“You look like a muntjac caught in headlights.”

Jamie felt the colour drain from her face. She started to feel light-headed.

"Jamie?" Linda jumped off her stool and grabbed Jamie's arm. "What's happened?"

"Oh… shit!" Jamie said slowly. She swallowed, her mouth dry. "Sarah Ekstein's back in London."

CHAPTER 9

"What?" Linda's question came out as a rasping whisper. "What does she want?"

"She's already been back in the UK for several weeks," Jamie said. "She's accepted a consultancy role at St George's Hospital in Tooting. Listen…" Jamie played back Sarah's message. Her final words: *"Please, Jamie, call me as soon as you can. We need to talk."*

Linda stood staring at Jamie, taking in the information she had just heard.

"I don't trust her. Why call me now? What does she want from me?"

"More to the point, what do you plan to do now?"

Jamie looked at the granite worktop. "I have no idea." Her brain was racing.

"You don't have to *do* anything, you know, Jay," Linda said, pouring her sister a coffee. "And you certainly don't need to make any spur-of-the-moment decisions right now."

"I'm not so sure…" Jamie drank her coffee. "I never did tell you the details of our split-up, did I?"

"Do I *need* to know?" Linda was cautious, adding quickly, "Actually, I'm not sure I want to know."

Jamie didn't elaborate.

"What can I do? Do you need me to stick around, or go?" Linda looked worried.

"I think I need to call her back," Jamie said eventually, peering into her coffee cup.

"You *think*, or you *know*? Because unless you know for sure...?"

"What would *you* do?" Jamie asked seriously.

"That is one question I'm not prepared to answer," Linda said. "But my say-so is pretty irrelevant. I remember how you were affected by the break-up the first time around."

Jamie could sense that her sister was biting her tongue.

Linda tried a different tack. "What do you hope to gain by raking all this back up again?"

"I'm not sure. Answers, I guess. If I'm being honest, I want answers."

"And how will that help where you are in your life right now?"

Jamie looked at her sister.

"I mean, how exactly do you see Sarah Ekstein featuring in your life today? Tomorrow? In your future?"

There was a pause. "I don't," Jamie replied quietly.

Silently, Linda nodded – the way she always did when allowing a person time to reach their own conclusions, rather than impose her own comments or judgement. "Do you want to talk this through some more?"

Jamie stood. "I'm going to call her back right now. Could you stick around, Linny?"

"Absolutely, hun," Linda said, growing ever so slightly taller in her seat, wearing her 'let battle commence' face.

"Here goes, then," Jamie announced as she picked up her mobile from the counter. She looked at the screen, hesitating, before tapping it in the palm of her other hand a few times. "Wish me luck." She marched past Linda.

Linda glanced at her watch.

Jamie took herself into her bedroom, pulling the door to behind her, knowing that Linda would be clock-watching.

"Jamie…?"

Jamie's heart raced. Even now, the sound of Sarah's voice affected her. She pinched the bridge of her nose and closed her eyes, hating that she had no control over her reaction.

"Ag, man! Is that you, Jay?" Sarah asked again. Her staccato-clipped accent was unmistakable, and as familiar as if they'd only spoken yesterday.

Jamie was blunt. "What do you want, Sarah?"

"How are you, my bokkie?"

Jamie was unprepared for Sarah's gentleness, or her use of that specific term of endearment. She only ever used it for Jamie. But it came, this time, too naturally from Sarah's lips. It implied contrition, which angered Jamie.

Sarah took control. "Can I see you?"

Jamie gave herself a second or two to consider the question. "Why?"

"Because I'm in town." Typically, Sarah's sentence
ended with an upward inflexion, making the statement sound like a question.

Another few silent moments passed.

Sarah followed through with, "And I would very much like to see you, Jamie."

Jamie closed her eyes.

"You're pinching the top of your nose, right now, eh?"

Sarah knew her too well. Jamie immediately released the grip across her nose. She could hear the amusement in Sarah's voice.

"This is encouraging – you're not giving me a flat *no,* then?"

Ironically, it was her tenacious persistence that had attracted Jamie to Sarah in the first place.

"Good to hear your voice again, bokk–" Sarah just managed to stop herself, mid-sentence.

Jamie was now four years wiser. She wasn't going to be sucked in again. "Why are you here – *now*, Sarah?" But she swallowed, with difficulty.

"I thought a coffee or beer somewhere might be a good plan, eh?"

A gentle tapping interrupted the conversation. Linda's face appeared, peeping round the bedroom door. She thrust an optimistic thumb up, nodding

vigorously, expecting Jamie to affirm that all was okay. Jamie replied with a pathetic partial nod and wave, hoping it was enough to convince Linda to stay put. Linda nodded in understanding and quietly closed the
door behind her.

Jamie finally emerged from her bedroom. Her plan of action had been agreed.

Linda got to her feet like an expectant father, but said nothing, allowing Jamie the time to volunteer the details freely. Jamie shuffled into the kitchen, deep in her thoughts. She loaded her mug into the empty dishwasher.

Linda couldn't remain silent. "Well? What did she want? I feel like I've been waiting for a jury to reach their verdict."

"I'm meeting her at The Lamb later." Jamie didn't look at Linda as she spoke.

"Why, for Christ's sake?"

"Because she's working in London… and it's been over four years since we broke up… and we are both adults."

"Sounds to me, baby girl," Linda suggested gently, "like someone hasn't yet reached a point of closure on this one."

Jamie's eyes stayed down.

"And being angry wouldn't solve anything," Linda said delicately.

"It wasn't an easy split," Jamie confessed. She could feel herself mentally withdrawing and was unwilling to elaborate, even to her sister.

Linda risked further probing. "Did she ask you to meet up, or did you ask her?"

"It was her idea," Jamie said, finally looking at Linda.

Linda nodded sagely.

"She screwed me over, you know?" Jamie said. "Royally! It was months before I sussed what was going on."

Linda sat trying to appear unmoved, but Jamie knew she was seething inside.

"No – I had no idea," Linda said, barely moving her tight lips.

"I know what you're thinking."

"It wouldn't be helpful to say what I'm thinking. You've finally started to talk about important stuff and I don't want to stop you."

Jamie thought on Linda's words.

"Do you *want* to tell me what happened?"

"Not much to tell..." Jamie took out a J-cloth from the drawer and rubbed at the spotless granite worktop. "Except that… I'd been living in her apartment, sharing the housework, washing and ironing her clothes..." Jamie's polishing became increasingly vigorous. "Sharing the bills, paying half of her fucking rent... I'm just glad I had the sense to buy this place on my own when I did. And, more importantly, that she never ended up sharing ownership for half of it."

"Your 'not much to tell' statement sounds like a tsunami of frustrated emotion," Linda said.

Jamie continued folding tea towels and moving things around.

"And stop that! I can't just stand here and watch all this pointless displacement activity." Linda took the cloth away and nodded towards the sofa, leading Jamie by the hand. She sat and patted the seat next to her. "Just come and sit down, Half-Pint."

Jamie took a deep breath and sat, exhaling loudly through pursed lips.

"You sound like you have the troubles of the world on these." Linda squeezed Jamie's shoulder.

Jamie sat forward and massaged her temples. "I was *so* bloody dense not to see the early warning signs." She pounded her thigh. "Her lies had been going on for weeks before I got wise. The old saying that 'love is blind' isn't far off the mark. If I'm honest, I didn't want to believe it. In the end, it was that classic old chestnut that was the giveaway." Jamie bit her bottom lip. "Unfamiliar perfume on your partner's skin? A pretty damn sure sign you're in trouble."

Linda nodded.

"And I've been battling with uninvited snatches of memory popping into my head recently."

"Time can certainly have a perverse, selective way of skewing perspective," Linda said. "It's all too easy to feed misguided sentiments by viewing shitty relationships through rose-tinted lenses."

Jamie speared her sister with a look. She had extraordinary depth of insight. Jamie's face grew hot, pricked by conscience. "I was *so* unbelievably dim." Jamie stood up and started to pace. "I need to know the details, Linny."

Linda considered Jamie's quandary. "Does it *really* matter?"

"Hell, yes!" Jamie almost shouted. "To *me*, yes. As soon as I had the evidence and courage, and told her I knew about her lies and cheating, she packed up and left. The day after I grilled her… she slithered off out of the firing line and buggered off to Jo-burg. She never contacted me again until today. I thought I'd put all that behind me."

"Why didn't you tell me all this until now?" Linda's eyes followed Jamie's distressed steps.

Jamie started biting at her thumbnail. "It's not *just* Sarah –" She pinched the bridge of her nose.

"Okay, so what else?"

Jamie shook her head, pushing away her train of thought, and veered down a different path. "Well, for one thing, you were caught up in your own life. It was about the time when Dave was between jobs and flitting back and forwards to America. You had enough to think about. It gave me the chance to throw myself into my work. Every cloud… Best thing I ever did, career-wise."

Linda gave Jamie one of her classic looks, which Jamie understood as: *Don't pretend that you haven't been hiding behind your work for years*.

Instead, Linda said, "That's two people you are angry with today." Then, in time-honoured fashion, she added, "And you know that anger is wasted energy, unless...?" she waited, inviting Jamie to anticipate her
next words.

Jamie completed one of Linda's favourite sayings: "Unless you channel it constructively and learn from it."

Linda clicked her fingers. "Exactly!"

Jamie stopped pacing. "I'll figure that out on my way there. I've got three hours to lose my anger and get constructive," she replied.

"Don't do anything you'll regret."

"Like what? Kill her and dump her body into the Thames?"

"I just meant don't be taken in by her swagger." Linda stood up again. "Besides, that's not exactly the smartest comment to make in front of a lawyer! Seriously, though, as I recall, she was a pretty smooth talker. She was in a relationship when you met her, wasn't she?"

"Yeah, she was. But I would never mess around with anyone who is already hooked up." It was a thorny subject that always got Jamie's defensive barrier up. "Anyway, it was Sarah who came gunning for *me*, not the other way around. And she had already ended her relationship before we got together."

"Your moral high ground was obviously very alluring and totally irresistible. And no doubt her being South African wouldn't have gone unnoticed on you, either." Linda gently punched Jamie's arm. "I know what a sucker you are for accents."

"I won't do anything silly. I just want some honesty from the woman. Some good old-fashioned honesty and answers to a few unanswered questions." Jamie moved back into the kitchen area and started gathering and stacking the breakfast plates and mugs. "You can stay around if you want. I'm going for a shower."

Linda attempted to inject some humour into the mix. "I hope nothing untoward happens to Sarah in the next few days. You've already alluded to her murder."

"Now who's being ridiculous?" Jamie was in no mood to trivialise.

"Right now, Jamie, I'm uncertain if I should stay or go. You are vulnerable. You've always let your heart rule your head and you have always been the optimist – seeing the positive in everyone. I know full well that you are not a pushover, but you are entering an emotionally charged situation. I suspected that Sarah will be fully aware of this, too, and will likely use this fact for her convenience. She doesn't see this as a date, does she?"

"Damn right it's not," said Jamie, stiffening.

"Just be careful. *You* may be thinking that, but does *she* know that?"

"Don't fret on my behalf. I'll make sure she knows it." As she spoke, Jamie felt a stab of guilt, knowing what she'd left out of her story just now was far worse than what she'd included.

"We've been so lucky, you know," Linda reflected.

"What do you mean?"

"With Mum and Dad's relationship," Linda said, looking down at nothing in particular. She closed her eyes. "They were perfect, and a hell of a tough act to follow – one of the best relationships I've ever known. He worshipped Mum, bless him, and she totally adored him. Her reading at the funeral was so moving, remember? Theirs was a special bond. How she got through the reading still astounds me, poor Mum. I couldn't have done it. He was the most amazing man I ever knew. Strong, reliable, loyal, steadfast... Dammit, I miss him."

Looking at the same arbitrary area where Linda was gazing. Jamie felt her stomach twist in a knot. She couldn't reply. Instead, she offered Linda a brittle smile. Jamie knew how close her sister had been to their father. He had been Linda's hero, rock and mentor, and Jamie knew she felt his loss dreadfully.

"Anyway," Linda said. "You get yourself in that shower. Once I've showered and dressed, I'm heading off. Promise me, though, you'll phone me as soon as you've finished with Sarah, okay?"

“Okay,” Jamie said, unconvincingly.

“Promise?”

“I promise.”

CHAPTER 10

Jamie allowed herself plenty of time to reach The Lamb pub in Conduit Street. She took her car, giving her a legitimate reason not to drink alcohol. Her mind needed to be clear and one step ahead of Sarah.

As she drove, she started to seriously question the wisdom of the meeting. Here she was, relatively unprepared and without a preconceived script in her head, while Sarah was a master at manipulation, no matter what the scenario. Jamie had learned a lesson from her misguided loyalty to Sarah and wasn't about to be trapped again.

There was a parking slot a short distance away from the pub. Jamie pushed numerous coins into the meter, paying for longer than she had intended to stay. Now, as she stomped through the streets, the nerves started. "Pull yourself together, woman," she told herself.

Sarah must have strategically planned to meet at this venue. Built in the 1720s, it was now Grade II listed, and one of Jamie's favourite buildings. They had come here on their second date together. The event was memorable, because of a discussion that had started about the pub's famous 'snob-screens': revolving glass panels, at eye level, set on either side of the counter. Originally erected during the class-conscious Victorian era, their purpose was to separate the sight of the lowly bar staff from the respectable, paying customers – the gentry. This arrangement served to encourage and even perpetuate social stratification. It was apparently the last remaining pub in London with this historical feature, and their conversation about it had been heated. The architectural detail fascinated Jamie, although its significance resonated painfully with Sarah, as a reminder of the apartheid years within her beloved South Africa.

Once in the pub, it was Jamie who spotted Sarah first. She had her back to Jamie, at a table just in front of the famous screens. She looked totally different, but her body language – the way she sat, the way she used her hands when speaking – was unmistakable. It seemed Sarah had reinvented herself during her absence. Her hair, once jet-black and below her shoulders, was now short, choppy and highlighted blonde. Though she hadn't needed to, she had obviously toned up. And a new pair of dark-rimmed glasses finished Sarah's new look. Loath to admit it, she appreciated – and was even a little ruffled by Sarah's physical appeal.

For Jamie, it was not at all unexpected to see that Sarah already had company. An attentive, bubbly, full-figured woman was stretched across the table, laughing at something that Sarah was saying. Sarah had the type of personality that drew people to her – like bees to a honeypot. Thankfully, Jamie was not the jealous type. On the contrary, she used to tease Sarah about her popularity. Jamie secretly enjoyed watching

other people flirting and engaging with her girlfriend, secure
in her total trust – or so she believed.

If only Jamie had known then what she knew now.

Today, she was prepared and ready. As she approached the table where Sarah sat, Jamie caught the tail end of the conversation.

"Yes, I love it there too," the other woman simpered.

Sarah smiled. "I'll hold you to that."

The woman looked jubilant. She gave Sarah a kiss then moved away towards the exit, like the cat that had just got the cream. As she crossed Jamie's path, she apologised, accidentally brushing against her arm on the way out. Sarah was blissfully unaware of the encounter.

Jamie spoke to the back of Sarah's head, devoid of emotion. "I see you've already made a friend."

Sarah turned, letting out a breathy "Eish!" She jumped up, her arms open wide. But Jamie raised her hand, palm towards Sarah's face. There would be no uncertain terms this time.

Sarah stepped back, looked Jamie up and down and gave an approving whistle. "You look amazing. Great to see you, bokkie." Having had her attempt at a hug thwarted, Sarah reached out instead to stroke the side of Jamie's arm. Jamie pulled away, and Sarah sat back down.

Resuming command, Jamie stayed standing. "Still spinning your webs, I see?"

Sarah gave Jamie a look.

"Why have you contacted me, Sarah?"

Sarah put her hand on the chair next to her, pulling it out from under the table. "Sit down, won't you? My God, woman, you're making me nervous."

"I doubt that very much," Jamie replied, still standing.

"Can I buy you a drink?" Sarah got up. "What about a bottle of our V.C., perhaps? For old time's sake?"

This was the pub where Jamie had introduced Sarah to Veuve Clicquot. The reference to it being 'our' V.C didn't work its intended magic.

"No. This isn't a date, Sarah. I don't plan on stopping. I've got things to do. What *exactly* do you want?"

"We can't talk while you're standing over me, Jamie," Sarah said, once again gesturing to the chair right next to her.

Jamie took the furthest seat away from Sarah and perched herself on the edge, indicating that she was ready to leave imminently. She looked at her watch. "Make it quick."

Sarah began a detailed, drawn-out narrative about all her past adventures, concluding with the fact she was now living in Brighton and commuting to London for work each day.

As Jamie listened, it became apparent that 'making it quick' was not on Sarah's agenda. She was extending their meeting for as long as she could get away with it. Sarah's ability to spin a yarn wasn't at all new to Jamie; Sarah had always had charm. Infuriatingly, she was still a great storyteller and extraordinarily affable. But the rub? Somewhere inside Jamie was the need to know. Even so, she was sufficiently in control. There was a time when Sarah's conversation would have rendered Jamie putty in her hands.

Eventually, Sarah spoke candidly. "This isn't the first time I've seen you."

Jamie questioned Sarah with her eyes.

"It was quite a few weeks ago, now… when I saw you."

Jamie's mind flitted to the possible times when this could have occurred without her realising.

"At The Coal Hole pub." Sarah added, then waited.

Jamie thought back. She often frequented The Coal Hole.

Sarah stared back at Jamie. "It was a busy night. I was on the balcony above the main pub, with a bird's-eye view of everything below. I first saw Alex and Gavin come in, with two other people… I assumed that you wouldn't be far behind them."

"I have no idea when you are talking about," Jamie said.

"You came in later, but didn't sit with Alex…"

"Why are you telling me this, Sarah? Why didn't you come and talk to me then, when you had the chance?"

"You came in with another woman," Sarah said. "I assumed that she was your girlfriend." She grinned. "But you left in quite a dramatic fashion, it seemed?"

Sophie! That had been the night when she'd got caught up in the altercation with Sophie's not-so-ex. "You were waiting for me, and you didn't come and talk to me because I wasn't alone? Why do I find that hard to swallow? Even if I *was* with someone else, it certainly wouldn't have stopped you from crashing the party in the past."

Nothing of what Jamie was hearing came as any surprise. The next part, however, was more of a shock.

"The way I treated you, and the way that I left things? That was poor form, Jay-Jay. I'm not proud of my behaviour. Hindsight has shown me that you were the best thing that ever happened to me."

Jamie's riposte was cut-throat. "For someone delivering such a slurry of shit, you didn't seem to be thinking too much about '*the best thing that ever happened to you*' when you were flirting with your friend as I walked in," Jamie jeered, using air-quotes to emphasise Sarah's words. The cynicism gathered force. "She left with enormous satisfaction plastered across her face. Whatever you said to her, it was obviously hugely engaging and thoroughly enriching."

Jamie was pleased with herself.

"Ag, man, are you jealous?"

"Jealous?" Jamie shook her head, aghast. "You're serious, aren't you?"

"It's nothing heavy," Sarah was flippant. "Turns out she loves Brighton too, and I just happen to know a great little bar just off the Lanes." She added as a post-script, "Nice little anties, though…"

Jamie realised her teeth were grinding.

Sarah casually sipped her drink. "Tell me, what else can I tell you about, just now?" Elbow rooted to the table, she rested her chin on her closed fist, then started. "Ag, man! I didn't catch her name."

Jamie laughed in spite of herself. "Your arrogance is astounding."

"Arrogance or confidence?" Sarah was smug. "Anyway, back to the important things. Tell me about the person I saw you in The Coal Hole with that night. I'll bet my rands that I can guess the situation?" She waved her index finger in Jamie's face in small, hypnotic circles. "She's neither serious nor current. Am I right?"

"I don't need to explain my movements to you, Sarah."

"I know I'm right, man!" Sarah said. "I know you well enough of old to be sure that you wouldn't be here now if you were in a relationship." Sarah's chin still rested on her closed fist, her attitude oozing self-assuredness.

"I'm single and I'm not looking," Jamie replied.

Sarah's eyes flashed. "Am I starting to melt the ice?"

"This is priceless, Sarah." Within a few minutes of being back in Sarah's company, all the anger and unanswered questions became completely irrelevant. "I need to stop wasting my time." Jamie stood up, very proud of the way she was handling the situation.

"So, is that it? All my efforts to find you again have come to this?" There was a new flash of disappointment in Sarah's eyes.

Those eyes! Jamie's diaphragm tensed.

Sarah reached out and gripped Jamie's hand. "Please don't go," she begged. She stood up and grabbed Jamie's other hand, moving in to close the space between them.

Jamie was swamped by fluttering palpitations, unprepared for such a visceral reaction, hating the emotion.

Sarah played her final card. "But you called me?" she said accusingly.

"Simple courtesy. Your voice message on my phone asked me to call you."

"No," Sarah said, adding, after several seconds' grace, "Before that." She tried to connect Jamie's eyes with hers. "You left an answerphone message on my cellphone… the other day…?"

Jamie thought a while, and then her eyes locked with Sarah's in a moment of realisation. "Shit, Sarah!"

"I could see from the balcony that night that something was stirring up a storm," Sarah continued. "You dashed out of the pub, Alex was bobbing up and down like a little duck – I'm guessing to try and see where you'd got to. Shortly after that, Alex and Gavin left also."

Jamie stared, taking it all in.

"Then, *bonsella!* I noticed something beneath the table where you had been sitting." Sarah searched Jamie's face. "There it was, right there by my feet, man… And as soon as I saw your key fob, I knew what I had to do."

Jamie was unable to talk. Silence filled the space where words could not.

Sarah went on, "A quick scribbled note on a beer mat, and the help of the cute fella behind the bar… and the rest? Well, I guess you know the rest, eh?"

With still nothing forthcoming from Jamie, Sarah pushed on. "I thought long and hard about that inscription… I would recognise that little key fob anywhere… and so sweet of you to keep it. That means a lot, bokkie."

Jamie guessed what was coming next, although she didn't need to hear it spelt out.

"I bought it for you on our first Christmas together, remember?"

Jamie certainly didn't need reminding. They had bought, on impulse, a little three-foot pine tree. Sarah had secretly commissioned a red leather key fob in the shape of a Christmas tree and had it engraved with the words: *First of many, my bokkie xxx.* It was the only decoration on their tree that year.

Hopelessly sentimental, Jamie had never brought herself to get rid of it. She was now wishing she had.

"I could give you the carrot on the stick, but what you chose to do with it was up to you." Sarah squeezed Jamie's hand. "I've never stopped loving you, Jamie."

*****

When Jamie finally left Sarah at the pub, she didn't return to her car; nor did she phone Linda straight away. She took herself for a walk through the quieter back streets of London, ending up on a park bench in Leicester Square Gardens. Only then did she take out her phone to make a call.

"So," Linda sighed, having heard the full account, "the anonymous key fob finder turned out not to be a stranger after all! But she's a grown woman, for God's sake. Why all the cloak-and-dagger nonsense?" She was clearly trying, with great difficulty, to conceal her lack of sympathy. "Meeting you face to face might have been a good place to start," she added. "She must have had zero confidence in your reaction for her to skulk around spying on you."

Jamie heard an exasperated harrumph on the other end.

"And she thinks she's still in love with you?"

"That's what she said."

"To be honest, I don't really care what Sarah thinks. What's important to me is how *you* feel about it, and what you plan on doing with that little scrap of information?"

Uncharacteristically, Linda didn't give Jamie time to
reflect on the question. Her approach slid from protective anger to a hailstorm of questions.

"So, what happened to that *take no bullshit* attitude that you were espousing this morning, Jamie? You were planning on getting answers from her, I thought – remember? Something along the lines of, 'Since when did lying and cheating become part of our relationship contract'? It appears that she manipulated the situation, and you allowed her to crawl under your skin."

Jamie said nothing, hearing the frustration and despondency in Linda's usually controlled tone.

"Has she?" Linda pressed.

"Has she what?"

"Succeeded in crawling under your skin?"

"If you're asking me if I'm giving the relationship another go – no. But it doesn't mean I won't keep in contact."

"Really?" Linda's voice expressed new concern.

"Linda, I'm capable of dealing with this." Jamie scuffed at the grass with the toe of her shoe. "And, yes, Sarah obviously hoped there was a chance of us getting back together. I put her straight."

"Good!"

"I won't pretend it was easy..." Jamie waited for a response that didn't come, so she continued, "If I'm honest, my own reaction is what horrified me."

"Uh-huh?"

"I was so taken aback by how I reacted," Jamie added. "I thought I had all that emotion under control. Even now, after all these years, she can still tug at my heart-strings. And that really hacks me off."

Linda thought. "You loved the woman," she answered honestly.

The corner of Jamie's mouth lifted. "Yes. Yes, I did. Thanks for that recognition, sis. I appreciate that."

Linda reined in the sentiment. "Yeah – but note my use of the past tense in that sentence. Don't you think for a second that I'm condoning your newfound friendship with her. It doesn't sound healthy."

"I'm under no illusions, don't worry," Jamie said, getting up from the park bench. She was beginning to feel the chill of the late afternoon. "If we meet up again, there's no chance of any reconciliation. It's me who's in control this time."

"Uh-huh," Linda said with uncontrolled scepticism.

"Anyhow, I'm bloody freezing out here. I'm off home now, okay?" Jamie started walking out of the park. “I’ve got a lot going on in the next few days, so I’ll call you mid-week, okay?”

“Sure,” Linda agreed. “Love you.”

“And please, don’t worry about me sis,” Jamie added.

“Tough!” Linda said, before ending the call. “Too late, it goes with the territory.”

CHAPTER 11

The following couple of weeks were busy. Jamie was trying to complete various jobs, resulting in a last-minute, two-day business trip to Edinburgh.

On Tuesday morning, she was sitting in the boarding lounge at Heathrow Airport when the phone call came in.

"*Miz* Barker?"

Jamie recognised the brand of disdain. "Mr Hunter."

"My client, Mr Silverton, is still waiting for your reply..." John stopped mid-flow, declaring his superiority.

Jamie was not budging. He was obviously waiting for an apology, or something similar. Refusing rise to the lure, she allowed herself an expedient pause before answering.

John's impatience won over his game-play. "Are you still there?"

"Yes, it's super to hear from you, Mr Hunter." Jamie's sincerity was entirely contrived.

"You have received my client's signed contract, have you not?"

"I have…" Jamie again suspended the flow.

"And?" John was sharp.

Jamie could hear his frustrated impatience. "Apologies, Mr Hunter, it's not the best time to talk.

You see, I'm at the airport and about to board a plane. I'll keep it short and sweet for you."

"Have you signed the contract, madam, or does my client require the services of someone who is reliable and competent?"

Jamie snorted a laugh, just managing to cover it with a cough. She had successfully wound him up. "Mr Hunter," she answered soberly, "I'm sorry to hear that you don't share Mr Silverton's confidence." She hesitated, keeping control. "Actually, I've just had a conversation with him." She stopped talking again, just because she could. "Hello? Are you still there, Mr Hunter?" she questioned, turning the screw just a little bit more.

"I'm here!"

"Oh, good – I thought I'd lost you then." Jamie wondered if he could sense her silently laughing at him. "Yes, I had a chat with Carl, approximately half an hour ago, actually. We already have a meeting pencilled in the diary this coming Friday – to finalise and sign the final contract. I assumed you'd be present?"

Nothing.

"But then" – Jamie stirred the pot some more – "I'm sure you're aware he's out of the country for a few months?" A pause. "His business trip in Europe? No? He's combined the trip with a visit to his villa in Saint-Tropez. He'll be gone for at least eight weeks and wants his property completed by the autumn...

I'm surprised you didn't know this." Jamie paused just long enough to conclude with, "Seems your communication systems need revising, John."

Again, no reply.

"So, anything else I can help you with today?" Jamie chirped.

The phone line went dead.

"Yesss!" Jamie gave a childish little celebratory punch in the air.

The call she'd received from Silverton that morning had been short and delightfully sweet. He delivered the icing on the cake, announcing that he was "officially handing the creative management reins" to her. The additional bonus was that their meeting on Friday would include the builder, engineer and surveyor. It came as a relief to hear that the rest of the project team would be there; she was reluctant to endure another session on her own with Silverton.

Now that Jamie had been given carte blanche to lead the project completely unhindered, she had a renewed enthusiasm for it.

More good news was delivered mid-week, when she discovered that John Hunter would not be present at the meeting. The next few months were panning out to be both interesting and creatively liberating.

Jamie rang Linda to share the good news.

"Why the *whole* day?" Linda complained. "That man is unpleasant enough to be with for an hour, but a *whole day*? Is there no other way around it?"

"I'm excited," Jamie said. "I'll be meeting up with the team."

A few hours later, Linda rang Jamie back, not entirely with altruistic motives. She had devised a plan to time-limit her sister's meeting with Carl. "Dinner at Le Gavroche is your get-out clause, Jamie. I've booked a table for us on Friday evening."

"You booked a table, just like that?"

"Well, I'm pretty sure that knowing the maître d' is a plus for securing a short-notice booking."

*****

Just as Jamie pushed open Carl Silverton's garden gate, the front door ahead swung wide open. Even from this distance, she could see through the hallway to the sunlight streaming in through the large bay window of the furthest room.

"My dear girl, how delightful," Silverton called. "You've been hanging around out there for quite a while. Early, eh? Couldn't get to me soon enough? Keen. Now *that's* the kind of enthusiasm I admire."

Jamie, who had indeed arrived fifteen minutes early to sort out her paperwork, realised that he must have been looking out for her arrival. It reminded her what a twat he was.

"Do come in –" Silverton locked the door behind them, then welcomed Jamie through with a grandiose sweep of his arm, completing the invitation by waving her down the hallway.

Recalling her first visit, Jamie was conscious of Silverton's lack of physical contact. She was cautiously encouraged. Had he taken account of her criticisms the other day? Was he demonstrating that he had taken them seriously? Whatever the explanation, Silverton was on the charm offensive, although his efforts seemed artificial.

Hearing the murmur of chattering voices coming from the far end of the hallway, Jamie made her way through to meet the rest of team. En route, she noticed the most obvious change since her first visit, was beneath her feet.

"The hallway looks incredible, Mr Silverton," Jamie said. "What a transformation."

Without the confetti of cigarette butts, the hall looked beautiful. Jamie also noticed the smell, the aroma of work in progress: paint, wood and varnish. She wondered if the fireplace was now fully uncovered and brought back to life.

"You've done a magnificent job." She crouched down to look closer, tracing between the joins with her finger. "It's impossible to tell the original tiles from the replaced or repaired ones."

Silverton looked down at Jamie, his little-boy face beaming. "I'm thrilled you noticed and approve, Jamie." His face relaxed into a serious stare. "I think we should ditch this Mr Silverton title, don't you? It sounds horribly formal, don't you think… for friends, I mean?"

Provided with a valid purpose, she extricated herself from Silverton's company to go and introduce herself to the others. She continued towards the drawing room.

Part-way along the hallway, Silverton stopped behind Jamie and grabbed her shirt at her elbow, just firmly enough to stop her from moving further.

"Carl, not Mr Silverton… It's Carl, okay? I wish to be addressed as Carl." He looked hard at her, still holding her sleeve.

"I'd prefer 'Mr Silverton,'" Jamie answered. "I address all my clients formally – it's less complicated to keep matters professional."

Silverton's appearance altered, yet again. His puppy-dog eyes fleetingly pleaded with Jamie. Releasing his grip on her arm, he flew into an unpredictable frenzy of energy and darted off ahead, up the stairs.

Automatically, Jamie followed, until she reached the foot of the stairs. Then she stopped.

Silverton was standing motionless halfway up, looking back down. "Upstairs," he growled. "Now, Jamie!" He disappeared around the corner at the top of the banisters.

The disciplined dog stopped dead. Jamie was shot down by the ferociousness of Silverton's tone.

Realising Jamie wasn't following, Silverton's face reappeared around the corner. He cocked his head a fraction – a question, waiting for Jamie's compliance. But he was detached, his emotional state ambivalent. His eyes flicked from wall to wall across the narrow confines of the stairway… brooding.

Then, a dull, metallic thud redirected Jamie's attention. She looked towards the noise.

The end of a thick, black leather belt was wrapped tightly round Silverton's clenched fist. He had dropped the buckle-end onto the stairs.

"Why?" he said. "Don't you trust yourself, Jamie?" Thin, tight lips and snake-eyes implied a salacious double entendre. He rhythmically lifted and dropped the metal buckle of his belt on the bare wood of the stair, like a heartbeat. The flat palm of his other hand braced his weight against the opposite wall. He leaned forward to lock eyes with her.

Jamie's mouth opened and closed as she struggled to find an answer. What did this all mean? The thought of being alone with him upstairs was disconcerting, but thankfully, Jamie knew she didn't need to be. She thought quickly and called up, "Show me later, Mr Silverton. I'd prefer any decisions we make to be seen and agreed by the whole team. Come and introduce me to them." Jamie turned, intending to join the chattering voices in the far room at the end of the hall.

Then the voices went silent.

They became... music?

The music... was a radio.

Where were the rest of the team? The engineers and surveyor that were promised? Jamie had to gain a sense of rational control. A change of subject would put this all into perspective. "So, how's the fireplace renovation doing?" She moved away, just out of Silverton's vision, around the corner at the bottom of the stairs. "That room was undergoing quite a transformation when I last saw
it." Jamie's agitation wasn't subsiding.

From where she now stood, she could see and reach the front door easily. To her left was the room with the fireplace; to her right, the front door. Either location was a good few feet away. The oddly positioned, enclosed, narrow stairs were approximately halfway down the long hallway.

Jamie could hear Silverton's footsteps slowly descending the stairs. The front door was closer than the back exit through the kitchen, but reaching either of them meant crossing Silverton's path at the bottom of the stairs.

Surely she was just being paranoid? But her fight-or-flight response was telling her to get the hell out.

Silverton was now at the foot of the stairs, ogling her round the bottom banister.

Jamie wasn't going to look at him. She needed to feel safe. "I've forgotten some paperwork," she bluffed. "It's still in the boot of the car."

As casually as her anxiety allowed, Jamie moved towards the closest visible exit – the front door. When she reached it, she found herself fumbling erratically, snatching at the handle several times with no success. "It's not opening!" she babbled, the pitch of her voice seriously betraying her alarm.

Silverton stood blocking the hallway, feet planted firmly apart in a rigid A-frame. The fingers of his hands were rammed into the front pockets of his jeans. His arms were straight, his elbows locked. His belt hung loosely round his neck, either end dangled in front of his newly half-unbuttoned, untucked shirt. He rocked audaciously on his heels, glaring predatorily. *What was he thinking?*

"Leaving so soon?" he castigated her. "You are turning out to be quite a wilful, naughty girl, Jamie – and you've been upsetting my friend, so I understand." Magician-like, he slowly revealed the key from his pocket, pinched between thumb and index finger, and dangled it close to his chest. "Security precaution," he smirked. "That bloody door lock needs fixing. Anyone could come in. There are some bad people out there, Jamie… Some *very* bad people."

The key wasn't offered willingly.

Jamie was convinced that Silverton was loving every single second. What was more troubling was that it was impossible to tell whether his behaviour was unsafe.

He slid the key back in his pocket.

Even with the banal, crappy pop songs droning from the far room, the rest of the house suddenly sounded dreadfully silent. Jamie could hear the blood in her ears pumping her heartbeat.

"It's that way." Silverton contentiously jerked his thumb a couple of times over his shoulder. "Through the kitchen door and down the side passage. Be my guest." His invitation to leave was not backed by action. He was stuck firmly in the middle of the hallway, showing no sign of shifting.

Jamie was still several feet away with no choice *but* to stand, facing Silverton.

"You upset my friend John the other day, didn't you?" Silverton didn't allow Jamie to answer. "That's no way to gain a man's respect. So why didn't you follow me upstairs just then, Jamie?"

Jamie didn't falter. "Where are the rest of the team, Carl? You said they were joining us?"

He ignored her. "I found your rudeness just now quite upsetting, Jamie." He looked hurt. "Your behaviour is intolerable. First, you upset my friend when he was simply doing his job, and now, you've made it very clear that you don't trust me." He took hold of the belt around his neck and gradually pulled. It slid off completely. Silverton held it swinging in his hand again. He pouted his lips in a humourless, fake show of petulance. "Boo-hoo!" He mimed the action – rubbing his eyes with his knuckles. "She doesn't trust me."

Jamie had no idea how she was expected to answer.

It seemed Silverton didn't want her to. "Wearing another trouser suit again, I see?" He glowered intimidatingly at her. "You're not selling your best attributes, Jamie. Is that to put me off? Either you don't trust *me*, or you don't trust yourself to be alone with me?" He partially slipped the fingers of one hand down the front of his belt-free jeans.

Jamie swallowed, not knowing where to look. Why would he do such a thing? What kind of game was he playing?

"Haven't you got something to collect?"

Jamie looked at him.

Silverton nodded down at the briefcase that Jamie had been diligently clutching the whole time.

"From your car, Jamie," Silverton snarled, irritated by her indecisiveness. "Your paperwork. Are you trying to provoke me?" He slowly took his hand out from the front of his jeans.

Jamie didn't need a second invitation to leave, but she had no choice other than to cross Silverton's path. What if he had no intention of letting her past? Was this cat-and-mouse game all part of some sick plan? Jamie drew courage from somewhere. "What are you doing, Carl?"

His face screwed up. "Doing? Trying to organise an exceptionally talented architect to come and fix my shit-hole; or so *I* thought."

Jamie was not going to risk putting Silverton's trust to the test. Unthinking, she powered past him. Once into the kitchen, Jamie gave a gasp of relief, finding that the back door had a key in the lock. She flung open the door as she fled, bolting around the back of the house down the side alleyway to the front garden.

CHAPTER 12

As she crashed through the front gate, Jamie almost collided into three other people on the street. Grinding to a halt, she was blocked yet again.

"Pardon – sorry, excuse us," said a woman from the group. The two men edged past Jamie through the garden gate.

"Someone's in a hurry," the woman said. Her sudden look of concern registered how close Jamie was to tears. "Are you all right, hon?" She glanced towards the house and then back at Jamie a couple of times.

Jamie usually cringed at the use of insincere terms of affection from strangers, but right now it was reassuring. After all, it seemed reasonable to question why she had just come running down the garden path like a woman possessed.

The two men in the group looked equally unsure. The older of them came back. "Are you sure you're okay?" He protectively rested his open palm on Jamie's arm.

Jamie stepped away, wary of receiving any further physical contact – even reassurance.

The younger man looked skittish, seemingly wondering what to do with himself.

"Are you *all* going in there?" Jamie blurted; her question was more an expression of relief than an accusation.

"Yes," the woman replied.

The three of them looked at each other uncomfortably, then back at Jamie.

"Do you *know* him?" It was the only lame and completely inadequate thing that she could say, and she realised she must be coming across as slightly unhinged. She was still trying to catch her breath.

"What's happened?" The woman was clearly worried. "Are you Jamie Barker? The architect Jamie Barker? Here for the meeting with Carl Silverton?"

With the timing of a well-rehearsed farce, the large front door swung open. The three new arrivals turned in unison. The younger man, his hand still outstretched in preparation to initiate introductions, dropped his arm mawkishly and abandoned his salutation.

Carl was standing masterfully on the threshold of his castle, presenting an ingratiating smirk. His shirt was buttoned up to the collar and neatly tucked into his jeans. He was wearing a tie. The belt that he had just wielded so provocatively was now being carefully threaded through the loops on the waist of his jeans. He fastened the buckle, pulling the belt tight, then stood upright, hands casually on each hip. "Ah, good – looks like you've all met. Come on in," he said, with perfect manners. "How about we do the formal introductions over a coffee?" He cast an incidental glance at Jamie. "Jamie Rose was just getting some paperwork from her car, weren't you, love?"

Demeaned and squashed, Jamie felt unable to even

correct Silverton's shitty introduction.

The three guests exchanged strained glances, each apparently unsure if they should be the first to leave Jamie's side. It was the younger man who broke away first. "Carl! Good to see you," he called, walking up the path towards the front door. "Coffee sounds like a brilliant idea."

There was another difficult pause.

"You go ahead." The older man made his comment to the woman, adding quietly, "I'll stay here and find out what's going on from Jamie Rose."

"No." Jamie appealed to the woman. "I'd rather *you* stayed."

The woman signalled an approving a nod, giving permission for her companion to go. He followed his colleague to the front door, where Carl welcomed them with a hearty handshake.

"The front door's not locked," he called down. "Just let yourselves in, girls." He directed one final, meaningless look at Jamie before closing the door behind him.

Silverton's behaviour was repulsive. Jamie didn't think twice before taking her leave. Already several steps nearer her car, she looked back at the woman. "I need to make a call." She didn't care how her abruptness was perceived; she had to speak to Linda.

Safely in her car, Jamie was far enough away from the house to think straight. It seemed probable that the three bewildered visitors were the project team. So, they *had* been invited after all? Had Jamie just made a complete twat of herself? Had she read too much into it all? And if she *did* phone Linda, what the hell would she say to her? That she was spooked when Silverton directed her to look at something upstairs? That Silverton was in possession of a belt that he later used to hold his jeans up? That he had locked the front door from the inside but told her where the back door was so she could easily get to her car? Put like that, it sounded insane. But underneath all this logic, there was something sinister about Silverton's mercurial behaviour.

Jamie phoned Linda, but the call wasn't connecting. She hung up and redialled, avoiding the answerphone. "Come on…come on…pick up, Linda..." She started to get jumpy, uncertain of her next move should Linda not be available.

The woman was still standing by the gate, staring at Jamie.

The phone connected. Linda took the call.

Jamie tried to recount her experience as quickly and succinctly as she was able. Succinct it wasn't. She fired off a barrage of emotionally charged ramblings, loaded with conjecture. Having tied herself into knots, Jamie was determined not to cry.

"Woah, Jamie, slow down," Linda took control. "Just stop there and listen to me."

Jamie did what she was told. Hearing Linda's no-nonsense tone, she knew it was sensible to listen.

"Jamie, I'm not clearly following what you've just said. Are you safe? You aren't hurt?"

"Yes, I'm safe and no, I'm not hurt."

"Right. Just stop and take a few seconds to calm down. I'm taking this seriously, okay?"

"Yes, okay."

"From what you've told me, you aren't alone now, right?"

"Yes, but…"

"Hang on," Linda interrupted. "Think about what's happened. Carl Silverton is a male chauvinist halfwit and a control freak. You've not only bruised *his* ego but made a fool of his lawyer pal, *again*. We know they are thick as thieves. From what I know about the underhand activities of John Hunter, Carl has learned a thing or two from his mentor. He is flexing his bully-boy muscles. He was trying to squash you firmly in your place."

"You think?"

"Okay, Jay, you just wait right there. Call the fucker and make some excuse for not going back in straight away – use your imagination. I'm not letting you spend any longer with that man without support. I can be with you in around twenty minutes, okay? Can you do that?"

"Am I overreacting? I feel like a jackass. Nothing like this has ever happened to me before."

"Not at all, Jamie," Linda said. "Don't you dare doubt yourself! Any woman would have reacted exactly the same way."

"Yeah, but honestly, *Linda*, I'm an architect for God's sake – *of course* he's going to ask me to look around the property."

"Look, Jamie." Linda was starting to lose her patience. "Semantics!" she said. "We could keep going around in circles with this. The fact is, you went with your gut. You've been subjected to a horrible ordeal with a bona fide wanker. Anyway, I wasn't going to say anything, but I've been doing a bit of digging of my own…"

Jamie was startled by the sound of tapping on her driver's window. It was the woman from earlier. "Is everything all right?"

Jamie didn't wind down the window but nodded and pointed a finger at the phone to her ear. She indicated her wishes by waving a brush off with the back of her hand, mouthing for her to go on in without her.

The woman nodded back at Jamie's request. She walked off, briefly glancing back, before going in to join the others in the house.

Linda listened to Jamie's silence, but cut her off. "Jamie…? Am I coming over or not?"

"What do you mean you've been digging?"

"Never mind that for now. Forget my last question, I'm just getting to my car. I'm coming over whether you like it or not. I'll be half an hour, max."

"Okay."

"Go back into the house, if you have to, but stay with the others, and keep your phone in your hand, okay?"

"Okay, thanks Lin."

"If you want a cover story, tell him you've got a lawyer coming over. Tell him I'm looking over the small print in the contract. He doesn't need to know I'm your sister. Anyhow, I want to assess this man for myself." Linda was sounding increasingly breathless. "Oh my God, I need to get fitter. I can't run in these bloody shoes…"

Jamie listened.

"Okay, I'm there."

Jamie heard the car door open and shut.

"I'm furious that my feisty, competent little sister has been side-swiped by such an abhorrent low-life."

Her engine started.

"Right, I'm on to it now, Jay. What's the postcode? I'll be there as soon as I can."

In the forty or so minutes that followed, Silverton was the epitome of the perfect host – affable, congenial and humorous. Faultless. Introductions were made, coffee was poured and proceedings for the day ahead were laid out. Silverton had kept his word: Paulo, Claudine and Luke were, respectively, the chief building consultant, surveyor and the structural engineer.

Remote and isolated, Jamie found it difficult pretending that everything was normal. The hypocrite that Jamie was with now was a person she had never met before. She had witnessed a very different Carl Silverton.

Jamie realised she had made a tactical error when she
told Claudine to go back into the house alone. She had missed an opportunity to enlist an ally.

There was an overwhelming discomfort amongst the group. Jamie was painfully aware of the tension - the elephant in the room.

A token knock on the front door was followed by a call. “Hello…? It’s Linda Harper. I’m here for Jamie Barker. The door was open... hello...?”

Silverton’s eyes homed in on Jamie.

“My lawyer!” Jamie announced without further explanation, and left the drawing room to collect her sister from the hallway.

There was no time for a private update, and Jamie was conscious that they could easily be overheard. Linda guessed as much, and went into professional mode, speaking loudly. “I do apologise for being so late – an unavoidable phone call directed me off track. I presume I’ve not missed anything of importance?”

Jamie pointed the way.

Linda glided with aplomb into the room ahead of Jamie. Her solid, stocky and well-proportioned figure was a statement in itself, but when she had on her kick-ass heels, her six-foot stature made her a force to be reckoned with.

Making a calculated guess, Linda marched up to Carl, ignoring everyone else. She thrust her hand forward, demanding his handshake. "Ah! Mr Silverton. I've heard all about you." She had already grasped his hand before he'd even had time to fully extend his arm. Locking eyes and smiling sweetly, she gripped, giving no obvious indication that the vice-like pain she was inflicting was utterly calculated.

Silverton's eyes widened briefly, and he winced ever so slightly. Jamie wanted to laugh. She guessed exactly what Linda had done, knowing that she was extraordinarily strong and had caught him unawares.

Linda then walked calmly round the group one by one, shaking hands and introducing herself, giving away nothing more than her name. Silverton stood watching.

The morning progressed smoothly and productively. Timescales were ironed out, details were agreed and materials were selected.

Linda's impromptu visit proved to be very helpful. Building and architecture weren't within her legal remit, but she seemed to blag it convincingly and was able to suggest and influence a few crucial tweaks. Most significantly, she insisted on making alterations to a couple of details in the contract – all to Jamie's advantage. It meant that Silverton was forced to wait longer for completion, which gave Jamie a satisfied sense of vindication. She secretly winked at Linda.

By 1:55pm, there was a timely pause in proceedings. Silverton made straight for his freezer. Then his halo slipped. "Lunch?" He took out a bottle of vodka, poured himself a large measure and offered a glass to the others. Everyone politely but stiffly declined.

Silverton shrugged incredulously at their refusal then belligerently splashed an extra slug into his glass. "Fuck it – all the more for me, then." He swung himself carelessly into his chair and brazenly rolled himself a marijuana joint.

At that, the mood became edgy, and the group collectively seized on the excuse of lunch to make their escape. Paolo suggested eating at a local pub and they agreed a time to reconvene for business in the afternoon.

As it happened, Jamie's role, for the purpose of this meeting, had come to a logical conclusion. The other three would return later to complete their work, but Jamie had no reason to stay. She started to pack up her briefcase, still feeling angry and compromised.

The sisters and Silverton were now alone. Jamie was standing in the doorway of the kitchen when Linda spoke. "So, Mr Silverton –"

"Please, Linda, call me Carl," he fawned.

"Please, Mr Silverton," Linda cooed back. "Call me Mrs Harper." She was stony-faced. Now it was Linda who was playing hard to read.

Silverton examined Linda, as if trying to fathom her meaning, while Jamie watched with interest.

"So, we have the contract sorted," Linda continued, strolling down the hallway. "And Ms Barker's work here will proceed once all the paperwork is amended, as agreed, and then finally signed off."

Jamie held back just outside the kitchen doorway.

"Absolutely!" Carl confirmed, following Linda through the hallway. "Jamie has come highly recommended. I want her to start as soon as possible." He lit up the joint again. "Lovely girl, isn't she? How long have you known her?"

Jamie followed. All three of them now stood by the front door. Jamie immediately noticed that the key had been left in the inside lock. Linda unlocked the door, one hand on the handle, ready to open. "So, this is how things are going to happen..."

Silverton listened, with an air of disparaging amusement.

"This job is going to run its course nice and smoothly." Linda opened the front door and walked out. Silverton followed.

Once she was a few feet away from the front steps, Linda turned to face Silverton. "When you return from your trip to Europe," she continued, "you will come back to an immaculate house, which you will be completely delighted with. After that point, you will never contact Jamie Barker again. Do you understand?"

"*What*?" Silverton clearly did not understand at all.

The atmosphere changed. Even with Linda present, Jamie couldn't get out of the house quickly enough. She scurried out and stood just behind her sister.

"From what I've heard about your vile behaviour, Mr Silverton, I shall advise my sister to have any future dealings with you through a third party."

"Your *sister*?" Silverton looked over Linda's shoulder at Jamie; his face was priceless. "What the fuck are you wittering on about?" He took a deep drag on his joint, flicking it onto the ground just in front of Linda's feet, exhaling the smoke slowly through his nostrils. "What a crying shame," he said, pushing his hands into his front pockets. "A threesome could be *so* much fun."

Linda shook her head. "Pitiful."

Silverton started to laugh.

"Oh yes, and one more thing, Mr Silverton."

"Please go on. I can't wait."

Indifferently calm, Linda took out and looked at her phone. "You'll need to find yourself a new lawyer."

Silverton's eyes narrowed but he said nothing.

"You've not heard?" Linda knew full well he hadn't. "In the early hours of this morning, John Tarquin Hunter was arrested and taken into custody."

Silverton's cock-sureness evaporated.

"I suppose it was only a waiting game before he slipped up. He's upset the wrong people this time and been a very, very silly boy." Linda let the man stew.

Silverton's chin dropped very slightly, his lips parting a fraction.

"Let's just say John Hunter is unlikely to practice law again. I have a feeling he will be enjoying a long stretch of time at Her Majesty's Pleasure."

"*What*?" Silverton's smooth exterior cracked.

"I'll arrange for Jamie's representative to be in touch," Linda told him. "It might be worth you looking ahead and consider broadening your own horizons, Mr
Silverton?"

Silverton was expressionless.

"Further education, perhaps?" Linda suggested. "How about enrolling yourself for that degree in Misogyny for Neanderthals?"

Staring wide-eyed at her sister, Jamie was surprised by her lack of subtlety.

Linda dropped her phone neatly back into her handbag. "You'd get first-class honours." She looked away, then back again, to deliver a mock parenthesis. "You know, a short while ago, I presided over a very interesting case – a complete bastard who was accused of false imprisonment with the intent of a sexual offence." Linda didn't reveal any further details. "Think on it, Mr Silverton." Tucking a wisp of hair neatly behind her ear, she turned to nod at Jamie. "I think our work is all done here. Ready to leave, honey?"

Silverton's hands curled into fists. He pulled out his phone from his pocket, nearly dropping it. Head down, he frantically pawed the screen then swivelled round, his back to the sisters, standing in his open doorway.

Jamie was a little in awe of her sister's unapologetic chutzpah. She smirked at Linda, turned to Silverton, and then coolly pumped two crisp bullets into the back of his head. She blew across the top of her extended index and middle fingers. In her head, she was finishing the job, blowing smoke from the barrel of a discharged pistol.

Revenge was sweet.

Job done, the girls left the premises – Linda strolling, Jamie strutting.

CHAPTER 13

Linda didn't go back into the office that afternoon. Instead, she went home. She had a job to do. She was waiting on some news for her next trial.

That afternoon, she received the confirmation she had been waiting for from a global pharmaceutical company. This time, John Hunter had become too greedy. He'd exercised very poor judgement with the wrong people, and sticking his mucky fingers into too many pies had finally seen the downfall of Hunter's little empire. Serious fraud, consorting with major criminals and drug-trafficking offences were his prime misdemeanours. Linda was to lead the prosecution and would relish every minute.

She sat down at her desk to ping off a few emails before regrouping to measure up her approach. She always followed the same routine for initial preparation, which took precisely one hour. One hour to brainstorm and sketch out the bare bones of a trial theme, which would serve as the foundation of her case. Its premise needed to be short and precise. Everything she crafted during the course of litigation would build on this theme: it would assist her in deciding what motions to file, which evidence to submit, which witnesses to interview, whom to depose and what questions to ask. This sixty minutes of preparation was her little nugget of gold. Her ticket to win.

Linda's strategy, quite simply, was: be first, be proactive, take control. She was masterful at being a step ahead of the opposing counsel. She made it her business to set the course of litigation, be the first to interview witnesses, to serve written disclosure, obtain records and facts to support her case, subpoena records from third parties and take depositions. With sworn statements taken from witnesses, she could then manoeuvre to lock them into their testimony. By driving her case ahead, she would show her opposition that she and her client were in control. Slam dunk!

Linda had a magnetic postcard stuck to her fridge that read: *Don't Sweat the Small Stuff.* She had crossed two lines in permanent marker over the word 'don't'.

In her line of work, the devil was absolutely in the detail.

One hour later, trial theme complete, Linda sat back, self-satisfied, with both hands clasped behind her head. "Damn, I'm good!" She pushed herself away from her desk, gliding on the wheels on her swivel chair. Time to relax and start getting ready for her night ahead with Jamie at Le Gavroche. She had worked up an appetite.

*****

Linda was standing in her bathroom, toothbrush at the ready, when the phone rang.

"You know what, Lin." It was Jamie. "I'm shattered and my head's all over the place after today…"

"What's that? I can't hear a bloody thing… hang on." Linda leant over her half-filled bath to turn off the taps. "Right, that's better. What did you just say?"

"I'm really not in the mood, after today, to go out for dinner tonight… are you in the bathroom?"

"Yes. Wearing a bathrobe and getting ready for my night out with my sister, who's just rung up to blow me out," Linda said. "I've skipped lunch, saved a damsel in distress, been working all afternoon… this superhero needs her meal tonight."

"Can you ask someone else?"

"No, I bloody well can't! I want some time with you, Jamie. I've only just managed to drag you out of your hermit shell, for God's sake. I want to have time with *you*. When was the last time that happened – when we've actually spent two nights out, just you and me, within the space of a few days?"

Jamie didn't reply.

"I'll tell you when – years!"

"I saw you last month. I spoke to you, too."

"Jamie – we happened to drive past each other and waved across the A10 rush-hour traffic. And you've called me twice."

"I'm just not in the mood tonight. And I'm not hungry."

"You're not in the mood for food? Is the Pope Catholic?" Linda said. "No one can ever not be in the mood for food – not in our family, anyway." She opened and sniffed into a Molton Brown bottle, then dribbled the contents into the bath water. "Jamie," she said gravely. "I know what all this is *really* about, you know."

"You do…?

"Of course I do. Why the stressy voice, you numpty?"

"Stressed voice? Was there?"

"Yes, there was. Look, stop getting so wound up, Jamie. Don't let today be associated with failure and fear. Carl Silverton really doesn't have that kind of power."

"Oh, *that* –"

"Don't belittle it, Jay. Fight back. Rewire your brain. Make a different connection and turn today into a positive memory." Linda listened to the hush again. "I can hear you taking in your big sister's words of wisdom," she said with a smile. "You know I'm right, don't you? And what better way to stimulate the positive, 'feel-good' receptors than with food?"

Jamie chuckled. "I always love your logic. You and your weird food psychology."

"That's me!" Linda said brightly. "I'm more like Dad than you in that respect. The foodie of the family."

"True."

"And, if we're going to feel good, we may as well achieve it at Dad's favourite restaurant with some of the best food in town."

"I can't argue with that," Jamie answered, sounding brighter.

"You know you just can't resist a soufflé suissesse."

"Your argument is very influential, sis."

"And let's not forget," Linda added, implying that Jamie needed persuading, "achieving and maintaining the feel-good factor is part and parcel of going for a cracking night out with your favourite sister. Am I right or am I right?"

"All right, all right," Jamie eventually caved in, swayed by Linda's enthusiasm. "I'll see you there."

"Fabulous!" Linda, said, turning the faucets back on. "I rest my case, m'lud."

*****

Sitting at Le Gavroche later that evening, Linda studied her little sister more intently than usual. It was obvious that Jamie wasn't herself tonight. In fact, she hadn't really been on top form for a long time; this recent period had been the longest spell of doldrums that Linda could remember. Her patience with her sister's indulgent spells of solitude was certainly being tested.

When Jamie's absences first started becoming more frequent, Linda put it down to the pressures and constraints of her work schedule. She totally got that – Linda herself was a self-confessed workaholic. The difference, though, was that *she* never let it get in the way of the important things in her life. Nowadays, Linda was simply hurt and confused by the way Jamie would fail to get in touch for weeks on end. But the most difficult part of this selfishness was the impact it had on their mother. She was the one who really felt the loss. Even so, Linda totally adored and indulged her little sister, always relishing and valuing the times they did spend together. She could forgive her sister anything.

"How's work going?" Linda asked.

"Busy – as usual," Jamie said.

Linda wiped the corner of her mouth with her napkin. "The sign of a class eatery," she remarked, "is their use of cloth napkins."

"You sound just like Mum," Jamie said, slathering butter on to her bread roll.

"Talking of Mum," Linda slipped in, relying on Jamie making that very association, "have you spoken to her recently?"

"No, but I'm planning on speaking this weekend."

"Good. She will appreciate that." Linda leant back as the sommelier approached the table, poised with the bottle in hand for the next taster-glass.

The sisters listened to the description of and explanation for the choice of matching wine. Two waiters glided to their table, placing the fourth of their nine courses from the 'Tasting Menu Exceptionnel'. Cloches were removed, again with synchronised precision, to reveal the meal.

"Oh my, would you look at that?" Jamie said, leaning over her plate and smelling the food.

Linda smiled. "We should bring Mum back here sometime. She loved coming here with Dad."

Jamie was too busy indulging herself to answer.

After all the tasting courses were complete, Jamie patted her tummy. "That was absolutely delicious," she concluded. "I think the venison was my favourite."

"And at least you aren't moping about in your flat all night," Linda said.

"I'm sorry I've been so hard to get hold of recently. Thanks for persuading me to come out. I always enjoy time with you. You do know that, don't you, Linny?"

"Hmm…" Linda peered through her half-empty wine glass at Jamie. "You aren't quite yourself," she said. "This doesn't feel the same as our usual evenings out."

Linda knew her sister very well. She had selected this venue for Jamie's benefit, knowing how her sister loved the dressing up to get ready, the theatre of the dining experience, the superb food and wine, and the brilliant double act that was the front-of-house twins, Ursula and Silvia. All this would have undoubtedly lifted her mood any other night out. But tonight, even a courtesy visit to the table by Michel Roux Jnr himself couldn't shake Jamie's malaise.

"I'm just feeling a bit low at the moment. This Carl Silverton incident has shaken me – more than I realised, I think. Sorry… I was determined I wasn't going to let it dominate the evening. I don't really want to talk about it."

At the end of the meal, as the sisters were munching petits fours with their coffee, it was Jamie who revisited the earlier events with Carl Silverton. "I was wondering – that sexual intent and imprisonment court case that you threatened Silverton with this afternoon?"

"I thought you didn't want to talk about it?"

"I didn't… but was that case true?"

Linda poured cream into her coffee. "Nope!"

"And did you honestly believe I might be at risk from Silverton when I rang you?"

Linda put her cup down, "I never assume anything." She folded her napkin and put it next to her on the table. "But I wasn't going to leave you there fending for yourself, on your own."

Linda watched Jamie as she gave the matter some thought.

"And your phone call earlier… You mentioned something else about Carl then? Something you weren't prepared to talk about over the phone?"

"Yes, I did."

“Can you tell me about it? Are you allowed to?”

Linda smiled. “Well, let me put it this way. I’m waiting on final and absolute confirmation tomorrow for a new case, which, honestly, is pretty much in the bag.”

“Right? And that’s connected to Silverton, how?” Jamie asked.

“I’m going to be as discreet as is legally prudent, and I’m only going to say it once. London is a small world in the great scheme of things. What goes around comes around… how do you think I knew about John Hunter?”

“What? John Hunter? Linda, how the hell are *you* involved with John Hunter?”

“Right now, that’s all I’m saying. But if there is a God, he sure works in mysterious ways.”

CHAPTER 14

When Sunday night eventually came around, Jamie was emotionally and physically burnt out. She was glad she'd made the effort on Friday night, but she had worked from home all weekend – partly through necessity, partly because she couldn't face the world outside. After the mayhem of the previous week, she planned to give herself some much-needed 'me time'. She took Monday off and bought a cinema ticket, buying herself a couple of hours' hiding in the make-believe of someone else's life.

As she left the cinema, the evening air seemed chilly – considerably cooler than recent evenings. Relaxed, but not quite ready to go home, Jamie decided to take herself for a quiet drink. The nearest, most obvious choice, if it wasn't heaving, was Alchemy. Jamie was less likely to bump into people she knew there.

*****

Alchemy was full enough to have a vibrancy, but there was no one she recognised. Jamie made her way to the bar – the same seat where she had witnessed Kate's showdown with her boyfriend all those weeks ago. She looked around at her surroundings as she had done on that first, accidental visit. It was strange being here alone.

She ordered a beer. “Is Kate in tonight?”

“No,” The barman looked at something under the counter – presumably a rota of some description. “Thursday and Saturday night this week.”

Good. At least Jamie wouldn’t have to avoid Kate, too. Watching the comings and goings of the people around her, she felt oddly detached. Even the few people that were there seemed loud and conspicuously sociable. She wondered if she stood out for being on her own. She let her mind wander.

“Another drink?”

Jamie had been sitting longer than she realised and the bar staff had noticed her nearly empty bottle. “No thanks. I’m off any minute.” She checked her phone, considering the options of transport for getting home.

Then Kate walked in.

Jamie found herself glancing fugitively all around her, although she wasn’t really sure why. But Kate was arm in arm with her companion, captivated and far too involved with their conversation to bother looking anywhere else. She guided him to a cosy table for two, just in front of the furthest archway – a safe distance away. Her back was to Jamie, but her friend, on the other hand, was in full view.

How bonkers would this be, if this was the infamous Chris? Jamie hadn’t seen his face before; he’d been hidden behind his upturned trench coat collar and the brim of his trilby. This man was very good-looking. Jamie noticed his eyes – not at all what she'd envisaged. They were kind. Jamie even pondered the idea that, had she been straight, he was just the type she would go for. Kate had very good taste.

Irrespective of what had gone on behind the bar that night, it was clear that the outcome of Kate's predicament had been a positive one. Kate looked happy, and, from Jamie's vantage point, she seemed pretty much loved-up.

Judging by her preoccupation, Kate had no clue she was being spied on, and wouldn't have cared a jot that Jamie was even there.

Kate's companion got up. Jamie realised it might even be her husband, although she hadn't ever noticed a ring on her finger. But what did that mean these days? He started towards the bar, eventually coming to stand right next to Jamie.

Of all the places to position himself. Jamie suddenly felt exposed. Finding an auspicious moment to slip quietly away now seemed like an unlikely plan. Jamie swivelled on her stool to turn away and face the bar, making herself as incognito as the situation allowed.

The man who had served Jamie and Rachel a few weeks earlier, was behind the bar. "Hello again." He nodded in recognition of Jamie and looked to the new customer.

"Two vodka tonics, thanks," Kate's friend said.

"If you're interested in trying something a little different, I can highly recommend our new range." The barman pointed to several coloured bottles on the back of the counter.

"That one looks interesting." He pointed to a bright orange bottle, with the word 'Chase' running vertically up the side in flouncy white writing.

"That's really good," the bartender said. "Chase Distillery's award-winner. Four times distilled, marinated in a copper pot still, with Seville orange marmalade."

"Go on then," the man agreed. "So long as your boss recommends it." He tipped his head towards Kate.

Following the direction of the nod, the barman laughed. "Oh, you're with Kate? She would indeed recommend it, sir – it was Kate who introduced the brand."

They struck up a courteous conversation, the friend sounding the real gentleman; there was a shade of plum in his very beautiful English accent. Jamie hadn't remembered it sounding quite so pronounced when he first spoke – but that was weeks ago, and his voice had been masked by emotion.

For Jamie, though, Mr Plum wasn't moving away from the bar quite fast enough.

Too late. Seeing Jamie, Kate came over, casually greeting her before turning to her staff. "Good to see you are peddling our best brands to the customers,

Kieran." She winked. "That's a really nice vodka. Good choice." She then looked back to Jamie. "That's one of your favourites too, isn't it, Jamie?"

Jamie didn't understand.

"Marmalade martini?" Kate prompted.

"Oh, right, yes." Jamie hadn't intended to be sociable, and here she was, fast becoming the spare-part to a romantic evening.

Kate looked at each of them – from Jamie, to the man, then back to Jamie again. "So, you two don't *actually* know each other, do you? Because that would just be too weird a coincidence."

They both answered together, with an emphatic "No."

"Ouch, that came out a bit unfriendly," said Jamie apologetically.

Kate's friend laughed politely in agreement.

"So," Jamie half-raised her beer as a parting salute. "Places to go, people to see... I'm out of here." She gulped down the remainder of her beer, misjudging the amount left in the bottle and her capacity to guzzle without choking.

"Steady," Kate chuckled, thumping Jamie's back as she coughed.

After her little theatrical entertainment, Jamie definitely wasn't staying any longer now. She got down from her stool. "Right then, I'm off." She looked at Kate. "Great to see that everything has worked out for you, Kate."

"Don't leave on my account," Kate's friend said. "I'm not stopping long. As it so happens –" He picked out his ringing phone from his back pocket. "Ta-da! That's my cue to move on." He took a quick drink from his glass. "Nice vodka, Kate. Finish mine off for me, will you? Got to get cracking." He leaned across to kiss Kate before leaving. "See you for dinner on Tuesday."

Knowing that he was about to leave anyway, Jamie didn't feel quite so bad.

Kate stood with a drink in each hand. "I can't drink them both alone." She looked a little coy, uncertain even. "Do you really need to go right now, or can you join me and finish your beer properly?"

Jamie looked at her watch, an automatic action that had nothing to do with knowing the time.

"I think we owe ourselves a chance to be polite and civil to each other, don't you think?"

Jamie had already stayed longer than planned. A few more minutes in Kate's company didn't seem too arduous. "Seems fair enough," she agreed.

"How did your evening go?" Kate asked eventually.

Jamie was cautious. "Which one? The fiasco you witnessed with Rachel is a story in itself. Certainly not one to go into now."

Kate half-closed her eyes. "I gathered that – I was the brunt of your frustration – as I remember."

"I can only say sorry, yet again," Jamie said, agitating the beer in the bottom of her bottle in small circles. She still didn't feel great about herself for that one.

"No need," Kate reassured her, sipping thoughtfully at her drink. "I was referring to what looked like a more successful meeting with the other woman who came to meet you later on." She looked at Jamie, sucking at her
straw. "A friend?"

"Linda?" Jamie was nostalgically evocative. "She's *more* than a friend. I love her to bits. The unique package of best friend, soulmate and the –"

Jamie didn't get the chance to share the many virtues of her wonderful sister. A sudden heavy crash sent Kate pitching unceremoniously off her seat, as a young man, tanked up with too much alcohol, stumbled past the table. He tripped up, just managing to stop himself from face-planting on the floor by lurching first onto Kate, and then ricocheting onto the table. He was far too drunk to realise the force of his fall. Most of his drink ended up shared between the table and her blouse.

The lad had no idea what he had done, but was already being firmly escorted to the exit by other customers. People nearby came over to check that Kate wasn't hurt. She hastily used her serviette to dab at her blouse. The guy behind the bar came around with a cloth to wipe up the remaining slop.

"I'll just go grab a t-shirt from the back room. This top is wet through. I think I'm probably *wearing* most of his pint." Kate pulled her saturated shirt away from her chest. As she got up, she asked one of her staff to go out and check that the man had moved on from outside the front of the bar. She didn't want him coming back.

Kate then went behind the counter and through a narrow door. She returned wearing an Alchemy Bar staff t-shirt and took her seat again. "Fool," she said gazing towards the exit. "That's one good thing about owning the place, I suppose – free change of clothes."

Jamie decided it would appear antisocial to leave for home so soon. She would make the effort and get to find out more about Kate, who seemed a nice enough person. It was a good opportunity to broaden her social circle. "So, was that Chris just now?" she ventured to ask.

Kate was hesitant. "Christian? I thought you said you didn't know him?"

Jamie answered, repressing a laugh, "Christian?" She was reminded of the daft conversation she had had with her sister about Carl and the Fifty Shades of Grey character, Christian Grey.

Kate appeared mystified by what Jamie found so entertaining.

Jamie took a hold of herself. "No, I don't know him – I just took for granted it was him," she explained.

Kate was obviously still puzzled, although Jamie recognised this wasn't an appropriate time to explain the joke. She tried, instead, to keep the conversation moving forward. "You looked very happy just now."

"Why wouldn't I be?" Kate answered.

Jamie didn't push it. It appeared that trying to talk to Kate about Chris was still a difficult subject for her.

After a nod of thanks to Kieran, who had brought over some fresh drinks, Kate went back to her earlier question. "Did you enjoy *your* evening the other night? It looked like you were celebrating. Champagne? Very
nice too."

"With Linda? Yes." Jamie said. "At least it was a relief from the awful event with Rachel. I'm sorry you ended up in the firing line with all that." Jamie started explaining the whole scenario involving Alex and the Rachel blind date incident, from start to finish.

"Wow!" Kate looked stunned. "If Alex is a friend, I'd hate to meet your enemies."

At least Jamie had now made her sexuality clear to Kate, which was a relief. She could relax on that score at least. She started fiddling with a beer mat, uncertain about how much more to tell this woman, who now seemed the easiest of people to talk to. She had already divulged a good amount of back-story about Alex and Rachel, but it would be good to turn this casual chat into something more meaningful. Jamie could envisage a friendship in the making.

Kate happily chatted on. “So, you and Linda appeared to have the evening all planned out?”

“Yeah – it was a good, fun night.” Jamie had almost finished her beer. “And it sounds like you've got dinner to look forward to with Chris on Tuesday?”

“Hmm… Dinner with Chris? I wouldn't say I’m looking forward to it, exactly.”

“Oh?” Jamie was surprised. She raised an eyebrow at Kate as she pushed her wedge of lime into the neck of her beer bottle.

“He’s a lovely man, but…” Kate thought about her explanation. “But he’s struggling at the moment – going through some tough times right now.” She sat back in her chair. “Look, you don’t seriously want to hear all about my boring life, do you?”

Hell, yeah! Jamie thought, but instead replied, “Of course. I feel like we’re talking like normal human beings, at last. Getting to know each other properly. It’s… nice.”

A broad smile gradually stretched across Kate’s face, flashing a perfect set of white teeth. Jamie observed the wonderful, expressive lines around her eyes and mouth. She still found them just as attractive as she had when she’d first noticed them several weeks ago. She was starting to get her head around the idea of developing a friendship with someone whom she found undeniably attractive. Typical – straight *and* gorgeous.

"Thank you. That's quite a turn up, considering the track record we've had so far." Kate, again, radiated warmth. "First, though, tell me more about Linda," she said. "How did you two meet?"

"Meet? How do you mean?" Jamie wondered how the conversation had suddenly returned back to her. "Linda met me here for a drink, I needed to tell her about Alex's interference and the blind date with Rachel. I was furious."

Kate's frown still lined her brow.

Jamie tried to help her obvious confusion. "I invited Linda to meet me here. She had never been here before." Jamie got out her wallet. "I'm getting myself a coffee, do you want another drink?"

"Put your money away, you don't need to pay – just ask at the bar."

As she waited to be served, doubts started formulating in Jamie's already addled mind. They weren't allayed by Kate's next words when she went back to the table.

"Actually, what I meant, just now," Kate continued, "was where did you *first* meet Linda?"

Jamie looked at Kate, who elaborated, delicately serious. "As in, date? Relationship? Girlfriend?" She ran out of alternative nouns. "She's your partner, right?"

Jamie screwed up her nose at Kate. "My girlfriend? Heck, no," she laughed. "Whatever gave you that idea? Linda's my sister! I already told you that when you asked me about her earlier."

"No, you didn't," Kate retorted. "You got as far as telling me you loved her, and she was your best friend and soul mate." Kate started laughing too. "Jamie! What else was I *supposed* to think? I would never have guessed you were sisters to look at you – not meaning to be rude or anything – but not only that, you two were completely into each other, acting like a couple. Anyone watching would have come to exactly the same conclusion." Kate was animated, talking with her hands. "And Linda – she was even rattling on about being in your bed before midnight." She took a breath from laughing. "In bed by midnight, with a hot chocolate, of all things! So sweet. I thought it was adorable."

Sweet? Adorable? To Jamie, this was exactly the type of patronising, twee comment that a straight woman *would* make. She wasn't completely sure if Kate was laughing *at* her, and it made her feel foolish. The situation wasn't helped by the suspicions that were crystallising in her head. "If you are taking the piss, you can sod off – I don't appreciate it!"

"Honestly, I'm not laughing, Jamie. I think it's…"

But Jamie's sensitivity rendered her deaf to explanations. Her defence was to throw back tit-for-tat retaliation. ""Before you start making jokes at my expense, *your* suspicious lifestyle doesn't exactly hold up to scrutiny, either."

"Pardon?" Kate seemed cagey. "What do you mean?"

"I totally respect your reasons for keeping your private life just that – after all, you don't *really* know me – but please, don't then start having a snide laugh about me and *my* life! Anyway, Kate," Jamie finally asked. "Who exactly is this Chris?"

It suddenly went quiet.

"Chris is…" Kate became sullen. "An old friend… but he's going through a very messy and acrimonious divorce. I'm sort of –" she took a swig of beer and searched for the words "– I'm helping him through it."

Immediately warned by how Kate was underplaying her story, alarm bells rang in Jamie's head. She was still trying to piece together all the various parts of information. Going through a divorce? Kate was having an affair with a married man! Jamie was no longer sure if she could be trusted. The whole thing had suddenly turned into a pathetic parody of the situation with Sarah.

Jamie snatched up her things. "I need to get home." She left Alchemy frustrated and angry. In all honesty, deep down, she was bruised and sore – she liked Kate just a little bit too much and needed a reason not to. Based on the evidence she had just heard, this was as good a reason as any.

Jamie had to get her head thinking straight, and at this moment, what she needed was sleep.

CHAPTER 15

Kate hadn't slept particularly well. There was way too much upset swimming around in her head. Jamie's wild histrionics hadn't helped matters, either. Who was *she* to cast aspersions?

But today was a new start. Today, she was meeting Richard to help him buy clothes for his friend's wedding. She would not allow her worries to mar her day ahead.

"That's your shoes and a shirt sorted," Kate said, as they walked arm in arm down Oxford Street. "What's next?"

"I'm all done with shopping today, sweetie." Richard organised his bags onto one shoulder. "I'll cobble together the rest of the outfit with something from my wardrobe."

"Okay, shall we plan another shopping spree some other time?"

"Well, I don't know about you, but I'm gasping for a cold drink. The Crown is just up ahead. Have you got time for a pit-stop?"

"I think so. What time is it?" Kate looked at her watch. Her mobile rang. She looked with trepidation at the screen. "It's Chris."

Richard walked slowly alongside in step, apprehensively glancing across at Kate every few sentences as she took the call.

Standing outside The Crown pub, Kate was still

ensconced in dialogue. "I'm going to go now, Chris," she said dispassionately. "This conversation isn't getting us anywhere. Perhaps we should talk again later?"

The call ended.

"That was all very matter-of-fact, sweetie." Richard said, impatient for information. He opened the door for Kate to enter the pub first. "I would even go as far as to say ice cold, if I might be so bold?"

"I love the shirt you bought earlier. How is it you always look so smart and immaculately groomed – even when it's not an occasion?" Kate scanned the food menu.

"Okay. I get it," Richard said. "You don't want to talk about it. That's fine… so what do you want to drink?"

"Coke with ice."

"I'm getting a cheese and pickle sarnie – want one?"

"No thanks, Rich." She put the unread menu down.

Richard dutifully went to buy the drinks.

"To answer your question," Richard said, as he came back with two Cokes, "none of this gorgeousness –" he waved a hand over the length of his body "– is accidental, believe me." He ran his fingers through his fringe and over his ear. "One should never skimp on one's appearance. One should always endeavour to look one's best, regardless of the occasion."

"You scrub up okay, I suppose," Kate grinned.

"And on that subject, my Granny Olga has a mantra."

"Oh, your lovely grandmother! How is she doing? I've not asked after her for ages."

"Well, she's home now, thankfully, but with a package of care for the short term, a nice occupational therapist and home care visiting twice daily to check up on her."

"That's good."

"Bless her. Anyway, Granny Olga has always said: never leave the house wearing underwear that you wouldn't put on to visit to your doctor."

"And I trust your bra and panties are fresh on this morning, Richie?" Kate chuckled half-heartedly. But it all came across as disingenuous; her thoughts were elsewhere.

"She has a point, though," Richard laughed. "You never know when the 'just strip down to your underwear' conversation is going to pop up at the doctor's."

"True." Kate wasn't really listening.

"Never put on in the morning what you wouldn't want to be seen dead in… that was her saying."

"Uh-huh."

"I'm at a bit of a loose end tonight…"

Kate followed the lines of tiny bubbles at they travelled up the side of her glass.

"What are your plans for later? Are you out anywhere?"

She poked at the bobbing cubes of ice with the end of her straw.

"A butt-naked man has just walked in with a massive boner."

Kate rubbed the condensation with her finger. She sucked the end of the straw.

"Kate! You aren't even listening, are you?"

"Sorry! What?"

"You are miles away. You've zoned out on me again."

"It's not just one thing, Rich, it's lots of things racing in my head at the moment," she said vaguely.

"It's that sodding call from Chris, isn't it?"

Kate slowly looked up at her friend. "Richard?"

"Yes sweetie." Richard looked back at her sympathetically.

"I need to talk to you." It was time to come clean.

"Again?" Richard was half-serious.

"The other day, when I told you about Chris and my brother?"

"Yes?"

Kate pushed her glass of Coke away to one side, sat forward and leant her elbows on the little table.

Richard's eyes widened.

"Sandwich, sir?"

Kate and Richard both leaned back in exaggerated unison, parting company like synchronised swimmers, to make way for the plate of food that was plonked down on the middle of the table.

"Can I get you anything else to go with that?"

"Sandwich? That's a stonker. There's about half a loaf there." Richard gawped down at the thick doorstop of a sandwich before him. "I'm risking a dislocated jaw with this bad boy."

"You've not had one of our famous door-stops before, then?" the server asked, smiling. "Enjoy!"

"Now, where were we?" Richard said, sizing up the slab of brown bread gripped in both hands. "How do they expect me to fit all this into my mouth?" He looked at Kate. Her chin was on her chest; tears splashed on to the table.

"Oh, my dear," Richard put his sandwich down. "Whatever has brought this on, sweetie?" He reached for Kate's hand.

"The other day?"

"Yes…?" Richard urged.

"I didn't tell you everything about Chris and my brother."

Richard reached for a paper napkin.

"There's a reason why my brother is like he is –"

"Okay?" Richard leaned in.

"I told you about how Tig got his name the other day; the link with your granny and the London Hospital? I showed you the photograph?"

"I remember."

Kate wasn't really sure where to start, so she just talked. "I had the very important job of choosing the decor for my new baby brother's bedroom. Dad was determined that the bonding with my new brother should start early. It was easy – I chose what I wanted – a Winnie-the-Pooh theme."

Richard smiled, and Kate smiled faintly back. "To complete the bonding, Dad bought the Tigger toy I told you about. The idea was that I should give it to my new brother when we first met."

"Lovely touch," Richard agreed.

"That first visit to see my newborn brother was all very confusing – excitement, mixed with the first twinge of sibling jealousy."

"It happens." Richard was trying to be helpful. "My sister is still green with envy that I was blessed with natural blond." His hand swept his fringe.

"After all the build-up of Tig's arrival, came a sense of anticlimax – well, I say I remember, but it's difficult to know how much is real memory and how much has been learned from all the times Uncle Peter and Auntie Joan have told me this story…" Kate saw Richard's eyes trying to understand what she was telling him. She needed to push on. "When I saw my brother for the very first time, I was completely underwhelmed by it all and really disappointed that he wasn't more interesting."

"Mewling pink blobs. Aren't all newborn babies like that?"

"I was all buoyed up for the grand presentation, but apparently, I threw the toy into the cot, very disgruntled, very bad-tempered. I yelled out: 'Here's Tig!' and it hit my brother in the face, setting off a cacophony of screaming – that I *do* remember," Kate said, smiling.

"What a great story."

"He was always known as Tig from then on. I'm told it was a story that my dad delighted in retelling over and over to anyone who asked about his name."

"How is that related to his behaviour, his ridiculous jealousy?"

Kate rubbed her eyes. "My very last memory of my family was twenty-five years ago, on a holiday to Cornwall."

Richard face relaxed into an expression that Kate couldn't interpret. She had veered wildly off-piste and knew Richard would be unable to follow. Kate looked down at the table again, worried that Richard's response, if it was negative, might be enough to stop her from talking. But she wanted to talk. She needed to talk. She inhaled, knowing that once she had started, she had to complete the story without interruption and without stopping.

"My brother was in the back seat of the car with me… listening to music on his earphones. Mum was navigating, as she always did… my baby sister, Molly, was fast asleep on Mum's knee."

"You have a sister?"

Kate's vision blurred but she was determined not to cry. She needed to connect with the moment. "Mum was in charge of the huge RAC map and she diligently directed my dad… mile for mile, junction to junction… she always did the same thing, every year, but the whole palaver was completely unnecessary… Dad was Cornish… he knew the journey like the back of his hand." Kate swallowed. "Dad was trying to decide with Mum where to stop off for our picnic lunch." Smiling wistfully at the memory, she realised that she'd never told anyone her story – actually spoken it out loud, in the way she had relived and seen it in her mind and in her dreams time after time after time. "Daft, really – we always ended up stopping at exactly the same place. I loved listening to Mum and Dad talking. They always laughed such a lot… and Dad had this look… It was only ever for Mum… even as a kid I recognised it to be a gentle expression associated with love and kindness. He often looked at her like that."

A thoughtful, youthful grin emphasised Richard's attentiveness. He was poised in his tell-tale pose: three fingers pressed to his lips.

Kate wiped a rogue tear from her cheek with her thumb. "Dad was trying to get my brother's attention – checking that he agreed with the choice of picnic destination. He couldn't hear a thing with his music hissing in his ears, so I dug him in the ribs with my elbow – harder than it needed to be but, my God, he screamed blue murder at me for it." Kate eventually met Richard's gaze. "Dad looked at both of us in the rear-view mirror, to tell me off. His eyes glanced between the pair of us. I remember his eyes, so vividly..."

"Oh my God!" Richard replaced the tip of his fingers to his mouth, in grim anticipation.

Kate kept going "I have a vague awareness of the lorry looming closer…"

"Oh my God," Richard repeated.

"Much later, I learned Dad had totally misjudged the braking distance…"

"Oh, Christ!"

"I never told you that, did I?"

Richard's hand was still over his mouth, as if he was preventing words from falling out.

"Neither Mum nor Dad had put on their seat belts, even though they religiously insisted that Tig and I always fastened ours." Kate sobbed a breath.

Richard plunged into his shirt pocket, handing over a blue silk handkerchief.

"Mum, Dad, my precious little Molly…" She could no longer control the tears. "All three were thrown straight through the windscreen. Killed instantly."

"Oh, sweet Jesus!" Now Richard began welling up.

Kate focused on one solitary place on a wall. She was fearful of looking away; she was fearful that if she stopped concentrating, the memories and the emotion she was experiencing would somehow be lost altogether. She used to have panic attacks sparked by the thought that she might one day be unable to see her family in her mind – that she might wake up one morning and not be able to remember their faces or their voices any more. "Tig had already unclipped his safety belt just minutes before to reach for the travel sweets in the front. The passenger seat in front prevented him from going through the windscreen, but the impact with the back of the seat was life-changing."

"And you?" Richard asked. "Were you hurt?"

"Apart from bruising and slight whiplash, no. But August 3rd is scratched on my mental diary forever. And it still feels like last week."

"And Tig? You used the words 'life-changing'?"

Kate let her Coke roll around in her mouth. "After the car smash, I went to live with my aunt Joan," she continued. "For three long months, I went with my auntie to the London Hospital. I had to be, I *needed* to be with my brother. Auntie Joan understood, but I'm not so sure about my uncle Peter… did I tell you he was my dad's brother?"

"Yes."

Kate thought a while. "It was also the same hospital where Tig was born. Can you believe that?"

"Just awful," Richard agreed.

"The whole experience was..." Kate tailed off. "I remember seeing Tig for the first time, lying pinned to an ugly Stryker frame. He had a metal bolt screwed into his skull… I didn't want to leave him there on his own. Every time I had to leave his bedside, I filled up with this wretched, black, bottomless sadness. That feeling stayed with me for years."

"Shock, I'd imagine. Did you have any therapy? Any counselling?"

"No."

"Nothing?" Richard asked, as if he couldn't bring himself to contemplate such a thing.

"A few afternoon visits to a nurse in the school first-aid room – a woman in a flowery, ankle-length dress who smelt of instant coffee and cigarettes. I remember she made me draw endless pictures. And she would ask me strange questions about what I'd drawn and the colour of the felt-tip pens I'd chosen, and she kept scribbling things down on a red clip-board." Kate sipped her Coke.

"That's appalling."

"It was much worse for Tig," Kate explained. She rubbed her forehead. "Recovery from surgery back then was a slow, laborious process. They were amazed that either of us survived, actually."

"Amazed? It's a bloody miracle!"

"Tig especially. He had loads of plates and pins to set his broken bones, followed by months of rehabilitation with relentless, intensive physiotherapy. It was touch and go if he'd ever walk again." She took a deep breath. "His body healed over time, although his mind never fully recovered from the trauma."

"Really?"

Kate nodded. "I watched the boy grow to become a very troubled, bitter man." Kate didn't feel the need to cry any more. Her emotion wasn't sadness – she was thinking about what her brother had become. "Drink and drugs gradually became his best friends. Then he started to try and control my life."

Richard leant forward, this time putting both hands over each of Kate's. He said nothing.

"As he got older, he began to get obsessively jealous of my relationships. He decided that as the man and the father-figure of the family, it was his role."

"But he was sick."

"Well, he didn't see it that way." Kate started picking at the skin around her thumb. "As far as he is concerned, me falling in love and starting a relationship is tantamount to him losing me." Kate started to well up again. "Tig has always been very quick to remind me that we are the only living family members left. That our family tree ends with the two of us, and somehow, he makes me feel like I owe part of myself to him. He hasn't said it in so many words, but I know he blames me for the accident."

"But it's so wrong," Richard said. He dragged his chair round to sit next to Kate, slipping his arm around her shoulders and pulling her in tightly.

"Maybe you understand now why I said I hate my brother?"

Richard released his grip to allow himself to look at his friend. "Kate, it's what your brother has become that you hate, rather than the person himself. He's not a well man."

Kate had distanced herself from her brother. She rarely saw him. When she did, it was through duty, and always swamped by guilt. She hated how it made her feel.

"I'm not going to let myself feel responsible for Tig any more. I need to choose between him and my future happiness with Chris."

"Totally behind you with that decision, sister, not that my opinion counts for a hill of beans."

"It does matter," Kate said. "You're listening. Thank you."

"It must have been so hard to visit him again in the same hospital, but in such different circumstances."

"It was horrific."

"And how are things with Chris now?"

"We're seeing each other tomorrow. I honestly don't know what the future holds for us. I guess we'll make some concrete decisions tomorrow."

Richard held Kate's hand. "Thank you for trusting me with that," he said and gently kissed her cheek.

CHAPTER 16

Linda was laughing. “I can’t believe she thought we were lovers. Mind you, it kind of makes sense when you think back to what the poor woman must have seen and heard between the pair of us.”

“I’m not really seeing the funny side of it at the moment,” Jamie said, unwrapping her burger. “I’m so sick of misreading people and then having to deal with the crap that comes with the consequences.”

“Oh, lighten up, Jay. Why throw the baby out with the bathwater?” Linda admonished. “Kate’s been as honest with you as she feels able to be. She’s still patching things up with Chris, by the sound of things. It can’t be easy for her at the moment.” She wiped off a blob of mayo from the corner of her mouth and licked her finger. “She could probably do with a friend, to be fair, and you’ve just basically pushed her away with your nose out of joint because she wasn’t telling you what you wanted to hear! Get over your straight-girl crush, for God’s sake.”

It was early evening in Hyde Park. Jamie put her burger down next to her on the rug and thoughtfully stuffed a few chips into her mouth. She chewed slowly.

“That’s the crux of the matter, though, isn’t it?” Linda said.

Jamie's brain was piecing the strands of information together. "I can't quite see it all clearly, just yet. I know
I probably overreacted, but it doesn't all quite make sense."

"I'm not going to hold your hand through this one, Jay. Kate seems a perfectly decent person, going through a tough time. She could be a really good friend if you gave her half a chance. Anyway, why the hell should she spill her guts to you? She hardly knows you."

"True. I did make that point on Monday night."

"Well, then!" Linda screwed up her burger wrapper.

"But she's having an affair with a married man…"

Linda slapped her hand on the rug next to her. "Jamie, when did you become so morally virtuous? It's none of your business what Kate does. Either go and patch up what could be the start of a decent friendship – God knows you could do with one of those – or forget about it and jog on." Linda slipped her sunglasses down onto her nose, then leaned back on the rug with a conversation-concluding grunt. "This is just wonderful. I miss not having a garden."

They settled for a short while.

"So, do you think that if I just…"

Linda sat fully upright with another loud grunt and unusual agility. "Just go!" She pointed across the park at nowhere specific. "Stop all this over-analysing and navel-gazing. Bloody well go and apologise to the poor woman."

"You think…?"

"Now!" Linda instructed, "But just cool down that hot head of yours – it'll get you into trouble."

Jamie got up and headed across the grass.

"Where are you going?" Linda called.

"Alchemy."

"Good!"

*****

When Jamie entered Alchemy, Kate saw her almost immediately, then disappeared through the little door at the back of the bar. Richard did a double-take and looked around him to discover an explanation for her actions. Seeing Jamie approach, he flicked his eyes skyward; he had his answer.

Jamie pitched up at the bar, with every intention of sitting this out. She ordered a coffee that she didn't want and sent a text to Linda: *#sighs Kate's avoiding me. I feel like I'm wading through treacle – 1 step forward and 10 steps back again.*

Linda's reply was quick: *She who wades through treacle learns how to clean boots spotlessly.*

Jamie sent back: ??? *LOL. Did they teach you that at law school?*

The answer: *Nope. ;)* Linda then followed up with: *Come back and enjoy the sunshine with me.*

The narrow door through which Kate had made her escape gradually opened, inch by inch. Two eyes peeped and blinked through the gap. The slapstick look of horror on Kate's face, when she realised that Jamie was sat right in front of her, was pure gold. The door
instantly banged shut again, its occupant incarcerated.

"Oops!" Richard witnessed the event. He sidled to the closed door, opened it a fraction, and peered in. "It's a store cupboard, sweetie – you can't stay there all night."

Jamie heard some mumbling from within, followed by movement. Kate reappeared with her arms full of crisps. "The crisps you asked for, Richard," she said, promptly marching out, dropping the packets onto the counter then walking haughtily to the far end of the bar. She didn't look at Jamie once.

"Did you even need those?" Jamie grinned at Richard's confusion.

"A few more bags of…" He looked at one of the packets and grimaced. "Gin-and-tonic-flavour crisps?"

Jamie laughed. "Yuck."

Richard gathered them up. "There's a very good reason why that particular promotional gimmick remains unsold." He opened the door and deposited the crisps back into the cupboard.

"Would you tell Kate I'd like to speak to her?" Jamie said.

Richard disappeared.

Kate returned, polishing a glass. This time, she was on the customers' side of the bar. "Are you all right?" she asked.

Jamie was not expecting the gentle touch. "I should be asking you that question. Yes, I'm fine. Actually, I came to apologise."

"Again?" Kate tossed the cloth over her shoulder.

"Look, life is too damn short," she decided. "Let's wipe the slate clean, eh? Come and sit down. That's if you've got time, of course…?"

Jamie picked up her coffee cup and followed Kate to a table. She sat down, then waded straight in. "All that stuff you said about Christian…?"

"Oh my stars, you don't hang about, do you? Something's obviously been playing on your mind."

"If I'm being honest, I feel disappointed and let down."

Kate sat up. "You do? Why?"

Jamie had climbed up on her soap-box without really thinking through her direction or conclusion.

"Can't you see the funny side to all this?" Kate asked. "The whole mad misunderstanding?" Then the giggling began again.

The mere suggestion of there being a side that could even be remotely amusing didn't sit comfortably with Jamie. She enjoyed a laugh and bit of tomfoolery as much as anyone, but this particular joke rankled. Unfortunately, Linda had hit the nail on the head – Kate mattered, but the feeling wasn't reciprocated.

The circumstances were made worse by what Jamie had discovered about Kate, and the home truths were hitting hard, reminding Jamie of her own emotional baggage.

"Oh, sod this crap," Jamie cried out, without thinking and without knowing what else to say. "You did this on Monday."

Kate laughed even more. "Why have you suddenly become so reactive again?"

Jamie's defensive hackles immediately rose. Kate was laughing at her yet again. Jamie launched her counter-attack before Kate could make her feel any more humiliated. "Why did you lie about Christian?" she raved. "Don't forget, Kate, I was here that night after he left. I heard your phone call. You were pleading with him not to leave you. And from what I can gather, you even chased him to the airport."

Kate's good-humoured animation vanished, instantly replaced by a deadpan, steely expression. "I don't honestly think it's just me that's misunderstanding the situation here, Jamie." She was calm and measured but turned her body away.

"You were pleading with him to come back, for God's sake. That's not the kind of conversation you have with a 'best friend'." Jamie used finger quotes to ram home her point. "Are you really expecting me to believe you're supporting him through a divorce? Sounds more like you're caught up in some messy extra-marital crap." For a brief second, Jamie listened to herself, shocked by her own outspokenness. But she knew she had to speak her mind.

Kate's eyes started darting round the room – questioning, searching, thinking – until, little by little, her poker face slowly diffused into an animated myriad of deep lines and expressive dimples. A snigger gradually erupted into boisterous, spluttering hilarity that just kept shuddering out in waves. Eventually, she gasped for air and flapped her hands every time she tried to speak.

"For fuck's sake." Jamie snapped. "That's right – you have your moment at my expense. I'm all done here."

Kate lunged across and grabbed Jamie's arm. She was suddenly no longer laughing. "Please, don't go. This is just all so crazy, Jamie." She stood up too. "Listen, the man who you met at the bar on Monday – Christian – he isn't the Chris that I rang when you were here that night."

"What?"

"No!" Kate quickly stopped herself from laughing again. "This is too mental."

Jamie's couldn't think straight. "What? But I don't understand…"

"And please don't storm out again! I'm really not laughing at you."

"But you phoned Chris after he left the bar that night. You used his name! That was him here last Monday, wasn't it?" Jamie pointed to the door, referring to the memory of the good-looking, posh English bloke.

"Listen to me… no, *he* wasn't Chris," Kate interjected. "And no, he didn't dump me." She was starting to gabble her words. "Yes, *he* is in America now, and he did come to say goodbye. But it's nothing romantic. Jamie, the man who you saw in here that first night… that man who came in to Alchemy and spoke to me before leaving, he isn't Christian… that man was my brother."

"Brother?" Jamie sat down again.

"Yes, my brother." Still standing, Kate had both palms flat on the table, leaning over across the table towards Jamie.

Richard came from behind the bar and hovered. "Can I clear these, for you Kate?" He looked at the clean glass and then at Jamie's still-full coffee cup. "Oh!"

"Just give us a few minutes, please, Rich."

Richard ambivalently raised his eyebrows at Kate before complying with her request.

"What do you mean, your brother?" Jamie asked again.

"Oh, my stars!" Kate said. "How long have you got?"

"So, the Chris who's going through the divorce…?"

"What?"

"You aren't having an affair with him?"

"What? Why would I be having an affair with Christian? He's a friend." Kate threw her hands in the air and plonked back down on her seat. *"O-kay,"* she began. "We need to clear up a few things here…"

Jamie sat and listened. She listened to the explanation of Kate's brother's birth, she listened to the story behind the horrific car crash, and she finally heard the full rocky history of Kate's relationship with Tig.

Now calmer, Jamie was lost for words.

Richard, who had been hanging around throughout, eventually returned to the table and took up position behind Kate. He bent over and kissed the top of her head. "Can I get you a drink, sweetie?"

"Tea, please, Rich," she said quietly.

"Another coffee?" Richard picked up Jamie's cold cup.

"Please."

"Coming up."

"You've had a hell of a time over the years," Jamie said. "So, you got sick of your brother's bullying and interfering?"

Kate nodded.

"I suppose you were more or less forced to do or say something?"

Kate nodded again.

"That's a tough call."

A thoughtful silence ensued. Richard brought over the drinks. As he left, he lightly squeezed Kate's shoulder.

Jamie loaded a spoonful of brown sugar into hers. "How did your brother take your news, once you'd caught up with him at the airport?"

"Badly… but it all had to be said. I didn't confront him without considerable prior thought. He needed to know how he had impacted on me and my life." Kate looked pained. "He knows I love him... it's just not good for either of us to be around each other any more. Tig leaving the UK was the right thing to do. After the accident, he became the most important man in my life, but as his personality changed and he went off the rails, our relationship took a battering. Eventually it fell apart completely." Kate waited quietly, allowing Jamie to think over what had just been said. "This is all very gloomy. I think we need to lighten up a bit, don't you think?" Kate suggested.

"Probably." Jamie smiled. "To be fair, though, I thought I was gate-crashing on a romantic date, last Monday."

Kate looked at her watch. "Do you have other arrangements tonight?"

"No."

"Me either." Kate looked hopefully at Jamie. "So, can I persuade you to have a proper drink?"

Jamie raised both hands in submission. "What the hell, why not? After what's just been unravelled, I reckon we could both do with one."

Kate jumped up. "I'm on it!" Glancing back over her shoulder, she added with a wink, "It's on the house."

Kate walked to the bar, Jamie followed her with her eyes, appreciating her exceptionally well-formed arse. She lamented with a fatalistic sigh, then pulled out her phone to message Linda: *Gossip unfolding - man who I thought dumped Kate that 1st night was her brother!!! Will tell u more later. With her now.*

Jamie looked back to the bar but couldn't see Kate. She sent another text to Linda: *PS Even if only a friend, she still has such a great arse.* Jamie finished the PS with a sad emoji face, then browsed her social media page while she waited.

Concentrating on her phone, Jamie was jolted back into reality by the appearance of a drink that was put down right in front of her. She looked at the glass, then at Kate. "Thank you," she said with a smile.

Kate looked back with wide eyes. "Marmalade martini," she said. "Remember?"

"I remember."

"Seemed appropriate – feels like we've come full circle." Kate sat down.

Jamie noticed Kate's eyes: in this light, they were an incredible, electric blue, able to hold Jamie's gaze with mesmerising confidence. Their depth and clarity were beautiful.

Kate raised her glass, “Cheers, Jamie...” She lowered her glass, without completing the toast. “It’s just dawned to me – I don’t even know your last name.”

“It’s Barker.” Jamie raised her own glass. “Yours?”

“Kate Adams.” She raised her glass again. “Cheers, Jamie Barker. It really *is* a pleasure to meet you.”

Jamie completed the salute, raising her glass fully to chink rims. “Cheers, Kate Adams.” She took a sip. “Wow, this is just as good as that first one.”

“Good!” Kate chuckled. “I wasn’t sure if you’d remember.”

General chat resumed between the two and drinks were finished.

“I wasn’t aiming to make tonight a late one,” Kate said.

“Is home far?”

“Stratford. And you?”

“Hyde Park.”

“Opposite ends of the city, then?” Kate checked her mobile.

Jamie checked hers too. Linda had replied: *Find out if she’s got an eligible sister hiding somewhere too – you never know! LOL Keep me posted, tiger! X.* Jamie smiled. She noticed Kate react with a questioning frown, but she refrained from asking.

"I would quite like a stroll." Kate stood up. "How are you getting home?" She was already zipping and buckling up her leather jacket.

"Probably the tube." Jamie got to her feet as well.

"Mind if I walk with you a while?"

They proceeded to make their way to Shaftesbury Avenue. Neither particularly taking the lead, they wandered along, chatting easily, picking their way through the narrow side streets.

"Oh blimey," said Jamie. "How did we get *here* so soon?"

Kate looked around her. "Where are we?" She wrapped her arms around herself. "I should have put something warmer on under this."

"I know a pub a little further on if you need to warm up a bit." Jamie wasn't feeling the cold, but she could see that Kate was starting to shiver. "Are you up for that?"

"Yes, let's." She opened her phone. "Richard is supposed to be giving me a lift back to Stratford. I'll give him a call – in case he thinks I've abandoned him." She called, giving Richard an estimated 'within the hour' return time to Alchemy.

One hour? Jamie realised that her evening with Kate was now time-limited. "It's a quirky old London pub," she said, aiming to stretch out the hour for as long as possible. "We could pop in to get warm, and I can call up a cab from there if you want – save you having to walk back to Alchemy."

"Okay, why not? I'll let Richard know. I'll call him when we reach the pub."

Jamie took the lead to their destination. "So, where do you hang out when you're not working? I'm guessing that socialising in your own bar isn't a regular thing?"

"I hadn't ever thought about it. I don't usually choose to go to Alchemy when I'm not working." She dawdled for a spot of window shopping. "It is a good place to start drinking before moving on to somewhere else, though." She looked at Jamie. "I'm probably biased, but I *know* just how good the cocktails are."

"Must be the way you make them," Jamie joked.

"I'll have you know, it's not just all for show, Jamie. Becoming a mixologist takes training."

Kate proceeded to spend several minutes explaining fervently that making cocktails was a serious business. Her passion was brilliant.

"But surely it's just chucking a few measures of booze into a jug with some ice and shaking it about a bit?"

"Absolutely not! It's performance art meeting science – like mixing chemicals for an experiment. It all has to be precise: proportional measuring and correct order of ingredient combination."

"You've given me a new perspective," Jamie said, with humorous gravity.

"Hence the name," Kate explained. "Alchemy – as in the medieval forerunner of chemistry."

“Ah!” Jamie understood the connection. She was getting a kick out of Kate’s enthusiasm – a trait she admired.

Once they were settled in The Lamb, Jamie went to the bar for a couple of Cokes. She returned to the table then reluctantly called a cab to collect Kate and take her home.

“Oh crikey, I nearly forgot,” Kate exclaimed. “I need to let Richard know I don’t need a ride home any more.”

“So… do you want to meet up again sometime?” Jamie had thoroughly enjoyed the latter part of the evening, although it was all happening too fast.

Then she heard steps coming up behind their table. “Hey, honey?” a familiar voice called. Jamie turned, tensing up.

It was Sarah.

CHAPTER 17

Kate watched the newcomer as she moved around to the side of the table and peered down her nose at Kate. Kate welcomed her with a smile, anticipating an introduction. Her greeting was blanked.

The stranger turned away from Kate and spoke directly to Jamie. "You didn't get back to me yet. Did you think any more about our conversation? How you feel about what I said?"

"No, I haven't thought any more about it," Jamie answered bluntly.

Kate scrutinised the interruption, puzzled by the withering look she had just received from this woman with the accent and no name.

"Were you even *planning* on getting back to me? After what we've been through?"

"*We* haven't been through anything, Sarah," Jamie answered.

At least Kate now had a name for the face. It was obvious that this situation had a past attached and that this Sarah woman clearly wasn't someone who deserved polite introductions.

"When I said I still love you, Jamie, I meant it."

Kate's head jerked back a fraction. She frowned. This was certainly an unexpected slant. Whoever this woman was to Jamie, she was bold, ruthlessly confident and clearly jealous.

"Do you mind?" Jamie said. "This isn't a good

time..." She looked briefly at Kate then back to Sarah. "And I'm not sure that we have anything more to say to each other."

"If you tell me you *want* me to go, I will leave." Sarah was steadfast.

Who *was* this woman? "Look," Kate intervened, unwilling to watch this horrible exchange escalate. She rose to her feet. "If you need to join me, Jamie, I'm going to wait outside for the cab, okay?"

"Yeah, bye –" Sarah subversively pulled rank. "Jamie's just fine here with me, darling." She pounced forward, seizing the opportunity to hijack Kate's empty seat. "Voetsek!" She scathingly dismissed Kate, waving her off with the back of her hand.

Kate didn't need a translator to convince her to leave these two to settle whatever grievance they had with each other. For sure, she certainly didn't need any more drama in her life. Jamie was on her own with this one!

"How dare you, Sarah!" Jamie sprang to her feet. "And Kate, don't *you* go anywhere," she ordered. The conviction in her voice was enough to bring the two other women to a standstill. Jamie looked at each of them in turn. "You are astonishing, Sarah. Do you *honestly* think you deserve a single minute more of my time – after what you put me through?"

Sarah didn't respond.

Then, the eruption followed. "So, for how long exactly *were* you screwing your boss's husband? And truthfully, Sarah? Were you *ever* planning to be honest with me, or did you believe you could just keep up the deceit ad infinitum and hope I would never find out?"

Kate's pulse quickened, shocked by everything she was hearing. She wondered what Jamie would do next.

"Surely you don't *need* reminding?" Jamie prompted. "Coming up to nearly four and a half years…? Remember? Eighteenth of June...? Remember? You came home that night drunk, stinking of perfume – and it sure as hell wasn't yours because it wasn't perfume at all, was it? It was fucking aftershave. God knows why I didn't recognise the difference." Jamie pinched the bridge of her nose. "Christ, Sarah, for all those weeks beforehand, you were feeding me like a dripping tap – introducing those little trigger words – telling me I was jealous... paranoid... insecure... distrustful. You were actually in tears that night, blaming *me* for hurting *you* with what you described as my despicable accusations."

Sarah's head was slightly bowed. She looked through her lashes at Jamie – defiantly penetrating.

"And to think I honestly started to believe it was *me* who was in the wrong. And you told me I needed psychiatric help. You even offered to do an assessment…"

Kate couldn't take her eyes off Jamie. She watched as Jamie's expression changed – hit by a bolt of mental clarity.

"You were gaslighting me, weren't you?" Jamie moved in closer to Sarah, then stepped back again, regaining her self-control. She turned to Kate. "You couldn't make this up. This feels like an episode of some shitty TV soap. I'm so sorry you are hearing all of this crap."

Cab forgotten, Kate had unconsciously leaned in closer to Jamie in sympathy.

"I told you then, and I'll say it again now," Sarah emphasised. "It didn't *mean* anything."

Kate recoiled. Sarah's words reminded her of the age-old, gross 'It was only sex' cliché.

"It meant nothing of any significance, Jamie," Sarah explained. "It was purely physical – just sex."

At that, Kate let out an involuntary little squeak, looking around to see if she was the only one watching this spectacle.

"You know what, Sarah? I'm further down the road, and I honestly don't give a shit any more." She looked down to the left at the floor, seeming to be considering the matter, then looked back at Sarah. "You know what? The other day, I was starting to think you'd hooked me back in all over again."

Sarah's face lit up. "And now?"

Jamie was having none of it. "What the *hell* makes you think there is a *now?* Why would I *want* to get involved again with a woman so deceitful and manipulative?"

Sarah gave no obvious reaction.

Jamie kept firing. "He was married with a two-year -old child, for Christ's sake."

"Oh, God!" Kate said under her breath.

"Jamie," Sarah said calmly. "I never made any secret of my interest in both men and women, did I?"

"That's not the point, Sarah, and you know it." Jamie was running ragged.

Sarah raised her voice slightly. "You are being unbelievably judgemental, are you not?" She locked eyes with Jamie. "It's only *one* commandment, and *everybody* sins."

"That's enough! I want you to take yourself as far away from me and my life as is humanly possible."

"Do you *really* mean that?"

Kate glared at Sarah. *Did she really just ask that question?* The gall of this woman was quite something.

Sarah got to her feet, but Jamie hadn't finished.

"You want something, don't you?" Jamie said, her eyes half-closed. "There's an agenda hidden here, isn't there? Why else would you come back and track me down? Why go about it all in such an underhand way? What's the motive, Sarah – and don't you dare say love, because we both know that's a crock."

"Ag, man, how do you suddenly have the moral high ground? No one is pearly white, and *you* are certainly no exception. Have you lost *all* memory of our past? Our happy times together? Our laughs?"

Sarah's eyebrow arched a fraction, implying subterfuge. "Our shared trust?"

Kate didn't like the feel of wherever this seemed to be heading.

"Our shared secrets...?" Sarah continued.

"Astonishing. You threw that in so deftly, you almost made me believe this was a normal conversation." Jamie was unable to conceal her sarcasm.

Sarah retained an obstinate frown. She allowed a few seconds for her words to be fully heard. "I'll be in touch when you're thinking straight again," she said, smiling with clinical duplicity.

"*Thinking straight?* There you go with the mind games. *My* thinking is just fine. It won't work anymore, Sarah."

"Won't it?" Sarah's manner was one of stony self-confidence.

Even through Jamie's shaken stoicism, Kate could see that she was cracking. This Sarah woman was quite obviously attempting to undermine Jamie and throw her into emotional free-fall. Kate knew precisely how that felt. She couldn't remain the bystander any longer. She moved to stand between the two rivals. "I'm pretty sure my friend has just politely asked you to leave."

Sarah was invincible. She brushed off Kate's intervention. "Really?" she mocked. "Ignorant moegoe." She looked at Kate, then at Jamie with equal repellence. "I'll be in touch," she promised, making it sound more like a warning. And with that, she was gone.

Jamie waited until they were truly alone. She tensed. "I am *so* angry!"

"I can see that." Kate put her hand firmly on Jamie's shoulder. "Breathe."

Jamie did just that – in, then loudly out again.

"Who was *she*? And what did she just call me? Mo-go…?" Kate was trying to hold back from laughing. "Is that even a thing?" She could see that Jamie was not in the mood for frivolity. Kate looked at her watch. "We might need to push the taxi back… wait, Richard! I've not called him yet." Claiming her seat back, she took out her phone.

Jamie sat down too. "Moegoe – it's an Afrikaans word – an insult."

"I see," Kate replied, then turned to her conversation with Richard. "I thought as much… No need for the cab, Rich is going to come and pick me up from here in about forty-five minutes. He's happy to take you home too if you want."

"That's good of him."

"In the meantime –" Kate got to her feet "– my round, I think. Alcohol, soft drink or coffee?"

"A coffee would be great, thank you."

"And don't you think that we're all done here. I want to know more about that Sarah woman."

Kate went to the bar to place the order, returning minutes later. “There you go, J.B. one coffee.” She put the cups on the table.

But something had altered in her absence. Jamie didn’t look right, and the atmosphere had suddenly turned dark. It didn’t feel so easy any more.

Jamie was looking sideways at Kate. She spoke slowly, hesitantly. “Actually, Kate –” she started. “You’re right… we’re not all done here.”

“Oh?” Kate delicately lowered herself into her seat.

“There’s something that you said earlier – something that still bugs me. Something you mentioned… I’ve scrutinised it from every angle, but it doesn’t add up at all.”

“Right… Should I be worried?”

“It’s to do with what you said… about Christian.”

“Right…?” Kate repeated, uncomfortably.

“Was he going through his divorce the night I first saw you, with your brother?”

“Yes. Why?” Kate now followed Jamie’s lead, looking askance at her.

Deep frown-lines formed between Jamie’s troubled brows. “It’s just that after your brother left Alchemy… the phone call, before you called the taxi… it just doesn’t make sense.”

“Which part?” Kate picked up her coffee. She needed something to hold.

“I understand the taxi ride, that it was your brother who you went to meet at the airport.” Jamie picked up her coffee cup too and paused to marshal the facts. "And you said earlier that it wasn't Christian that you were talking to. But on the phone, you were going on about desperately needing to meet him… you said you couldn't let the conversation be goodbye… you told him you wanted to fight for the relationship. 'For us' were your exact words." Jamie's eyes defied Kate's. "So, who exactly is the Chris that you were on the phone to?"

Kate's head dropped. "Chris?" she said, putting down her coffee. "So, you overheard all that too?"

"You didn't exactly make your conversation very private."

Kate looked up. "It was only a matter of time, Jamie…"

Jamie's eyes questioned.

"The Chris I was speaking to…" Kate pushed her mug to the side. "It wasn't Christian… and Chris isn't a he. This Chris is a she. Not Christopher – Christine."

"A *woman?"* Jamie sat bolt upright.

"That would be the logical alternative." Kate couldn't repress a chuckle, but she lowered her eyes, nervous of how Jamie was taking this new information. "Yes, a woman."

The two friends sat for a moment, slightly strained and contemplative. They both sipped their coffee but didn't look at each other.

It was Jamie who spoke first. "Do you mind if I ask you about Christine?"

"I don't mind at all," Kate said, relieved for the conversation starter.

"So, are we talking friend or relationship here? I don't want to presume," Jamie said.

Jamie's dilemma struck a chord with Kate. "As did I with you – not wanting to presume." She slowly lifted her eyes from her coffee cup to Jamie. "Jamie, Chris is a woman who I'd been seeing for nearly eleven months. My brother, Tig, hated her – well, not her per se," she qualified. "But he hated how serious I was about her and, selfishly, the loss he believed it meant for him – losing me, I mean. He was an absolute pig to her. Abusive and rude, sending threatening emails, letters through her door. When he started trying to get at her through her place of work, she went crazy. She got to the point of seeking legal advice to take out a restraining order. Understandably, she couldn't maintain her relationship with me while all this was going on."

Jamie sat with her hand over her mouth as she listened. "Good God!" she said at last. "That's quite some curveball. I did not see that one coming."

"No, I gathered," Kate said. "But then I also didn't want to assume you were gay when we first met. It's not the kind of conversation you tend to strike up with a person you hardly know."

"No, I can understand that." Jamie looked worried.

Kate sat and watched Jamie assimilate this new slant.

"And Christine?" It was now Jamie's eyes that lifted furtively from her cup. "How did *she* take the news about what you'd told your brother? Happy? Relieved?"

"Initially? Yes. Long term? No, it wasn't meant to be. I should have sensed it. The idea of us getting back together again was all very chocolate-box. The reality was, we had both already moved on. It only took a week or so for us both to finally acknowledge it."

"Well, I reckon that if she'd really wanted you, she wouldn't have left in the first place. But maybe that's just me being an unrealistic, fluffy romantic." Jamie smiled. "That's what my friend Alex calls me, anyway."

"Nothing wrong with a bit of fluffy romance," Kate decided. "If nothing else, it was all a catalyst. It forced me to see sense, make some overdue life choices and realise what I did and didn't want."

Jamie nodded.

"And I'm in a good place now. As a matter of fact, I've got something in the pipeline for tomorrow night," Kate said. "Handy little things, these dating apps."

"Oh?" Jamie said with a wry smile. "I beg to differ."

Kate laughed. "Says the voice of experience."

"Yeah, too right."

Kate finished her coffee. "Well, I'm already out later than I meant to be tonight. I'm going to sit nearer the window, so I can see when Richard arrives. I'm just visiting the toilet first."

On her way back from the bathroom, Kate noticed Jamie was smiling at something on her phone. "At least something has made you smile tonight," she said.

"It's just a message from my sister." Jamie followed Kate to a window seat.

"So, as this seems to be turning out to be a night of show and tell," who is Sarah, then?"

Jamie inhaled unwillingly.

"Assuming you *want* to tell me?" Kate said. Trying to sweeten the pill, she made a disclosure of her own. "My brother had a real knack for making me feel totally crap about myself. I thought I was turning into a fruit loop at one point… oh dear, that wasn't very politically correct, was it? Did I really just say 'fruit loop'?"

Jamie beamed.

Sensing she had found a way in, Kate folded her arms onto the table and leaned forward, head slightly lowered. "You mentioned four years? So, is Sarah a recent acquisition, or one of old?"

"Yes, in a nutshell – to continue the fruit and nut food theme! It's been a long while since our relationship ended."

"Serious, then?"

"Basically, Sarah screwed me over and went back to South Africa."

"Are there any more ingredients of information to add to this fruit and nut cake?" Kate was tickled, and judged it safe to prolong the silliness, even though their talk was touching on serious matters.

Jamie too, seemed comfortable with it. She proceeded to relay an abridged version of her relationship with Sarah.

The pub was gradually thinning out.

Kate's phone buzzed. She checked the message with a dimpled grin. "Our carriage awaits," she said. "Hyde Park for you, wasn't it?"

CHAPTER 18

With Jamie in the back seat and Kate in the front of Richard's car, the two women now had no opportunity, or special reason, to talk.

Jamie re-read the message she'd sent to Linda while Kate had been in the loo: *All hell just broke loose!!! At Lamb pub & Sarah just appeared!!! Am still with Kate... and just let slip she's only freaking gay!!! Nothing romantic. She's not interested. Can I call u when I'm home?*

The drive home was dominated by Richard's chin-wag bitching to Kate: he moaned about the attitude of bolshie customers, chatted about his grandmother and filled Kate in on the changes in the bar staff duty rota and stock updates.

Jamie's phone pinged. It was Linda's reply: *Cor! What a drama! No need for 'new hat' shopping then??!* Jamie laughed out loud, catching Richard glancing curiously in his rear-view mirror at her. She sent back: *Nah! I'm over str8-girl crushes. Kate seems to be squaring up to be a trustworthy friend.*

As Richard pulled up outside Jamie's place, Kate hopped out of the car to open Jamie's door and say goodbye. She moved forward, her face just inches from Jamie's. Taken completely off guard, Jamie moved off centre to regain her personal space. As she did so, Kate's lips missed Jamie's cheek, brushing gently across the corner of Jamie's mouth.

The pit of Jamie's stomach flipped. That microsecond of brazen physical attraction was palpable. Her response was to return the kiss politely, on her cheek, with a friendly pat on the back, then pull away. But the execution was all very clumsy and embarrassing. The unexpected spontaneity of Kate's action was a shocker.

Jamie's gawky reaction obviously amused Kate but she politely said nothing. Her lack of response was not helpful. It simply made the whole event feel even more cringe-worthy.

They swapped mobile numbers.

"Catch up sometime soon, maybe?" Kate called out of the passenger window, before Richard pulled away.

"Yeah, sure," Jamie said. "And good luck with your date tomorrow."

"Thanks."

The car pulled away.

Kate didn't seem too fussed about firming up a date to meet, but Jamie realised that, in spite of everything, "sometime soon" wasn't soon enough.

Back in her flat, Jamie slumped down fully clothed on to her bed, thinking through the significance or otherwise of what had turned out to be an eventful evening. She gave Linda a call.

"Why are you so chewed up by Sarah's interruption?" Linda said. "You are bigger than that. Having experienced it first-hand, you're hardly unprepared for Sarah's ability to get inside your head. And still you let her rattle you. Why?"

"I just don't trust her."

"But you say that like you've only just found this out. You know she's a pile of crap, so why even give her the time of day? I don't get it."

Jamie could hear Linda's patience dwindling.

"There's absolutely no reason any more to have Sarah be any part in your life, so why are you even giving this airplay, Jamie? What am I missing here?"

"Missing? Nothing…" Jamie dived in. "I'll sort it," she said, intending to quickly conclude the conversation.

Linda yawned. "You're an adult and I'm not your keeper, Jay. I'm going to bed." She closed the phone call on a tactful positive. "It was good of Kate to step in on your behalf, though. She gets my vote on that score. Sounds like she has a backbone."

Getting ready for bed, Jamie stood in her bathroom, staring at herself in the mirror. She leant forward over the basin, eyes closed, allowing her forehead to rest against the cold glass. She sighed heavily. Trying to reason made her brain race and her head ache; she was unable to shake the nagging voice of her conscience. She knew she had been economical with the truth. She had failed to tell her sister about Sarah's reminder of their "shared secret".

Jamie gradually stood upright, following her own reflection in the mirror. Her eyes moved across to the unsightly cracked and broken wall tiles. Instantly, the memories were conjured up again: horrible memories of actions charged by aggression and anger.

Jamie was afraid – fearful that Sarah's shared secret tipped the balance of power in her favour. It was hard to imagine that Sarah had once been her most trusted, loyal friend and partner. She couldn't just forget about her implied threat. Perhaps this was *exactly* what Sarah had intended – to take control so that Jamie had no other choice *but* to stay in contact? For several days, Jamie was hounded by a clawing anxiety, unable to believe that Sarah could really let sleeping dogs lie.

*****

The following week, Linda arranged to meet Jamie at The Coal Hole for a late Sunday-afternoon drink. Their vague phone conversation about Sarah had worried her. She planned to choose her moment and tactfully ask Jamie to clarify.

The two sisters had only been in the pub for ten minutes. They had just ordered drinks and found a place to sit. Linda didn't get the chance to ask Jamie about the phone call.

"I thought I would find you both in here, eventually. I've been hoping to track you down." Sarah stood by the table between the two sisters like a macabre spectre. She pulled up a chair from the next table to join them. "This won't take long," Sarah promised, looking at Linda. Then she turned to Jamie: "I'm very sad that you were so quick to bad-mouth me the other day in front of your friend."

"What is it you want, Sarah? I'm having a night out with my sister and you aren't welcome," Linda challenged.

Sarah stared at her prize. Jamie knew the look. Sarah meant business.

"Ag, man! You, of all people, Jamie, casting the first stone? Isn't that hypocritical?"

Linda looked to Jamie for an answer.

"I was honestly hoping we could try again."

Jamie was aware of Linda's eyes burning into her for a response.

Sarah kept going. "I was an idiot to have cheated on you, and I know that I haven't behaved in a way that I'm very proud of. But that was years ago. Truthfully, I'm a different person now."

"Really?" Linda asked. "I doubt that, from what I've seen so far of the allegedly 'new' you. You still seem to be every inch the twister and schemer." The voice of reason, the front-line protector, looked reassuringly towards Jamie. But Jamie was agonisingly speechless. "Jamie?" Linda prompted.

"I couldn't ever trust you again," Jamie said.

"Shame. I'm planning on moving back here – settling for good this time."

"Really?" Linda cut in. "Were you intending Jamie to be a part of your next move towards securing your permanent residency, Sarah, or is this the next thing you are working towards?"

"I don't like what you're implying, Linda. That's a crappy insinuation. I don't *need* your sister for anything, but I do *want* her in my life again. There's a difference between *need* and *want*."

"And I don't *need* or *want* your kind of relationship, Sarah," Jamie said, this time answering with forceful conviction. "I'm done with tying myself up in knots over you."

"Amen to that," Linda agreed.

Sarah addressed Jamie. "Is this it, then?"

"*I* certainly heard my sister loud and clear," Linda said. "I think you need to start listening, Sarah." Linda loomed large, in full big sister defence-mode.

"You have made your point crystal clear. *Both* of you have," she concluded tersely. Sarah then opened and looked into her handbag. "Jamie has been very quick to cast me aside as the distrustful cheat…"

"What are you saying, Sarah?" Jamie asked.

"I'm not carrying your shit with me any more, is what I'm saying." Sarah pulled a plain, sealed envelope from her bag.

Jamie moved forward, her hand poised to take the letter. But she wasn't the intended recipient. Sarah pulled the envelope away from her outstretched hand, handing it, instead, to her sister. "You need to see this, Linda," she said. Pulling her bag onto her shoulder, she stood up and addressed Jamie. "Even if you don't want to hear this, Jamie – I loved you, I still love you and will always love you."

"What are you doing?" Jamie was nervous.

"I'm doing this for your own good." Sarah about-turned and left without a last glance back.

Linda was dumbfounded, perilously holding the envelope between finger and thumb. She tore the seal open. "What *is* this?" She pulled out a sheet of lined paper and unfolded it – eyes all the while on Jamie.

With the paper now removed from the envelope, Linda started to read.

Jamie watched Linda's eyes ferociously devour the handwritten words on the page. Her face, paralysed with concentration, intermittently contorted.

Finally, Linda scowled at Jamie, thrusting the letter towards her. "What is this, Jamie?"

Jamie snatched away the paper, unable to absorb its contents rapidly enough. She could feel the hot anxiety drain from her face, turning into cold, blind panic – fuelled by the knowledge that this bomb had been primed for detonation long before today…

Linda,

Jamie has made it quite obvious that she no longer wants me in her life. If that is how she wants it to be, then I can no longer hold on to her. However, I'm not going to exit Jamie's life looking like the bitch from hell, leaving her smelling of roses. A paragon of virtue she most certainly is not!

In short, I no longer feel any obligation to carry my share of Jamie's conscience, as I did for the most part of four years. I am about to give you some home truths that Jamie did not have the guts to do.

Two days before your father died, he asked Jamie out for lunch. You were in New York at the time. He admitted two things to her. What he confided in her that day was cowardly and pernicious.

First, your dad was having an affair with a colleague from his work for over two years. He told Jamie that he was about to tell your mom and then file for a divorce.

Jamie was understandably and profoundly concerned about what this information would do to the family. But your dad managed to reassure Jamie that this news wouldn't be so devastating for your mom, because they had already been going through the motions in an unhappy, loveless marriage for many years. Their relationship had, effectively, long since ended.

Your dad also told Jamie that he and your mom had, for years, intentionally kept the breakdown of their relationship hidden, as they wanted to protect you and Jamie from the heartache.

I also need to tell you the second part of this whole sordid story, which I know will be extremely difficult for you to hear. Where your family has let you down, I will simply be honest with you. Linda –you are not your father's daughter. Your mom and dad split up a few months after they started dating. Your mom met someone else and fell pregnant. He was not able to deal with the responsibility of being a father, so disappeared completely. A few weeks later, the man you believed to be your father came back on the scene, eager to rekindle the relationship with your mom. Your mom told him you were his. He never knew the truth until the day that Jamie was born, when your mom finally confessed everything.

Having offloaded all this onto Jamie, her dad made her promise not to tell you any of this information. He knew how much it would hurt you and he didn't want you to think badly of him. He swore to Jamie that once the divorce had gone through and the dust had settled, he would tell you and your mom about the other woman in due course. He also intended to tell you that you weren't his daughter. Your father told Jamie that your mother had vowed to take this secret with her to the grave. She never intended for you or Jamie to know. He never forgave your mom for her deceit and was no longer prepared to allow her to opt out of all responsibility for the truth.

Jamie dutifully kept her promises, trusting her dad's word. I know all this because it was too big a secret for Jamie to carry alone. She told me everything. I, in turn, became unwillingly complicit in their deceit – I'm the only other person that knows the truth.

Finally, Linda – I'm sorry to say that isn't all. It's also about time that Jamie was exposed – not just for the devious liar she is but for her dangerous and abusive aggression, that ultimately drove me away from our relationship in the first place. I wash my hands of it all.

Sarah Ekstein.

Jamie finished reading and dropped the note to the table. "I can explain, Linny." But she had no idea where to begin.

Ashen-faced, Linda snatched up the letter and shook it. "This makes no sense. What does it mean? Tell me this is all some fucking Mills and Boon crap."

Linda's eyes were chilling, expressing an emotion that Jamie had never seen.

"No, I'm so sorry, Linda. It's not crap," Jamie said softly, her voice catching in her dry throat. "I love you. You will always be my big sister, no matter what…"

"*No matter what*? What kind of statement is *that*? Make sense, Jamie."

Linda's inevitable shock and anger were brewing.

"Just let me think a minute… I don't know where to begin, Linny. There is so much more to this than what Sarah has written…"

"Start somewhere, for fuck's sake!"

Then the floodgates opened. Jamie's words spewed and she couldn't stop. "I had no idea about you. Dad loved you like his own, but everything he told me about his broken relationship with Mum was bollocks. I had no reason to doubt him at the time. Mum has been living in her own little world of denial all these years." Jamie wiped silent, brimming tears that refused to stop. Her mind felt scrambled. The look in Linda's eyes and her indescribable expression were unbearable. Jamie continued to gabble, trying to relay the facts as rapidly as possible, trying desperately to make things right. "It was only three days after Dad had taken Mum out to dinner that I met him for lunch. It was two weeks before you were due to come home from New York. I knew something was wrong straight away – it was only Dad sitting at the table, without Mum. That was when he told me about his affair... two days later he was dead..."

Linda stared blankly at Jamie.

"I was with Mum when she phoned you in New York to tell you Dad had died. She was devastated. She broke down over the phone. She had no idea he was cheating. They had enjoyed a romantic dinner just the weekend before. That night, he even asked her to renew their wedding vows." Jamie's sentences were now running into each other. "There was no indication that anything was even wrong with their relationship. Do you see? Dad was lying to us all. He was a weak and pathetic cheat."

Linda was still excruciatingly mute.

Almost lost for ways to present her case, Jamie finished with, "You are still my sister and I love you to bits, and what Sarah wrote about me is a lie." She felt sick – every word sounded hollow and inadequate.

Linda looked away, hard and emotionless, at some remote, unidentifiable place beyond Jamie's shoulder.

"Linda," Jamie persisted, pained by the realisation that her sister was unable to look her in the eye. "It was only two days after my lunch date with Dad that he had his heart attack. What could I do? He dumped his guilt on to me, cleared his conscience and then dropped down dead. I was grieving for so much more than his death, Linny. I was in shock, too. I was so confused and upset." The tears were now flowing freely down Jamie's cheeks – too many to wipe away. "Talk to me, Linny. Say *something*."

Linda's eyes narrowed. "Four years," she said at last, pointing out the facts. "You've known all of this for four years?"

Jamie nodded contritely.

Linda nodded back slowly.

Jamie could see the hurt. She reached out for her sister's hand – more to satisfy her own need for reassurance than to console Linda.

"Don't!" Linda yanked her hand away from Jamie's grasp as if avoiding the contamination of her touch. She stood up.

Jamie immediately stood up too.

"Just *don't!"* Linda reiterated sharply, definitively, forcing Jamie to withdraw. Without saying another word, she was gone.

Jamie's legs buckled.

*****

Jamie had been sitting motionless for what seemed like ages. Then the realisation hit her: The one person she would usually call for support and reassurance in such a situation was the very person she had just hurt and disappointed so badly. Linda – Jamie's sister and heroine, the indefatigable crusader for all things fair and morally indubitable – had walked.

Jamie was numb, too undeserving and ashamed to sob openly now that Linda had gone. She could only imagine the torment that was going through her sister's mind right now.

From behind the serving counter, one of the bar staff was rubber-necking. Jamie cast her eyes down at the crumpled paper abandoned in the middle of the table.

The barman approached; Jamie was unaware – caught up in her introspection. He leant forward, reaching in to clear the glasses and remove the discarded paper. "Can I clear this for you?"

Snapping out of her reverie, Jamie slammed her palm on top of the letter.

The barman was jolted. "You okay?"

"Thanks, yes… I… I'm okay."

The barman held back a second. “Are you sure?”

“No… yes… Could you get me a whisky?”

“Certainly, madam.”

“Actually, make it a double, please,” Jamie added.

The barman nodded.

Now that her secret had been so shamefully crowbarred out of the shadows, Jamie had a burning need to share her burden. This had been her secret for so many years that she had almost forgotten what “normal” felt like.

And should she tell Alex? The two had not spoken since the blind date set-up, just sent a couple of texts at the most. A week earlier, Facebook had informed Jamie that Alex wasn’t even in the country. Up popped several photos of her glugging fancy cocktails, basking amongst beautiful, half-clad young people on a beach somewhere in Spain. Jamie had no idea if Alex was even home yet.

In truth, Alex’s absence was a respite that Jamie was actually glad of – a fact that hadn’t particularly occurred to her until this moment. At this time, she needed to talk with someone who would listen, be supportive, wise and nonpartisan. She didn’t need to get an ear-bending, or be read the riot act. Jamie was already well aware of the monster she had inadvertently created.

Jamie flicked open her phone contacts, scrolled through the names, then waited for her phone to connect. “Hi...? It’s Jamie. I was wondering, are you free at all...? For a chat...?" She left a pause that stretched out longer than she'd intended. "Something's happened with Linda… and Sarah… It's all been just horrible… I could do with a friend right now..." Despite her best efforts, Jamie ended abruptly on a short, breathy gasp. She couldn't camouflage the tears.

"Yes," Kate replied, without hesitation. "I'm free, Jamie… I'm coming to get you, right now. Where are you?"

CHAPTER 19

On her way to find Jamie, Kate wondered what on earth could have happened to have prompted the call. She hadn't known Jamie that long, and although they had shared some pretty personal experiences, surely Jamie had other friends higher up the pecking-order, and better established than she, to call up in a crisis?

As soon as Kate arrived, she registered what a state her friend was in. Jamie wasn't crying *now*, but it was obvious that she had been, and she looked grim.

Jamie saw Kate and burst into tears.

"Come on, you." Kate took charge, taking Jamie by the hand and standing her up.

Jamie was compliant.

"Try and hold it together. My car's just outside." Kate walked Jamie to the pub door. She didn't want her friend to go through the shame of a public meltdown, which seemed both highly probable and imminent.

Jamie followed Kate, still hand-in-hand, to her car. It was, as she had said, literally just outside the pub, parked precariously on double yellow lines. Already, a beady-eyed traffic officer had pounced on it and was writing out a ticket ready to stick on Kate's windscreen. Taken unawares by the pop of the car door lock, he looked up. Kate didn't give him the chance to put the parking ticket on her screen. She took it from his hand. "Thank you, officer."

"You understand why I have issued this ticket, do you madam?"

"Yes officer." Kate smiled and opened the passenger door to let Jamie in. "And it's worth every penny. Have a lovely afternoon." She got into the driver's seat and shut her door. "Right, your place or mine?"

"Mine, I think."

Kate pointed at the satnav on her dash. "Put in your postcode."

Jamie did as instructed. They drove away, leaving the bemused-looking officer standing on the roadside, watching the car as it disappeared up the road.

Kate looked across at Jamie. Her eyes were closed, and she had leant her head back against the seat. Kate took the cue and turned her music on: the low, rich, chilled slide of smooth, smoky jazz.

As she drove, Kate realised she was rather enjoying the moment. She couldn't speak for Jamie, but she was totally at ease simply listening to the music, without feeling under pressure to alleviate the quiet with conversation. It was one of those qualities that people talk about valuing in others, but seldom actually experience – it was a compliment.

Kate's thinking shifted to a time somewhere in the future: she could picture herself doing just this – sitting in silence and driving, listening to music – only in her imagination, she was cruising with her new girl along the freeway on Route 66, on a Harley, or sitting in a vintage classic Cadillac convertible, the wind blowing through her hair.

She turned into the visitors' parking area in the underground car park. They pulled up just next to where Jamie's own car was parked and got out. "Lead on, J.B.," she invited, gesturing with her open palm.

She hadn't expected to be visiting Jamie's home quite so soon, if at all. Once inside the building, she was struck by Jamie's surroundings. It looked like an expensive gaff. Jamie had done very well for herself.

"How are you doing?" Kate asked, as the lift doors opened onto Jamie's floor. "Are you all right?

"Not really," Jamie said.

Kate smiled and squeezed her arm.

Inside the apartment, Kate was even more bowled over. Jamie's home was astonishing. Modern, immaculate and enormous. She had only ever seen places like this on home make-over TV shows. This was completely out of her league. She was very relieved that Jamie hadn't suggested they drive to her own microscopic one-bed flat.

Kate tried her best not to look too much like a kid in a sweet-shop. The child in her wanted to run from room to room, exploring all the spaces, and finish up skidding in her socks across the length of the living room, just to emphasise the sheer size of the place. Her own little flat barely had room for a double couch. "Wow, this is beautiful," she said, looking all around her. Resisting the temptation to go and have a nose around in the kitchen, she walked towards the streaming light of balcony windows. "And this view is just fantastic."

Jamie pulled open the bi-folding doors, taking in a long, deep breath.

Kate spotted Jamie's framed print above the white leather sofa. It caught her eye for being bright and bold but mostly because it was the only piece of artwork in the whole room. It seemed odd to Kate that the walls were so sparsely decorated – particularly since Jamie was an architect. "Life is not about waiting for the storm to pass, it's about learning to dance in the rain – what a great saying. I love that."

Jamie said nothing. Kate let her be.

Drawn back to the kitchen area, Kate noticed the crazy little flecks of glass shimmering within the light-grey granite worktops. Every surface was completely clear of utensils – all but a funky-looking coffee machine in one corner that looked able to prepare every type of coffee under the sun.

"Can I make you a coffee, perhaps, before we talk?" Kate was itching to play at being a barista, and, while she was at it, get a chance to peek at the contents of the sleek and elegant kitchen cupboards and drawers. They all fitted flush, reflecting the light and adding to the sense of space and grandeur.

"No thanks…" Jamie spoke with her back to Kate, facing her balcony, overlooking the park beyond. "I need a drink. There's a bottle of French burgundy chilling in the fridge, if you want to join me?"

Kate found a single bottle of wine and numerous bottles of beer in the pathetically sparse Smeg fridge. She looked at the label – Le Cailleret. "Holy moly!" She continued to scan the bottle – Puligny-Montrachet 1er Cru. Thanks to her job, she could recognise an expensive bottle of plonk when she saw one. It seemed a strange contradiction to find this calibre of wine within a fridge so bereft of anything nutritionally substantial. She started opening and closing identical cupboards and drawers, searching for glasses and a corkscrew.

"There's a switch on the wall to the left of the coffee machine," Jamie called from the balcony. "If you're looking for glasses and a corkscrew. Give it flick, but stand back a bit when you've done it."

Kate pushed the switch, and there followed the sound of mechanical whirring. She was rewarded by the gradual, silky-smooth emergence of a fully equipped, cleverly concealed mini-bar, hydraulically propelled forwards from a panel on the wall.

"Superb!"

With hands full, Kate walked through and joined Jamie, who was now sitting at the balcony table outside.

"I thought you'd like that little gizmo. I designed it myself," Jamie said. "Bear with me – I'm feeling pretty crap right now, but I'll snap out of myself once

I've talked this through. I promise not to be quite so morose for the whole evening."

"Just be whatever. It doesn't bother me how you are. I'm not going to pretend I'm not intrigued by your call. And me of all people? We hardly know each other."

Kate put the glass, bottle and corkscrew on the table.

"Only one glass? Aren't you joining me?"

"I'm driving." Kate jiggle-mimed turning a little micro-steering wheel.

Jamie smiled at Kate's action. "I didn't even think," she said.

"I never touch a drop if I'm driving," Kate explained. "It's not worth the risk. I'm fine with a coffee." She went back to the kitchen to collect her cappuccino. "Actually, I cringe when I think of the number of times Tig got behind the wheel so shitfaced, he could hardly walk straight, let alone drive. It was impossible to tell at one stage if it was the drink or the drugs he was taking."

"Really? What a fool," Jamie agreed.

"Yeah, tell me about it." Kate echoed Jamie's sentiment, but guessed from Jamie's vacant answer that she wasn't fully engaged. "The one and only time my simple-minded brother was pulled over by the police for driving under the influence," she continued, "it was all my doing."

"Was it really? How?" Jamie's interest was roused.

"I had to do something. His days were numbered

before he killed someone."

Jamie listened sombrely.

"I would never have lived with that on my conscience. I had to do what I thought was right. He had no idea it was me who had called the police on him, until his lawyer opened his mouth during the court
hearing."

"Ouch!"

"Oh, my stars, listen to me. Enough of my doom and gloom." Kate pulled her chair forwards. "I'm gutted, though!" She gestured to the bottle to lighten the mood. "That is a beautiful drop of burgundy you're about to drink alone there, and your mini-bar is awesome. It's like being in a Bond movie."

Jamie put her feet up on the seat of the chair next to her.

"You've obviously got a lot on your mind." Kate brought the conversation back to why she was there.

"I've just had a thought," Jamie lifted her feet off the chair. "You *could* have a couple of glasses, if you wanted to. I've got a spare room that's all made up. You can leave your car overnight in the visitor parking bay."

"Okay, go on then," Kate said, almost without thought.

"Oh!"

It didn't sound like an enthusiastic response. "Although, don't feel obliged to offer…" Kate said quickly, backtracking.

"No, no – you read that wrong," said Jamie. "I didn't expect a reply that quickly… actually, I thought you'd say no."

"Oh, I see." Kate got off her chair to look over the balcony. "You have a superb view of the park here – but if I'm stopping, I'm not going to drink half a bottle of wine on an empty stomach." She ventured into Jamie's kitchen, aware that the food options in the fridge were not just limited, but practically non-existent.

Jamie must have read her thoughts. "I'm guessing a pot noodle and hunk of cheese doesn't float your boat as a culinary option, then?" She screwed up her face, then shook her head. "I'm not usually such a crap host… but I generally have more warning with my invited guests, and this was rather impromptu."

"Please don't think I'm ungrateful, Jamie, but this burgundy is wasted on me without a meal to do it justice." Kate was penitent, uncertain of Jamie's reaction. She softened the blow with, "Hey, but I'm happy with a beer and curry take-away, to be honest."

A half-smile lifted Jamie's features. "That's exactly the kind of comment my dad would have made. He would never drink a good wine without decent food to compliment it."

"Sorry to be a killjoy. It just seems like a waste of good wine otherwise. Are you sure you're okay with that?"

"I'm fine with that – although, to be honest, I'm not that hungry right now."

"Well, I'm hungry and you shouldn't drink on an empty stomach." Kate was already heading back to the fridge to put back the unopened wine bottle and go in search of beers.

"The second drawer on the right of the fridge – there are a pile of take-away menus. I don't care what you choose. Get extra of what you want, I'll pick at yours."

Once she'd ordered the food, Kate joined Jamie outside. "So, you mentioned your father a while ago – but it was in the past tense...?"

"And the reason for me calling you in the first place," Jamie said. "I think you'd better start by reading this." She pulled the folded paper from her pocket and handed it to Kate. Piece by piece, she helped Kate put together the jigsaw – the circumstances of her father's duplicity and Linda's reaction to the letter.

"This is incredible. What a nightmare…" Kate said. "So many questions." She looked back at the words. "The bit where Sarah describes – where is it – your 'abusive aggression'?" She looked at Jamie.

"No, believe me, it's absolutely not how it sounds. And I didn't even get to explain that part to Linda."

"So, how *was* it, then, exactly?"

"I know exactly what she's referring to. Sarah has totally twisted the truth. It happened on the day when she walked out."

"I'm already building up quite a vivid picture of this woman, and it's not particularly pretty."

"Trust me. She's a nasty piece of work," Jamie said. "At the time, it had only been five weeks since our father had died, and I was carrying the stress of my own burdens – knowing what I knew."

"Uh-huh."

"I had just finished moving my stuff from Sarah's flat to this apartment – we had been planning to move in together for weeks. Sarah hadn't yet sold her place."

"How long had you two been together before this?"

"Three years."

"Wow!"

"Well, the plan was that, once settled, Sarah was going to move in with me here and share the payments on the mortgage. That was around the time when the crevices in our relationship really started to rip open. It all came to a head one Sunday afternoon, over four years ago." Jamie glanced at Kate. "That was when the balance of the scales finally tipped."

"I'm listening," Kate said, feeling particularly uncomfortable. She repositioned herself, preparing to listen to Jamie's explanation of the day in question…

CHAPTER 20

Four years and six months previously, on that fateful Sunday afternoon, Jamie had been standing in the doorway of her bedroom, watching Sarah. She was sitting on Jamie's bed eating a cheese sandwich. Jamie was already irritated that she wasn't sitting at the table or in the kitchen to eat.

Sarah's concentration was riveted elsewhere. Chomping unconsciously and grinning moronically at her mobile phone, she didn't seem to notice that Jamie was even there. With every bite, chew and swallow, with every irritating, ugly rumination, Jamie's disgust and anger gradually swelled inside her. "You do realise that I know, don't you?" she said, the strained tremor in her voice revealing her inner anguish.

Sarah didn't even flinch.

"I know about Annette and her husband, Paul..."

Sarah's eyes moved away from her phone screen to look straight ahead, though she carried on chewing – giving no indication that Jamie's words had been acknowledged.

"Sarah," Jamie continued, stepping into the bedroom, "I know about your relationship with Annette's husband. I know how long it's been going on."

After one final swipe of her screen, Sarah placed her phone next to her and turned to look at her partner. Her next words were carefully primed. "Jamie, my bokkie. I'm worried for you," she said, with the authority of a therapist conducting a client session. "You need psychiatric support."

Sarah was calculated, icy-cold and totally composed.

Not Jamie. She grabbed the closest object to hand and hurled it across the bedroom with a guttural scream. The force with which she used to throw the glass paperweight released her pent-up passion. At that instant, Jamie didn't recognise herself. She knew she had fully intended to hit the target.

Sarah darted to the side, only just avoiding the missile. It ended up flying through the open door of the en-suite bathroom, ricocheting off the tiles above the basin and smashing them.

No further conversation was necessary.

*****

As she told her story, Jamie stared fixedly across at the park. At last she looked at Kate. "Sarah left the flat immediately and never returned. That incident ended the relationship and, shortly after, she left the UK and went back to South Africa."

"What astonishes me is why the heck you stayed with her for so long. Does your sister know all of this?"

"Not the detail. She knows Sarah cheated on me,

but she has no idea about the circumstances, or how Sarah subjected me to months of drip-fed lies and systematically eroded my confidence and sense of mental stability. And now, she's used her knowledge of Dad's secret to her sick advantage." Jamie pinched the bridge of her nose. "I truly meant to kill her that day…"

"I don't mean to trivialise the seriousness of it all, but the fact is, you didn't kill her," said Kate reasonably. "I realise I'm stating the obvious, but you really need to tell Linda about this – as soon as possible."

By 11:53pm, Kate and Jamie had eaten most of the food and had each drunk four bottles of Peroni.

"Any more to drink?" Jamie was already retrieving a bottle of Prosecco from her mini-bar.

The conversation had moved on. Though it had started as a heavy-going and difficult evening, Jamie was now more relaxed, enjoying the free-flowing, open and honest chatting. The alcohol probably helped, but she felt increasingly at ease with Kate, and she was beginning to believe she could rely on her new friend.

Standing in the kitchen, Jamie enthusiastically explained to her the mechanics behind the workings of her mini-bar. She even pulled out her technical drawings from a drawer to illustrate a detail.

Kate responded with a tipsy chuckle. "As an architect and designer, J.B., I can see you're in your element here. Is this your way of getting your own back for my lecture the other day? Trying to convince you that mixology is actually a science?"

Jamie laughed, too. She rather liked the new nickname that Kate had coined for her. "I reckon it just goes to show how passionate we are about our interests, I suppose?"

For her part, Kate had hidden gifts too – a creative soul. When she wasn't managing Alchemy, she was developing her artistic abilities. She had completed a degree at the Royal College of Art, then did her Masters. Now she was at the point where she could exhibit her work.

"I'm even starting to sell stuff," Kate said.

"Impressive." Jamie admired all forms of creativity. "Let me know when you have your next exhibition, and I'll be there, for sure."

At 1am, they were still hunkered round the table on the balcony, enjoying another humid, early Monday morning. The two women had reached a comfortable respite in the conversation and were now sitting quietly, sipping coffee, gazing at the park and the skyline beyond.

It was Jamie who broke the silence first. "I can't tell you how much your time and company has meant to me tonight. Thank you, Kate."

"And I thought *I* had been going through a rough time recently," Kate said, checking the time on her phone. "Where's *that* time gone?"

"It's all relative. The struggle you've had with your brother is no less valid than my family chaos. We have more in common than I realised."

"Seems so. Who'd have thought it all those weeks ago, when we first met?"

They fell silent again.

"Mind you, it now makes total sense," Kate mused. "The reason you bit my head off the other night, when you thought I was having an affair with my friend, Christian…"

"Yeah, sorry about that. Infidelity is always a touchy subject for me to deal with – for obvious reasons."

They compared their commonality of experiences, having both been let down or disappointed by people they loved and trusted.

"So, before we finally go to bed *this morning*," Kate said pointedly, emphasising the number of hours they had talked, "how are you going to broach all this with your sister? What's your plan of action?"

"What's really hard," Jamie explained, as she started to gather empty bottles, "is that I've gone through all the textbook emotions – anger, denial, isolation, sadness..." Her arms dropped by her sides, her hands still full of bottles and wineglasses. "But what's even tougher is that I feel like I've never been

able to truly let go. I'm not sure if I've ever come to terms with my parents' deceit, and I've never really had the chance to grieve my dad's death. I've never spoken to Mum about it. She went into denial when she found out she was pregnant, and then Dad came back into her life. Mum and I have sort of gradually drifted apart, and I allowed my relationship with Linny to follow the same path, really. I feel like I've been floating through the last four years like a rudderless ship in the middle of the ocean,
with this huge cargo of guilt."

"You certainly have." Kate stood up and started to help clear the remaining bottles.

"The only thing in all this that has ever remained constant, real and dependable is my amazing big sis. I don't give a rat's arse that she's my half-sister. Even when I found out the truth from Dad, I think it made me love her even more. I would do anything for her."

"Have you had any reason to think she feels differently?"

"No – but let's be honest, this is quite a game-changer."

Kate thought for a second. "Well, to be fair," she said, emphatically pointing an empty beer bottle at Jamie, "if you think about it, it's also about your need to have permission to let go and grieve."

"How do you mean?"

"The person who could give you permission to share your burden was your dad. But it was his selfishness that put you here in the first place. He made you promise under false pretences. By holding you to that, he has denied you the chance to let go of your burdens. It's like you've not had permission for closure."

Both women walked back into the apartment and put the glassware onto the kitchen counter. Jamie, looking thoughtful, went back and locked the balcony doors.

Kate started picking up her belongings from the sofa – her rucksack and hoodie.

"I guess a good night's sleep is what I need. Maybe I'll call Linda in the morning," Jamie decided.

Hearing voices, and having just woken up, Amelie poked her little head curiously around the door from Jamie's bedroom. She gave a provisional little mew, then padded slowly across the room towards Kate. The cat stopped halfway, sniffing the floor.

"Oh, my word, you've got a pussycat? She's so cute," Kate fussed. She knelt, scratching at the floor with her nails, encouraging Amelie to come and play. The cat didn't need a second invitation: she scampered over to Kate and promptly dropped to the floor, flipping over onto her back to expose her tummy, legs outstretched in the air.

"Kate, meet Amelie – Amelie, meet Kate," Jamie said with a smile. "You've made a friend for life there. She doesn't ask for tickle-tum from just anyone. Usually it's only me she trusts."

Kate was in her element, and Amelie was loving the attention, too. After the cat had enjoyed a thorough fussing, Kate got to her feet and yawned, suggesting it was an opportune time to retire.

Jamie showed Kate to her room, ensuring that she had everything she needed and was comfortable. "There's a brand new toothbrush still in the packet – feel free. It's in the bathroom cabinet." She pointed to the en-suite.

Kate looked around the bedroom. "Crickey, even your spare room is huge. If this is a guest room, *your* bedroom must be just about the same square footage as
my entire flat."

"Have a look around in the morning, if you want."

Kate threw herself backwards onto the bed in a star shape. "It's a cloud. Bliss."

Jamie laughed, enjoying Kate's simple gratitude. She was a fascinating mixture – a gentle soul, naively excited by a coffee-maker and a fancy kitchen, yet able to recognise the quality of a fine wine. Jamie was finding yet more appealing facets of her to warm to.

"Do you need a wake-up call in the morning?"

"No, thanks." Kate was still horizontal, eyes closed. "But if I'm still asleep when you get up, just come and pull the covers off. It usually takes a baseball bat over the head to wake me in the mornings." She opened her eyes and lifted her head. "Are you off out early tomorrow?"

"I need to be somewhere for nine-thirty. You?"

In the soft glow of the bedside light, Jamie was struck by the shadow on Kate's cheek, cast by her amazingly long lashes. Her make-up-free complexion was beautifully smooth and clear.

Kate sat up. "No, I'm fine until eleven. I'm going to view a venue for an upcoming exhibition."

"You mean your own show?" Jamie was impressed.

Kate looked proud of herself. "Hopefully, with a group of about eight other artists to spread the hire cost."

"Fantastic. Let me know the opening date. I'd like to
see your work."

"Certainly will. You'll get the first day viewing invite." Kate flicked open her phone to show Jamie pictures of her artwork. She patted the mattress next to her.

Jamie sat next to Kate on the side of the bed to look at the images. She nodded studiously, making all the right noises, but she wasn't overly keen on the style of the few paintings she saw. "I tell you what," she said. "We could always save the burgundy for next time and have a decent meal to go with it?" The invitation came before Jamie had even realised what she was saying. "But I'm afraid I'm not much of a cook."

"Jamie, if you're sharing a decent bottle of wine like that with me, it's only fair that I do the cooking, I reckon. I *love* to cook and I'm chuffing good at it too, even if I do say so myself." Kate blew on her nails and buffed them on her shoulder.

"Sounds good."

Just before getting up to leave the bedroom, Jamie took the initiative and leaned forward, determined this time to be the one in control of the cheek-kiss. "Thanks for coming tonight – goodnight then." But before she could get to her feet, Kate responded with an alcohol-enthused hug, nearly toppling her over.

Then Kate flopped back again. "Sweet dreams, Jamie," she said, with eyes closed.

*****

The next morning, they left the apartment together, each heading off their separate ways. Kate opened her driver's door, stopping just before she got in. "Are you going to try and talk to Linda later?" she called.

"I can't believe I'm saying this about my own sister, but I'm really nervous." Jamie stood by her own car, several feet away. "I couldn't cope with rejection from *her,* too." She thoughtfully tossed and caught her car keys in her hand a couple of times. "Actually, I think I might just wait until she calms down – give her more time."

"You want my opinion?"

"Go on...?"

"From everything you've told me about your sister, she doesn't sound like she'll let you down. She probably just needs time, I'm sure she won't leave you stewing for too long. She may be shell-shocked, and even angry – but from what you've told me about her, she doesn't strike me as cruel."

Jamie nodded.

Kate looked at her watch. "If you're still undecided by five o'clock, and assuming that Linda hasn't contacted you already, how about you call me? We can decide together what to do next."

Jamie didn't answer.

"What do you think?" Kate cajoled.

"Yeah, okay." Jamie smiled. "Thanks, Kate."

"No problem, J.B. I think I'm just as keen as you are to see this happily concluded, you know." Kate gave a wave and got into her car.

She edged her car forward a few feet and stopped closer to Jamie, who was still standing by her car. Kate wound down her window. "Thank *you,* too," she said. "The value of our chat last night works both ways. You've helped me also. I've come to a few decisions of my own – I need to make some changes in my life, too." Kate held Jamie's eyes, the way she had done that very first time in Alchemy, after sliding the bowl of peanuts to Jamie.

Jamie's stomach turned. She loved Kate's warmth and ability to calm muddy waters with a touch or a look. Nice though it was, it was also bittersweet. Jamie knew she couldn't accept the feeling. "Seems we've been good for each other in different ways."

"Seems so," Kate agreed. She waved goodbye, drove to the exit, then turned right out of the parking lot.

Jamie followed her out, but turned in the opposite direction. In her rear-view mirror, she watched Kate's little car disappear slowly into the maze of London streets.

CHAPTER 21

It was just coming up to 6.30pm when Jamie finally started packing up documents into her briefcase. As was often the case, she was one of the last to leave the building for home. At certain points on her walk to the lift, Jamie stopped to take in the views through the glass panels across the water of Canary Wharf.

At the front desk in the grand reception area, she pulled out her phone, checking again to see if there was anything from Linda. There was nothing. She was at a loss as to what to do next. She'd never been in this position with Linda before.

Even as kids, they hadn't ever seriously fallen out. Disagreements never amounted to much, or were quickly resolved with apologies and hugs under the watchful eye of their father, the mediator. It was he who had instilled this attitude into his daughters' mind-set. Jamie's dad would always lead by example, citing his own solid, loving relationship with their mother as the ultimate model of perfection. He indoctrinated his daughters with the understanding that, as sisters, they were forever tied by blood – which, like the sanctity of marriage, was strictly a forever bond that should never be broken. The irony of it now was mind-numbing.

Jamie's phone buzzed. It was a message from Kate, checking to find out if Linda had contacted her yet, and offering to call for a chat if not. Jamie gave it some thought but she was so tired that she could hardly even think straight. She sent a message back: *'Still no word from Linda. Don't worry about calling, I'm only just leaving the office now. How are you fixed this week for meeting up?'*

Jamie put her phone away and walked to where her car was parked. She'd forgotten to ask Kate how her visit to the exhibition venue had gone, so messaged back to find out. The reply came back: *'Very excited. Whitechapel Gallery is booked! 8 of us are exhibiting. Got 6 months to get creative. BTW – hang on in there with your sister – she's bound to crack. I'm free Sat if that works for you? X.'*

Jamie replied to congratulate her and agree to meet up on Saturday. She put her phone away, disappointed that Saturday was ages away. At least she had enjoyed the thrill of seeing an 'x' at the end of Kate's text.

At home, she unwrapped the sandwich she'd grabbed from the local deli and flicked on the TV to a random channel. But after several minutes, she realised that she'd not heard any of the programme. She was too distracted, still fretting over Linda.

Her mobile rang. "Linda?"

"Hello, stranger," the voice chirruped. It wasn't her sister.

With a silent sigh, Jamie anticipated a bombardment of questions – every one of them asked without the slightest interest in hearing the answer. Her prediction wasn't wrong.

"So, where have you been hiding yourself away then? Have you purposely taken yourself off the social scene, or are you just trying to avoid me? What have you been doing with yourself? Oh, my good God, Jamie, you'll *never* guess who I met the other day...?"

Jamie wasn't given the opportunity to reply. The silence was temporary.

"Only Sarah Ekstein!" With no imminent response forthcoming from Jamie, Alex offered a reminder. "Your ex-girlfriend?"

How thick *was* Alex? As if Jamie needed to be told who Sarah was! This was one of those occasions when she was unable to tell if Alex was attempting to goad her into a reaction, or just being witless and insensitive.

Alex continued to gush, barely able to contain herself. She was a coiled spring. "You *did* know Sarah's back in town, I take it? Did she contact you yet? She said she was planning to. Can you believe it, though? She just walked into the bookshop, the day after I got back from Spain – literally, it was completely unexpected. She said she'd taken a gamble that I still worked there, and you'll never guess what...? I ended up going down to stay over for a couple of nights at her new place in Brighton. She's got herself a beautiful flat by the sea in Adelaide Crescent towards Hove way – and, seriously, she is *such* a laugh. You two really should hook up again – just as friends, I mean," Alex added.

Jamie wondered if Alex had actually recognised the idiocy of what she was saying. "Thanks for the afterthought," she said sarcastically. "Have you only just considered how I might be feeling about all this?"

Undeterred, Alex rattled on. "I'd forgotten what fun Sarah was to hang out with. Do you remember the laughs we all used to have? We did loads of reminiscing about the good old days." She stopped. "Oh, my God!" She spoke with an artificial Brooklyn accent. "The good old days? Listen to me, I sound like my mother!" She dropped the Fanny Brice impersonation. "Mind you," she added, "they do say daughters eventually turn into their mothers – God help me." She laughed maniacally.

Jamie couldn't listen to any more drivel. "What the hell did you do that for, Alex?"

"What do you mean? Do what? Turn into my mother, you mean?"

"Why do you always have to be such a twat, Alex?"

"You're not still mad at me, are you, Jamie? I can't believe you haven't got over your hissy-fit about the blind date."

The last time Alex had spoken to Jamie had been the day when her botched blind date had crashed and burned.

Jamie got to her feet. "What possessed you to agree to see Sarah? Without telling me?"

"Why wouldn't I see her? Sod off, Jamie – you can't dictate to me who I can and can't see. What's your problem? She's nothing to *you* anymore. Why the irrational over-reaction?" She bridled. "Actually, Jamie…"

Jamie prepared herself.

"I'm now thinking you were so wrong to dump Sarah. She's wonderful. I'm entitled to be friends with her – and I don't need your permission."

"Bloody hell, Alex – you just can't help yourself, can you? Some friend you are." Jamie clicked off the TV and threw the remote at the sofa.

"Well, she obviously hasn't been in touch with *you*," Alex carped. "And if you must know, since you've forced my hand, Sarah was afraid that *exactly* this would happen."

"Exactly what would happen, Alex?" Jamie was now pacing the floor.

"That you'd be bolshie and immature about it all. I might as well tell you," Alex sniffed. "Sarah expressly asked me not to tell you that she had seen me until she had got in contact with you herself. But you've gone and made me *have* to tell you now, haven't you?"

"And your loyalty now lies where, Alex?"

"Loyalty? What are saying? I don't understand why you're being so tetchy. She's only an ex-girlfriend. I'm not exactly breaking any laws."

"Believe me, Alex, you don't know the half of it – and yes, I *am* pissed off." Jamie was already part-way down the hallway of her apartment. "Look, I'm not continuing this conversation over the phone. We need to talk face to face. I've got my jacket in my hand. Wherever you are, just get yourself to The Coal Hole, *now*!"

Alex's timbre changed, her voice becoming fainter and more upbeat. "Oh, go on then – I'll have a brandy and Coke, and a packet of salt and vinegar crisps –"

Only then did Jamie notice the babble of voices and music in the background. She stopped walking. "You haven't got Sarah there with you, have you?"

"God, you are suspicious, aren't you?" Alex said mordantly. "Get a move on yourself, *missy*! I just happen to be at The Coal Hole right now, in fact."

Jamie could hear Alex mumbling again to whoever was with her – hushed and inaudible.

"Alex...?" Just as she was about to ask Alex to repeat herself, the phone line went dead.

Jamie couldn't get to The Coal Hole quickly enough. As she drove, she felt consumed by dread. What if Sarah was there with Alex? How would she would react? It was horrible to think that Alex would even concoct such a sly plan.

Even if Jamie was wrong and Sarah wasn't there tonight, what was Sarah playing at? It seemed a great deal of preparation had gone into her various stage-managed reunions – the key fob, the letter, and now the meeting with Alex in Brighton. Was Sarah's letter to Linda planned? Had her scheme been brewing for weeks? Months? Years, even?

It was easy to see how Alex had got caught up in it all. Back then, she and Sarah had become very good friends. They had had a social life independent of Jamie. Could it be that Alex had secretly been keeping in touch with Sarah in her absence over the last four years? Perhaps Sarah had premeditated her goal, and been subtly preparing, almost grooming Alex to get her on side, ready for this moment? Right now, Jamie would put nothing past Sarah and her capacity to stoop so low.

She decided to keep her mouth firmly shut about Sarah's actions, including the letter. She wasn't going to be the first to give anything away, and she wanted to discover exactly how much Alex knew about Sarah's actions and motives. Now Jamie thought about it, Alex's behaviour hadn't exactly been exemplary just lately. This profound dissonance made Jamie question – doubt, even – if Alex could be trusted at all. This apprehension was a new and very real, uncomfortable feeling.

*****

At The Coal Hole, Alex was sitting on a stool and chatting to Darren, who was serving at the bar. He saw Jamie before Alex did, and mouthed a hello at her as she walked towards the counter.

Alex looked round. "Hello, fancy seeing you here."

Jamie forced a stressed exhale, only then realising she had been holding her breath since entering the pub, anticipating having to face Sarah. To her enormous relief, her nemesis was nowhere in sight.

Jamie nodded back a hello to Darren but declined a drink, then stood just behind Alex. It was busy but not Friday-night heaving. The man sitting next to Alex finished up his drink and offered Jamie his stool before leaving.

"I ended up in A&E the last time I saw you, I'll have you know," Alex said.

"What?"

"I ended up with a bit of your bloody glass in my foot. From your broken coffee jug."

"It was your mess, Alex, not mine." Jamie initial sense of relief was fast disappearing. "Even now I'm still finding shards of glass on the floor. It's been difficult enough with Amelie padding around. Thank God I've not got a baby or toddler crawling around the house; it wouldn't all be so amusing then, would it?"

Alex tutted loudly. "*You*? With a baby?" She looked momentarily shocked, and her mouth puckered – an ugly expression that resembled a cat's arse.

"What the hell is going on, Alex?"

Now that they were face-to-face, Jamie could see that Alex looked different. Her hair was long and highlighted, she was tanned, and her make-up was applied more thickly than usual. Only the dark circles under her eyes didn't fit with her general air of someone who had only recently been on holiday.

Alex picked up on Jamie's stare. "What do you think of the new look? I've been getting some remodelling tips." She proudly flapped, primped and stroked her ponytail over the front of her shoulder. "I've gone for
extensions and a blonde vibe. Like it?"

"It's different – but if I'm honest, for someone who's only just come back from holiday, you look done in. Or hung over? One of the two."

"Why aren't you having a drink with me? What's wrong with you? Is it Lent or something?" Alex gurned absurdly at her own joke, looking to Darren to join her in the jocularity. He wasn't listening.

"I'm not here for a social visit. Why did you meet up with Sarah?"

"Sarah?"

"Yes, Sarah. How is it that you've started cosying up to her after all this time?"

"Cosying up?" Alex screwed up her nose at Jamie. "That's a very immature term to use. Get over yourself."

"I'm not here on a whim, Alex," Jamie told her. "I have a very good reason for asking. I need to know what Sarah's been up to."

Alex was characteristically oblivious to Jamie's infuriation. To the contrary, she was bouncing with enthusiasm – outrageously excited to inform Jamie of her recent rendezvous with Sarah. It emerged that Alex had no more to add than what she had already related on the phone. She wittered on about what a fantastic time she'd had in Brighton, and that she'd even got to meet a couple of 'new' friends through Sarah.

Alex's visit to Brighton appeared to be nothing more than a casual outing between two old friends. It was also apparent that Alex knew nothing about Sarah's recent contact with Jamie, or about her letter. What still concerned Jamie, however, was that Alex obviously viewed Sarah from a totally different perspective. The extent of her grasp of the facts, or rather lack of them, became apparent during the conversation.

"I nearly forgot," Alex said. "You never told me about the outcome with the key fob. Did you ever discover who returned your keys?" She swirled the ice-cubes in her brandy and Coke with the straw. "I've already done my detective work. Darren couldn't tell me anything. Apparently, it was a one-night temp working at the bar that night. He was given the keys and handed them over to Darren at the end of the night shift." She sucked her drink through the straw, self-satisfied.

"Since you've asked," said Jamie, "I did find out who it was."

"Oh?"

"It was all Sarah's handiwork, actually." Jamie was keen to see how Alex would react.

The straw dropped from Alex's lips. "*Really*?" Her eyes flickered. "Why didn't you tell me?" Then she added, after brief contemplation, "Actually, why didn't Sarah tell me? She had plenty of opportunities to do so. I was with her for two days."

"And you are more upset by the fact that snide Sarah didn't trust you? More upset by *that* than my feelings? Do you care at all for how I feel about this, Alexandra?" Jamie stepped off her stool. "Lesson number one, Alex. Never, *ever* allow yourself to be hoodwinked into a false sense of security with Sarah Ekstein – she's a snake in the grass and ready to strike. Trust me, you can't rely on her."

"Why didn't she just call you, instead of playing hide and seek with your keys? Why did she do that?" Alex stood too, ready to follow Jamie. "What did she want?"

"Don't bother getting up. You don't need to follow me out. I'm going home."

"What? You haven't told me anything. What *exactly* has Sarah done?"

"Basically, Sarah is hell-bent on causing trouble and she is just too shit-scared to be open and transparent with you about it."

"So, what's happened?" Alex was defensive – protective, even.

Jamie folded her arms. "Are you asking because you are concerned for *me*, or because you are upset that your buddy, Sarah, didn't trust you enough to keep you informed?" Jamie looked Alex squarely in the eyes.

Alex said nothing – a rare event. She was obviously mulling things over.

"Alex." Jamie was firm. "The fact you even need to consider my question speaks volumes." She pulled her car keys from her pocket. "See you around sometime. I'm out of here."

"Really? Seriously...?" Alex hardened, ready to strike back. "You've told me nothing to convince me I should do or have done anything differently."

"If you must know," Jamie said, "why don't you ask Sarah yourself? Get her perspective on why I am so goddamn livid?"

On the brink of leaving, Jamie added, "I'd give anything to be a fly on the wall for that conversation – assuming, that is, that you haven't totally switched your allegiance by then."

Alex took a couple of seconds to think. "Jamie – what's with all this cryptic shite? Are you going to credit me with any trust and integrity? Whatever's happened with you and Sarah, it's obvious you have no plans to tell *me* about it. No. Sod off, Jamie – I'm not playing guessing games with you. Who do you think you are? My mother?" She flung her blonde extensions obstreperously back over her shoulder and stood upright.

"You have no idea, do you?" Jamie said categorically. "There is a great deal of wisdom in that old adage to keep your friends close and your enemies closer."

"There you go again, Jamie. Why does everything have to turn into such a crisis with you? You are *so* cynical. If you must know, it's Sarah's great advice that's prompted my mini make-over. Nothing that Sarah said or did while I was in Brighton has given me the slightest reason to believe she is anything but kind, generous and, if you want my honest opinion, misunderstood."

"Misunderstood?" Jamie said. "*Me*? Cynical?" She let out a disbelieving snort.

Alex stood, saying nothing. Right or wrong, she wasn't in the habit of backing down.

"Right now, Alex…" Jamie wasn't going to listen to any more. "I'm only looking out for myself. Believe me, I've got bloody good reasons to cover my back where Sarah is concerned. I suggest you think very carefully before you jeopardise my friendship."

"Just stop being such a drama queen for once in your life," Alex threw back.

"Your sycophantic kowtowing is pretty sickening, Alex. Choose your friends wisely!" Jamie warned.

"Why don't you just put it all behind you? You have the perfect opportunity to forgive and forget and be grown up about this."

Jamie couldn't bring herself to even respond. She left. And as she drove home, she wondered if any of what had just been said had even breached Alex's notoriously thick skin.

CHAPTER 22

Thursday lunchtime came and went. Jamie's resolution to give her sister some cool-down time was short-lived. Over the last three days, she had sent her sister a few messages and a couple of voicemails. Linda hadn't replied to any of them.

Jamie knew that the current week was an especially full and busy one for her sister. She prayed that Linda's lack of contact was down to her simply having limited time. Trying to convince herself of this, though, was little comfort.

Already struggling on three nights of virtually no sleep herself, Jamie was now feeling quite ill with worry. Her head was crammed with all manner of explanations for Linda's lack of response – all of them negative.

Before leaving work to go home, she phoned Kate.

*****

Kate had just finished her afternoon shift tending the bar and was about to hand over to Richard. Hearing her phone's ringtone, she threw a tea towel over her shoulder. "It's Jamie," she told Richard, and took the call.

Richard clapped his hands together with a thrilled little squeal. He stuck both thumbs up approvingly.

"Shh!" Kate mouthed, slapping at the air a couple

of times to stop him interrupting. She turned her back to him for privacy.

"Jamie," Kate said eventually after hearing about Jamie's most recent incident with Alex. "If you can't wait until Saturday, I could meet you tomorrow at seven-ish, if you're anywhere near Alchemy at that time? I'll be in between shifts, and have arranged to meet someone later, but I'll have a little over an hour before then. Is that any good? It gives us a bit of time to make a start on thrashing out a modus operandi for your sister – if you want to, that is?"

"I would *so* much appreciate that, Kate," Jamie sighed.

Kate could hear the relief in her voice.

"I'm getting myself completely screwed up about all this. Are you sure you've got the time?"

"Of course I have. I wouldn't have offered if I didn't. But, listen, if I'm not there when you arrive, just wait for me. I shouldn't be too long. I'll let Richard know to look out for you."

"No problem."

"And we can still keep Saturday as planned if you want – if Linda hasn't contacted you by then. I'm worried about you. I can hear it in your voice, Jamie. You sound anxious and stressed."

"I wish I could see through to the conclusion with such calm optimism."

"Please let me know when you're home safe, okay?"

"See you tomorrow." Jamie sounded distracted.

"Positive thinking. Have faith," Kate said. "Call me." She put her phone back in her rucksack.

"This is all coming along very nicely," Richard said excitedly.

"Whatever you are thinking, Richard Walker, don't!" Kate warned, allowing a little chink of fun to filter through her serious message.

"Really? Ha! I could smell the aroma of a Sapphic romance blossoming from day one, sweetie."

Kate reacted sharply. "You and I might be friends, Richard, but while you are under the roof of this building, I am your boss. Your opinions about my personal life are neither appropriate nor welcome."

Richard looked stunned.

"And being gay doesn't give you special permission to play at being my agony uncle."

Richard's chin dropped. His eyes almost closed, and he glared at Kate. "Ouch! I certainly felt *that* bitch-slap well below the belt." He leant forward with both hands on the back of a chair. "That's fine with me, Kate, if that's the way you want to play it." He looked like he'd just sucked on lemons. "But since when has my offering an opinion ever bothered you before?" He snatched up a cocktail menu off the table – for no other purpose, it appeared, than dramatic effect. "If you don't want me to get involved, don't cross boundaries and don't move goalposts. You've *always* told me about your problems, and what's going on, Kathryn. Now, when it suits you not to, you shut me down. Just don't expect me, in future, to still be your emotional therapist at the drop of a hat. You can't have it both ways. That's not the way friendships work." He stood upright, retaining his dignity. "Anyway," he added, pushing his fingers through his hair over his ear, "I obviously can't stop here lollygagging, I've got work to do – mein Führer!"

"Oh, crikey." Kate realised how she must have sounded.

Richard had already sashayed to the opposite end of the bar.

Kate followed. "Wait, Rich," she called after him. "That was completely uncalled-for. I'm sorry. Please forgive me. I've had a lot on over the last few days – I didn't mean to be such a cow, and you *are* more to me than just a colleague, you know you are."

Richard stood with his back to Kate, then gradually turned around. "Trust me – I'm feeling the pain of your stress right now. Someone must have poked a stick into your cage. You've *never* spoken to me like that before – *ever*!" Richard was wide-eyed, a little frown attempting to furrow his botoxed brow. But then a wide, consoling grin gradually spread across his face. "Come here, you," he beckoned eagerly, gliding forward to meet her halfway. "Come and get a Ricky-hug." He moved in and enveloped Kate in his muscular arms for a long, ungrudging hug. "And if you don't want to tell Uncle Richard all about it, I'll

understand. But you do know –" he kissed the top of her head "– that I'll find a way of dragging it out of you at some point, sooner or
later."

Kate smiled into Richard's shoulder. "Look, Rich, I'm meeting Jamie here tomorrow night at seven." She hoisted her rucksack on to her back. "If I'm still not back when she arrives, make her welcome – look after her, okay?"

Richard looked impish.

"And be nice," Kate warned. "She's had a tough time recently."

"Absolutely!" Richard saluted. "Any friend of yours…"

"Anyway, I've got a hot date tonight, if you must know. I need to go home and get myself looking beautiful."

"You kept that one quiet, you minx! Have fun. Be good."

But Kate was worried about Jamie. Their phone call had made it obvious that she was really struggling. Kate realised that she had to step up into pole position if she was going to be any kind of worthwhile, meaningful support to her new friend.

CHAPTER 23

Jamie's phone call to Kate certainly made her feel a little better, but she needed time to cool off. She was still incensed by Alex. Instead of driving straight home, she took a convoluted route around her neighbourhood, eventually circumnavigating Hyde Park. The detour was longer than it needed to be, and Jamie found that the time she was wasting was not particularly helpful, or safe. Her muddled-up anger was getting in the way of her concentration and road sense.

She arrived home wiped out, frustrated and still feeling angry. In the basement parking lot, she sat in her car and checked her phone again, hoping for some word from Linda. "Come on, Linny, please call." Her phone battery was close to critical, so instead of making a call, she sent Linda a short message: *'I love you, sis. Call me when you're ready x'*.

Leaving her jacket on the driver's seat, Jamie inhaled a deep breath. She didn't yet feel any more relaxed, and her black mood was compounded by the sticky heat of the evening. She couldn't face being boxed in by four walls and a night of tossing and turning into the early hours.

Her head was starting to ache. She needed to shake it off before it became a migraine. Hyde Park was only minutes away. What she needed was a stroll in the open air across the park amongst the trees – on a route she knew like an old friend.

As she left her building, she was aware of the rumble of a motorcycle somewhere further up the road. Once outside into the night, she turned left but was then blinded by the ferocious blue-white glare of a parked car's full-beam headlights.

"Sort it out!" Jamie averted her squinting eyes as the piercing beam sent a stab of pain to her already aching head. As she approached the car, the muffled boom of loud, bass-heavy music pulsated from within. The driver's-side window was pimped with opaque, black-tinted glass.

"Turn off the damned lights, arsehole," Jamie muttered as she passed the driver's door. She sped up to reach the shelter of the darkness, a few feet ahead and beyond the glare from the vehicle. But the car pulled off and drove away.

After several minutes, spots of light rain started to fall. It was too dark to gauge from the clouds whether it was setting in for the night. Even without a coat, she was committed to completing her head-cleansing stroll, but the uncertain weather caused her to divert from her original plan. Instead, she decided to take a shorter, circular walk that cut across Grosvenor Square Garden and round the block back to home.

The shower stopped. The only evidence that it had ever started was the distinctive post-rain cocktail of ozone and nitrates – a pungent, earthy smell, now lingering in the air.

Jamie liked the quaintness of this particular street: its narrowness, which made it unsuitable for most modern transport, the original Victorian lamp-posts still preserved and positioned further apart, allowing for blissful little pockets of darkness in between. Jamie was in heaven – basking in an oasis of peaceful serenity amidst her recent chaos.

As she continued, all she could hear was the soothing, steady tick-tick of her boots on the pavement. The air was, at last, a little cooler. Jamie's headache was subsiding.

But then the silence was fractured by a dull, thumping noise some distance away. As it grew louder, she realised the interruption was emanating from a car's speakers. Finally it cruised by, slowing down as it drew parallel to Jamie, presumably searching for a place to park, or simply lost within foreign surroundings.

Then Jamie recognised the opaque windows: it was the same car that had been outside her apartment earlier. The reverb of the heavy bass was familiarly unpleasant. Were there *any* places left in the world where a person could experience absolute, uncontaminated silence?

Thankfully, the car moved on, and the music stopped. The driver manoeuvred into a vacant space several cars away, further up the road. For the second time that night, Jamie walked past the parked car. This time she was curious. What kind of person would have so little respect for the neighbourhood – polluting the street with such a God-awful din?

As Jamie passed, the driver within stirred, and the far-side window slowly opened. The passenger seat appeared to be empty. The driver leant across the vacant seat to attract Jamie's attention. It was too dark to see clearly. Jamie's instant reaction was to hang back a bit, assuming she was about to be asked for directions. She leant down, peering through the partially open window, expecting to be spoken to. But the driver said nothing, and the window slid back up.

Realising her misunderstanding, Jamie moved away. Already, the walk had worked its magic and blown away the cobwebs. She picked up her pace – she was ready to get home and try to get some much-needed sleep.

Behind her, a car door clicked open then clunked shut. There followed the heavy footfall of metal-heeled shoes click-scuffing on the tarmac. The pace was purposeful, the destination unclear.

"Jamie!" A voice barked, a command to a disobedient dog to come to heel.

Jamie peered behind her into the shadows. On the evidence of just one word, she was unable to recognise the voice. The strained gruffness was unidentifiable. The footsteps slowed down. Jamie watched the dark figure move towards her, weaving needlessly between parked vehicles.

"You arrived home very late tonight, Miss Barker – for a school night."

At that point, Jamie was in no doubt who the mystery driver was.

Carl Silverton was striding down the middle of the narrow road towards Jamie, still intermittently obscured as he walked behind each of the stationary cars. To Jamie's ears, the sound of his steps had taken on a very different feel. Somehow, knowing they belonged to *him* made all the difference. Silverton, still in the road, finally got to where Jamie was standing. They were now separated by a parked Range Rover. This barrier created by this substantial chunk of metal between them was ephemeral. Silverton sauntered past the driver's door of the Range Rover and came around in front of the vehicle. He stepped onto the pavement and stood to face Jamie, just a car length away. His fingers were casually pushed into his trouser pockets, legs straight, feet hip-distance apart – a stance that Jamie knew well.

Though she had no immediate reason to, Jamie felt edgy.

"Don't you know?" Silverton warned. "It's dangerous for a girl to be walking the streets all alone at night."

Jamie answered with a feeble, nervous laugh. "It's safe as houses round here..." She was figuring out how to quickly conclude this unexpected encounter. "We aren't living in Victorian London any more, Carl."

"Mr Silverton – to you," he corrected, with more than a hint of venom. "That privilege is afforded only to my friends, or for those with whom I have a *professional* relationship."

Jamie didn't understand. Which of the two categories – if not the latter – did *she* fit into? But this was neither the time nor place to find out. She shuffled very slightly from one foot to the other.

Silverton took a couple of steps forward. He removed a packet of cigarettes from the breast pocket on his shirt. He used his mouth to pull one from the box, then lit it, taking in a long, deep drag, filling his lungs to capacity. The strike of the match and glow of the inhalation illuminated his sallow face. His hand trembled. He swallowed and released the smoke slowly through his nostrils.

Now Jamie could see his features clearly. His face glistened with the sheen of perspiration, but his eyes were empty. He looked haunted. This looked like a man battling the effects of substance abuse.

Jamie's heart-rate quickened. Her physical response was shockingly instant, and sickeningly familiar. "Is this an accidental or calculated meeting, Mr Silverton?" She was trying her best to sound calm, but knew she was failing miserably. She hoped Silverton was too wasted to notice.

Silverton stood swaying very slightly, blinking with repressed energy.

"What do you want?" The question seemed spineless, tenuous.

Silverton just stood leering and dragged on his cigarette.

Jamie was now convinced that his presence here, right now, was no coincidence. But why had he come? She could only imagine he had a score to settle. This thought heightened her already escalating anxiety.

"Haven't I warned you before, Ms Barker?" He threw his fag butt at her feet – an act of defiance. "There are some bad people out there. Some *very* bad people."

Jamie didn't need to hear any more. Too much of what she was seeing and hearing was reliving her previous nightmare. She mustered the mettle to take control. "I need to go..." She faltered, adding, "I'm meeting my sister, actually." Even as she spoke, Jamie knew that she sounded wretchedly unconvincing.

Silverton was motionless, flaunting his dominance.

Jamie acted on her chance to go – to get past him, and get the hell out of the place. At least this time, she was on *her* turf, and out in the open: a small advantage.

As Jamie moved forwards, her path was flagrantly blocked as Silverton crouched into a bizarre goalkeeper's stance. His legs were bent, his arms and fingers fully outstretched to either side of him. Jamie bobbed from left to right, like some over-enthusiastic basketball player trying to wrong-foot the other team. Barely exerting any effort, Silverton countered and sidestepped, ready to intercept and block her every move – testing her.

"Leaving me so soon?" he taunted. "This is becoming a habit, Jamie. How depressing. You're giving me quite a complex."

"I need to go – my sister is waiting for me," Jamie blabbed.

Propelled on a wave of panic, she barged past Carl and ran. Her refuge would be Shepherd's Place: a narrow cut-through further up the road off Brook Street. The alleyway was only about 250 feet long, and the far end merged at a T-junction, to Lees Place. From here, she would have one of two options – head left or right, to secure her escape.

Now committed, Jamie continued running hell for leather, only stopping when she had finally left Brook Street and successfully escaped around the corner to Shepherd's Place. Here, Jamie had no choice but to stop; she was physically incapable of taking another step. She tucked herself into the darkest spot that she could find, in a shadow cast by the wall of an adjoining building. Clasping at the pain in her chest, she gasped for breath, nearly at the point of retching. After a few moments, although her chest was still tight, her pulse and breathing had calmed a little. But time was deceptive. The dash to reach her sanctuary had seemed interminably longer than the time it actually took. She skulked in the shadows, cowed by a chilling silence.

Turning her head slightly, Jamie strained to listen past the everyday, peripheral sounds of the night. A motorcycle cruised by along Brook Street. It slowed down, then moved on, but she couldn't hear footsteps any longer.

Where was Silverton now? Jamie hadn't formulated a plan for what to do if he followed her. Someone needed to know where she was. She pulled the phone from her pocket. Her battery was no longer critical – it was lifeless. She stifled a cry of panic in her throat and froze. In the distance she heard the motorcycle again.

Then the slow, click-scuff of metal-heeled shoes resumed. Their exact proximity was unclear, but they were close. Too close. It didn't make sense. Jamie hadn't heard Silverton follow her. Surely she would have heard those distinct footsteps pounding the street after her?

The footsteps stopped.

Silence again.

Jamie stood, unyielding. Waiting. Listening. Her breathing was erratic and her blood was coursing through her veins. She needed to push herself further into the shadows. She stepped back, her back against the wall, forcing herself into the shadows as far she could possibly go. But as she stepped back, the click of her own boot-heels, to her ears, cracked like a gunshot.

Fuck.

Silverton had been following the direction of her steps; the sound of his footsteps resumed, this time gathering pace. Suddenly, he lurched forward from out of the gloom like a deranged Jack-in-the-box and lodged both palms flat on the wall, either side of Jamie. She was securely pinned – lasciviously caged.

A newly lit cigarette hung from the corner of his mouth, the heat of its burning tip almost touching Jamie's cheek. She could smell Silverton's sour breath.

"Perfect timing," his voice rasped.

Keeping one hand on the wall, Carl leered down at Jamie. His face twisted into a rictus. His stare penetrated, but his eyes were lifeless. His other hand very gradually slid down to the front of his trousers, where his fingers lingered. His eyes raked the full length of her body.

Jamie swallowed, unable to move and unable to bring herself to look down at his hand. She had to maintain contact with the viper's glare. She needed to understand what his eyes were telling her.

Then Silverton put his hand into his trouser pocket.

He pulled something out. It was only when he had brought the object up to eye level that Jamie realised it was a scrappy sheet of folded paper. The sense of relief was massive.

But Silverton wasn't finished. He moved his grip several times around the sheet, opening and closing his hand, to mould a roughly scrunched-up cylinder. Then he offered it up to his cigarette – which was now held between his front teeth. After several drags, the paper in his hand had caught light and was burning freely.

Just as he was on the point of burning his fingers, Silverton let the ashen remains drop to the floor. He ground the ball of his foot over the top of it. All the while, his inscrutable eyes were fixed on Jamie. He eventually relaxed the one remaining arm still holding him to the wall. "Our contract." He pointed to the charred remains on the ground. "Now null and fucking void, you ugly, devious bitch." He grabbed Jamie's arm.

She yelped, more from shock than pain. Jamie then got a brief glimpse of the man behind this mask. It was evident that this was just the reaction he wanted. He was enjoying her pain. She watched his jaw muscles flex through gritted teeth. Jamie tried to pull herself free, but his grip became tighter as he pulled her out of the shadows.

"Why don't we go for a walk together and have a little chat with your sister? I feel the need to have a bit of quality time with her. You being there too will make it extra special." He wiped the back of his other hand across his mouth and scratched his crotch.

Jamie mind was free-falling into a tail-spin; her reason was momentarily numbed. Then something within her reacted. With immense force, using all the strength within her, Jamie brought her knee up between Silverton's legs. The full force of the impact was evident as he cried out and doubled over.

Now free, Jamie bolted. Once she reached the end of Shepherd's Place, the adjoining T-junction was her security.

About halfway down the alleyway, Jamie stopped. The adjoining wall was brightening, lit up by the beam of an approaching headlight.

There was a motorbike crawling around the corner into the far end of the street. It stopped, motor idling, blocking the exit where Jamie was aiming her escape. The rider didn't get off. Even with the echo from the high walls of the buildings on either side, Jamie could tell that this was not the silky-smooth purr of a Triumph triple. This wasn't Gavin's bike. For a brief spell, when Jamie had first heard the engine, her immediate prayer was that it might be so. No. This rider's style was distinct. Every few seconds, he would aggressively and pointlessly rev the throttle – a typical engine-ignorant, boy-racer technique. She realised this engine was more immediately familiar; she had heard the same bike passing nearby a few times this very evening.

But then, a different panic set in. Silverton must have enlisted an accomplice.

The only escape routes, at either end of the narrow road, had now been sealed. Jamie was the fly, caught in the carefully constructed web. Her response was immediate: unthinking. Jamie took a breath and screamed, as loud, as long and as piercingly as she'd ever screamed in her life.

Then, in reaction, the predators both moved towards her – closing in on their prey.

CHAPTER 24

Speed was clearly on the side of the motorcycle.

Silverton had backed off and halted his pursuit. He was now observing, presumably satisfied that the biker would reach Jamie before he did.

Jamie's attention switched to that which presented the most immediate and impending threat. The headlight was gradually edging nearer, but the pace lacked urgency. The bike was crawling along, barely moving. It appeared that the rider was holding back. Watching – waiting for the right time to pounce?

Jamie was engulfed by the hollow sense of time standing still. The reality of this living hell meant there was no point in running. Where would she go? Glancing back, she was no longer able to see Carl. Where had he crept off to now?

The bike unexpectedly accelerated towards Jamie, pulling up right next to her. The rider was now visible – he was clad from head to toe in black leathers and a black, full-face helmet. A gloved hand lifted the visor, face still partially hidden.

"Get on…"

Jamie was cautious. She didn't respond right away.

"Jamie? It's Kate. Get on!"

"Kate?" Sick wave of relief, Jamie climbed on to the back of the bike.

Kate accelerated past the entrance where Jamie had last seen Silverton. "Go left," Jamie called over her shoulder, knowing that Silverton had parked his car on the right, further down Brook Street. She continued to call out instructions, telling her where to turn, intending to take a round-about, back-street route to safety. She wasn't going to risk being followed again.

Several twists and turns later, Kate stopped the bike and pivoted around. "This is as far as I'm going. You're not wearing a helmet. I've already paid off one parking fine for you," she joked. "I'm not about to risk losing my driver's licence as well."

Jamie obediently got off the bike. She had no idea how much of her ordeal Kate had witnessed. Did she realise how serious it was?

"You didn't call me," Kate explained. "I asked you to, as soon as you got home, and I was worried when I didn't hear from you." She kicked down the side-stand, dismounted and removed her helmet, carefully balancing it on the seat of the bike. "I'd swear I saw you earlier, walking along the road, just outside your car park," she said. "I wasn't sure to begin with. It was hard to make out clearly and I was too far away."

Jamie had her arms wrapped around herself.

"Jamie, you're shaking like a leaf, woman." Kate moved forward and held firmly onto either side of her shoulders, trying to steady and reassure her. "That *was* you running along the street just now, wasn't it?"

Jamie nodded. She was still hugging her body, trying to stop her tremor.

"I *thought* it was you. Damn it, I should have gone

with my instinct earlier." Kate unbuckled and unzipped her leather jacket and put it round Jamie's shoulders. "Who was that man with you just now?"

"Shit, shit, shit!" Jamie's final utterance came with a sharp punch to her thigh.

Kate took a circumspect step away.

"This is all such a sodding, shitty mess, Kate…" Jamie dissolved into tears.

"Listen, we're not that far from yours. I'll park up my bike and come back for it later. You aren't going home on your own tonight. What's happened?"

"Can we just get home first?" Jamie pleaded.

"Of course we can. Let's get you home right now."

*****

Back at Jamie's flat, Kate took charge of providing hot, sweet tea.

"After seeing how fragile you were at Alchemy earlier, I had already decided to call you back after work and check up on you. You said you would call when you got home. I did text you a few times, but you never replied and I wasn't able to leave voice messages." Kate put tea in the pot and got a couple of mugs from the cupboard.

"I'm really sorry I didn't call you. It completely slipped my mind. My charge was low, and my first thought was that I needed to message Linda, before

my phone battery died," Jamie said, flopping down onto her
sofa. "Then I went to get some air."

"That explains it."

"I didn't go home right away," Jamie said. "I went for a drive around the block for a while – to clear my head."

"When you didn't answer your door, I thought I'd hang around for a while. I rode around on the Harley for a bit – I did wonder if you'd maybe gone for a walk," Kate said. "It was lucky I spotted you when I did. Who was that man?"

"That scumbag was an ex-client – Carl Silverton."

"Scumbag?" Kate came and sat next to Jamie on the sofa. "Well, now is as good a time as any to tell me about this scumbag." She handed Jamie the tea. "Two sugars."

Jamie put Kate fully in the picture with everything about Carl Silverton, including the details of what had happened at his house the day Linda had intervened.

"His actions tonight –" she said at last. "He was not a happy bunny. A bully with a score to settle." She stirred a slow figure of eight with her spoon in her tea.

"Jamie, the man's dangerous. He sounds like a psycho – the kind of creepy weirdo you find yourself reading about in the morning paper. I didn't imagine it, then? Did I see him trying to pull you away from the wall? I thought at first that I couldn't be seeing clearly. It was difficult enough in the dark, with you being so far away, but you know when you see something that your brain doesn't want to compute? I kind of did that for a bit. Once I recognised that it might be you, I drove back round to the alleyway. I could see a scuffle going on. My God, I'm *so* glad I took the decision to come back and check. I had no idea it was so serious. What was he saying and doing? What did he want?"

"Trying to make me take him to my sister," Jamie explained.

"Take him to Linda? Why? What do you mean?"

"I was flustered. I gave him some idiotic smokescreen that I was going to meet Linda. It was a crap excuse, but it was the first thing I thought of at the time." Jamie explained further – about Silverton's relationship with John Hunter, and the recent disclosure of Linda's legal involvement.

"Crikey, Jamie, I'm *so* glad I came back." Kate put her cup down. "Oh God, look at me, I'm shaking now." She sat on her hands. "Did he hurt you?"

"No. No, he didn't hurt me. He's obviously thoroughly pissed about Linda's involvement with his lawyer-friend." Jamie put her cup down, too. "And it looks like the contract for the property renovation is dead in the water. Silverton performed a private pyrotechnic show, just to clarify any misunderstanding."

Kate looked puzzled. "Are you *really* that bothered about the contract?"

"No. You're right. Linda was exactly of that same opinion. Anyway, it's no longer just about me." Jamie pinched the bridge of her nose. "He's turned it into something personal. Linda is involved now, and I'm not prepared to compromise her any more than she is already."

"You need to let Linda know what's happened, Jamie. You should call the police. You have no idea if this man is planning to rear his head again. You and Linda are potentially in danger. The police need to know about this."

Jamie balked at the idea.

"He physically touched you, Jamie, with intent to – " She shook her head. "It doesn't even bear thinking about. You're being irresponsible if you don't. If *you* don't call the police as the victim of an assault, then I'm ringing right now as a witness." She got her phone out of her jacket pocket. "I'm serious, Jamie," she scowled, to emphasise the gravity of her intent.

*****

The next few hours did not go as Jamie had planned. She reluctantly took Kate's advice. At gone two in the morning, rather than being tucked up in bed, she was escorting an efficient WPC and her ebullient counterpart, fresh out of police academy, out through her front door.

“So you’re not going to press charges?” Kate said, as Jamie returned to the lounge. “Is that wise?”

“I never said I intended to press charges. But at least it’s officially on record if Silverton tries anything again.”

Kate looked agitated. “I’m not sure that your decision was the right one, but it won’t do any good to argue the point.”

“I wish Linny was here,” Jamie said flatly. “I’m missing her.”

“I know you are.” Kate gave Jamie a hug. “You need to sleep now, though, yes?”

Jamie nodded. “Will you stay too?”

“I hoped you’d say that.” Kate seemed relieved. “I am so tired. The thought of driving home is not appealing right now. You must be exhausted, too, after what you’ve been through today.”

They crossed the lounge towards their respective rooms. Jamie stopped. “Kate? Don’t take this the wrong way,” She was apologetic. “But would you mind bivouacking down with me tonight? I really don’t want to sleep alone, and I feel like I need the company.” She rubbed her forehead, anticipating a rebuff.

“Take it the wrong way? I’ve cut short my date for you. It could be the only action I’m getting tonight,” Kate said with a grin.

“What?” Jamie’s reaction was pure, off-guard embarrassment. She certainly hadn’t expected *that* as an answer, and neither had she banked on Kate's humour cutting quite so far down to the bone. To make such a joke, it was plain that Kate had no idea how Jamie felt about her. Kate's harmless, witty little quip had delivered quite a bruising blow.

"That was a stupid thing to say, Jamie – a crass and tactless joke. I'm sorry."

This pitying apology only made things worse. "Let's forget it, okay? I know you didn't mean anything by it. We're both tired and I'm still fretting about Linda." The deep ache within Jamie jolted her into acknowledging that her sense of loss was not only about Linda. "Sleep well, okay?" She walked to her bedroom, adding, "And thank you again for tonight." She shut the door behind her and closed her eyes.

The timing was crap.

Next morning, the atmosphere was still decidedly difficult. Standing in the kitchen, both women stood politely sipping cups of tea.

Jamie felt she'd just walked on to a film set – at the part when the protagonist wakes up after a drunken night out, nursing a mother of a hangover, only to find a stranger lying naked next to them in bed. She couldn't stomach parting company with Kate on such a tense note, and took a gamble to break the ice, relaying her movie-scene scenario to Kate.

Kate listened, then chuckled. "My God, that's a reassuring injection of humour," she said. "You've just helped to paper over the crack of *my* dim-witted comment last night. I was feeling awful this morning, Jamie."

At least any misunderstandings were now unequivocally quashed; they knew where they both stood.

Standing by Jamie's car, they parted with a peck on the cheek. Kate had declined an offer of a lift to her bike, preferring to walk the short distance.

"By the way," Jamie called from her car, as she slowly crawled alongside Kate.

Walking to match the speed, Kate called back, "What's that?" and cupped her hand to her ear.

"A biker chick," Jamie called, slipping on her Ray-Bans. "You kept that very quiet. Yet more hidden skills?"

"I don't like to reveal all my cards in one hand," Kate called back, a huge grin creasing her face.

"A poker player too, eh? Are there any limits to your talents?"

"You'd better stick around to find out," Kate said. "See you at seven tonight? Don't forget I'm likely to be a few minutes late."

"Sure, no probs."

"And fingers crossed for word from Linda today," Kate added, holding her thumb up to emphasise the good-luck sentiment.

Jamie hit her car horn a couple of times by way of signalling 'over and out', then pulled out towards Canary Wharf and a manic day ahead.

*****

Back at home after work, Jamie showered and changed with a heavy heart. Linda still hadn't been in touch. It had now been five whole days. She'd never left it that long before making contact. The same, Jamie realised, couldn't be said of her track record of reliability. Maybe this time, Linda was giving Jamie a taste of her own medicine?

Jamie walked into Alchemy a little late. Seeing that Richard was on duty, she went straight to the bar. He was talking to the younger, fresh-faced lad who had been there on the afternoon when Jamie had tried to salvage the blind date debacle with Rachel.

Richard greeted Jamie with all the effervescent enthusiasm of a cruise ship entertainment rep. "Well, hello, Jamie. Kate's running a bit late tonight. She's asked me to tell you to wait. She shouldn't be long; she knows you're coming."

"Okay, thanks for that," Jamie replied.

"Drink while you wait, perhaps?" Richard stood, polishing a glass in anticipation. "Should I give her a call to get her moving, perhaps?"

"Erm, no, you're fine. She knows I'm here."

"And what about a drink?" Richard tried again.

"Just tonic with ice and a slice, please." Jamie sat up at the bar. She checked her phone – more through habit than reason. It also provided a convenient foil.

Jamie wasn't feeling sociable and was trying her best to put Richard off from engaging her in small talk.

"No gin in that? Single? Double?" Richard held the ice-filled glass tantalisingly beneath the London Gin shot-dispenser.

"No thanks."

"Are you sure?" Richard shook the glass.

Jamie paused before answering, surprised he was even asking the question. "Yes, I'm sure," she said, staring at him.

"You *sure* you're sure?" he asked again, this time with the glass poised beneath the dispenser, ready to push and release the liquor. He jiggled the glass again, more vigorously than before. The ice chinked enticingly – an incentive for Jamie to change her mind?

His persistence was starting to irritate her. "What's the matter with you, Richard?"

At that, his face fell, his high spirits quashed.

"I've told you already what I want. Tonic, ice, lemon slice. No gin. I don't want any gin, okay? No alcohol! Can I make that any clearer?" Jamie had been unusually firm, but she was satisfied from Richard's expression that her point was at last being heard and understood.

Richard remained remorseful, his attention now caught by something going on behind Jamie. A hand gripped her shoulder. She turned.

"Richard *is* looking after you, I hope, Jamie?" Kate asked doubtfully, glowering at the repentant Richard.

"Oh, Kate…" Jamie realised it must have been the arrival of his boss that had curbed Richard's exuberance. She wondered how much of her ranting Kate had overheard. "Yeah, it's fine, Richard's looking after me..." She was unconvincing but looked at Richard, knowing she was saving face for him. "Look, sorry, Richard." Jamie looked back at Kate. "Of course, he's looking after me. I'm just not in the mood for being cross-examined about what I've ordered to drink."

Richard looked bashfully at Kate, then turned to Jamie. "No, you're absolutely right, Jamie," he cut in. "It's *me* who should be apologising. I was just trying to make a friend of Kate's feel welcome… as instructed," he said pointedly in Kate's direction.

"You're at work, Rich, not entertaining guests at home," Kate said, but she wasn't overly serious. "And I'll have the same as Jamie to drink, please."

Richard looked surprised at the request.

Entertained by this face-off between the two, Jamie wondered if Kate's unlikely choice was to make a point: demonstrating solidarity for Jamie's embarrassing predicament, with a dig at Richard for creating it.

Richard prepared and set down Kate's drink. He mimed a smack on his wrist and mouthed a repentant "sorry" to Kate before scuttling off and making himself busy.

"No harm was done," Jamie said. "Richard only meant well." She called over to Richard. "Thank you for making me welcome, Rich. That was kind."

He responded with a beaming smile and blew Jamie a kiss. He then pointedly stuck his tongue out at Kate before quickly disappearing.

Jamie caught Kate's eye. Both women recognised an unspoken acknowledgement of his cheek, and fundamentally good intentions.

"You've just got to love him," Kate whispered. "But

don't tell him I said that," she added with a wink.

CHAPTER 25

Kate returned to the moment. "So, we've got –" she looked at her watch "– just over an hour and a half. Do you want to stay here or go somewhere else?"

"Have you got another date?"

"If by that you mean a different person, no. This is meet-up number three with Catherine, the same woman."

"Oh." Jamie said. "Getting serious, then?" She realised she didn't actually want to hear the answer, so changed the subject. "Let's stay here. Here's okay with me."

Kate called across to Richard. "Rich, if anyone wants me in the next hour or so, I'm not here, okay?" He doffed an imaginary cap at her in reply.

"This way." Kate led Jamie through the middle of the three back arches. Jamie had never ventured into the inner vaults of the bar. The arch was more like a tunnel. Twelve or so feet long, it was lit by spotlights on either side of the walkway, illuminating the full arch of the tunnel in a soft, orange light. The arch opened into a circular, tiled floor area. Branching off from the circle were three separate seating areas, recessed into the brickwork like igloos: secluded little snugs, all with their own colour-themed array of comfy sofas covered in cushions, huddled around an upturned beer-barrel table. Like the main bar, each barrel was adorned with a flickering, low burning candle.

It was far bigger and went further back than Jamie had imagined. "This place is full of surprises," remarked Jamie, looking all around her at the wonderful surroundings. "I'm half waiting to see Fagin and Oliver Twist huddled round a table, counting out their day's pickings."

"Glad you approve. That's the kind of vibe I was after. When I first saw it, the naturally arched architecture screamed out Hogwarts Castle – you know? The Dungeon of Spells?"

Jamie could see exactly what she meant. She nodded in agreement. "Ingenious!"

Kate led Jamie to the furthest pod. The two women sat, each with their tonic and lime.

Kate cut straight to the point. "Why are you doubting your sister's ability to see sense? She's an intelligent woman."

"She's probably hurting and feeling just horrible," Jamie said. "She must be wondering right now, who can she trust?"

Kate took a couple of sips from her glass and gave the question ample thought. "I know I've only met Linda the once, but it is so obvious she's sound, and she clearly loves you dearly. I'd put money on her doing the right thing. Trust her, Jamie. Trust her to make the right decision, but let her do it in her own time. She'll come round, I'm sure she will."

"And if she doesn't? What kind of timeframe would you put on this?" Jamie asked, still hoping for a magic wand to make everything okay again. "And what about our mum? What the hell do I say to her? My relationship with her hasn't exactly been a bed of roses these past few years."

"Crikey, one step at a time, J.B.," Kate said. "You can't solve everything in one day."

"I guess so," Jamie agreed, but she wanted quick solutions.

"So, tell me more about Alex and Sarah?" Kate held her tonic and lime in both hands.

"What else do you want to know?"

Richard poked his head around the corner, raising his hand up and down at Kate, like a student waiting to be picked by the teacher to answer a question. She gave him a look that told him his presence was not welcome.

"Someone out front is asking for you," said Richard apologetically.

"I didn't want to be disturbed, Richard. Can't it wait?"

"No!" He was adamant.

Attention aroused, both women stared at Richard for clarification.

"No, I mean, they're not asking for *you*, Kate, they're asking for Jamie."

Jamie immediately tensed. "Man or woman?"

But Jamie's pursuer wasn't prepared to wait to be summoned.

"Woman!" The announcement came simultaneously from Richard and from a voice from within the tunnel.

"Process of elimination. I thought I would find you here," the voice said.

Richard cast a forlorn glance at Kate. He had failed to protect Kate's privacy. His authority had been ignored.

A woman emerged from the archway. Jamie leapt up out of her chair and let out a breathless squeal.

"Oh my God," Kate echoed.

"Linny!" Jamie catapulted across to her sister for the longest, tightest hug of her life, not willing to relinquish her grip until she was sure Linda wasn't going to turn around and leave again. She was close to tears.

Linda returned the cuddle.

Richard looked at each woman in turn, hunched his shoulders and opportunely made himself scarce.

Linda looked over Jamie's shoulder and nodded at Kate. "Hello again."

"I think I'm almost as pleased to see you as your sister is."

Linda gradually started to unwrap herself from Jamie's limpet-like embrace. "I take it you have been told what's happened, then?"

Kate nodded, and glanced timidly at Jamie.

"I'm so, so sorry for all this, Lin," Jamie said. "I understand if you're angry."

"We need to talk, Jay," Linda said, gravely.

Hearing those words, Kate stood up. "Please come and sit down, Linda. I've already got plans tonight. I wasn't staying long anyway." She turned to Jamie. "We can still meet up tomorrow night if you want to. Unless, of course, you need to be with your sister?" She looked to Linda for confirmation.

Jamie now wondered who was trying to reassure who.

"That is totally fine with me if you do, J.B.," Kate smiled openly at both Jamie and Linda. "We can meet up again any old time."

Jamie instantly picked up on Linda's fractional lift of the eyebrow on hearing Kate's affectionate 'J.B.' nickname.

"I don't mind you staying, Kate," Jamie said. "You've been amazing these last few days." She then looked to Linda, adding, "If you're okay with that?"

Kate launched in quickly with, "That's a very lovely thing to say, Jamie. But this *really* is none of my business." She was clearly not going to put Linda in the position where she needed to give her consent – willingly or otherwise. "This is a conversation that should only be shared between the two of you." She bent down and gave Jamie a kiss on the cheek. "Call you tomorrow, okay?"

"Thank you, Kate," Linda said.

"Be kind to each other," Kate added before leaving.

*****

Linda needed to read the letter again, this time, *with* Jamie. They went over it together several times – unpicking, dissecting and questioning every sentence.

The emotional untangling that ensued was frank and painful but cathartic.

"You know," Linda said, "I couldn't speak to you over the last few days – actually, I couldn't speak to anyone. I needed time to process everything."

Jamie sat holding Linda's hand, which Linda now held out willingly and without any of the reservation of their last encounter.

"I remember Mum's phone call that awful day. It's still etched on my brain like it had only happened this morning." She spoke slowly, thoughtfully. "When Mum told me Dad had died, she gave no clue whatever that she was trapped in a marriage that was long since over. Totally the opposite. She was inconsolable. I literally dropped everything in New York and got the next available flight back to the UK."

Jamie nodded. She remembered every single event, and every single conversation at the time, unfolding like some horrible bad dream.

"Do *you* know who my biological father is?" Linda asked.

“No idea,” Jamie answered. “All and everything I know is exactly what Dad told me over lunch that day.”

“And you’ve never told Mum about it, or asked her?”

Jamie shook her head.

“Idiotic question,” Linda said. “What on earth *could* you have said or asked, under the circumstances?”

“Indeed,” Jamie agreed, grateful that her sister was now on the same page.

Linda cupped her other hand over Jamie’s. “I’m so, so sorry you’ve had to carry this all these years.” Her eyes filled. “It must have been unbearable.”

“You just do what you have to do, I suppose.”

“But then,” Linda said after a short pause, “I must say, I always did feel... how to put it...? Different.” A droll smile suggested she was trying to lift them from the quagmire. “I mean, look at the pair of us. And I don’t just mean my love of Jimmy Choo stilettos and handbags, versus your passion for pulling engines apart, and murdering furry creatures running across a field with your shotgun.” Linda stopped to reflect a moment. “I’ve always wondered how I inherited this frizzy red mane.” She lifted her hair off her shoulders and let it flop back down. “That wasn’t part of the gene pool – and what’s more, look at your figure and mine. You’ve always been a skinny-Minnie, whereas look at me…” She patted her tummy. “Mum and...”

Linda swallowed, struggling to speak his name. "Mum and *Dad*, they were built like beanpoles, too."

Jamie smiled.

Linda shook her head vigorously, as if exorcising painful reflection. "So what about Mum? I'm going to see her next weekend. How about we go together as a united front and talk to her?"

"You're right," said Jamie. "Things can't possibly stay the same, can they?"

Linda mouthed a "nope".

It was late. The conversation had started to repeat threads that had already been discussed. Linda put her keys on the table and made noises to indicate she was ready for home. But Jamie couldn't let her sister go – not quite yet. She plucked up the courage to confess what had happened with Carl Silverton the night before.

Initially, Linda was furiously protective. This gradually turned into pensive rumination, which finally concluded with a cool, "That vacuous bastard has very foolishly underestimated me."

Jamie watched an uncomfortable tension writhe across her sister's face. Her countenance hardened.

Linda took out a packet of cigarettes from her handbag. "I need a smoke." She stood up, took out her phone and swiped the screen with her thumb. "I won't be long." She walked slowly back through the arch, and she pressed her phone to her ear. "Hi, it's Linda Harper…"

No more than ten minutes later, she returned and sat down. "Carl Silverton has mixed with some very nasty individuals," she said, as if the previous conversation had never been broken. "But he has totally misjudged the loyalty of his little group of cronies."

"What do you mean?"

"Retribution. John Hunter has a very loose tongue and a big mouth. I gather he's angling to plea-bargain then dump everyone else around him in the shit rather than find himself in it on his own."

Linda thought some more, in the way she always did

when weighing up options and solving problems. Jamie had just seen something in her sister's eyes that didn't sit well with her; Linda never promised what she couldn't deliver. "What are you thinking, Linda?"

Linda gave Jamie a hug. "Don't you fret. You don't need to worry about a thing, Half-Pint." She looked at the time. "And I need to go home."

Jamie watched her sister organise herself.

"Your friend Kate…" Linda said as she buttoned up her jacket. "I like her. I like her a lot."

"Me too," Jamie said. "But I need more than just a new close friend in my life, Lin. I need to take a leaf out of her book."

"Oh?"

"It's about time I spread my relationship net a bit further afield. Kate's on a date tonight."

"Maybe her date has some single friends?"

"To be honest with you, I don't know how I feel about meeting one of Kate's love interests."

"Uh-huh?" Linda sympathised, dubiously. "You're right, though. I think you need to move on." She lifted her handbag off the table. "So, you won't be enlisting Alex's help with this next phase then?" she teased.

"Watch it," Jamie laughed.

CHAPTER 26

Jamie woke up earlier than usual, for a Saturday, so took advantage of the 6am start. Before the traffic became heavy enough to break the silence, she was out on the balcony with a coffee and a book. She had given her conversation with Linda some serious thought. Her plan for the day was devoted to pro-activity. There were various jobs and bits and bobs that she'd put off doing for way too long. It was time to put her house in order, in more ways than one.

By 11:30am, the flat was clean (by far the least time-consuming of her chores). The spare room-cum-dumping-ground had been sorted out into neat piles of "keep or throw" clothes, shoes, books, magazines, paperwork and general stuff. The end result: a floor now covered by a sizable square footage of boxes and bin liners. A small skip-hire's worth of get-rid, and a pile of items worth a trip to the charity shop.

Jamie's phone rang.

"Hiya." It was Kate. "How did it all go with Linda after I left?"

"It was okay, thank God. We had a long talk about everything, cleared out a lot of cobwebs. Talking of which, I'm doing a bit of spring-cleaning of my own today, or should that be summer-cleaning? Anyway, the end result is the same. I'm chucking out a load of tat…"

"Good for you!"

"And how was your night last night?" Jamie knew she couldn't really avoid asking.

There was no answer on the other end. The silence was interrupted with mumbling. A conversation was taking place away from the phone – a woman's voice merged with Kate's.

"No need to answer *that* question, then," Jamie interrupted, slightly embarrassed. "The dulcet tones of the morning after, eh?"

"Sorry, what was that?" Kate said. "I was talking to Catherine."

"Oh, nothing much." Jamie found herself babbling self-consciously to fill the gaps in the conversation. "I might just take a leaf out of your book and take a look at a few of those dating apps later today."

Kate didn't answer.

"Kate?"

"About tonight…" Kate began.

"Tonight? That's a good point," said Jamie, pre-empting her. "We don't need to meet up now, do we? I mean, things have been resolved with Linda now. Happy ever after all round."

"Okay," Kate said. The talking in the background continued. "Are you sure?"

"Absolutely!"

Was Kate asking by choice, or because she felt she ought to? Jamie hedged her bets. "Let's keep it open, maybe? See how we're both fixed later?"

"Okay. If not, maybe we'll catch up soon?"

"Yeah, sounds good. Have fun…" Jamie ended the call feeling unreasonably deflated. She knew that Kate wasn't an option, but it didn't stop her feeling flat. "Positive thinking, Jamie Barker," she told herself. She would pick herself up, dust herself down and move on.

Jamie looked around at all her stuff. One of the last items to be boxed was a jacket that she'd pulled out from the depths of her wardrobe. A "worn-only-once" denim jacket, bleach-splashed and patched with tartan. As she shook it and brushed it down, a plan came to fruition. "You need recycling again, my friend."

Where better to start putting herself back out there for new romance, Jamie concluded, than where it had all begun, all those weeks ago? Her next stop that afternoon? Brick Lane. An overdue offer of a coffee date with a certain American sales assistant was on the cards…

*****

It seemed strange loitering outside Contemporary Retro after all this time. First, Jamie did a bit of window shopping to check if the woman was even working there today or, indeed, at all any more. She walked past the shop and casually peered in. On the second sweep of her reconnaissance, Jamie noticed a sign in the door: *Half Day Closing Today at 1pm.* Ten minutes to go, but still no sign of the assistant. Third time lucky: having decided that this patrol would be her last, she spotted the woman returning from the back of the shop.

Jamie timed her move carefully. She moseyed in and poked about through a rack of clothes, listening to the delicious Texan drawl as a sale was finalised with the only other person in the shop. He left, and, seconds later, the assistant pounced to turn off the mix of 70s and 80s tunes that had been playing to the customers. Instead, the bohemian sound of Doria Roberts blared from the speakers. Singing along at the top of her voice, the Texan woman started tidying up. She didn't realise Jamie was even there. Now, just when Jamie wanted to get her attention, the music was so loud that even heavy steps and throat-clearing had no effect. Jamie was right next to the till when the woman eventually turned with a start.

She turned down the music. "Why, hello there, ma'am. Pardon me." She put down the things she'd gathered up. "I didn't hear you coming in."

Jamie pointed somewhere above her head at hidden speakers. "Doria Roberts – great album." She lifted her chin towards the ceiling, hoping the genre of music was not just coincidence.

The assistant clicked off the tunes. Her head tipped slightly to one side. "Erm, yeah. She's great, isn't she?" There was uncertainty in her voice. "So, is there anything I can help you with? We're about to close." She glanced at her watch.

Jamie took the folded denim jacket that she'd carried in over her forearm and opened it out to present it. "I've brought this in," she said. "I've only worn it once."

The sales assistant looked more closely at the jacket, then scrutinised Jamie. "Well, hello again. Everything all right with your purchase, ma'am? It was a good few weeks ago when you bought this item, as I recall. And I'm afraid we don't do refunds on our stock."

"Oh!" This was difficult. Jamie hadn't anticipated that Ms Ripley would actually remember her. What made it even more awkward was that she'd misunderstood Jamie's reason for returning the jacket. "No, no, the jacket's fine, thanks." Since she hadn't planned her next move, she just kept talking. "You must know your stock intimately to remember that long ago?"

"It's quite a distinctive item, ma'am," she said, pointing to one particular badge on the lapel. "That jacket belonged to me."

It was the denim jacket she remembered, rather than the customer. Jamie's original plan to hand it back for resale now seemed redundant. But Jamie had nothing to lose, so she went straight for the jugular. "I realise this might sound odd, and if I've misread this, I'm going to look like a right numpty."

The woman's face was a mixture of amused confusion.

Jamie just kept going anyway. "Do you drink coffee?"

The woman's eyebrows lifted. "Pardon me?" She spoke calmly.

"Can I take you for a cup of coffee, maybe?"

Totally out of the blue, her response was disarmingly direct. "Are you hitting on me?"

"No, no, I..." Jamie instantly retreated.

The woman's eyes opened, her nose wrinkled. "Do I *look* gay?" She looked disgusted and sounded angry.

That was all the response Jamie needed. She realised her disastrous faux pas and she couldn't take it back.

"Oh no, this is so embarrassing," she said. "It's my mistake. Please accept my apology."

"I can't believe your nerve," the woman continued, solemnly.

"Look, I think I should just go –" Jamie turned to leave. She just wanted to get away.

The background music was back on again but this time, to the sweet strain of K.D. Lang's 'Constant Craving'. The satire of the track was almost laughable.

"Hey?" the woman called after Jamie. "As you're headed that way, you can stick this up on the inside of the door as you leave." She took something from beneath the counter.

The odd request added to the whirlwind of confusion and Jamie, on autopilot, found herself politely doing what she was asked. She reached out to take a brightly coloured flyer, but the assistant didn't let it go. It was just for a few seconds, but a few seconds too long. The woman leant in close across the counter. Whatever the intention, her actions felt uncouth and ill-judged.

Jamie pulled back.

The woman threw her head back to let out a deep, husky laugh. "Why, I'd love to come join you for coffee, Jamie Barker."

Jamie recoiled, reminded of Carl Silverton. How did she know her name?

"Forgive me. I'm still getting to grips with your quaint sense of humour over on this side of the pond." The woman was still chuckling to herself. "Hey, look. I apologise for kidding around on you just now. I was just having a bit of fun… And for your information –" she was unable to hide her delight "– I *am* into women and you can close your mouth now."

Jamie closed her mouth but hadn't yet found her voice.

"I'm Cindy, by the way." She offered her hand.

Taken off guard, Jamie returned a reticent handshake.

"And if you're wondering how I knew your name…?" Cindy allowed for just enough time to build the anticipation for her answer, "You came in here with a woman, a few weeks ago? Before you came back to buy the jacket?"

"I did," Jamie confirmed guardedly.

"She spoke your name."

"Did she?"

Cindy laughed again. "And you paid by credit card that other morning."

Jamie remembered the incident.

"You put your card the wrong way up in the scanner. I put it back in the machine for you and noticed – well, I looked, to be strictly accurate – at the name on your card…"

Jamie wondered what was coming next.

"I remember these things," Cindy winked. "Anyways, you'd kinda caught my eye already. But, hey," she giggled. "Talking of stalking, I don't think it's me who needs to be explaining myself. You weren't exactly subtle just now – or a few weeks ago, for that matter."

Jamie had started out with a goal in mind, but she hadn't expected the chase to be quite so easy.

Cindy helped her out. "I noticed you with your friend. You'd been doing a terrific job of prowling outside my shop. I thought you were casing the joint and sussing out your mark. Y'know what? I was close to calling the cops." She let out another gravelly laugh. "There are places back home that would greet you with both barrels of a shotgun if you prowled around on a person's property like that." Meanwhile, Cindy busied herself, closing drawers, tidying her desk.

Jamie felt her face redden.

"Oh, my! Would you look at you, honey?" Cindy misread the reason for Jamie's embarrassment. "I wasn't *really* about to pull a gun on you… The Second Amendment – it's a law we have in the States."

Cindy got her coat and keys, and moved towards the exit, turning off the main light switch by the door. "So, time for a coffee, huh? Where are you taking me?" She swivelled the Open sign in the window to Closed and set the alarm. Opening the door, she invited Jamie to step outside first, then locked up the door behind them.

"Gregory's Café okay with you?" Jamie asked. "It's just around the corner."

"Sure," Cindy agreed. "You've discovered the art of speech, then?"

All the while, as they walked, Cindy was chattering non-stop. Jamie failed to get a word in but wasn't too bothered. She was enjoying Cindy's enthusiasm, and she liked the way the woman held herself; graceful, almost gazelle-like in stature.

Once at the café, sitting across the table from each other, Jamie was struck by the deep brown of Cindy's eyes – almost black against her dark olive skin and short, ebony hair. She was gorgeous. Her quirky, deep laugh was a mismatch, but very seductive. Even the guy serving the coffee flirted with her, and she evidently loved the attention and consequences of being so attractive. Where others might have found it a burden, she revelled in it.

They spent the next couple of hours chatting and getting to know each other, although the balance was one-sided: Jamie asked lots of questions but limited what she revealed about herself.

"An architect, huh? Sounds important. So if I was to google you, who would I be looking for?"

Jamie handed over a business card.

Cindy laughed. "Smooth! And I didn't even get to ask for your number, huh?"

Jamie pointed her teaspoon at Cindy. "You never know when you'll need an architect."

"Ohhh… wielding a teaspoon with intent? Masterful too, huh? I like that."

Jamie smiled, wondering about her next move.

"So, who was the woman with you, that first weekend?" Cindy asked. "Your apathetic companion?" She scooped the milk-foam from the top of her cappuccino and licked it slowly off the back of her spoon.

Jamie was intrigued by the seduction.

"Not your significant other, I'm guessing?"

"Alex? Good grief, no. She's just a close friend. Do you think I would be here if she was more than that?"

Cindy erupted into laughter. "Oh, my lord," she gasped, clapping her hands together gleefully. Already strong to the point of parody, her Southern American twang intensified. "You sweet little thing, you – are you for real? Are you telling me you've never cheated?"

"No!" Jamie replied, with unprecedented vehemence.

"Not even overlapped a little between relationships?"

In light of Jamie's recent experiences, this was not a good conversation.

"This *is* just an innocent cup of coffee, ya know – not some shady, clandestine lovers' rendezvous," Cindy said.

Jamie squirmed on her chair.

"Well?" Cindy's eyes narrowed. "Would you rule it out if it was?"

Jamie tensed. She sat upright – a subconscious, guarded reaction.

"Oh, pushed buttons there, huh?"

"Not at all," Jamie lied.

"Sure I have."

Jamie shifted her gaze to the bottom of her coffee cup, mindful that she was being studied. Cindy leant forward and slipped her hand across the table. She stroked her thumb over the back of Jamie's hand. "Hey, look," she said softly, "it's none of my business anyhow. Another coffee?"

Something in Jamie wanted the touch to last longer, struggling with an uncertain yearning. Wasn't this why she had orchestrated the meeting? Wasn't her intention to get to know more about Cindy? Widen her net?

Jamie glanced at her watch. It was nearly three in the afternoon. "So, I need to make tracks now…" She partially stood up, deciding how to present her invitation for another meeting.

"Sure. No worries." Cindy was sluggish, suddenly preoccupied with something far more interesting on her phone.

Jamie took the initiative. "How about meeting up again tonight?"

"Huh?" Cindy remained side-tracked, examining her phone.

Jamie persevered. "I'm easy about where to go, if you're up for it?"

Cindy tilted her head slightly, apparently pondering Jamie's invitation, but her eyes were still on her phone. Without looking up, she answered slowly, "Yeah, as a matter of fact, I do have other plans already..."

There was a difficult silence while Cindy continued flicking and tapping at the screen. "I guess I could put them on hold for tonight," she continued. "But if something lands on my lap in the meantime…"

Mind games and rejection were the last straw. Jamie was not in any frame of mind to be dealing with any more asshattery from anyone. "Look, I don't need any favours, thanks." She stood up. "This is to cover the coffee." She tossed some coins on the table.

"What?" Cindy got up too, staring at Jamie for answers, alternating her gaze between the money on the table and Jamie. "What's wrong? Did I just miss something? What just happened here?"

Jamie was beyond appeasing. The sense of déjà vu could not be ignored. She made a private resolution not to let her poor judgement catch her out – yet again. Whether it was Cindy's wit or just lack of awareness, she didn't care; either way, it had started to grate. The shine was wearing off, and she had lost the motivation to chase any longer.

"I swear to God, I just don't get how you Brits think…" Cindy looked shell-shocked. "So, later? Can I still call you?"

"If you're free, fine. If not, no worries. No big deal…

thanks again for the coffee." Jamie turned to leave.

"Your jacket," Cindy called.

Jamie had left it on the back of her chair.

"Keep it. I'm recycling it," Jamie said, and left the café.

*****

Jamie was pacing the streets through Spitalfields when she received an unexpected message from Kate: *Are you still free tonight?* Jamie genuinely didn't know what the evening held in store, but knew she needed to be direct with her reply. She sent back: *Not too sure right now. Got a possible date on.* She waited a couple of minutes before curiosity prompted her to text: *Why?* But she'd waited too long – Kate's reply crossed Jamie's, and it read: *That was quick work. Have a good time. Catch up soon.* No response to Jamie's last question.

Irrespective of recent events, Jamie was feeling upbeat and positive. She'd reconciled with Linda, and still had to be thankful for finding a new friendship to develop and explore with Kate. There were possibilities with Cindy that she had yet to pursue, and, to be fair, the Texan had seemed quite keen to follow up with another meeting later, despite Jamie's hot-headedness. Things were looking up.

CHAPTER 27

Late afternoon came and went. Jamie hadn't heard anything from Cindy, so she messaged Kate back: *Looks like I'm free tonight after all. Are you still at a loose end tonight?*

A good half hour passed before Kate replied: *Okay then. Shall we stick to original Plan A and meet up at Alchemy?* Another twenty or so minutes passed before Jamie received: *What's your sister up to tonight? Ask her to come along too, if you want? I've not really met her properly, yet. X.* Jamie loved the suggestion: *Great plan. Will ask her!*

*****

Within ten minutes of Linda's arrival, she and Kate were acting like two lifelong buddies at a reunion party. They shared a similar sense of sparky wit, a gift for repartee, which Jamie thoroughly enjoyed watching and being a part of. Halfway through the evening, Linda had already organised a date with Kate to join her and her husband for dinner.

"Oh, and by the way," Linda said, "if you want to bring your friend – what's her name? Oh, yes," she clicked her fingers, jogging her memory. "If you want to bring your friend Jamie along too – feel free."

Kate was grinning from ear to ear. "Oh, if I must. I suppose it would be ungracious not to."

"Oh great," Jamie laughed, loving the fact that the pair of them had hit it off famously. "This is like having *two* sisters to battle against now."

"You'll cope, Half-Pint," Linda teased.

Kate looked quizzically amused, needing clarification.

"Childhood throwback," Jamie explained. "My nickname."

"It's only meaningful," Linda qualified, "to those of us –"

"Laura Ingalls? Little House on the Prairie?" Kate interrupted, recognising the reference.

"Yep!" Jamie confirmed. "Mum and dad even considered calling me Laura."

Another reference to their father pricked an emotional bubble. The humour and chat were punctuated by a reflective silence – Linda clearly feeling it more than anyone else. The moment lingered and passed. Jamie appreciated that Kate was naturally able to take the stillness in her stride.

Her phone rang – an unknown number. "Hello…?"

"Jamie Barker?"

"Cindy, hi…"

Kate and Linda looked at each other, then to Jamie, hearing an unfamiliar name. They both stopped talking.

"I'm sorry about earlier. I should have explained myself better. I've got family over to visit and we were trying to coordinate meet-up dates and times…"

"That's okay, I understand."

"So, about your invite earlier…? Is it still on?"

"I've made other plans now, actually." Jamie transferred the phone to the other ear. "But what about next week? Could we plan something next week some time?"

Linda nudged Kate and gave her a knowing wink. "So while she's all tied up," she said in discreetly hushed tones, "I gather there's someone new in your life…?"

Distracted, Jamie got up, knowing she wouldn't be able to concentrate on just one conversation. She went outside.

"So, you have my number. Call with me details," Cindy said. "We can pick up next week… are you in town now?"

"Yeah, with my sister and a friend."

"Okay. Well, I'm in Covent Garden. Are you far…?"

"Alchemy. It's a cocktail bar." Jamie answered without thinking. As soon as she'd revealed her location, she had a gnawing feeling that she had unintentionally opened up her oasis, her secret haven to an outsider. She knew it was absurd, but she suddenly felt exposed. It was clear where this was going, and she wasn't sure how she felt about it.

"Okay, yeah, I know it. It really is just round the corner. I've not been there before…"

Jamie wasn't sure if Cindy was angling for an invite. She wasn't ready. "So next week then, yeah? I'll contact you."

Jamie walked back into Alchemy to find Linda and Kate laughing over something they were sharing on their phones. "What have I missed?"

"Not much," Linda said. She snapped her phone shut, with Kate still chuckling.

The evening drew to a natural close.

"I need to get home," Kate said.

"I'll give you a lift if you want, Jay," Linda said. "I could run you home too if you want, Kate." Linda gave her offer another thought. "Although I suppose I should find out where home is first. If it's outside London, we might have to rethink that offer."

"You're welcome to stay at mine, Kate," Jamie said. "I'll ride you home in the morning. I've got a client to see at nine-thirty in your patch."

"That makes sense," Kate said. "It means that Linda doesn't have to faff about with a detour to take me home."

"That's sorted then," Linda agreed.

Excited by the change in Kate's plans, Jamie suddenly remembered she'd not changed the spare room bed sheets since Kate's last stop-over.

*****

"I feel like I've known your sister for ever," Kate said, as she unlaced and took off her shoes just inside the front door of Jamie's apartment.

"I'm just made up that she's okay, and, more to the point, is still speaking to me." Jamie put her pumps into the shoe box after Kate. "I was worried sick… I'm glad you like Linny. She likes you too, you know."

Kate smiled.

"I wasn't kidding when I said she was amazing," Jamie said.

"You certainly got that across, Jamie. You described her to a tee." Kate walked to the kitchen. "Talking of which, fancy a cuppa before hitting the sack, or do you want to go down straight away?"

Jamie laughed in her head at Kate's unintended sexual innuendo. Hastily she looked away, stopping herself from making a childish comment, "Go on then. I'll have a cuppa with you." Jamie took a seat on the bar stool tucked under the narrow counter. "Glad to see you're making yourself so at home – it's nice."

"Thank you for helping to make me feel so welcome," Kate replied, as she started to prepare a tray for the tea. She peered over her shoulder at Jamie and echoed, "It's nice –"

Jamie smiled.

"That's how friends *should* be, right?"

Jamie gave a thumbs up. "Absolutely!"

Tea made, the two sat chatting over the events of last few days.

"I've been meaning to ask you all night," Jamie said. "How's the new relationship?"

"Catherine? I was talking to Linda about her earlier on." Kate picked up the sugar bowl and took it to the counter on the far side of the kitchen.

Jamie followed her, even though it was no more than a few feet away.

"And Cindy?" Kate asked in return. "That's a new name on the block."

"Early days. Putting my toes back in the water." Jamie picked up the bowl that Kate had just put on the counter and put it into a cupboard.

"We're getting there… slowly," Jamie said.

"Seems so," Kate agreed.

They both wandered back to the counter and sat opposite each other.

"The other day, I started a conversation that we didn't finish," Kate said.

"Remind me." Jamie turned the first page of a magazine next to her.

"I was asking you about Alex and Sarah."

"Oh yeah, I remember. What were you going to ask?" She closed the magazine and turned her attention to the teapot in between them.

"So." Kate shuffled her bottom into her seat, her elbows on the table, as if preparing for a serious session of something profound and meaningful.

"Reason, season, or life?" Her question was surprisingly ebullient.

Jamie stopped pouring herself a top-up. "What do you mean?"

"Well, I have a theory." Kate did another wiggle-shuffle in her seat.

Jamie smiled.

"I truly believe that people enter our lives for one of three main purposes – either for a reason, for a season, or for life," Kate explained. "In my experience, this applies to everyone I've ever known."

"Sounds like an interesting theory. Explain."

"Well, those that come for a reason help us to solve something, teach us something, or enrich our journey through life in some way."

"Right...?"

"Okay, keep up with me on this. And those that come for a season are more like acquaintances, people who come and go in life. People that you get to know through work or through other people – but they are transient, and don't stick around."

"Interesting..."

"And, as the final one implies, there are some people who really make a difference. They are the ones who are special – they are the ones who are valuable – worth hanging on to and help to make you a better person. The 'lifers' stay with you, as the term suggests, for life."

Jamie took a sip of her tea. "Well, Sarah, I'd say, comes under the 'reason' category. The reason for her existence, I reckon, was to teach me what damage an unequal, unhealthy relationship can do. I've learned what I *don't* want – that's for damn sure." Jamie shuddered. "It's funny. Linda has always been adamant that no one can *make* a person feel anything. She reckons that it's an emotional reaction to an external

stimulus. She used to say that about Sarah."

"So, basically we choose to allow someone to make us feel crap?"

"Yep."

"Clever, and true."

"It's an empowering theory; not so easy to carry through when you're feeling emotionally vulnerable."

"And Alex?" Kate asked. "Reason, season or life?"

"Hmmm, an interesting one, that one."

"Why?" Kate's head tilted.

"I suppose she should come under the 'life' category, although it's more like a friendship of habit –" Jamie was perturbed by her own thoughts.

"It's just a bit of fun, really," Kate said. "I don't mean to make you feel uncomfortable."

"Not at all," Jamie said. "It's quite an interesting way of looking at things, though. I'm liking the analogy. It certainly makes you think." She slurped at her tea some more.

"Do you socialise with her much?" Kate asked. "Alex, I mean. Do you two meet up a lot?"

"We used to – most weekends – although lately, not so much," Jamie said, giving thought to what she had just said.

"And the letter? Does she know about Sarah's letter?"

"No idea. I don't think so."

"If she did, would that change anything – how you feel about her? Your friendship?"

Kate had relaxed into her seat, her posture inviting Jamie to talk freely. "I don't know, actually. I've not thought about it," Jamie said, staring at the table – but analysing the matter. She traced her finger around the rim of her mug. "Since you mention it, she has been *particularly* annoying just recently. Well, she's *always* been a pain in the arse."

Kate smiled.

"But just more so lately, I guess," Jamie concluded.

"Have you come to terms with her rekindling the friendship with Sarah? You don't feel as if she's been disloyal? I mean, what kind of friend would do that? Wowzers! You must have damn good padding on that hide of yours."

Kate had clearly formed her own opinions.

"Quite honestly, Kate, it doesn't surprise me at all, really. At first, I was upset with her… to be honest, Alex has always had that 'I'll do exactly what I want' kind of attitude. She's always been a law unto herself."

Kate wrinkled up her nose.

"Welcome to my world," Jamie chuckled. "And I suppose, to echo Linda's phrase, anger is wasted energy, unless you do something constructive with it."

"You're used to it?" Kate asked, amazed.

"Something like that."

"Okay, well, since Alex is still part of your social schedule, how do you feel about organising a girls' night out? The four of us – Alex and Linda? Give me a chance to meet her properly."

"Hmm…" Jamie said, unsure of how to elaborate. "Alex and Linda – not the most auspicious of combinations."

"Oh?" Kate said, leaning forward to hear more.

"It's just that there's never been much love lost between them. Linda doesn't have time for Alex."

"Any particular reason for that?" Kate looked even more curious.

"Basically, they don't get on," Jamie explained. "It goes back years – they've never seen eye to eye. Ask Linda to tell you about it when you next see her."

"I might just do that," Kate said. "I'd still like to meet her, though. I'm intrigued."

Jamie went into the kitchen. "I'm peckish." She rummaged about inside a cupboard.

"And for you," Kate said. "You have yet to discover if Cindy is a reason, season or lifer."

"Who knows? Early days." She held up an unopened packet. "Fancy a Rich Tea biscuit? It's all I've got, I'm afraid."

"Go on then," Kate said. She watched Jamie cack-handedly trying to locate the tab around the packet, to open the biscuits. "Beer, cheese, wine and Rich Tea biscuits… you really are terrible at looking after yourself, aren't you?"

"I'm lucky – I can afford to be." Realising she probably sounded arrogant and boastful, Jamie quickly qualified her statement with, "I am capable, just lazy. I suppose my priorities in life have become a bit skewed over the years." She sat down and offered Kate a biscuit from the packet.

"I'd best get myself organised then – with that dinner I promised to cook for you." Kate munched on her Rich Tea. "And get some decent food inside you."

Jamie washed down the dry clod of biscuit sticking to the roof of her mouth with a slurp of tea. She watched Kate struggling in a similar fashion. "And I think my bottle of Le Cailleret is a better alternative to a pot of PG Tips and a dry Rich Tea?"

"Deal!" Kate offered a confirming high-five. "When?"

"Crikey, you don't hang about with your social calendar, do you?" Jamie said.

"No, I don't," Kate replied, opening her phone organiser. "But it's all a bit of a tight squeeze – I need to see where I can fit you in on my diary..."

Jamie's hackles rose ever so slightly as she braced herself for a rebuff.

"The problem is," Kate continued, "I'm trying to organise my social calendar and fit you round a dinner date with a certain barrister friend of mine." Kate put her phone down. Mischievous and elfin-like, her face lit up.

Caught again, Jamie wagged her finger at Kate, and took another biscuit. As she chewed, she found herself returning to Kate's theory. "Going back to 'reason, season or life'," she began.

Kate looked up from her phone. "Uh-huh?"

"In your opinion," Jamie smirked, her bottom lip still touching the rim of her mug, "which of those three categories do *I* fall into?"

Kate flashed a smile, disclosing a beguiling dimple, and peered over her mug too. "Are you fishing, Jamie Barker?"

But Jamie didn't need to answer. The look they exchanged at that moment communicated meaning beyond words. They both put their drinks down and leaned across the counter – an action that was as natural as it was spontaneous.

Their lips met.

Unlike the gawky, unexpected caress that had caught Jamie off guard last time, this kiss was long, deep and searching. This time, Kate was fully and willingly participating, and Jamie simply went with it. It was the most honest and meaningful physical contact that she'd experienced for a very long time. Resting on the counter, her arms ached to pull Kate close. But the moment was over all too quickly. Jamie had imagined but hadn't dared to hope that this would ever turn into a real possibility. She leaned back onto her seat, and breathed in.

Kate leaned forward, her elbow on the table, propping her chin on the heel of her palm, her fingers curled, covering her mouth. "Do you have *any* idea how long I've wanted to do that?" she said, her eyes half-closed.

"Really? You kept that well hidden. Not as long as me, I bet," Jamie said.

"That first night – I didn't give you a free cocktail for no reason," Kate said, beaming one of her dimpled grins. "Well, it was a subtle hint, I thought. I certainly don't give drinks on the house to just *any* customer. I had to tread carefully – I wasn't sure at that point if you were gay."

"And I was pretty much smitten, too, as soon as I saw those eyes of yours." Jamie reached out and traced her finger along the smile creases, framing Kate's eyes. "Your crow's feet... and your eyes... they're beautiful... just stunning." Jamie could hardly believe she was touching Kate's face.

Kate's eyes widened briefly. "You and your simple pleasures."

"Your eyes – I've never seen blue quite like it."

"Tinted contacts," Kate said.

“Really?” Jamie was evidently disappointed.

Kate nodded the confirmation slowly, heightening Jamie’s sense of disappointment. But her nod tantalisingly transformed into a grinning shake of the head. “Nah! Only kidding,” she teased. “They’re both my own corneas.”

Jamie groaned and buried her face in her folded arms on the counter in front of her.

Kate chuckled. “You were bedraggled and rain-sodden, as I remember – but, my stars, you were hot as hell.”

“Even with my dreadful hairstyle malfunction?”

Kate’s eyes sparkled. “Yup,” she laughed impishly. “Particularly that.” She drank the last of her tea. “It was seeing you with Linda that made me think I didn’t have a chance. What she said to you convinced me you were a couple. Mind you, you threw me when you asked me to stay over and keep you company in your bed...”

Jamie’s jaw dropped a fraction.

“You looked horrified when I suggested I might actually be up for that option,” Kate said. “I’ve never backtracked so quickly in my life.”

“What? I thought you were joking – having a laugh,” Jamie admitted. “I was so disappointed. I thought you were letting me know you had no interest in me – in *that* way.” This was all news to Jamie, and she was loving the revelation. Suddenly something occurred to her. “And what about Catherine? I haven’t even got off the starting block with Cindy, but you and Catherine…?"

"I was telling Linda earlier," Kate replied with a smile. "We've knocked it on the head. We agreed last night it was a no go. My mind was too full of someone else…"

It was years since a woman had spent longer than a weekend in Jamie's home. That night, Kate didn't sleep in the spare room.

CHAPTER 28

"The totally refreshing thing is," Jamie explained to Alex, as she slid and held her briefcase under the table in the Cole Hole pub, "None of this feels an intrusion. She's so… easy."

"And it's taken you nearly three weeks to introduce me to Little Miss Easy?" Alex pouted, making herself comfortable opposite. "She didn't sell herself when I saw her in that dreadful bar. She wasn't exactly brimming with personality that night. Actually, she was quite surly."

"A completely unfair comment," Jamie said. "I've told you – you know *exactly* why Kate was upset that night."

Alex tutted. "I've just endured twenty minutes of hearing about Kate this, Kate that…"

"Look, Alex, if you don't want to meet Kate, I suggest you leave now."

Alex rolled her eyes.

"You agreed to this, Alex. You were all up for it when you heard that Kate wanted to meet you."

Alex flapped and primped her fringe in the reflection of the window, then looked at her watch. "What time is she supposed to be coming, anyway? I can't hang about here all night."

"What's wrong with you?" Jamie eyed Alex. "I've not seen you like this before. You aren't nervous, are you?"

"Of course not! I just think you should have told me sooner, when all this lovey-dovey fluff started with Kate. I feel like the tail end of the loop – the last one to know."

"That's rich, coming from you, under the circumstances. It didn't cross *your* mind to consider *my* feelings when you rekindled your friendship with Sarah."

"Yadda, yadda, yadda." Alex made a puppet-like yapping gesture with her hand. "That's not the same at all."

Jamie was angrier with Sarah than with Alex. What Sarah had done was unforgivable, whereas Alex's reconnection with Sarah was more understandable. After all, Alex already had a previously established close friendship with Sarah. She knew nothing about the letter and was ignorant of all the destructive things that had gone on during and after the relationship broke down. And why *would* Alex know? Jamie had never confided in Alex in that way. The truth of it now was that Jamie had moved to a very different place. She didn't really care that much any more if Alex and Sarah were friends again. Sarah no longer had any kind of hold over Jamie, and Alex would almost certainly become just another of Sarah's casualties. She'd learn.

Jamie suddenly jumped to her feet. "Here she is…" She smiled, looking beyond Alex, and moved forward to greet Kate with open arms.

Alex didn't turn around and didn't get up.

"Hello, Alex." Kate gracefully glided into a chair. "It seems we've already met briefly – a while ago." She offered her hand for Alex to shake.

Alex stayed firmly in her seat. She held out a hand, extending it just far enough to be an inconvenience for Kate, who was forced to stretch right across the table. Their fingers had barely touched before Alex retracted her hand.

"So, you're a waitress, are you?" Alex wasted no time drilling down to the nitty-gritty.

"Alex!" Jamie said. "Kate's not even sat down yet." She turned to her guest. "Can I get you a drink?"

"Just a coffee. Can I help come and carry?"

"No, you stay and talk to grumpy-guts."

Alex already had her phone out. She was either distracted or choosing not to hear the insult.

Jamie left them to it, confident that Kate would be quite capable of holding her own. At the bar, she waited her turn behind several other people. As she stood, she looked back to the table. Alex had her back to her, Kate was in full view. Jamie wondered how the meeting would pan out, and, right now, what they were saying to each other…

"Your question just now," Kate said, pushing her rucksack under her chair. "I'm the owner of Alchemy, if that's what you mean?" Smiling, she sat down properly, making herself comfortable.

"Oh, really?" Alex said. "I'm pretty much familiar with most of the cocktail bars in London. Well, the *good*
ones that is."

"I suppose most people tend to socialise in the places they know, rather than try somewhere new." Kate put her phone on the table next to her. "Even so." She looked at Alex who was not looking back, "You didn't stay long enough to get the feel of the place. To be fair, you *were* more concerned with trying to get Jamie home safely that night."

Alex didn't answer.

"You should come on over again one night – give it another try. Bring your friends."

"No – it's not for me." Alex had already made her mind up. "To be honest, I wouldn't choose to go there."

Kate was sizing up the opposition. Although she'd been warned ahead of time by both Jamie and Linda, she was still astonished at Alex's rudeness. She couldn't yet figure out if this was an honest opinion, or if Alex was simply chucking her rattle out of the pram. Kate was willing to allow Alex the benefit of the doubt.

Jamie set Kate's coffee down in front of her. "So, who would have thought," Jamie said, looking in turn at the women on either side of her, "that my stumbling on Alchemy in the pouring rain all those weeks ago would lead to the three of us meeting up here now?"

Jamie placed her hands on Alex's and Kate's shoulders, and squeezed. Unifying gesture complete, she excused herself.

"Who'd have thought?" Alex mimicked dryly to the back of Jamie's head as she walked towards the loo.

Still hoping that she had misconstrued Alex's surliness, and allowing her the opportunity to redeem herself, Kate pressed on. "So, I hear you two go back to school days?"

"We do." Alex offered nothing more.

Kate took a breath. She was trying to understand the appeal of this lifelong friend of Jamie's. Why she was giving such a negative vibe? If this was how it was going to be, Kate realised she would struggle long-term. She absolutely was *not* going to waste her time trying to decipher or sidestep Alex's nonsense.

"Alex...?" Kate was emphatic.

"Kate!" came the sarcastic echo.

Alex made eye contact with Kate and held her gaze in a challenging glare.

"I like to think I'm pretty astute." Kate returned the stare, unblinking. "And I'm not one for mincing words –"

Alex's brow raised a tad.

"Am I imagining this tension, or do we need to clear the air here – preferably before Jamie comes back? I'm sure you'll want to spare her this unpleasant atmosphere."

"I'm not holding my breath." Alex was bold, brash and loud. "I've seen Jamie float in and out of too many dead-end relationships these last few years. It's a pattern she's got into. She doesn't seem to suit serious commitment. I'm naturally sceptical."

"You're naturally sceptical about what?" Jamie piped up, now standing behind Alex.

Alex instantly turned to face Jamie; her face flushed.

"We were just talking about politics," Kate announced.

Lips pursed in the shape of a Polo mint, Alex said nothing. Kate nearly laughed, to Jamie's bemusement.

All eyes were now on Kate, although each of the other women expressed totally different emotions. Jamie's expression was that of curious amusement; Alex's, however, was more difficult to interpret, although Kate couldn't imagine that Alex would appreciate feeling beholden or indebted to anyone – particularly the present company.

"Alex was just telling me she is naturally sceptical about politics –" Kate's excuse eased the tension, but she could tell by Jamie's flickering glances that she was suspicious.

Seemingly unaware she had let Alex off the hook, Jamie fired up the conversation in a different direction. She and Alex started chatting more freely, sharing memories – stories about their school days, previous social events and mutual friends. As the evening evolved, Kate watched and listened to the two friends laughing and joking with each other. Alex was thawing, and she was certainly more civil than she had been at the beginning of the evening. Kate had already heard so many negative things about Alex; it was a relief to see a different, more pleasant side emerging.

Jamie drew Kate into the conversation, inviting her to join in with the jokes and laughter. Then there was a critical moment – carefully timed by Alex to be unseen. Jamie had gone to order a coffee. Alex immediately ceased her jovial conversation, replacing it with a humourless, vacant glare, cutting Kate off completely. It was brief; it was calculated; it was deliberately spiteful. Jamie reappeared, and Kate continued chatting as if nothing had changed.

Alex clearly didn't want Kate to feel too relaxed just yet, if at all. Indeed, Kate was now uncertain if she could warm to Alex – ever. Her behaviour was boring, immature and exhausting. But one thing was sure: Alex had made her opinion clear, and Kate had yet to figure out how to deal with that.

CHAPTER 29

The days soon turned into weeks. As far as Kate was concerned, she was glad she had only met up with Alex a couple of times with Jamie since that first uncomfortable meeting, and always with others, as a group of friends. Thankfully, she had never been in a position where she was alone with her. Indeed, Jamie didn't see Alex on her own, either. Kate decided there was no point in telling Jamie what had happened that night. It was all pretty much water under the bridge, and Alex certainly didn't deserve the attention that raking it all up would bring.

However, Kate's apprehension towards Alex was reignited by an incident that unfolded at Alchemy, one Tuesday lunchtime…

It was a quiet start to the afternoon. Kate was taking the opportunity to check up on the stock. She was bent down, sorting out shelves underneath the bar. As she bobbed up, she spied Alex walking in through the entrance. Behind her – Sarah Ekstein.

Something felt wrong. It was an unspoken assumption that Alex had simply moved on from being a part of Sarah's social life. They hadn't yet spotted Kate, so she stayed ducked down and hidden, intending to keep it that way.

Richard, who was standing next to Kate, watched her crouching on the floor. "A new game, perhaps?"

He was bemused. “If it’s hide and seek, I don’t rate your chance of winning, if that’s the best you can do.”

Kate grabbed Richard’s knee.

“Oh, sweetie,” he joked, gyrating his hips.

“Richard!” Kate forced a sibilant whisper. “The two women who just walked in...”

Richard surveyed the entrance area but didn’t understand who Kate was referring to.

“It’s Alex and Sarah,” she hissed. “They’ve just walked in.”

“Damn, girl… no way?” Richard said, quietly excited. He had never met them, but he certainly knew *those* names all right.

Kate crouched behind the bar and dropped further to the floor. She sat down, back against the counter, knees hugged to her chest. “I’m not here,” she told him.

Richard doffed his imaginary cap. A naughty-schoolboy grin slid across his lips. “This, I *must* see,” he said under his breath.

Kate looked up at the back wall – to the large mirror behind the bottles of alcohol on the clear glass shelves. From this vantage point, she could see the pair’s reflection. Contrary to her initial assumption, it appeared that it was Sarah, and not Alex, who was the leader of this expedition. Sarah was now in front. She marched towards the bar, looking all around her, acclimatising to unfamiliar surroundings. Her sweeping panorama had all the methodical precision of a hawk. Was she looking for something? As she strode through the room, Alex was scurrying (a little reluctantly, Kate thought) a few paces behind.

"I thought you said she would be here, Alex?" Sarah said, when they reached the counter.

Richard's ears pricked up.

"We may as well sit down, as we're here now. Anyway, Sarah, we can always ask someone." Alex unwittingly revealed their identity to Richard.

"Ladies!" Richard was eagerly on the case, greeting the two women with a plastic smile. "What can I get for you?"

Kate looked up nervously at Richard, with pleading eyes. She realised her friend had complete control, and he was basking in it. Kate held her face in her hands.

This wasn't a game, and she hoped that Richard could be trusted.

Alex ordered and paid for the drinks, then they each sat on a stool at the bar. Sarah was now sitting in the same place where Jamie had sat that very first night for her marmalade martini.

"Is Kate here?" Alex asked Richard, getting quickly to the crux of their visit.

"Not right now," he replied, flawlessly cool, polishing a wineglass. "But…"

Kate flinched.

"I can pass on a message for you, perhaps?"

Richard just couldn't resist.

"Yes," Alex began.

"No!" Sarah barked, directing a glare at her. "No," she added, a little less aggressively, this time to Richard. "No messages." She looked back again to Alex. "I'm not playing Chinese whispers, Alex. We need to talk face to face, not pass the parcel, second-hand."

"Is Kate working at all today?" Alex asked Richard.

"No, I don't think so."

Kate was relieved at his quick thinking. He was right next to Kate; she was virtually leaning up against his leg. It was just where he loved to be, in the thick of it all. To him, the fun had only just begun. She knew he was itching to see this through and she was praying he would be subtle.

There were now other customers waiting to be served, but Richard was going nowhere. This was all way too interesting for him. He served them quickly, then returned back to where the action was unfolding.

Kate, meanwhile, scanned the narrow confines of her temporary prison for a way out. She had two options: the little door on the far right, which led only to the store cupboard, or the archway on the right that curved round to the back, the inner vaults and public seating areas. If she were to leave by the main entrance, she would still need to reveal herself. Even going out through the fire exits meant walking past Alex and Sarah. Kate had no choice – she was forced to stay put for the duration.

"Ag, I'm sick of all this shit, man!" Sarah announced. "*I'm* the one trying to patch things up. *I'm* the one all set for meeting and making friends. But it's Jamie who's throwing the spanner in the works. I've called her, I've messaged her. She's refused to reply. What else can I do?"

This version of Jamie's attitude certainly did not ring true to Kate. Jamie would have told her if Sarah been in contact… wouldn't she?

"That's not the impression that *I* was given," Alex said, in a tone of voice that suggested she was also trying to make sense of something that did not make any sense at all. "You haven't been in contact with Jamie for a few weeks, have you?"

Kate didn't hear Sarah answer. Had she replied at all?

"So, am I right in thinking you've only spoken to her a couple of times since you came back to the UK?" Alex asked.

"That's right," Sarah said. "But only on the phone…"

Kate involuntarily tensed.

"And let me tell you," Sarah continued, "I'm so glad *you* saw sense. I always could rely on you. I would have found all this very hard and painful without being able to rely on your friendship. I've been devastated by all this."

Kate had her hand over her mouth. She wasn't sure how Alex was reacting. Her reflection was now just out of view of the mirror, and she didn't reply.

"I would dearly love to meet up and make friends with Kate," Sarah proclaimed.

Kate's eyes popped open, hearing this flagrant lie.

"I really don't understand why Jamie's behaving like this," Alex said. "All you're doing is trying to rekindle a friendship, and she's throwing it back in your face. I don't understand why that is so hard for her."

Kate now realised that Alex really had no idea about the full story, and certainly had no clue whatever about Sarah's letter.

"Anyway, I'm not holding my breath on this one, with Kate," Alex went on. "I can't see it lasting."

Alex moved her stool closer to Sarah. Kate could now see her reflection again.

"Don't get me wrong, I'd love Jamie to be settled and happy," Alex said. "I just don't think she chooses her relationships very wisely. This has all happened so quickly, and I've always said Jamie was an idiot to let you go."

Kate was wondering how it could possibly be that Alex was Jamie's friend for so many years yet was so blind to not see how unhappy and destructive the relationship with Sarah had been. How could she have missed the signs?

"Well." Sarah lifted her glass to Alex. "Let's drink, at least, to one old friendship that *has* stood the test of time." She raised her glass higher. "To us!"

Alex clinked her glass against Sarah's. "To us!"

"I need your friendship more than Kate does, Alex," Sarah said firmly. "You wouldn't break my confidence,
would you?"

"Of course not," Alex replied.

"Another drink, ladies?" Richard asked. He'd been listening with interest to the whole thing.

Kate wasn't happy. She glared up at Richard and poked at the face of her wristwatch several times, indicating that she'd already been trapped behind the bar for quite long enough and didn't wish to be trapped even longer.

Richard didn't notice.

"You'd get your buddy another drink, wouldn't you?" Sarah asked.

"Sure," Alex agreed, delving into her handbag for her purse.

Drinks served, Alex said, "I didn't mention this before, Sarah, but when I spoke to Jamie a while ago, she was pissed off about something. It was just after I'd met up with you in Brighton."

"Oh man, that was a wild weekend, wasn't it?" Sarah chuckled, reminiscing. "*So* much fun."

"Jamie mentioned to me – about something that you'd said or done to upset her?"

Silence.

"She wouldn't tell me herself. She told me I should ask *you* about it…?"

Further silence.

Alex continued. "She said I should get *you* to explain..."

Now three of them – Alex, Kate and Richard – were
waiting on the answer with bated breath.

"I have absolutely no idea what you are talking about," Sarah replied, with a hint of anger – intending, most likely, to shut Alex down.

Shocked, Kate pressed her palm to her mouth, hushing the sharp intake of breath that she was sure would reveal her whereabouts. Even Richard, who was playing a credible game of bluff, was struggling with what he was hearing.

Sarah downed her drink. "Well, if Kate's not here, there's little point in outstaying our welcome. I'll postpone introductions for another time." She slipped down off her stool and was already walking away. "I'm so hungry. Do you want to come and get food with me? I need a burger. I'll buy you this one."

Sarah walked out of Alchemy as quickly as she'd entered. Alex was not far behind.

"Bloody hell. Can you believe that, Richard?" Kate was struggling to her feet. "The devious cow is lying to Alex too. She has no intention of owning up to what she's done to Jamie." Now upright, Kate brushed off the seat of her jeans. "What does she think she's going to achieve by lying? How long does she think she's going to carry that off before she's found out?" She stared at the closed door through which the two women had just left. "I can't believe Alex is so gullible that she'd swallow all that crap. Is she mad?"

"It would appear," Richard observed, "that the South African Ice Maiden has successfully trained her new
lap-dog to come to heel."

"Why did Sarah want to come and talk to *me*, particularly, I wonder?" Kate mulled over. "What on earth was she planning on saying to me? More to the point, what the heck do I tell Jamie?"

Eyes skyward, thumb placed under his chin, index finger curled over his closed mouth, Richard adopted a 'thinking' pose. "Absolutely nothing!" he said firmly, after some consideration. "Do nothing, and say absolutely nothing."

"Don't you think Jamie should know about this?"

"Difficult though it might be for you to believe," said Richard, reassuringly cradling his hand beneath Kate's elbow and leading her to a table, "and knowing how fond I am of a little mischief-making, this is one situation where I can see no good in stirring the shit any more." He pulled out a chair for her.

"Really?" Kate was not at all sure. "Don't you think I owe it to Jamie to tell her about this?"

Richard bounced into one of his frenzies of energy, grabbing for a pen and paper, which he always managed to find from somewhere on such occasions. This time, it was squirrelled away in a drawer near the till. He was preparing some of his legendary words of wisdom: traditionally, this was an approach that was passed down from his beloved Granny Olga. It was a visual technique, helping you to spell out various options, choices and consequence pathways. The purpose was to make decisions more easily in tricky circumstances.

Sitting down next to Kate, he enthusiastically began to scribble down an intricate jigsaw of names, arrows, cause-and-effect boxes and outcomes. Kate humoured him, confident that, although sometimes quirky and long-winded, his advice was generally fair and reliable.

"The bottom line," Richard finally summed up, "is to decide what you are trying to achieve, and who you are likely to hurt or upset by passing on this knowledge. Who are you doing it for, and why? Is it for you – to clear your conscience? Or for Jamie – because she needs reminding some more of what a skanky bitch her ex is?" He keenly tapped the end of his biro where he had written the words "skanky bitch".

Richard let Kate think on the matter awhile, before saying, "Sometimes, my dear, keeping your mouth shut is the most difficult but the best thing to do. My

Granny Olga taught me: if what you plan to pass on is not going to heal or mend, why repeat it at all? All you end up doing is creating mean or hurtful tittle-tattle. Why do that? You end up being no better than the person who started the trouble in the first place." With that, Richard put his pen down and folded his arms conclusively. "This could backfire on you," he warned. "Are you prepared for that?"

Kate had now seen Alex from a completely different perspective than Jamie's. She thought some more. "I don't know," she said at last, "I'm going to need some time to think about it." Her dilemma was clear. She could keep her mouth shut, but risk being exposed later on. How would Jamie react if she was to find out about this overheard conversation? Was she prepared to lose Jamie's trust – jeopardise everything?

CHAPTER 30

Six months on, Jamie was finding that being with Kate was positive and uncomplicated. She was starting to get her mojo back, and her earlier fears about commitment had gradually been dissipating. Moreover, other important life decisions and plans were being made. Jamie was less inclined to be so easily irritated by Alex, and for now, Kate was content to maintain the status quo, and have as little as possible to do with Alex.

Today, Jamie was on a high. She busied herself cleaning and tidying her apartment. She was planning how to rearrange furniture and put balloons and banners up in time for the party that night.

"All this cleaning," Alex criticised, "is a pointless exercise. Your place is *always* OCD spotless."

But not even Alex could rain on Jamie's parade today.

Tonight's party would be a celebration on two counts. Yesterday, Kate's opening night for her exhibition had been a huge success. She had already sold eight of her pieces and had set up two other venues for future shows. Reason number two for the celebrations: the spare room was no longer a dumping ground stuffed full of Jamie's old clothes and unwanted junk. It was now freshly painted and wallpapered, with empty drawers that would be filled the very next day. A second toothbrush had taken up residence in the bathroom, making Jamie smile every time she saw it. These days, she looked forward to waking up every morning next to another person – more precisely, next to Kate Adams.

Jamie wanted tonight to be one that everyone would remember, bringing together friends, family and loved ones. Even her mum was going to be there.

That morning, Jamie put Alex on vol-au-vent baking duty, and Gavin had been coerced into carrying all the junk down to the skip outside. Jamie packed a few last bits and pieces into a cardboard box, ready for Gavin to take down – a few magazines, some cleaning cloths and a leaking can of oil that Kate that used for her motorbike. Earlier that day, Jamie had accidentally dropped the oil onto her antique Persian rug while attempting to put it back in the cupboard near the front door. She had spent a while trying to remove the stain, and the smell. Unfortunately, she was a captive audience to Alex's idiotic wittering on the periphery. "You do realise you can't replace that old thing once you've eventually scrubbed a hole right through that rug?"

Once the final box was in the skip, Gavin left the apartment to pick up some much-needed mid-morning coffee and doughnuts.

Pastries in the cooker, Alex moved to the other side of the kitchen into the lounge area, to await the coffee break. She perched herself on a bar stool and was running her finger absentmindedly down the creased spine of a well-thumbed paperback book. It was open and face down on the counter; clearly, Jamie was midway through reading it. “I think this one is ready for the skip. Real books get so tatty. Why do you still waste shelf space rather than reading e-books?” Alex said. “One day, Jamie, you might get in touch with the current century.”

It was no surprise to Jamie that Alex’s attention had been caught by the title and cover illustration: a long, thin bullet, encased in a solid cube of ice, overlooked by the embossed title: Colde and Rainey – A Rainey Bell Thriller. Alex picked it up and scanned the open pages, apparently drawn in by the sentence she’d started reading. "I’ve not heard of this author; it’s not a book I’ve come across. Is it any good?" Her eyes were still glued to the page.

"Yeah, it's great," Jamie replied. “This is the second time I've read it. It’s part of a series. Best to read them in order, though. The storyline and characters make more sense if you do.” Jamie nodded at the cover. “An American author.”

Alex flicked through and read a few more pages. “Oh!” She clapped the book shut and tossed it across the work surface as if she had just suffered an electric shock. It slid off onto the floor. "It's about lesbians…"

Jamie frowned. "Lesbians? What do you mean?"

"It’s about two women having babies, isn’t it?" Alex was deadly serious.

“No,” Jamie corrected. “It's actually a thriller about a veteran Special Agent who happens to have kids with
her wife. Why? What’s your problem?"

Alex elucidated. "Well, that's just plain wrong. Two women? I mean, keep what you get up to in your own bedroom, so long as I don’t think about it for too long – but two women having babies? That's just not right – inflicting a lifestyle choice onto a child. A choice that they have no control over, I might add. The kid is highly likely to become an innocent victim of bullying throughout their school life: labelled as something out of a freakshow, just because two gays want children. It's really selfish, actually – not that I'm homophobic or anything."

“Christ, Alex!” Jamie was used to Alex’s asinine remarks. However, this was particularly disturbing.

“Oh, come on,” Alex added. “It’s not like I’ve ever hidden my views.”

“Listen to yourself – lifestyle choice? *Choice*? *Freakshow*? That’s quite an obscene opinion you’ve just put out there, Alex.” Jamie was finding it hard to keep her composure. “What *exactly* are you saying? You certainly kept that little sting in the tail to yourself over the past few decades.”

Alex was clinical. “No, I haven’t. You've just never explicitly asked me for my opinion.”

“I can't believe I'm hearing this bullshit,” Jamie said.

But Alex wasn't finished. "I'm just relieved that you're too old to have children. Mind you, it's a bit rich to think that even with the adoption route, the gays seem to get a priority pass over a normal couple like Gavin
and me."

"*What*? Where has all this suddenly come from?"

"Just my opinion. Anyway, children should have a mother and a father. It's a bit like the whole gay marriage thing. I never could understand why your lot weren't satisfied with just having a civil partnership. After all, it's not a *real* marriage anyway, is it?"

Jamie pinched the bridge of her nose, trying to release the negative stress that was threatening a migraine.

"Don't get me wrong, Jay, it's not personal or anything."

Jamie's gut twisted. She started to feel sick. "This is hideous," she muttered. She slowly moved her gaze from the floor in front of her feet, to an unfixed sequence of objects – stepping stones across the room – until she met Alex's eyes. "Oh Jesus," she said quietly, as a mental light switched on. "I've been burying my head in the sand with you all these years, haven't I? Do you honestly have *any* regard or respect for me or my feelings?"

Alex inspected Jamie, with dead eyes.

Jamie exploded in a fit of intense fury. "Fuck you, Alex. *Fuck you*!" She spat the words. Hot tears of anger and despair welled uncontrollably. Jamie ferociously blinked them back. "Why not finish the fucking job and kick me in the teeth too?"

Amelie mewed plaintively, reverting to an anxious kitten. She cowered behind a chair leg, too frightened by the angry voices to move.

The front door swung open. Gavin had let himself in, armed with a bag of doughnuts and a carrier loaded with four coffees. Pushing the door shut with his foot, he called out, "Jamie Barker raising her voice and swearing? It must be serious." He was laughing as he kicked off his shoes in the hallway. "No chocolate sprinkled on your cappuccino, right, Jamie?" He entered the room but stopped in his tracks, taking stock of the catastrophe before him. The gravity of the situation became all too apparent when Jamie swung round – red-faced, nostrils flared and swallowing hard to fight back tears.

"Cat-fight? This looks dangerous. What have I missed?" He had an imbecilic grin plastered across his face as he rubbed his hands together.

"Just leave!" Jamie pointed to the door.

"What...?" Gavin set the drinks and doughnuts down. "Why?"

"Both of you," Jamie ordered, still pointing. For now, she had managed to regain control. Her fury was contained. "I mean it – just get out of here. I want you both to leave my home."

“Fine!” Gavin high-tailed it out into the hallway, buzzing with excitement. Jamie could hear him pulling on his boots as if he couldn’t get them on quickly enough.

“Bloody hell, Jamie,” Alex was cautiously jovial. “Call me when you've calmed down after your little meltdown, yeah?” Her supercilious defiance was considerably less confident than usual. It was almost as if she sensed, for once, that she couldn’t be certain Jamie would loyally make that call.

Standing tall, Jamie started to walk towards her balcony, unable to look at Alex. She needed air. Alex maintained her controlled pig-headedness, but she unexpectedly lacked conviction. “Be a diva, why don't you?”

“Leave her be, Lex,” Gavin called to his wife from the hallway. “If that’s the gratitude we get for helping her out, she can sod off.” He couldn’t resist twisting the knife with a final, verbal jab. “Jamie’s world always has been, always will be one fucking train smash after another. Bloody good riddance. And once I’ve closed this door behind me, Jamie, I won’t be coming back through it again.”

This was the tip of the barb that Jamie had been stung by weeks ago, and Gavin had just been handed the perfect opportunity to hook it in.

Alex, however, chose to neither challenge nor contest any of it. Instead, she snatched her handbag off the back of the nearby dining chair. The shoulder strap snagged on the backrest. She pulled harder. The chair toppled and crashed to the floor. The oven timer started to beep: the vol-au-vents were cooked. The comic timing was both ironic and pitiful.

Ordinarily, Jamie was the appeaser, the white-flag bearer, using humour to gloss over the cracks. Not this time. This was a chasm. After thirty-plus years of knowing Alex, Jamie felt something had just been broken – smashed. And in that split second, she realised that it couldn't be repaired. Jamie had heard enough. Alex's voice had become white noise.

"Leave my door key on the table on your way out," Jamie ordered, without turning. "Linda was right," she continued, having turned to look at Alex. "You *are* toxic."

Alex's expression suggested raw, open emotion – something Jamie had never seen. She scrabbled in her bag for the key and threw it onto the sofa. As if priming herself to add a final line, she opened her mouth, but couldn't find the words. Without picking up the fallen chair, she turned on her heels to leave.

"You are no longer welcome in my home, Alex." Jamie spoke with imperative calm to Alex's back. "Ever!"

For a millisecond, Alex froze mid-step. She didn't turn. Instead, she kept going and joined Gavin in the hallway.

The front door slammed shut behind them.

Amelie surreptitiously emerged from behind the sofa and padded hesitantly to Jamie's feet, mewing for reassurance. Light-headed and nauseous, feeling as though she had been taken down by a kick to the back of the knees from phantom steel-toed boots, Jamie slumped, her back against the wall.

Motionless for minutes, she was engulfed by silence.

Then she crumpled.

It was a good hour before Jamie felt able to talk to anyone. She wanted to speak to Kate, but the person she *needed* to talk to just happened to be five minutes' drive away. Linda was on her way over to help with clearing and preparations for the party.

When the door-intercom trilled, Jamie almost didn't answer the call. But as soon as she heard Linda's voice from downstairs, she was overcome with relief. Incapable of speaking, she buzzed her sister up, leaving the front door ajar.

"How's it all going, hun?" Linda called from the hallway. "What still needs doing? Okay if I get myself a cuppa first? Where is everyone?" She came into the room to find Jamie sitting on the sofa, sobbing uncontrollably into her hands.

Right now, Linda was exactly the remedy that Jamie needed. Shrewd and pragmatic, she could unpick the emotion from fact, and she listened calmly to Jamie's account.

"It was unbelievable. I realised I was looking into the eyes of a stranger. You know what? It was worse than that – it was like she was the enemy." Jamie had now moved beyond the tears to a peculiar kind of numbness.

Even though she didn't like Alex, Linda was scrupulously fair, enabling Jamie to make a balanced evaluation of it all. "You are probably the most loyal and steadfast person I know, Jay. But you've always spoken of Alex like someone you have been rubbing along with just because she's always been around. There's been an uncomfortable dissonance between you two for a long while."

"I've never known life without Alex. She's become a kind of…"

"Habit?" Linda suggested.

"Yeah, I guess so."

"Not all habits are necessarily healthy."

"So, when are you planning to quit the nicotine, then?" Jamie asked, half-seriously. Linda didn't answer. Jamie realised she was being petty and offered back a wink.

Linda moved to the kitchen. "Cuppa?"

Jamie nodded.

"That good old British cure-all and elixir of life – a pot of builders' brew, Rosie Lee." Linda filled up the teapot. She started the ritual of organising the tea paraphernalia on a tray. "To my way of thinking," she added, picking up again on her original point of reference, "a person should look at friendships as they would any relationship. If the negative traits of that person more frequently outweigh the positives, you need to step back and take stock. No point in having negativity crowding your karma – life's too short for that shit." She brought the tray and set it down in front of Jamie.

"True," Jamie agreed.

"So, when you realised that your relationship with Sarah had disintegrated, you cut ties, yes?"

"Eventually – but as you know, it was ugly and complicated."

"But you knew that the balance had shifted over time. No relationship ever stays the same. It either evolves and grows, or it becomes stagnant and directionless. People grow apart. Goals become different and you find yourselves having less and less in common. It happens."

"You should have seen Gavin. He was loving it. I could almost hear his excitement. I think he was relieved, hoping it meant he wouldn't have to share his wife any longer."

"Very likely," Linda agreed. "He must have been waiting to deliver that exit line for decades." She noticed the book that Alex had discarded earlier and picked it up from the floor. "A Rainey Bell thriller – don't you just love a kick-ass defence attorney? I fancy myself as a bit of a Molly Kincaid." Linda's eyes glinted, and she gave one of her crooked grins. "Is Alex still in contact with the delightful Sarah?"

"Who knows? She's not spoken of her for ages. I don't think she would tell me any more, even if she was," Jamie said.

"They are well suited to each other. In my opinion, they're both the antithesis of a healthy friendship."

"I don't think my brain can cope with any more dissecting." Jamie held her face in her hands and massaged her temples. "My head hurts."

Linda moved next to her sister and put her arm around her. "Whereas," she continued, still holding on tight to Jamie. "The lovely Kate is the polar opposite of both Sarah and Alex. They're deadwood."

*****

The party that night was a great success. The earlier showdown with Alex had made Jamie realise, that a huge weight had been taken off her shoulders. Alex and Gavin didn't return to the party, so she was able to switch off completely and throw herself into the celebration.

Linda was right. Too much in Jamie's life recently had turned out to be deadwood – she had started the process of culling.

At one pivotal point that evening, Jamie had taken herself outside to her balcony. She looked across at London as the world went by beneath her. She listened to the happy buzz inside behind her – the sound of her loved ones. She breathed in the cool evening air – long and deeply.

The touch of hands on each shoulder made Jamie turn, suddenly flanked by her mother and sister.

"It's just perfect seeing you both together like this." Their mother gathered up her daughters in for a hug. "Dinner at Le Gavroche the other day was wonderful. Thank you so much for treating me." She pulled her girls in tighter. "And I'm so, dreadfully sorry…" She sighed, resting her head on Linda's shoulder. "For everything…" She lifted her head and looked up at them both with pained, tired eyes. She quickly pulled the girls in again. "You know I love you both equally, don't you my darlings?"

Jamie swallowed. "We love you too." She looked to Linda.

"Very much," Linda reassured. "And it's still early days, mum… we're all healing." She moved a strand of greying hair from her mother's fringe and tucked it behind her ear.

When the last couple finally left, Kate looked around the room at the dinner plates and general post-party debris. "Let's clear up this mess in the morning."

Having consumed a bottle of champagne, and a couple of generous slugs of 16-year-old Lagavulin, Jamie was drunk. She was ready to fall into bed. It was the kind of evening where the level of goofing around and frequent belly-laughs had made it a perfect end to a magical day.

"I'm pissed…" Jamie giggled, half stumbling over the arm of the sofa. Kate, more sober, sprang into action to stop her lurching into any more furniture.

"Great party, huh?"

Kate agreed wholeheartedly.

"By the way, what was it you were going to say earlier?" Jamie asked. Her head was resting on Kate's shoulder as Kate guided her towards the bedroom.

"There's something I need to tell you," Kate said.

Jamie was already unbuttoning the front of her shirt as they walked, and was now thrashing her arms about, having forgotten to take out her cufflinks. Kate reached across to help Jamie out of her straitjacket.

"You taking a shower?" Jamie asked.

Kate put her arm round Jamie, her hand resting on Jamie's hip. She slipped her fingers just under the waistband of Jamie's jeans, her thumb gripping her belt to help steady her direction.

"I'll talk to you in the morning," Kate answered quietly. "When you're in a fit state to listen."

Jamie looked unwaveringly into Kate's eyes. "I love you too."

Kate grinned as she guided the sleepy Jamie across the room.

The route to the bedroom was convoluted. Kate sniffed at the air. "What's that smell? I've noticed it all evening." It was wafts of the spilt WD-40 oil, mixed with household cleaner – Jamie's attempt to clean up the stain on the carpet earlier.

"It's Dad," Jamie said, slurring her words. "He's been cleaning the damn guns again." She chuckled wistfully at her childhood memory.

Kate had no idea what Jamie was saying. "You *are* drunk," she chuckled, having never seen Jamie in quite this state before.

They showered together in silence. Words were superfluous. Kate propped Jamie up every now and again to stop her from leaning on the inside of the shower cubicle. All the while, Jamie's eyes were closed, a grin permanently plastered across her face. Kate mirrored Jamie's smile. She wiped the soap suds away from Jamie's closed eyes and kissed them.

Once showered and dry, they stumbled haphazardly into bed. Jamie looked at Kate's naked body. Physically, she was exquisite. Jamie nestled sleepily into the warm flesh of Kate's perfectly formed breasts. The faint musky smell of her perfume still lingered on her freshly clean skin. Jamie nuzzled in, lulled into a blissful, soporific state of relaxation.

Kate's fingertips gently stroked Jamie's shoulders. Jamie smiled, recognising the familiar pattern of the touch, as Kate gradually worked down Jamie's spine in small circular motions. The shower had sobered Jamie up enough that she could guess the next move, like a grandmaster chess pro. Her body stiffened, and she arched her back, tingling with anticipation.

Straight away, Kate picked up on her lover's response and increased the pace, eagerly taking control.

Jamie couldn't recall ever being as happy, contented and complete as she was at this moment, right now. When she finally fell asleep that night, the following thirteen hours were the longest, deepest and most peaceful sleep she had experienced for many years.

*****

The next morning, Kate and Jamie lay entwined, motionless and blissfully unaware of the radio alarm clock's London news headlines: *Missing for five days – multi-millionaire bank tycoon – recovered from Docklands waterfront – fatal gunshot to the back of the head..."*

The dark storm clouds had just started gathering overhead. But for now, and if only for one night, Jamie Barker had, at last, danced in the rain.

Printed in Great Britain
by Amazon

66001476R00251